Praise for Katie McDonald mysteries!

THE SUDOKU MURDER

"This intriguing first in a new series from Freydont introduces mathematician and Sudoku whiz Katie McDonald. Katie, a self-professed geek who works for a hush-hush government think tank, returns to her hometown of Granville, N.H., at the behest of her former mentor, P.T. Avondale. Katie is shocked to find Avondale frail and preoccupied, his beloved puzzle museum in serious disrepair and dire financial straits. Before Katie can make sense of the situation, she discovers Avondale murdered in his office—slumped over an unfinished Sudoku puzzle that may provide a clue to the killer's identity. She tops the brash new police chief's suspect list and decides to solve the case on her own, not only to clear her name but to save the Avondale museum from the wrecking ball. Readers will want to see a lot more of the intelligent and endearing Katie." —*Publishers Weekly*

"Entertaining fare for mystery-reading Sudoku addicts."
—*Booklist*

" . . . I know those brainiacs are out there just waiting for a book dedicated to their favorite game. This is it. Enjoy."
—*OnceUponaRomance.net*

"This charming read is wonderfully told, and intriguing, as the reader is caught up not only in the investigation of the murder but the detail of the puzzles woven in the storyline. This is one stupendous mystery not to be missed." —*coffetimeromance.com*

SUDDEN DEATH SUDOKU

"Whether you like Sudoku or not this series is a fun, c͠
cozy mystery series that any mystery lover will er͠
—*fallena͠*

"A good, old-fashioned murder mystery...."—*bookgas͠*

SERIAL KILLER SUDOKU

Katie McDonald Mysteries
by Shelley Freydont

THE SUDOKU MURDER

SUDDEN DEATH SUDOKU

SERIAL KILLER SUDOKU

From Running Press Book Publishers

SERIAL KILLER SUDOKU

A Katie McDonald Mystery

WITHDRAWN

SHELLEY FREYDONT

RUNNING PRESS
PHILADELPHIA • LONDON

9 8 7 6 5 4 3 2 1
Digit on the right indicates the number of this printing

Library of Congress Control Number: 2009927136

ISBN 978-0-7624-3711-5

Cover design by Whitney Cookman
Interior design by Alicia Freile
Typography: Berkeley, Crackhouse, and Interstate

Running Press Book Publishers
2300 Chestnut Street
Philadelphia, PA 19103-4371

Visit us on the web!
www.runningpress.com

Puzzle answers: page 351
Puzzle credit to come

This is for puzzle lovers everywhere:
those who enjoy the mystery, accept the challenge,
and don't quit until they find the answers.

3					1	9	7	
		1	7	5			4	
4		9	3				6	
	2				5		9	1
1				3	7			2
5	4		9				3	
	3				4	5		7
	8			7	6	3		
	1	5	2					4

SOLUTIONS BEGIN ON PAGE 351.

CHAPTER

ONE

KATE MCDONALD SHOOK the rain off her umbrella and shoved it into the crowded umbrella stand just inside the door of Rayette's Bakery and Café. After three days of torrential rain and accompanying flooding, the town was a mess. And so was Kate.

She ran her hand over her wild red curls. Even with double gel, it still managed to frizz. She smoothed it back, pulled it down, and stepped through the arch into the café.

"Katie, where have you been?" Rayette Lansing, the queen of the sticky bun, slapped her hands on her navy blue skirt, sending clouds of flour into the air. She was wearing a white apron, but somehow her hands always found their way to her skirt.

"At the museum, tax time," Kate said, looking around the small café. Most of the tables were filled, but no one was chatting. All heads were bowed over the round white tables. "Don't tell me they're saying grace."

Rayette snorted. "Honey, that would be a Godsend—so to speak. They're reading the *Free Press*."

"The *Granville Free Press*?"

"The one and only."

"Since when did the 4-H fair elicit this kind of attention?"

Rayette pursed her lips, creating dimples in her apple cheeks. "The fair got bumped. They're reading about the murders. Johnny," she called to the counter boy, "we need a latte over here— to go."

"Murder?" The question squeaked out as Kate tried to wrap her mind around the idea of another homicide in this small New Hampshire town that hadn't seen a murder in ten years—that is, until she'd returned last fall. Since then . . . she didn't want to think about it.

"Mur*ders*, plural."

"Murders?"

"If you hadn't been holed up in the museum all last week, you'd know. But no worry. It's just a serial killer stalking Boston."

"Oh," Kate said, relieved.

Erik Ingersoll folded his newspaper and pushed away from a nearby table. "Ayuh," he interjected, making no bones about the fact that he'd been eavesdropping on their conversation. "And as long as he stays there, it's fine by me."

Kate flushed. She'd been thinking the same thing.

"Anyway," Erik continued as he searched his pants pockets for change, "that's old news. Today it's about the local murder."

"*Alleged* murder," said his breakfast companion, Jason Elks. Jason and Erik were both members of the museum board and the Arcane Masters Puzzle Club the museum sponsored. Like all good Granvilleites, they argued as much as they agreed.

"It don't say 'alleged' in the *Free Press*," Erik pointed out.

"The *Free Press* is covering murders?" Kate asked, feeling more confused than ever. What was going on with their friendly neighborhood weekly?

"Tess Dougan has gone missing. And Henny out of the blue decides to make himself a new garage. Buried her in the concrete foundation. Ayuh."

"Holy . . . um . . . cow," Kate said. "I thought she went to stay with her sister."

"Ayuh. So did everybody else. But she isn't there. Nobody's seen her." Erik shook his head, setting stomach and jowls to wobbling. "Chief Mitchell's gonna love digging that up."

"Don't you take anything the *Free Press* says as fact," Rayette said. "Getting people all het up over nothing."

"I'm just saying . . ." Erik picked up the check and handed it to Jason. "Your day to buy."

Jason took the check and squinted at it.

"Don't you go questioning my math, Jason Elks," Rayette said.

"I'm not questioning nothing, just can't see worth a damn since I broke my glasses."

Rayette took the check from him. "Ten-seventy-eight for two gourmet breakfasts. Count your blessings."

"Gourmet, *hmmph,*" wheezed Erik. "Looked like oatmeal to me."

"Tasted like gourmet baked oatmeal with raisins, bananas, walnuts, and maple syrup," Rayette countered. "Not to mention the four cups of coffee you drank." She poked him in the chest, depositing a white, powdery fingerprint on his dark corduroy shirt.

"Wait a minute," Kate said, muscling her way into the altercation. "I don't get it. This is the *Granville Free Press*, right? They don't write about things like murder." She frowned. "Besides, it's Thursday. The *Free Press* comes out on Friday."

"Did." Erik shook out the paper and pointed to the banner. "It's a daily now. Got a new owner. What's the feller's name, Jason?"

"Finnegan Tucker. Ran a weekly over in Laconia. Now he's bought out George Franklin and moved here."

"Right. Finn Tucker. George and Arlene are moving out to Minneapolis to be closer to the grandchildren. Sold it for a song."

"That's him sitting right over there." Jason nodded to a table where two men sat over coffee. One was of medium build and had sandy blond hair that curled tightly to his head. He was busy scribbling in a spiral notebook. The other man sprawled in the chair across from him, his long thin legs stretched out and his arms crossed. A long dark-brown ponytail hung over the back of his chair.

"Finn's the blond," Erik said. "The hippie is his staff photographer. Don't know what's happening to this town."

"What's happening," Rayette said, nudging him toward the door, "is you're blocking my entrance, and I got people waiting for a table."

"We're going—just as soon as Jason pays the bill. And get a whole handful of those mints while you're at it, Jason."

But Jason didn't move toward the cash register. "Uh oh. Look who just came in."

"Oh damn," said Rayette. She snapped her fingers toward Johnny, who immediately put down a pitcher of steamed milk and disappeared into the kitchen.

Kate turned around to see who had arrived and stepped back.

The fumes enough should have warned her. Henny Dougan, the least-liked man in Granville, staggered through the archway, waving a bottle of cheap liquor and a crumpled copy of the *Free Press*.

"Guess he read the article about Tess." Erik took a step back, leaving an opening wide enough to let Henny pass.

Rayette stepped in to fill the gap, feet parted, fists on her hips. "Henny Dougan, I don't serve drunks. So you just turn yourself around and go home and sober up."

Henny lifted the newspaper, reeling from the effort. "Where's Finn Tucker? I'm gonna kill the muth—"

"You watch your language. I got women and children in here. Now get."

Johnny stepped up beside her. "Chief Mitchell's on his way."

The counter boy was the same height as Rayette and just about as stocky. They stood together shoulder to shoulder, blocking Henny's way. Henny towered over them, or would have, if he could have stood up straight.

"I'm gonna kill 'im. Where izhe?"

All eyes drifted toward Finnegan Tucker, who sat grinning cheekily at Henny from across the room. His eye caught Kate's and he winked.

"Mr. Tucker's just asking for it," Kate whispered to Jason, who seemed to be trying to hide behind her.

"Whatcha sayin' 'bout me? Damn lies!" Henny lunged toward Kate and Jason.

Johnny stepped between them and Henny round-housed him. Johnny ducked; Dougan missed, but the momentum of the punch pulled him with it and he fell into Johnny. The liquor bottle flew out of his hand and crashed onto the wooden floor.

Patrons ducked, shoved back chairs, and scuttled toward the opposite side of the café, some carrying coffee cups and plates with them.

Rayette grabbed Henny by the shirt collar and attempted to drag him toward the door.

Henny flicked her away. "Don't make me hurtcha, Ray," he mumbled. He stood swaying on his feet, scanning the crowd, though how he could see anything was beyond Kate. Her own eyes were watering from the revolting odors of liquor, body odor, and unwashed clothes.

He spun back toward the room, knocking a stack of new menus off the counter.

"That does it." Rayette righted herself and marched back in for another round. Erik grabbed her and held on.

The outer door opened and two young police officers hurried into the bakery section, their heads bobbing as they looked around for the trouble. They were followed by the chief of police, who quickly surveyed the scene and motioned to the two officers to follow him into the café.

Kate's stomach did a little flip, as it always did when she saw Brandon Mitchell. *Tall, dark, rugged . . . upholder of the law.* Totally inappropriate reaction, she reminded herself, and she stepped aside to let the chief do his job.

He moved past them in deceptively easy strides and, with one efficient movement, twisted Henny's arm behind him and force-marched him toward the door.

Henny let out a shriek, but after one jerky movement succumbed. "Kill 'em," he whined, "kill 'em." And then he burst into tears.

The chief handed him off to the officers, who wrinkled their noses but trundled him toward the exit door.

"Lemmego," whimpered Henny.

"You'll go once you've sobered up," Brandon said. "Give him a nice comfy cell where he can sleep it off."

"'Bout time you got here, Chief," said a voice from somewhere within the crowd.

"Like to see *you* do it faster," said another.

Kate rolled her eyes. The Chief was nobody's favorite. He had come from Boston, and he'd only been in Granville a year. An outsider, he was tolerated at best. But his general lack of acceptance didn't stop the natives from taking sides. If one person complained about him, there was somebody ready to stick up for him, even if they didn't mean it. It was the Granville way.

The chief glanced at Kate and she smiled in reaction. She quickly wiped it from her face only to see it transferred onto the chief's. He turned to Rayette. "Do you want to press charges, or shall I just arraign him on drunk and disorderly."

"Just let him sleep it off, then let him go," said Rayette. "I don't want to get on his bad side. He's mean when he's drunk. Mean when he isn't, come to think of it. But he would never have come in here except for that article in the *Free Press*. You can blame that on Finn Tucker. Practically accused Henny of killing Tess and burying her body."

"I saw it," the chief said. "It's not really my jurisdiction, libel. But I'll talk to Finn Tucker all the same."

"See that you do that," said Erik, who had grown cocky ever since the chief *hadn't* arrested him for murder the previous winter. "He's sitting right over there. Bumped the announcement of the Cambridge Killer Sudoku winners to make room for that garbage."

"And the 4-H fair," added someone else. "Our kids didn't take care of those animals all winter just to have their hard work and award ribbons ignored."

"That's right."

"You tell 'em."

"Aw, shut up. Everyone knows who got which ribbon. And everybody knows who won that puzzle thing. God knows Erik's told anybody who would listen."

"Twice."

Erik narrowed his eyes until they were slits in his chubby face. "You'll be singing the same tune, Ben Hollowell, when your next Monster Wheels meet gets ignored."

"Just as long as there's no more talk about murder."

"Better than having nothing to talk about."

"Better than reading about murder in Granville."

"You gonna dig up Henny's garage, Chief?"

Everyone seemed to have forgotten that Finn was sitting right there, and Finn seemed to be enjoying this immensely.

"That's enough," Brandon broke in.

Immediately, the heckling died down and people began returning to their seats.

The voice of authority, thought Kate and smiled, though she knew that in another second, they would switch gears and return to complaining about the "new" police chief.

Brandon caught her smiling and walked toward her, but just as he reached her, an all too familiar voice rose out of the crowd.

"Katie. *Yoo-hoo!* Katie! Over here."

Brandon winced.

Kate stifled a groan. Her Aunt Pru's tall, lanky figure rose up from the seated patrons like a flagpole. She was standing at a table by the window, waving furiously.

It wasn't the "Katie" that made her cringe. Everyone in Granville still insisted on calling her "Katie" though she'd been Kate for years. It was the Katherine Margaret McDonald that her aunt's "Katie" implied.

Great, Kate thought. *Caught me talking to the chief.*

The chief took a step back. "Guess I better get back to work. Kate. Rayette." He nodded toward the two women, then turned on his heel and strode out the door to the street.

"Guess you're staying for breakfast," said Rayette, squatting down to pick up the menus. "I'll send Lynn over to take your order."

Resigned, Kate threaded her way through the closely placed tables to say hello to her aunt.

Today Pru was dressed in a purple running suit with a bright yellow stripe down each leg. Her hair, dyed blue since Kate had returned home last fall, was swept up in a fancy twist. Kate had seen the same hairdo on several of the ladies who frequented Karen's Kurls in the last few weeks.

Across from her, Alice Hinckley, Pru's longtime friend and main squabblemate, sat perched on the edge of her chair, wisps of white hair pulled back into a bun, her hands in her lap, and a white cardigan sweater draped over the shoulders of a floral print shirtwaist.

"Morning, Katie," said Alice, looking up at her with sparkling blue eyes that held just a touch of impish humor.

"Sit down," Pru invited, brooking no argument. Kate sat in one of the two vacant chairs at the table. "It's a disgrace. A man that drunk at this time of morning."

"At any time of day," corrected Alice.

"I'm thinking this is still last night for Henny," Kate said.

Pru pursed her lips.

Alice leaned forward. "Do you really think Tess Dougan is buried under their new garage?"

"I'm sure she's alive and well and living the good life." At least Kate hoped Tess Dougan was alive and well. There had been far too many murders in Granville lately.

"Well, I say there's never smoke but there's fire. Ayuh." Pru punctuated her sentence with a snap of her napkin.

"Unless it's totally fabricated by the newspaper," said Kate. "I hear the *Free Press* has a new owner."

Alice put down her cup, patted her lips, and returned her napkin to her lap. "He looks like a very nice young man."

"Hmmph," Pru said. "Finnegan Tucker. He brought his own news photographer with him. Like we need another photographer in Granville."

Kate broke in before Pru started in on her praises of Sam Swyndon, a good local "boy" and until recently the *only* photographer in town.

Sam was Pru's number one candidate for husband. Kate's husband. He was the nephew of Elmira Swyndon, one of Pru's many friends and Granville's police dispatcher. Kate and Sam had gone on several dates, but neither of them was hearing wedding bells.

The waitress came over with a menu. "Hi, I'm Lynn, and I'll be serving you this morning."

"Hi Lynn." Kate smiled at the young woman. "You're new here."

"Yes, ma'am. I came over from the Brick House after we had that fire last month."

"Oh yes. I read about it," Kate said.

"In the old *Free Press*," Pru said.

"Yes ma'am." Lynn placed the red leather menu in front of Kate. "I'll be right back to take your order."

"That sweater is a lovely color of blue, Katie," Alice said. "It matches your eyes."

Kate glanced down at her sweater. She'd dressed for the weather that morning, not for fashion. She always kept a pantsuit at the museum in case she needed to look official, but she wore slacks and sweaters for everyday. There was nothing she could do about her hair.

She stole a look at her aunt, who always had an opinion on both her clothes and her hair, but for a change Pru was scrutinizing the back of Finn Tucker's head.

"The idea. Turning the *Free Press* into a daily. There's not enough news in the whole county to make up a daily. So he's got to write about all that nonsense."

"There's a new serial killer in Boston," Alice said with more excitement than censure.

Kate nodded to Lynn, who had returned to fill her coffee up.

"Hmmph, Boston," said Pru. "Just like them to have a serial killer. Ayuh. And don't think I didn't see you talking to that . . . that chief of police."

The change of subject was so abrupt that Kate nearly choked on her first sip of coffee. "I was saying hello. Just being friendly."

"Hmmph."

"Now, Pru, you leave Katie alone. She was just showing proper respect."

"Alice Hinckley, you must be getting dotty. Who fined you for selling jam without a license? I just ask you that."

"That was last year. And we've come to an understanding since then."

"Some understanding. He paid for the license. You're nothing but a traitor."

"I'm no such thing. I just give credit where credit's due."

"Well, never mind," Pru said, suddenly perking up. "Look who just walked in."

Alice and Kate both turned to look. Kate felt a little stab of disappointment to see that the chief hadn't returned.

Norris Endelman, owner of Endelman Garage and Auto Parts, was taking a chair at a table near the door.

"Now, if you'd played your cards right, young lady, you could be Mrs. Endelman by now. Norris has job security. He's big and strong and if any serial killers do decide to come to Granville, he could protect you."

"Heaven forbid," said Alice and crossed herself.

Kate felt like following suit, only she was Presbyterian.

Pru sighed heavily. "If you aren't going to marry Sam, you might as well marry Norris."

Lynn returned to take Kate's order.

"I really can't stay. I've got to finish up the museum's taxes. I'll just have a latte and a sticky bun—to go. I'll pick it up at the counter on my way out."

"You can't live on sticky buns," Pru said. "Ever since you became curator at that old museum, you hardly have time for anything."

"But she's done such a lovely job of restoring the museum." Alice reached across the table and patted Kate's hand. "Professor Avondale would be so proud."

Kate smiled and stood up.

"Hmmph. P. T. might be proud, but even he would agree she works too hard."

Privately Kate doubted it. Puzzles had been the professor's life. "I'm just really in a hurry today. Besides taxes, Johansson's is delivering the new chairs for the boardroom. A gift from Marian Teasdale, and I want to be at the museum when they arrive."

"Well, you just stop by Norris's table and say hello on your way out. And be sure to have a wholesome lunch."

It was still raining when the chairs arrived late that morning. Kate watched from the circular front porch as two workmen in yellow rain slickers maneuvered them though the wooden gate and up the sidewalk to the front door of the puzzle museum.

Kate stood admiring the new chairs long after the delivery truck had driven away. They were heavy-framed with cushioned leather seats. They looked substantial. Smelled fresh and filled with promise. They would last a long time.

And so would the museum.

Finally, she closed the door on the board room and walked back down the hall, pausing to look into each exhibition room on her way. Every room had a fresh coat of paint, thanks to her apprentice Harry Perkins and several other teenage boys. The exhibit cases shone with polish and Windex, thanks to Alice Hinckley and the Granny Activist Brigade, known affectionately—and sometimes not so affectionately—as the GABs.

It was a far cry from the neglected Victorian mansion it had been when the professor had summoned her home. Back then, the paint was peeling, the old sign sagging and unreadable. Half the overhead lights were burned out, and the exhibits were covered in dust. The backyard maze, once a favorite attraction, was completely grown over.

Kate sighed. Thinking about those days was always bittersweet. The house and the museum had belonged to her friend and mentor Professor P. T. Avondale, a brilliant, reclusive man who had been her only friend when she was growing up as a neglected child genius in Granville.

Now the museum belonged to her, and one day it would belong to Harry. She'd promised the professor she would take care of the puzzles *and* his apprentice.

It was a promise she would never break. She smiled with satisfaction. It was just a beginning, but the Avondale Puzzle Museum was on its feet again.

Alice came in at one o'clock. She and the GABs took turns manning the front desk. They'd stepped in when Kate had lost her secretary, and they enjoyed it so much that Kate had kept them on. When she'd suggested payment, they became insulted, and she'd never mentioned it again, though she did donate to their favorite causes.

Since the museum didn't open until two o'clock during the

school year, Kate made herself a peanut butter sandwich, got a can of Coke out of the ancient refrigerator in the downstairs kitchen, and went upstairs to wade through an accumulated pile of bills, notices, and professional announcements, hard copy and e-mail.

As she sat down behind the old kneehole desk and popped open her soda, she heard the familiar clunk that told her Aloysius, the museum's Maine coon cat, had jumped down from the bookcase and was on his way to check out her lunch.

He leapt to the desktop in a flash of gray-brown fur and curved his feather duster tail around the stack of Sudoku books at the corner.

"Hello, Al." Kate reached over to scratch behind his ears while he rumbled a low purr and kept an eagle eye on her sandwich.

"Sorry fella, but you are too f-a-t. It's expensive, nutritional canned food for you until further notice."

"Yeow," Aloysius said and swiped at her sandwich. She barely managed to snatch it out of his way. With a look of disdain, the cat jumped from the desk and padded over to the professor's—now her—big wingback chair near the fireplace. He jumped to the seat, made his ritual three turns, then curled up on the cushion and returned to his nap.

The rain continued to fall as Kate opened her tax preparation folder. As a theoretical mathematician, she always enjoyed putting her knowledge to practical use, even when it meant taxes. She was soon immersed in the pleasure of number crunching.

The outside world faded away as the rain and her own concentration created a cocoon in the comfortable, darkly wainscoted office. She wasn't aware of another thing until Harry burst through the door at four o'clock.

Harry was fourteen, almost six feet tall, all arms and legs with copper hair and freckles that spread from ear to ear. He dropped his backpack on the floor and stood over her, broadcasting excitement. Kate clicked out of her tax program.

"Good day at school?"

Harry gave her a look.

Harry, at best, was bored at school. He had so informed her when they first met; he'd said he was only an almost genius, not as smart as Kate or the professor. But Kate had her suspicions. Brandon had considered sending him to a private school, but Kate convinced him a home life was more important—just as she'd convinced him to let Harry move in with him in the first place. She still thought she'd made the right decision.

"Guess what?"

"You aced your chem test."

"I always ace my chem test."

"English?"

He reached into his back jeans pocket and pulled out a crumpled copy of the *Granville Free Press*.

Kate groaned. "Et tu, Harry?"

"Huh?"

"Everybody was reading it at Rayette's this morning."

"Oh, the article about Henny Dougan. This is from Saturday. Much cooler. You know I told you the chief had a house guest."

Kate remembered. She never thought someone like Brandon, so self-contained—for lack of a kinder term—would ever entertain guests in his personal space. He and Kate had been sort-of friends for half a year, and he'd never once invited her to his house.

"Uh huh."

"He's wicked cool. He and the chief used to be partners back in Boston and—this is the coolest—he was working on the serial killer case before he came here on vacation."

Harry slapped the paper down in front of Kate. "How cool is that?"

"Very . . . cool," said Kate. "I wonder that they let him take a vacation in the middle of an investigation."

Harry frowned—for a nanosecond. "Hel-ck. They have the entire Boston force working on it. Detectives get leave time just like everybody else."

Everybody but her, it seemed. Not that she minded. There was no place she'd rather be than at the museum.

"He's been telling me all about it. The things that aren't classified, I mean. And I have some theories."

Kate shuddered. Harry was an ace at codes and ciphers, and Kate had long ago given up the hope that he would find a nice safe occupation like dentistry or veterinary sciences until he took over the museum. She'd even accept the idea of a desk job for him with the CIA or FBI, decoding terrorist threats. That should be safe.

After all, she'd been working for a highly classified government think tank herself before giving it up for the museum and moving back here permanently. And she'd never been involved in anything more dangerous than trying to get the last cup of coffee from the community coffee pot.

All the same, Harry's increasing interest in crime and enthusiasm for detecting made her cringe.

He propped one hip on the desk, knocking over the Sudoku books stacked there. He didn't seem to notice. "See. This guy has been able to elude them so far because his victims and the locations appear random. But what if. . ."

He broke off long enough to reach down for his backpack, knocking over more books. He pulled out a dog-eared stack of paper, shoved the books he'd just knocked over out of the way, and spread several sheets out in front of Kate.

Kate couldn't help but smile. How many times had the professor been just this oblivious to his surroundings when he was excited about something? Her throat constricted.

"What?" asked Harry, his pencil stub arrested above the page.

"What, what?" echoed Kate.

"You've got a kind of sappy smile on your face."

Kate shrugged. "Just enjoying your enthusiasm."

It was all Harry needed to rocket him into a long, convoluted explanation of his killer profile. "I've been working with Ted—that's the chief's friend. And he says I have a really analytical mind." Harry grinned. "Duh."

"Duh, right back at you," said Kate. "So, have you and Ted narrowed down the suspects?" She couldn't imagine Brandon taking part in this armchair investigation. He had strong opinions about Harry's and her involvement—read: meddling—in detective work.

"We're still working on it," Harry said.

"So tell me about Ted."

"Oh, you'll probably meet him when the chief comes to pick me up. We're going to Rayette's for dinner. Man, since she started staying open at night, our eating habits have sure improved."

"No more pizza?"

Red crept up Harry's face until the rest of his face matched his freckles. "Sometimes. But I hardly have to pay anymore. Just when I get really PO'ed at something. The chief . . ."

"You don't have to tell me," said Kate. "He's having a harder time cleaning up his language." It was a game they had started originally to eliminate four-letter words from the teenager's vocabulary. He'd been living with an abusive uncle until Kate had foisted him on the chief. He knew words Kate had never heard of, and *she'd* worked for the government.

She and Brandon knew he would never succeed at the local

middle school if he didn't clean up his act, so they made up the three-cuss-words-and-you-buy-pizza rule. It worked fairly well— Harry had toned it way down. Kate, who didn't use expletives that often, had gotten better. Only Brandon still had to buy a lot of pizza. Kate blamed his job as chief of police, but she still let him buy dinner.

"Yeah, well. After meeting Ted, I kind of understand the chief better."

"Oh?" This was intriguing. Kate didn't think she'd ever understand how Brandon's mind worked. Then again, she wasn't a rocket scientist in the social skills department. Too many brains, according to Aunt Pru.

"Yeah. They used to be partners, the chief and Ted. That's how Ted got his limp."

"He has a limp?"

"Yeah. Pretty bad one too. You kinda have to concentrate not to stare, ya know? But I'm getting used to it. Anyway. They were conducting a raid that went south and the chief got it in the gut—"

"He was shot?"

"Yeah. But it was a long time ago and it didn't hit anything important. Just broke a couple of ribs."

Kate swallowed bile. She'd never thought about Brandon's former life as a Boston detective, and he sure didn't volunteer any information on his own.

"So Ted went back to drag the chief out of the line of fire and the bast—*bad* guys plugged him in the leg. Shattered the humerus bone. Totally."

Kate shuddered. "How awful."

"Yeah, it's kind of amazing. He really gets around okay. And man, the guy has some biceps."

"Well, I can hardly wait to meet him."

"He wants to meet you too. I told him all about you and the museum."

"And our experiences in detecting?"

"Yeah, but only when the chief wasn't around, and I swore him to secrecy."

Kate let out a heartfelt sigh. "Harry . . ."

"I know. The chief would be seriously PO'ed. Don't tell him."

"No problem." She didn't want the chief seriously PO'ed at her.

2		9		6			8	1
	7			8		2		
	6		7		3			9
	5			7	9			6
	8	3			6	1	2	
7			8				5	
3			2		5		7	
		7		1			9	
8	9			4		3		2

CHAPTER

TWO

CHIEF MITCHELL WALKED into Kate's office at six o'clock, accompanied by a man Kate assumed was Ted. He was two inches shorter than the chief's six feet. Stockier and with an overly built-up torso and a receding hairline.

He shook Kate's hand. "I hope we're not interrupting."

"Just taxes and e-mails. They can wait."

"I've been looking forward to meeting you. Harry's told me all about you and your puzzle-solving skills."

Hopefully her museum puzzles, and not the other. Kate glanced at Brandon, but he seemed preoccupied.

Ted looked amused. "Says you're a world champion."

"Eastern United States champion. In Sudoku. But that was several years ago. I'm too busy to compete these days."

"I can understand after seeing this place. Harry gave me a quick tour when we came in. I had no idea there were so many different kinds of puzzles in the world."

"I'll give you a more in-depth tour if you have time while you're here."

"Would love it. Are these the ones you do?" Ted picked up a copy of *Samurai Sudoku* from the desk and flipped through it. He puffed out air. "I wouldn't know where to start."

"That's one of the more difficult ones. It uses overlapping Sudoku grids in such a way that their corners form a quincunx." She cringed inwardly and flashed a quick look to see if Ted's eyes were glazing over. She'd been practicing her people skills like crazy, but she still tended to slip into geek mode when talking about puzzles.

But Ted seemed interested. He leaned over the desk and read off several titles. "*Magna Mega Sudoku, Hypersudoku, Killer Sudoku.* I like that title. More along my line."

Kate smiled. What the heck was wrong with Brandon? Why didn't he say something? "Since you're a detective, I can see where the title would have a certain appeal."

"Now here's something I know. A Rubik's cube." Ted picked up the black cube that Kate used as a paperweight.

"Actually it's called a Sudokube. It's based on the same principles as the Rubik's cube, except given the nature of numbers, there is more than one solution."

"Well," said Ted, returning the cube to the desk. "It's Greek to me. I guess I'll have to stick to means, motive, and opportunity."

They smiled at each other.

Kate wished Brandon would take up the slack in the conversation. He knew how bad she was at small talk.

"Um, Harry says you're on vacation. We have lots of things to do around here." Too late, she realized that most of those things—like kayaking, hiking, and spelunking—might be impossible for a handicapped man. She felt the heat rush to her face.

Damn red hair. She could never hide her feelings. Her complexion always gave her away, which was a real disadvantage when dealing with the chief, who seemed to always bring out her fiercest emotions and who never showed emotion himself.

"I've made Bran promise to take me fishing. Now that he's given up big city crime for the cushy life of a small town cop, I expect him to know all the best spots."

Kate glanced toward Brandon, who just stood there like a stump, obviously not even paying attention to their conversation.

But he fooled her.

"Saturday," he said, so suddenly that Kate started. She saw something flicker in his eyes, but it passed so quickly that she wasn't sure she'd seen it—or what it meant.

He might be chafing with an extra house guest. He had taken Harry in against his will, and there had been some intense readjustments on both sides. Maybe a third person was just too much.

She heard Harry bounding up the stairs. A minute later he swung through the door. "I locked up. You guys ready to go? I'm starved. Want to come, Kate?"

There was a moment of dead silence, and then Ted said, "Sure, Kate. Would you like to join us?"

Kate shook her head. "I've got a huge amount of work to catch up on with tax season being upon us. Plus this stack of puzzles just came in the mail and I'm dying to get started on them."

And how pathetic was that, to choose an evening at home alone with a glass of wine and a puzzle instead of dinner out with two attractive men and a teenager who liked her company.

"You're welcome to come along," Brandon said belatedly.

"Thanks, but I can't tonight. Enjoy yourselves. Have you been to Rayette's yet, Ted? Excellent food. Her pot roast is fabulous, and her chicken—" She stopped, suddenly aware that she was babbling. "Have a good time."

She breathed a sigh of relief when they finally left. Brandon had insisted she come down with them and dead-bolt the front door. She watched from the window as they walked down the sidewalk toward Main Street—three men out on the town. Then she fed Al, gathered up her new puzzle books. and went home to eat leftovers in front of the television.

The first thing Kate saw when she walked into Rayette's the next morning was the stack of *Free Press* papers.

"Finn Tucker must work twenty-four-seven," she said to Rayette. She stuffed a dollar into a canister with the initials GFP printed on it and took a copy.

Killer hits Manchester. Will Granville be next?

"Manchester? The Boston serial killer?" Kate scanned the few paragraphs and turned to page three to read the continuation of the story. Page three was blank. So was page two. She turned the paper over. Page four was filled with pictures of cows, pigs, and chickens with proud youngsters displaying award ribbons. The 4-H fair had finally made the news.

Kate dropped the paper and picked up another copy. Its middle pages were blank too.

"Unfortunately," said Rayette, handing her a latte to go, "while Finn was having dinner here last night, someone broke into the *Free Press* office and took a sledge hammer to his printer. He'd only printed half the pages for today's edition."

"That's terrible."

"He swears he'll have the paper up and running by tomorrow. The poor guy. I think he sank every penny he had into purchasing the paper. There's just the two of them, Finn and Fast Eddie."

"Fast Eddie?"

"Eddie Blair, the photographer. Finn calls him Fast Eddie. He canvassed the area for pictures of the 4-H fair and got them printed in the paper. Nice guy, even if he does have a ponytail that's longer than half the girls in Granville."

"Did they catch who did it?"

"Not yet. But my guess is they won't have far to look."

Henny Dougan, Kate thought. At least he'd gone after the printer and not Finn Tucker's head.

"Well, I gotta get back to work." Rayette adjusted her white apron. "Damn if I don't think I've gained another pound or two. I tell ya, middle age is a bitch."

She snagged three menus off the counter and gestured to a group of women who'd just come in.

"See you tomorrow?" she asked.

"First thing," Kate said. "It wouldn't be Saturday without a sticky bun straight from the oven."

"Better make it seven. I've got a busy day ahead. I'll leave the front door open." Rayette led the women to a table and Kate headed to the museum.

The rain had slackened off to a drizzle, though there were more ominous clouds in the sky.

With all this rain, we'd better have May flowers out the wazoo, Kate thought grumpily and got into her Toyota. She parked at the curb near the museum. As she walked up the sidewalk, the sun made a brief appearance before disappearing again.

Spring was definitely on its way, though they would probably get a couple more fast but fierce snow or ice storms. April was like that. In New Hampshire, a white Easter could happen as easily as a white Christmas.

And now some crazed nut case was headed their way. If one

could believe the *Free Press*.

But to trust a paper whose sole content seemed to be scandal and rumor? Finn Tucker was just guessing. There was no way one incident of murder could point to the serial killer moving north. The Manchester murder had to be pure coincidence.

It would take all of her colleagues at the Institute of Theoretical Mathematics to calculate the odds of the Boston killer making his way up I-93 to Granville, systematically stopping to kill, and leaving a trail of clues behind him.

Yellow press. That's all the *Free Press* article was, she decided. Finn Tucker had taken advantage of an unrelated murder to instill curiosity. And frighten half the population. He'd spun the story in order to sell papers. And it had accomplished just what it was meant to do.

He might not be making friends here, but he sure had their attention.

There is something inherently frightening about a serial killer, Kate thought. A crime of passion she could sort of understand intellectually as long as one didn't know the victims. But serial killing seemed so random. No obvious reason as to what set it off, where he would strike next, or who the victim would be. Someone you knew? Or even yourself.

Unfortunately there was no formula that could take human quirks into account. *Much less the mind of a maniac.*

Kate shuddered. She wasn't fanciful at all, but she was just spooked enough to turn on the lights in each of the exhibit rooms before she went upstairs to the office. She stayed fairly calm until she reached the hidden puzzle room. Usually, this room was inviting, with pictures hidden within pictures: an old man emerging from a craggy mountain, a group of picnickers appearing within a bowl of flowers, all inviting you to be part of the discovery.

It could also be a little creepy. Kate remembered the times after the professor's death when she'd been loath to enter it. In those days, each hidden face seemed to pop out, not to amuse her, but to accuse her of not acting soon enough to save him.

It felt totally creepy today even with the bright lights and freshly painted walls. The old man suddenly took on the guise of murderer, the people in the floral arrangement, the unsuspecting victims. She quickly peered into each corner, then sprinted up the stairs to the office, where she turned on the lights and shut the door.

At least here she felt safe. And there was plenty to do to keep her mind off potential serial killings. Besides finishing up her taxes and answering all the e-mails she'd been neglecting, there were the new expansion plans to study before the next board meeting and the next fundraiser to organize in order to pay for the necessary improvements.

Even with the addition of P. T.'s Place, which was an interactive puzzle room for kids, and an additional exhibition room on the second floor, they were still crowded. Many of the exhibits were still in storage.

At one time, Kate had planned to expand to the third floor where the professor had kept his private quarters, but Harry became so upset that she'd given up the idea. Now Kate's dream was to eventually build out the back of the first floor: a large room for displays, a library for the puzzle books, and an atrium filled with plants and comfortable seating and a view of the privet maze that took up most of the backyard.

She and Rayette had even discussed putting in a coffee bar.

Yet the idea of a serial killer drawing closer to Granville niggled at her mind, kept her from concentrating completely. It was the bane of a puzzle solver, or a mathematician: the need to know. Why? How? What if?

Her field was theoretical mathematics. The government had been quick to realize its usefulness in applied mechanics. And even Brandon Mitchell had begrudgingly recognized that the mathematical method had been pivotal in solving more than one murder.

Kate opened her e-mail and sighed at the sheer numbers. Some she could delete. Some were industry advertisements—these she would either file or delete. There were quite a few that required answers.

She went doggedly to work, staving off the image of a killer that lurked in the recesses of her mind. *Damn Finn Tucker and his lurid headlines.*

A crash sounded outside the window. The wind had picked up, and she knew it was just a falling tree branch—not a serial killer. But she couldn't stop the thrill of fear that rippled up her spine.

It was a stupid, illogical reaction, brought on by the power of suggestion. She was playing right into Finn Tucker's manipulations: He had her imagining all sorts of things. There was only one thing that could stop an imagination run wild.

Knowledge.

Kate closed her e-mail account and logged on to the Internet.

With Aloysius kibitzing—by attempting to bat at the key pad as she typed—Kate surfed the net for articles about the Boston serial killer. There weren't too many details. The Boston police were playing this one close to the chest.

The victims were both male and female. They had been found in seemingly unrelated places; a walking path, a grocery parking lot, an alley between a row of town houses, under an overpass. The last victim was discovered lying on a park bench as if he were asleep. There was no mention of the method of killing.

Kate searched for the Manchester murder. A suburban housewife, mother of four. The husband was cooperating with the police.

A terrible tragedy, but too many unknown variables and nothing to connect it to the Boston killer. The murders had to be pure coincidence.

Harry bounded up the stairs at three-fifty. He tossed his backpack on the floor by the desk and peered over her shoulder, holding a giant double-decker sandwich away from the computer. "Whatcha doing?"

"Finishing up a bunch of e-mails. How was dinner last night?" she asked, hoping he hadn't heard about the Manchester murder.

Harry frowned. "Okay. But a bunch of people came up and hassled the chief."

"Because he took in Henny Dougan?"

"Nah. Nobody cares what happens to him. They were afraid the serial killer was headed toward Granville now."

"Well, he's not," said Kate. "There's no need to worry. But we should always be smart and take precautions."

Harry gave her a look.

"I mean it, Harry." She frowned. "Wait a minute. The Manchester murder was in this morning's paper. How did people know about it last night?"

"Somebody heard it on his CB and was spreading doom and gloom. Sometimes the people in this town act like a bunch of nut cases."

"You'll get no argument from me," said Kate. "I assume the chief reassured them."

"Yeah. But then Ted told them they were safe under the—get this—watchful eye of the police. Which everybody knows is a joke, cause the only watchful eye is the chief, so they started giving him sh—*a hard time* about his force being so young. And asking how he planned to protect them."

"Poor Brandon."

"Then they turned on Ted and told him to mind his own murders. Then the chief got called out to the Winslow farm, 'cause their creek overflowed with all the rain we've been having and their bridge washed out. Rayette had to pack up his dinner."

Harry heaved a sigh. "It was still in the fridge this morning. I don't even know if he got home last night. He was gone when me and Ted got up."

"Rough night," said Kate sympathetically. It didn't seem like the chief ever caught a break.

"Why can't people be nice to him?"

"They're just making him pay his dues. They don't really mean it. Look at Jason Elks. He's lived here for fifteen years and they still give him a hard time."

"It isn't fair."

"No. But it's the Granville way." Kate touched his arm. "They just like to razz him. If they really hated him, they'd have driven him away by now."

Harry scuffed over to the wing chair and slumped into it. He reached for one of his cipher books from the side table, fumbled in the caddy for a pen, and opened the book.

He was acting just like the professor when he didn't want to deal with his problems. And just like in the old days with her mentor, Kate turned on the hot plate for tea before sitting down in the second wing chair and opening her own puzzle book.

Saturday morning began wet and chilly and uncomfortable, but at least the rain had held off. It was a day for staying in bed—which

Kate would never do, even if there weren't hot sticky buns waiting for her at Rayette's.

It was barely seven when she reached the bakery. She found a parking place right in front since Rayette wouldn't be open for business until nine.

A bell tinkled as she open the front door. No one was in the front yet. The waitresses wouldn't be in for another forty-five minutes or so. The big copper espresso maker was gurgling, so Johnny was already here. Rayette must be in the kitchen because the outer rooms were filled with the sweet, spicy smell of hot sticky buns.

Kate stepped behind the counter and went through the swinging door to the kitchen. Two huge pans of sticky buns were placed on the cutting table. The kitchen was empty, but the back door was open.

Kate walked across the room and peered out into the alley. Rayette, Johnny, and Calvin, the new chef, were standing side by side staring at a row of metal trashcans.

"Rayette?" called Kate.

Rayette looked up. There was a big smudge of white icing across her cheek. The rest of her face was just as white. She opened her mouth, closed it, then mutely pointed to the row of trash cans.

Kate hurried down the pavement and pulled up short.

Henny Dougan lay sprawled against the cans. Kate shook her head. He must have passed out in the alley during the night. At least it wasn't freezing, just wet. But he sure didn't look good.

His head lay in a puddle, pillowed by a square of soggy newspaper. His hair was matted. His clothes were filthy and clung to him where the rain had seeped into the fabric. And the smell, a combination of vomit, urine and—Kate covered her nose with the edge of her rain slicker and tried to breathe through her mouth.

"Is he all right?" she asked hopefully.

Rayette shook her head. Johnny and Calvin just stared at the motionless figure.

Kate inched closer, leaned over, and peered down at him. "Henny, wake up." Then louder, "Henny."

Henny didn't respond. He didn't groan or turn over to go back to sleep. He just lay there.

"Shit," Kate said, staring down at the body. *Shit.*

One thing was perfectly clear. Henny Dougan might have started out drunk, but he'd ended up really dead—and it wasn't the booze that killed him.

CHAPTER

THREE

KATE'S PURSE AND Sudoku book fell from her hands as she fumbled in her rain slicker pocket for her cell phone. She pressed 4, the speed-dial number for the Granville police station.

Elmira Swyndon, the office secretary, dispatcher, and soother of ruffled feathers, answered with a cheery, "Good morning, Granville Police."

"Elmira." Kate gasped in air—she must have been holding her breath. "This is Kate McDonald."

"Hi, Katie. What has you calling us this early on a Saturday morning? Nothing serious, I hope."

"We have trouble over at Rayette's."

"Not that no good Henny Dougan again? The chief just had him in here a couple of days ago, drunker than a waxwing on fermented mulberries."

"It's Henny. But he isn't drunk. He's dead." The last word wobbled out. Kate sucked in more breath and concentrated on not crying.

There was silence at Elmira's end of the line, then, "I knew he'd drink himself to death one day."

Kate was afraid it wasn't liquor that had killed him. Once she was close enough, she'd seen the narrow red line that bisected his throat from ear to ear.

"I'll send the chief."

"Thanks. In the alley out back," Kate added quickly before Elmira hung up.

The four of them stood together watching the body—a safe, upwind distance away. Not that Henny was going anywhere. Rigor had come and gone, and Henny Dougan was as limp and soggy as the day-old newspaper that lay beneath his head.

Ironically, Kate could see a piece of the headline from yesterday's *Free Press*: "Murd—"

It seemed like forever before she heard footsteps running down the alley from the street.

"Thank God," she said as Brandon Mitchell reached them.

He looked tired, the hollowed-eyed gaunt look of too little sleep and too much on his mind.

"He's over there. I think he was —"

The chief held up his hand. "Kate, I had a washed-out bridge one night, downed power lines last night. So *don't think.*" It was a warning as much as it was a statement. He'd have no patience with interference today.

Then she saw Harry sprinting toward them, and at a slower, more awkward pace, Ted Lumley. All three of them were wearing jeans and fishing vests, but they wouldn't be seeing any fishing today.

"I thought I told you to wait in the truck!"

Harry skidded to a stop.

"Ease up, Bran," said Ted, sounding slightly out of breath. "You can't have a ten-fifty-four and expect him—or me—not to be curious. I'll keep him out of your way."

Rayette looked a question at Kate. "A ten-fifty-four?"

"A possible dead body," Harry volunteered.

Brandon shot Harry a look. Harry lifted his chin.

"At least stay out of the way."

Ted put a hand on Harry's shoulder.

Brandon knelt by the body. "Anybody disturb the scene?" he asked over his shoulder.

Kate looked at Rayette.

"Calvin shook him with his foot. Nobody wanted to touch him. He'd kind of . . . had an accident."

"That's what happens when people die." Brandon stood up and reached to his belt for his cell: a brief conversation, which Kate knew must be to the county crime scene investigator and another call, most likely to Sam Swyndon. Sam had gotten the job of police photographer by default, being the only photographer in town and because he was Elmira's nephew.

He didn't like the job, and he really didn't like Kate's involvement in what seemed like an increasing spate of murders. He was going to have a fit when he saw her now.

The chief rehooked his phone. "Who found him?"

"Joh—" Rayette cleared her throat and started again. "Johnny did. He came out to recycle some vegetable boxes and . . ." She finished by gesturing vaguely toward Henny. "And he called me and Calvin."

Brandon turned toward Kate. "And how did you manage to be on the scene?"

Kate stifled her annoyance. "I always have an early breakfast with Rayette on Saturdays. Girl time," she ended with a shrug.

"Figures.

"It's noy my—"

"I'll need to get a statement from each of you. But for now, everyone go inside. Take Harry with you. And, Kate, no comparing notes. Rayette, you'll have to put up the closed sign."

Rayette snapped out of her stupor. "I will not."

"Rayette, there's been a—"

"I know there has. And I'm sorry the man is dead—I guess—but I'll be damned if he's going to wreck my busiest breakfast day of the week. It took me long enough to build it up. Sorry, Chief. But there it is."

The chief deliberated, looking back at the body. Kate wondered what he was thinking. She knew he must have seen the ligature marks on Henny's neck. "All right," he said at last, "but not one damn word."

"Chief!" Kate and Harry exclaimed together.

He gave them an evil look that shut them both up.

Mutely, they all turned toward the bakery door. Brandon caught Kate by the shoulder, stopping her. "I don't want a damn panic on my hands," he said in a low voice.

She nodded. She understood, and he knew she did. She would do her part to keep things quiet.

More footsteps. Sam Swyndon was moving at a brisk walk toward them. His step hesitated when he saw Kate. Brandon's hand dropped from her shoulder. Kate turned to face Sam, who was scowling at Brandon.

Honestly, Sam was almost as bad as her Aunt Pru when it came to protecting her from the chief's "attentions"—not that the chief had ever paid her any of those kind of attentions. Just business and exasperation.

"Amazing that the part-time photographer arrives at the scene before my officers," the chief said sourly.

Ted shook his head, but he seemed more amused than concerned over the situation. Maybe he'd just seen too much murder in his line of work.

"What are you doing here?" Sam asked, moving closer to Kate. He must have been asleep, because his hair stuck up in tuffs over his forehead and one side was smashed flat against his head. He was wearing jeans instead of the slacks and buttoned-collar shirt he wore at his photography studio, and Kate could see the edge of a white T-shirt beneath his hunter's jacket.

"I was going to have breakfast," Kate said a little too sharply.

"Hmm." Sam turned his scowl back toward the chief.

The chief looked as bland as a rock. "Over there," he said, indicating the body. "Go inside, Kate." He walked away from both of them.

"I'll talk to *you* later," Sam told Kate, and began setting up his equipment.

Kate lingered when she saw Paul Curtis, one of the three young officers under Brandon's command, hurrying down the alley. Benjamin Meany, who had retired from the force nearly twenty years before—and whose sole duty was emptying parking meters when his rheumatism allowed—accompanied him.

"Oh God, give me patience," muttered Brandon, almost groaning the words. Before the two policeman had made it halfway down the alley, another man sprinted past them: Finn Tucker. Eddie Blair was right behind him, his pony tail flapping against his back as he snapped pictures on a digital camera.

"It's a parade," Ted said and burst out laughing.

"Curtis, get those two out of here!"

Finn skidded on the wet pavement and ended up forehead to chin with the chief.

"Tell me, Chief Mitchell," he said in an excited tenor that held a faint Irish accent. "How long was the body here before it was found?"

Fast Eddie eased past him toward the body. Without taking his eyes from Finn Tucker, the chief snagged him by the elbow and grabbed the camera.

"Hey, police brutality," Eddie groused, and attempted to reclaim his camera.

Brandon held it out of reach. "You're obstructing justice and tampering with an investigation in progress."

"So it's a crime scene, is it?" asked Finn, shoving a tape recorder under the chief's nose.

"It's going to be if you don't move that machine and get yourself and your assistant here out of this alley."

Paul Curtis and Benjamin Meany stood by, waiting expectantly, though Mr. Meany looked more eager than the twenty-four-year-old Curtis.

"Come along, son. And don't upset the chief," Meany said.

Finn ignored him. "Was it murder, chief? Has the Boston serial killer struck in Granville?"

"There's an investigation under way. No cause of death has been established. When the details become public knowledge, you will be free to print them. But if you print anything—anything at all—that causes a panic in this town, you'll be looking at jail time. Now back off."

"It's Henny Dougan, boss," Eddie said, craning his neck to get a better view of the body.

"You don't say." Finn tried to muscle his way past Brandon. The chief barred his way expediently by throwing out his arm and catching the newspaperman across the chest.

"Hey, you—"

"Son, why don't you let the police do their work." It was Ted. Kate noticed he had a way of sounding friendly and authoritarian in the same sentence.

"And who would you be?" asked Finn. He shoved the tape

recorder in Ted's face. Ted stepped back, his leg gave, and he threw his arms out for balance, inadvertently knocking the tape recorder out of Finn's hand.

Finn juggled for a frantic moment before reclaiming it, but by then Ted had moved away.

"Curtis, Meany, show these gentlemen to the street."

"You've got my camera."

"Which will be returned to you once all pertinent photos have been wiped. Curtis, give him a receipt."

Officer Curtis pulled out a notebook and, after fumbling in his pockets, pulled out a stub of pencil.

"But my camera's necessary for my line of work."

"Then you can wait at the station until I've finished here. You can wait there, too, Mr. Tucker. I have a few questions for both of you."

"Hey, you don't think we—"

"Curtis."

Benjamin Meany stepped to Finn Tucker's side. "This way." He motioned to Curtis, who took the other side.

They finally moved away while Finn danced between the two officers trying to get a last look at the scene.

After a sullen look at the chief, Fast Eddie followed.

Ted leaned over and picked up Kate's purse and Sudoku book off the ground. Both were wet and covered with mud; the books pages were crumpled and torn.

He smoothed out the pages and read the cover. "Killer Sudoku. Appropriate." He handed the book and purse to Kate.

"Thanks."

"Kate. Inside. Now."

"What are they doing?" asked Harry, trying to peer over Kate's shoulder.

They were in the kitchen, perched on the counter next to the industrial-size sink, trying to look out the small window that overlooked the alley.

"I can't tell. The trash cans are way off to the left, and I can't get a clear view." All she could see were parts of Sam as he shifted positions to get another angle of photos. The chief's head popped in and out of view as he moved around the area, stopping, kneeling down, standing up again.

It was like a jigsaw puzzle with pieces missing. Kate longed to just open the door and see the whole picture.

She hadn't mentioned the ligature marks to anyone, not even Harry. Since she, unfortunately, had been involved in discovering a body—several bodies—before today, Kate knew the drill. Don't talk, don't speculate.

Johnny sat on a stool, his head lowered between his knees. Calvin moved along the row of open shelves, shaking his head and mumbling to himself. Rayette paced the length of the kitchen, looking worried.

Calvin lifted a huge glass bowl off the top shelf and set it on the stainless steel work island. He opened the fridge and took out four cartons of eggs and began to crack them one-handed into the bowl.

"Yo, Johnny, my man, I totally relate to the ick factor, but shouldn't you be checking the coffeemaker?"

Johnny's ashen face appeared above his knees. He caught sight of the eggs and lowered his head again.

"Leave him be, Calvin," Rayette said. "The coffee can wait . . . for a few minutes . . . What's taking the chief so long?"

Calvin rolled his eyes toward Kate and cracked another egg.

The door opened just then, and Kate and Harry jumped back.

The chief, followed closely by Ted, eased in the door and closed it behind him. He raked his fingers through his hair and looked around the kitchen.

Rayette pounced on him. "How much longer are you going to be, Chief? My waitresses will be here in less than a half hour."

"Jee—" He caught himself and sighed, a sound awfully close to a growl. He took a breath. "I'll get initial statements now. Then I guess you can have your kitchen back. But stay out of the alley. The county crime scene van is on its way."

"They're getting faster," Harry commented.

Ted chuckled. "Practice. They told Bran they were going to requisition a van just for Granville."

"Funny," Brandon said dryly. "Do you think we could get a couple of cups of coffee?"

"Sure," Rayette said. "Johnny?"

Johnny looked up.

"Oh, never mind. Back in a sec."

"Calvin, you first," the chief said.

Calvin kept beating his eggs. "I don't know anything but what you saw. Johnny goes out back to dump the boxes and stumbles back inside looking green as an overripe avocado. All he can do is point and pant, so I went outside. Saw Dougan. Called Rayette."

"And none of you touched him?"

"Only with my shoe, like Rayette said. I mean, the man was nasty. You saw it. Would you touch—well, I guess you had to. I feel for you. It was bad. We all knew he was dead. He'd—*you know*—lost it all, everywhere. . . Makes you think twice about dying. "

Johnny groaned.

Kate had to swallow hard as the smell of eggs wafted toward her.

Even Harry looked pale.

The chief stoically moved on to Johnny, who had little to add.

Rayette returned with the coffeepot and poured out cups all around.

Calvin moved to the refrigerator and took out a milk carton. He had to squeeze between the chief and the center island to reach a bag of flour. He dropped it on the work table.

"Not to appear crass," Calvin said, sounding as if he didn't care one way or the other, "and it's not like I don't enjoy the company, but could you all get the hell out so I can work?"

"Calvin," Rayette snapped.

"Sorry, but the guy was a drunk and an asshole. And if you want the Saturday brunch special ready in time for Saturday brunch, I. Need. My. Space."

The chief gave him a considering look. Opened his mouth, then shut it.

Kate breathed a sigh of relief. Calvin could be grateful that he wouldn't be whipping up crepes from a jail cell.

"Hell and damnation, Calvin," Rayette said, "stop being an ass and cut the chief a break." She turned to Brandon with a smile. "Since you can't cuss, I'm doing it for you. Be grateful. How much longer are you gonna be?"

"As soon as—" The chief was interrupted by a loud clap of thunder. "Shit." He headed for the door.

"I'd better round up all those umbrellas people have left behind," said Rayette. "Sounds like you're gonna need them."

Before the door closed behind the chief, Kate heard him order, "Get a tarp out of the trunk and set up a shelter. And Curtis . . . try not to touch the body."

"I think I'll just go help out," said Ted and went out to the alley.

The chief stuck his head back inside. "I'll have to take your statements later. I don't need to remind all of you not to discuss this matter."

They all shook their heads, except Calvin, who saluted with his wooden spoon.

Kate could swear she heard the chief grinding his teeth.

"Kate, would you mind giving Harry a ride home?"

"No way," Harry said as Kate said, "Sure."

"Harry."

"Can we at least have breakfast first?"

"I guess. But stay away from the alley and don't speculate out loud. And go straight home or to the museum when you finish." He pulled the door shut without waiting for an argument.

"I think Harry and I will go see if Rayette needs help," Kate said.

Calvin grunted. "Could you get that package of Canadian bacon out of the fridge on your way out? Right side."

A groan came from Johnny's bowed head.

Kate reached into the double-door refrigerator and lifted out the slab of bacon. Her stomach rebelled, and she held it at arm's length until she could slide it onto the island.

Calvin shook his head at her. He took the plastic wrap with each hand and rolled the bacon onto a wooden cutting board with a flourish. "You better take Sir Barf-a-lot with you." He picked up a wide carving knife.

Johnny pushed to his feet. Kate and Harry dragged him out of the kitchen just as a large *whack* resounded behind them.

	3	1		4		2	9	
		7	2				4	
	6		7		1	8		
1				2		5	6	
4				6				9
	7	8	5		9			4
		6	1		2		3	
	1				6	4		
	2	5		8		6	7	

CHAPTER

FOUR

KATIE PICKED AT a piece of dry toast and watched Harry tuck into a plate of scrambled eggs, bacon, a side of banana-walnut pancakes, and his second glass of milk. She took another sip of coffee and wondered if this was just the resiliency of teenagers or if Harry was becoming way too cavalier about murder.

Henny Dougan had definitely been murdered, and unless she'd missed her guess, which she rarely did when it came to details, Harry had also noticed the marks on Henny's neck and merely tucked the information away to discuss later. This couldn't be a normal reaction to death from a fourteen-year-old, she told herself.

Maybe Brandon was right. Living around so much violence couldn't be good for a teenage boy, especially not after all the violence Harry had been subject to during the years he lived with his hateful uncle.

Living with the chief might be introducing him to just a different kind of violence. But it was also teaching him justice and fair play. Harry needed a good, solid male role model, and you couldn't get much more solid than Brandon Mitchell.

Kate put down her cup.

The new waitress, Lynn, appeared at her elbow to refill it. "Hi, Harry. Haven't seen you and Chief Mitchell here for a couple of nights."

Harry flushed and swallowed hard. "He's been real busy."

"Well, don't make yourself a stranger." She winked at him.

Harry watched her move to the next table. "She's wicked hot," he said dreamily.

Kate dropped her fork. It clattered on her plate. "What?"

"Lynn, the waitress. She's—"

"Oh my *Lord!* Harry, I'm not ready for this."

Harry grinned.

"And neither are you. So eat up and let's get out of here."

Kate had chosen a table against the wall close to the door to facilitate an easy departure if news of Henny Dougan's death became public knowledge. So far they'd been left alone, but Kate knew it was only a matter of time.

The Granville grapevine gathered intelligence as fast as any Homeland Security network. And when the news did leak out, everyone would come to her—the go-to girl of the GPD—as if she had a private line to the police force. Which she didn't. Which didn't make any difference. The good people of Granville "knew what they knew," whether it was the truth or not.

She could barely sit still wondering if the CSI van had arrived, if the body had been taken away to the county morgue. She had an overwhelming urge to go into the kitchen and peek out the window, but that would set a bad example for Harry.

So she sat, trying to look unconcerned as unanswered questions roiled in her mind.

Who would want to kill Henny? Nobody liked him, but mainly they just ignored him.

Had he smashed Finn Tucker's printer? Had Finn found out and killed him? It was far-fetched. No one would kill over a printer, unless the new editor of the *Free Press* had a history of violence. Which was possible.

Tess Dougan was apparently missing. If Henny had really killed her, might someone be out for revenge?

She considered and dismissed the idea of an itinerant vagrant passing through town. *That's what people always hope for in these cases—a stranger,* she thought. *Not one of us.* It very rarely happened that way.

Or worse still, could the *Free Press* articles about the Boston serial killer have triggered a copycat murder? Or even worse than that, had the Boston killer gotten tired of Boston and moved on to Granville—

Absurd. Her imagination was mushrooming out of control.

"Aren't you hungry?" Harry asked. The words were muffled by a mouthful of pancakes.

Kate looked down. Little pieces of toast lay crumbled in a pile on her plate. "Not really."

"Because of the—"

"Harry," she warned. She was distracted by a sudden commotion in the entranceway. "There she is." Jason Elks hurried toward the table where Kate and Harry sat.

"I think it's time for us to split," said Harry, cramming a last piece of bacon into his mouth as he stood up.

"Too late," Kate said. "You might as well sit back down."

Jason came to a stop, blocking their escape.

Erik Ingersoll muscled his way closer. "Is it true that Henny Dougan is dead in Rayette's alley?"

If he'd meant to be discreet with his *sotto voce* question, he had sorely miscalculated. It echoed across the café.

The rustle of reaction, the scrape of chairs, and they were surrounded by a half dozen diners.

"What's this about Henny Dougan?"

"Dead," said Erik.

"Behind the bakery," added Jason.

All heads turned toward the kitchen door, then back to Erik and Jason.

"Musta drunk himself to death."

"Probably fell over in a drunken stupor and hit his head."

"He's been asking for it for years."

"Do you think they'll still dig up his foundation?"

"Maybe it was the guilt that did him in."

"Who found him?"

Erik turned on them, hands on his hips, and took an expansive breath that strained the buttons over his barrel belly. "If you'd all just hold on a sec, that's what I'm trying to find out from Katie here."

They turned to Kate.

"Did you find him, Katie?" they pressed.

"You sure got some kind of sixth sense or something. How many does this make?"

"At least three, or was it four?"

Kate shook her head as her cheeks flamed with embarrassment. "Not me."

"Then what are you doing here?" asked Erik.

"Having breakfast."

There was a collective sigh of disappointment.

"Erik probably made the whole thing up." This idea was met with murmurs of agreement.

"I did not. Jason and I ran into Finn Tucker and his photographer on our way over here. They were hurrying back to the paper offices to put out a special edition."

"Not another special edition."

"Never heard of such nonsense."

"He'll have to lower his prices. Can't spend a dollar every time there's a special edition."

The crowd suddenly parted, and Rayette pushed her way through. "I got people waiting for tables . . . so if you're all finished. . .?"

"Did you find Henny Dougan's body out back?"

"No," said Rayette with a snap of her teeth. "Now go sit down."

Grumbling, everyone returned to their seats to eat and speculate. Kate was pretty sure there would be lots of people detouring to the alley after breakfast.

Rayette collapsed into the free chair next to Kate. "Ghouls." She raised her hand and Lynn appeared with the coffee pot, snagged a mug off a nearby table, and filled it for Rayette. She topped off Kate's cup and asked Harry if he wanted another glass of milk.

Harry shook his head, suddenly tongue-tied.

"The girl's on her toes," Rayette said after Lynn walked away. "I'll say that for her. Got her and Holly alternating day and night shifts. I'm even thinking about taking on a third girl. Johnny helps out with the rush, but he doesn't have Lynn's *je ne sais quoi*." Rayette grinned at Kate, then pointed her finger at Harry. "And don't you go getting any ideas—her *je ne sais quoi* ain't for you."

Harry blushed and concentrated on pushing a forkful of pancake though the syrup on his plate.

"Maybe I should have closed up for today."

"Well," said Kate. "Closing the café isn't going to bring Henny back."

"Not that we'd want him back." Rayette let out a gusty sigh. "Ah hell, that was very un-Christian of me. But he was such a low-down scoundrel, and if he really killed Tess . . ."

Kate shook her head. "No evidence. But it's an academic question now."

"It's just that it's taken me so long to make a go of the café. I'm finally convincing people that life is more than just sticky buns and muffins...." She sighed again. "But I still feel pretty low. I mean there's a dead man in my alley."

"It sure hasn't put a damper on their appetites."

Rayette shook her head. "It boggles the mind. Though I'm not complaining." She pushed herself up from the chair and wiped her hands on her skirt, the apron forgotten as always. "I'd better get back to work." She cocked a finger at Harry. "And I'm telling Lynn that you're only fourteen."

Kate had to force herself not to detour by the alley on her way to her car. Harry didn't have such scruples.

"I better tell the chief we're leaving. Guess there won't be any fishing today."

"I know," said Kate. "I'm sorry."

"It's okay. Henny was murdered, wasn't he?"

Kate quickly looked around, but the sidewalk was empty. "I have no idea, and I wouldn't mention the subject if I were you."

"I won't. 'Cause if it's murder, everybody will get on the chief's case. Like it's his fault that Henny Dougan is a drunk and maybe killed his wife. I wonder if they've taken the body away."

Kate shuddered. "You're getting much too grisly for me, Harry."

"Let's just check it out!" Harry took off around the corner. Kate had no choice but to follow.

A knot of people was standing at the entrance to the alley, peering in.

"Harry, the chief doesn't need us adding to the craziness."

Harry shoved his hands in his pockets. "Can't see anything anyway."

Kate steered him back to Main Street and the car.

When they got to the museum, Alice was already sitting behind the reception desk, her stamp pad and ticket dispenser lined up in perfect order.

"'Morning, Katie. Harry, I thought you were going fishing today."

"Henny Dougan bit it in the alley, so the chief had to cancel. Is Ginny Sue here yet?"

"Up in P. T.'s Place, setting up for puzzle hour."

Harry took the stairs two at a time.

"Dead?" Alice whispered when Harry was out of hearing.

"Dead," Kate said.

Alice clasped her hands together and closed her eyes. "Lord have mercy on him. The Lord knows he'll need it." She clicked her tongue. "And on Chief Mitchell's day off, too."

"It was really gross," Harry was saying as Kate stepped into the interactive puzzle room. He was sitting on the craft table, swinging his feet.

Ginny Sue Bright was standing on a stepladder, dressed in jeans and a yellow sweater, looking as bright as her name and as chipper as the primary-colored walls. She was holding a stack of large construction paper.

She saw Kate and climbed down. "Katie! How *awful.*" She dropped the papers on the table. "Are you all right?"

Ginny Sue was one of the few people who could show concern and still be upbeat at the same time. She and Kate had been in the same grade at Patrick Henry Elementary and Valley High School, but had only become friends since Kate had returned to Granville.

Now they were not only best friends, but in addition to her duties as a fourth-grade teacher, Ginny Sue was on the board of the museum and ran the museum's Saturday children's program. She also ran two afternoon Sudoku sessions to help children improve their study and thinking skills, and she'd started a Numbers Busters class for kids having trouble with basic math skills.

She was an indefatigable pixie, with long auburn hair that swirled softly about her shoulders and made Kate green with envy. Kate unconsciously smoothed back her own unmanageable hair— a hopeless gesture in this weather.

"What's on for today?" she asked as Ginny Sue carried paste jars from the supply cabinet and placed them on the table.

"Pattern puzzles. Then once we solve them, we'll glue the pieces on the construction paper to take home and show their parents. They can hang them on the wall or put them on the fridge for the whole family to enjoy." She took out baggies filled with colorful paper shapes and dumped them into plastic bowls.

Kate picked up a few and arranged them on the tabletop. "Hmm," she said, rearranging her initial design. "Matching edges, repeated color . . ." She took a few more pieces and placed them next to the pieces she'd arranged. "Nice."

"I think the kids will like it, and I have some larger, simpler designs for the younger kids."

Kate scooped up her puzzle and redistributed the pieces in the correct bowls. "Are you going to hang here, Harry?"

"Yeah, I guess."

"I'll call the chief and let him know where you are."

The chief didn't answer his cell. Kate didn't expect him to. She left a message and tried not to think about what she'd seen in the alley that morning. But the image of Henny Dougan lying in the filth, that ring of cut skin around his neck—ugh.

When she'd first seen it, she'd just assumed it was dirt. But she hadn't spent years in a government think tank without learning to take in all the details and assume that each random element fit into a pattern until it could be discounted or confirmed.

The scientist in her, the inquisitive nature, had made her take a second look. Something had cut Henny's throat. *A knife? Or a piece of wire?*

The flood gates of speculation opened. *Why? Who? How? What would leave that kind of mark?*

She closed the office door, turned on the intercom in case anyone needed her, and logged onto the Internet.

She had a number of investigative and forensic sites bookmarked in an innocuous file labeled *parabolic coordination system,* which had absolutely nothing to do with the bookmarked sites but sounded boring and esoteric enough to keep anyone curious from opening the folder.

She checked the sites for descriptions of ligature wounds. The ligature marks on Henny's neck had been narrow and as far as she could tell from her cursory look, fairly deep. No finger marks, though it was hard to tell with all the dirt and other stuff. And not a soft material like a scarf. But she read every description and looked at every picture. She opened another page, and there was the same wound as Henny's—in color. Narrow, deep, and lined by inflamed flesh. There was no question in her mind now.

Strangulation by means of a thin wire. Garroting.

Conjuring horror movies and tales of the Inquisition, Kate Googled *garroting*. Ten minutes later, she knew more than she ever needed to know about that method of killing.

Used during the seventeenth century as a means of torture, a garrote consisted of a collar attached to a chair that tightened around the neck or drove a spike into the spinal cord of the person being interrogated.

Later, simplified and made portable, it became a line with two handles; chain, wire, fishing line, even scarves were used to asphyxiate the victim. Garroting became a favorite among assassins—and serial killers—since it was completely silent.

She discovered Web sites she had never imagined and had no intention of entering ever again. Disgusted and dismayed, she clicked out of Safari, took a Sudoku puzzle book off the stack on the desk, and carried it over to the wing chair.

She picked up a pencil and immediately felt better. She began to mechanically fill in numbers until the images of death faded away and she settled into the safety of logic and the firm ground of mathematics.

At a quarter to ten, Kate went downstairs to welcome the Saturday puzzle time participants. The first two children to arrive were the Wallstadtler twins, Devlin and Dean, two twelve-year-old demons, who dropped their five-dollar activities fee on Alice's desk and jostled past Kate to the stairs.

"Hey," Kate called after them. "No running." They slowed for one step, then one of them shoved his brother out of the way and bolted first up the stairs.

"Time to send out another newsletter reminding parents of the museum rules," Alice said.

"I'll talk to the boys' mother," Kate said. "Most everyone else is well-behaved."

"If you ever see her. You should inform her that we're not a babysitting service."

Kate picked up a black knit hat with the initials NYC monogrammed in red. "Less than two minutes and they're already losing stuff. Shall I toss this in the lost and found box or take pity on the mother and leave it here for her to find?"

"I'll take it," said Alice. She let out a ladylike snort of disgust. "Doesn't even have his name in it."

The door opened and two girls came in.

"Hi, Jenny."

"Hi, Ms. McDonald," said Jenny, a towheaded eight-year-old. "This is my friend Samantha."

"Now there's a child who's been taught good manners," Alice said as they watched the two girls go up the stairs hand in hand.

After that, they arrived en masse, fifteen in all. Chattering and laughing, they filed up the stairs and out of sight.

Kate stood at the bottom of the stairs, listening. All was quiet.

"I don't know how she does it," Kate said. "I'm just glad she does."

Ginny Sue really knew how to handle kids. It was more than her experience as a fourth grade teacher, Kate thought. It was her whole attitude. Upbeat without letting things get out of hand. Inspiring while keeping order. Instilling enthusiasm while curbing attention deficit.

Ginny Sue and Harry were responsible for the success of the Saturday morning programs, and Kate was grateful. She would have run screaming from the room the first time Devlin Wallstadtler poured puzzle glue over Kelly Cuzack's waist-long pigtails.

Ginny Sue had merely tucked Kelly's head over the sink and rinsed it out.

She'd then put Harry in charge of keeping the boys in line, and so far there had been no more mishaps.

It was great to have the museum alive with kids and parents. The evening puzzle clubs were thriving, thanks in part to Rayette, who insisted on providing snacks for each one. Ginny Sue's youth programs were growing rapidly.

Life is good, Kate thought. If only she didn't still miss the professor so much.

Kate stacked her lunch plate in the kitchen sink and stood sipping a cup of coffee, staring out the window. Rain gushed out the gutters and dropped off the eaves of the gables. The leaves of the privet hedge that formed the popular maze were shiny and green.

"Think you can spare another cup?"

Kate jumped as she recognized the voice. She turned around, and her answer died on her lips. Brandon Mitchell stood on the old linoleum, hair dripping, police jacket shiny with rain, and looking miserable.

"Oh dear," she said. "Well, if it's any consolation, you wouldn't have gotten much fishing in today."

"Are you kidding? This is perfect fishing weather."

It was cold and wet and dismal. And they called her weird.

She got down a mug and filled it with coffee. Then she reached into the linen drawer and pulled out a dish towel. She handed it to him with the coffee.

He accepted both gratefully and took a sip before putting the cup down and scrubbing his hair with the towel. It left it standing in dark little spikes and looking . . .

Yikes! She was doing it again. "Have a seat."

Whatever people skills she'd learned from all those books and all her practicing in the last few months flew out the window whenever the chief was around. She didn't want to look too closely at the reason. She had a feeling the scientific method wouldn't be too much help in this case. And she wasn't about to use anything else.

The chief shrugged out of his wet coat and draped it over the back of his chair. Then he sat watching her, as if he was expecting her to start pumping him for information. She was dying to do just that. She sat down across from him.

"I'm here in an official capacity."

"Room C."

"What?"

"The interrogation room at the police station. That's what this feels like."

"I'm not interrogating you. I just want a statement." He pulled a notebook from an inner pocket of his coat. Opened it and looked at its limp pages. He clicked his pen and waited.

"I went to have breakfast with Rayette. We do that almost every Saturday. I arrived at the bakery a little before seven. When I got there, no one was around, so I went through to the kitchen. There was no one in the kitchen, but the back door was open, so I went out to the alley. Rayette, Calvin, and Johnny were there staring at something. When I got closer, I saw that it was Henny Dougan.

"I called his name, but it was pretty obvious that he was already dead. I, uh, saw his neck. He was garroted, wasn't he?"

Storm clouds settled in the chief's dark eyes as he looked up at her. "Don't—"

She heard a rattle coming from outside the window.

"What was that?"

The chief was on his feet. "What?"

"A noise outside. Like someone raiding the trashcan."

"Your fat cat, perhaps."

At that moment, Al nosed open the dumbwaiter and padded into the kitchen, dry and haughty. He checked out the chief, then went to stand by his food dish.

Kate ignored him. "So . . . was Henny garroted?"

Coffee sloshed in the chief's cup. *"Dammit, Kate!"*

"Pizza," she reminded him.

"I'm not at liberty to—"

"Discuss the case. I know. But was he? His wounds looked like it."

After a struggle, the chief's frown morphed into a smile. "You're something else."

"I'll take that as a yes. But why someone would want to murder Henny is beyond me."

"That's why you have a police department. Though I wish I'd kept him in jail. Maybe he would still be alive."

"Maybe," Kate said. "It isn't the Boston serial killer, is it?"

"No. There's nothing to worry about."

Another rattle. Kate jumped up. "Somebody's out there."

She headed for the door, but the chief was right behind her. He grabbed her by both shoulders and held her back. "Wait here."

A crash outside drowned out his last word.

He strode to the door and threw it open. Kate hurried behind him, but she stayed in the doorway when he stepped onto the small porch.

A trashcan had fallen over and garbage bags were spilled onto the ground. And sprawled among the bags was Fast Eddie Blair, camera in hand.

"Smile, Chief Mitchell," he said unrepentantly and clicked a series of pictures.

"You're trespassing." The chief stepped toward him, but Finn Tucker, rain dripping into his eyes from the brim of his yellow rain slicker, sprang out from behind a bush.

"Ms. McDonald. Are you a suspect in the murder of Henny Dougan?"

CHAPTER

FIVE

KATE STARED AT him openmouthed.

Chief Mitchell stepped in front of her.

"Do you suspect her of killing Mr. Dougan?"

"No comment."

"Brandon?" exclaimed Kate, using his name out of pure shock.

The chief's nostrils flared, like a bull about to charge. But he held on to his temper. "Everyone is a suspect until proven otherwise. Including you and your sidekick."

Finn Tucker's eyes widened marginally. He recovered his assurance almost immediately. Dripping and smiling, he turned on his tape recorder and stepped onto the porch. "Any leads?"

"No comment. You have thirty seconds to leave the property."

"If Ms. McDonald isn't a suspect, is she assisting you in the investigation?"

"No," Kate said, "I'm only cooperating with the police."

Brandon winced. "*Twenty* seconds."

"Our research shows that you've helped the police in former murder cases."

"Ten."

"What is your relationship with Chief Mitchell?"

"Time's up." Brandon surged down the porch steps.

Finn hopped nimbly out of the way, but he hadn't taken the wet, slippery paving stones into account. His feet flew out from under him and he sat down hard.

Brandon advanced on him, reaching for his firearm.

Before Kate could even yell "No!" Fast Eddie jumped between them, dragged Finn to his feet, and herded him toward the gate at the side of the house.

"No need for violence, Chief Mitchell!" Finn called over Eddie's shoulder. "Just doing our job." He gave them a cheeky grin before Fast Eddie hustled him around the corner of the house and out of sight.

"Idiots."

Kate followed the chief back into the kitchen.

"They thought you were going to shoot them."

"Yeah."

"Were you?"

He raised his arms out to his side. There was no holster on his belt. "I left it in the squad car." A slight shrug. "But it worked."

He brushed at the front of his uniform, now as soaked as his coat. Ran his hands over his dripping hair, a futile effort if there ever was one.

Kate handed him a dry dishcloth. "Did you see his reaction when you said everyone was a suspect?"

The chief stopped scrubbing his face and looked at her over the edge of the dish towel.

Kate winced. "I know you did. What I meant was—"

"I know what you meant. Kate, please, *please*, stay out of this."

"I intend to, but he might have a motive if Henny smashed his printer. Maybe that's far-fetched but . . ." She sighed. "It's just . . ."

"That you can't help yourself. But for Harry's sake—and mine—please. Mind. Your. Own. Business."

Kate's cheeks flared.

Brandon's face softened, maybe. "And don't get all huffy. Until we discover what the motive was in killing Henny, everyone is at risk. I just want your promise to leave the investigation to the professionals."

"I'm not getting *huffy,* and your people skills are worse than mine," she said, and huffed out of the kitchen.

"Kate. . ."

Kate's cheeks were burning and she knew she was being unfair, but she couldn't help it. She'd just made a simple suggestion and the chief had nearly bitten her head off. Well, maybe it hadn't been that bad, but it still hurt.

He caught up with her in the hallway. "Would you just be reasonable?"

"I'm always reasonable. And you didn't have to be so mean."

"I apologize. But I haven't slept in forty-eight hours and I'm a little short of patience."

"Accepted, but it's not like I want to get involved."

That got her a raised eyebrow before he shrugged back into his wet police jacket. "Thanks for the coffee." He strode down the hall, gave a quick nod to Alice, and went out the front door.

"Good-bye, Chief Mitchell," Alice yodeled and turned an inquiring eye on Kate. "Are you two spatting again?"

Kate shrugged. "He thinks I'm an interfering busybody."

"That's because he's a man." Alice nodded wisely. "But as far as men go, a girl could do worse."

Kate blinked. *Is Alice suggesting . . . ? Good Lord, just the mention of the subject will give Aunt Pru a coronary.*

Choosing to ignore the suggestion, Kate returned to her office. She was embarrassed, perturbed, and anxious. She couldn't separate her feelings and didn't really know which emotion belonged to which situation: the murder, her relationship with the chief, Alice's matchmaking, or Pru's potential reaction.

That is the problem with emotions, she told herself. Too random to classify.

Sometimes she longed for the days when the professor could ease her bewilderment with a new puzzle and a cup of hot chocolate. He always seemed to know just what would make her feel better, even when she was totally unaware of it.

In the solitude of the office with the drip of the rain and the brush of the tree limbs against the window, Kate could almost feel the professor's presence.

When they'd renovated the exhibition rooms, Kate insisted on keeping the office just as it had been. The big desk, the worn Oriental carpet, the two wing chairs placed before the fireplace. The ceiling-high bookshelves with their arcane books. The old crystal ball, given to the professor by a Rumanian gypsy, was still sitting atop an oak pedestal—with only one minor change. Once it had been attached to a pedestal that hid a secret lock. Now it sat free in a wooden frame.

Everything else was as it had always been. Not as a shrine to her dead mentor but because it was cozy, safe, peaceful. And home.

At the end of two hours, Kate heard the kids filing out of the interactive room. She went outside to admire their finished puzzles and say hello to their parents.

Today, Kate noticed, there was a larger group than usual waiting in the foyer. *Must be the rain*, she thought. Usually they congregated on the sidewalk or stayed in their cars.

They turned as one when Kate came down the stairs.

"Is it true Henny Dougan was murdered in the alley behind Rayette's Bakery?"

Not the rain, Kate thought. They were all waiting to hear the details of Henny's death.

"Did you discover the body?"

"Of course she did."

"Please," Kate interrupted, glancing meaningfully at the children. "Henny is dead. But the police haven't determined the cause as far as I know." *And you can thank me for not escalating the murder rumor, Chief.* "But this really isn't the place or time for this discussion."

"She's absolutely right," said Laura Cusack. "Come along, Kelly. Jenny's mom invited us to go out to the highway for Burger King with Jenny and Samantha. Come along, girls." She scuttled her group out the door and the others soon followed.

"Lord," Alice said. "What's wrong with those people? Scaring those poor children out of their wits."

Kate shook her head, though she suspected that the little darlings, who were raised on Freddie Kruger and Lara Croft, were tougher than they appeared. A frightening thought.

As the last group filed out, Izzy Carmichael came through the door, his heavy mailbag slung over his shoulder and a stack of mail in his hand. Izzy had been mailman since Kate had been a kid and shorter than his five-three. Now he was smaller than she was and seemed to have shrunk even more in the last year.

"Hi, Izzy," said Kate.

"Parents giving you trouble?"

"No, they were just curious about Henny Dougan."

"Ayuh. You should see the crowd over at Rayette's. She could probably retire on her lunch business today."

"People are just plain old ghoulish," Alice said and took the mail from Izzy.

"Has Chief Mitchell got any leads?" asked Izzy.

Kate shrugged.

"I don't think so," Alice said. "He was here this morning and cranky as a bear."

"That was because he caught Finn Tucker and his photographer spying through the kitchen window."

Alice pursed her lips. "Well, I *never.*"

"That's what you get when new people move into a town. No respect for people's privacy." Izzy hoisted his mailbag to the other shoulder, then hesitated. "I did hear of something, but I don't know if I should pass it on or not."

"Of course you should." Alice leaned forward. "You have a duty."

Kate resigned herself.

"You know my regular route is here in the historic district."

Kate nodded.

"Well, Rufus Sykes's been out with a slipped disc, so me and Andy Dee are splitting up his route till he gets better. I got the south end of town. Thing is, I delivered the mail to Jumpin' Jack's this morning."

"That bar on the edge of town?"

"That's the one. Not the kind of place any decent folks would go. Sees a lot of bikers and people from the hills. But thing is, when I was there this morning, the guy who owns it, Jackson Fletcher, stopped me to shoot the breeze. And he told me that Henny Dougan had been drinking there last night till after midnight."

"Good heavens," Alice said. "Did he tell Chief Mitchell?"

"Jackson? Heck no. He and the chief have already had a couple of run-ins. There's definitely some questionable activities going on there. Not to mention the clientele. I know the chief has had to break up several fights."

Kate thought of Brandon taking on the people who habituated a place like Jumpin' Jack's and shuddered.

"I'm sure the chief will investigate Henny's movements up until the time of death."

"Ayuh. I'm sure he will, but it could make his life easier if somebody told him about what Jackson said."

"Why don't you tell him?" asked Kate.

Izzy stretched his neck as if his uniform had suddenly grown too small. "Ordinarily I would. But I wouldn't want it to get back to Jackson."

"Is he dangerous?"

"I don't know for sure, but I don't want to take any chances. If it got back to him that I told the chief things, he might take offense. If you see what I mean."

Kate did. "I suppose you want me to drop a hint in his ear."

Izzy nodded energetically. "That's just what I was thinking."

"He won't like me butting in."

"No, but he'll listen to you. Now I'd best get on with delivering the mail or there won't be nobody happy on my route." He walked to the door but stopped with his hand on the knob. "And Katie, you might tell the chief that Jackson doesn't want to get involved."

"Right," she said. Izzy walked out the door, and it seemed to Kate he was looking a little taller than when he walked in.

"Well," Alice said. "I guess you'd better telephone Chief Mitchell."

"I guess. But I doubt if it's necessary."

"Maybe not, but you should always cooperate with the police." Alice shot her an impish smile.

"You should know."

Fortunately, the chief didn't answer his cell phone. Kate left a message that began simply, "I don't know if this will help," then detoured to, "And you probably already know this, but. . .," then devolved into a hopeless jumble of explanation, mixed with apology and embarrassment, and ended with "Henny Dougan was at Jumpin' Jack's last night until after midnight. And I know you probably already know . . ." When she started repeating herself, she hung up.

The phone rang. The chief was calling her back, and even though she had caller ID, she answered, "Avondale Puzzle Museum."

"Would you like to try that again?"

Kate made a face at the phone. "And good afternoon to you too."

"Not likely. How did you learn about Henny's whereabouts?"

"Uh . . ."

"And no hemming and hawing, please."

"I hope you're more approachable with other, um, tipsters." She heard him stifle a groan and felt vindicated. "If you must know, Izzy had to deliver the mail out there today. The regular mailman was out with a slipped disc. The owner told him."

"And Izzy told you."

"Well, yes."

Kate knew he resented the fact that people fed him information through Kate. It was the one way they could continue to keep him an outsider without actually obstructing his job. Brandon didn't understand that it was just the Granville way.

"He doesn't want the owner to know he ratted."

There was a long silence. "He could have saved my staff a lot of legwork if he'd just come to me in the first place."

"I guess that means you already knew."

"Yes."

"Don't be mad at him." *Or me.*

"Kate."

"I mean it."

"I've got to go. Thanks for the . . . tip."

He hung up as that last bit of sarcasm reverberated in her ears. Another conversation mucked up because once again she was caught in the middle. Because he always disconcerted her.

She dropped her head in her hands. "What is wrong with you? You're a mathematician, for heaven's sake. And you're an idiot."

"Nah, you're a genius," said Harry, coming into the office. "But focus for a sec. There's somebody I want you to meet."

Kate looked up. A girl, almost as tall as Harry, stood next to him. She was rail thin and pale and wearing tight black low-rider jeans held up by an industrial strength chain link belt, a black midriff tee, a black leather jacket covered with myriad zippered pockets, and black knee-high boots with three-inch heels.

Her hair was black except for two thin, purple braided tresses that hung on each side of a center part and partially covered her black-rimmed eyes. Her mouth was a slash of black lipstick across a pale face.

"Hi." Kate was having a hard time assimilating the contrast between the girl and Harry, whom the chief had managed to transform from a dirty, foul-mouthed misfit into a stylishly clothed, clean-cut young man. Brandon would have a fit if he backslid now.

Harry gave his companion a little nudge, but she just scowled back at him, sank into one hip, and cracked her gum.

"This is Wynter."

Kate looked from Harry to the girl. "Hi . . . Winter?"

"That's Wynter. With a Y." The girl cracked her gum again and gave Kate a look that dared her to contest the spelling.

"Ah," Kate said, not being able to think of anything else to say.

"She just moved here. We're in the same chem class. She just kind of came in the museum to check things out, and well, I guess, we're going to hang out in town."

"Great," Kate said. And she would be left to break the news to the chief. "Maybe you should—"

Harry gave her a desperate look and a quick shake of his head. He didn't want her to mention the chief. Or that he was expected to check in if his plans changed.

"See ya." Harry hustled Wynter with a Y out the door.

"But how long—"

The door closed

Great, just great, Kate thought. She was already on the chief's least popular list. Now she was going to have to tell him that Harry had left the museum without telling him and that he was "hanging out" with the only Goth in town.

CHAPTER
SIX

SUNDAY MORNINGS AT the First Presbyterian Church were not just for prayer, contemplation, and the forgiveness of sins. They were also the central exchange for the week's gossip. And this Sunday was no different.

If anything, it was even more frenetic. There was a distinct rustle as Pru and Kate walked down the aisle to their regular pew. Heads turned, then bent to whisper. Kate felt acutely uncomfortable. They'd probably heard she'd been on the scene when Henny Dougan's body was discovered.

As often happened in a town the size of Granville, there was a finely tuned grapevine, and even though someone might be instructed not to divulge information, it was an exercise in futility. Word had gotten out that Henny Dougan's death was no accident, not natural in any way. Henny had been murdered, and speculation and curiosity were running wild. Even the quiet organ music wasn't putting this crowd in a soberly religious mood.

Kate noticed that Brandon and Harry weren't in attendance. They didn't always come. The chief's duties sometimes coincided with church services, and Kate suspected that other times the two of them just played hooky.

As she and Pru slid into their pew, Gilda Malone turned around and gave Kate a piercing look.

"Hmmph," Pru said. Gilda settled back in her pew.

Pru pulled Kate down to the seat. "Nosey Parker," she whispered. "She probably heard that you found another body."

"But I didn't."

"And in church too."

Before Kate could protest again, the organ music swelled and the choir, followed by the acolytes and Reverend Norwith, began the processional down the aisle to the chancel. Everyone stood and opened their hymnals.

Elmira Swyndon paused in her singing long enough to frown at Kate before continuing down the aisle. Kate began to feel a terrible premonition. Elmira couldn't be upset that Kate had been on the scene—Elmira was Kate's chief informant.

She knew everything that happened at the police station and everything that happened in town. It had been during one of Kate's fact-finding excursions that she'd met Elmira's nephew Sam. And Elmira kept tabs on that too.

Sam must have said something that set her off.

He hated that Kate had anything to do with murder. But also, Sam could never think clearly around the chief. His desire to protect her was gratifying, but a little annoying. It wasn't like she made a habit of finding bodies. She'd only wanted coffee and a sticky bun.

The choir filed into the choir loft and Reverend Norwith climbed the steps to the pulpit. When the hymn ended, he spread out his hands.

"Welcome, my friends, on this day of our Lord. Please join me in prayer."

Kate bowed her head with everyone else, but she was a little anxious, wondering whether he would mention Henny Dougan's demise. When he came to the amen, he still hadn't mentioned the death, and Kate began to relax.

It wasn't until the prayers of intercession that Henny was mentioned. Gilda stood and shot Kate another harsh look over her shoulder before saying, "We should pray for the soul of Henny Dougan, who lost his life yesterday. He wasn't much liked, but he oughta be prayed for."

Gilda sat down again and another person rose with another prayer.

Pru nudged Kate's arm. "She doesn't even know the man."

Kate, who always drove Pru to church, tried to leave right after the service, but there was no way she was going to get Pru away before the coffee hour.

Simon Mack waved for them to join him, and Pru guided Kate through the knot of churchgoers to where Simon stood. He was a spare man in his seventies with a tonsure of white hair and a penchant for three-piece suits. He was wearing one today.

He was Pru's good friend, and Pru fondly called him the "oldest living lawyer in Granville." Which was the truth, since the only other lawyer in Granville was forty-seven.

Simon had helped Kate when she'd been suspected of murder the year before, and he'd been a good friend since.

"Mornin', Pru, Katie. Would you —"

Tess Dougan's name wafted over the buzz of lowered voices. Kate strained to hear what they were saying, but it was gone.

"Sorry?"

"I asked if you and Pru would like to join me for lunch at the Bowsman Inn?"

At that moment, Elmira Swyndon bustled up to them. "Now, Katie, I want to talk to you."

Hopefully not about Henny Dougan.

Though Elmira always knew more details than the rest of the town, she managed not to become the focal point of everyone's questions. *It must be her grandmotherly nature*, thought Kate. The comfortable softness of her pleasantly plump body, the beginning-to-gray hair waved back from her forehead and sprayed into a helmet of curls. Her pleasant demeanor that gave the illusion that she didn't know everything about everything that passed through the police station.

"Have you seen this morning's *Free Press*? I think you should sue them for—"

She was cut off by a voice saying loudly, "There's Katie. Let's ask her."

"What about the *Free Press*?"

Elmira pursed her lips. "I just hope you know what you're doing."

"Elmira, I don't—"

"Katie, are you helping Chief Mitchell solve this case or are you just messing around?"

Kate stared at Roy Larkins, who rarely came to church, and who avoided Brandon whenever possible, since the chief, in his third week on the job, had stopped Roy for not having an inspection sticker. Roy had never gotten the truck inspected in the ten years he'd owned it and didn't see why he had to get one now.

The chief impounded the truck for two weeks until Roy promised to bring the vehicle up to passable condition, and Roy still held a grudge against him.

"Neither," Kate said, confused. "I'm not—I don't—"

"Well, the paper says . . ." A crowd was beginning to form around Kate, and she shot a helpless look toward Simon and Pru.

Simon stepped forward. "Roy, folks, this is not the time or the place." Pru grabbed Kate's elbow and spirited her away, nodding to Reverend Norwith as they passed. Simon followed a half step behind.

They didn't stop until they were outside on the lawn.

"Darn men," Pru said. "Don't know any better than gossiping on a Sunday and right there in front of Reverend Norwith."

This from someone who had just learned that Therese Plumtree's baby was one of those (wink, wink) seven-month deals, that the Turnbulls were getting a divorce (it was about time), and that the Arnos' youngest son had just been arrested for possession of marijuana (which is about what you'd expect when kids go out west to college).

Kate let it pass; she was still trying to figure out what Roy was talking about.

Since the museum opened at one, she turned down Simon's invitation to lunch. She'd have to grab a latte and a sandwich from Rayette's.

She stopped in front of the bakery and parked in one of the last available parking places. The café was already filling up with the after-church crowd.

As Kate stepped out of her Matrix, the sun broke through the clouds. *At last*, she thought, knowing that it was probably just a tease. April weather was just as fickle as the other months in New Hampshire—sometimes worse.

There were only two copies of the *Free Press* left on the counter. Kate paid her dollar and picked up a copy.

Rayette caught sight of Kate and hurried over. Her cheeks were rosy pink, her platinum bob was disarranged, and she was wearing flour everywhere.

"Holy cow," said Kate. "The place is packed."

"I think we broke some kind of record already. I had to send Holly out to the Market Basket for more eggs. *And* I had to whip up another tray of biscuits on the fly. Calvin's cooking isn't any better than it was last week, so I must have Finn Tucker to thank for it."

"No way," Kate said. "They could just buy their paper and leave. Nobody's making them have breakfast with their scandals."

"Yeah. You're right." said Rayette, sounding pleased.

Lynn came up with Kate's latte. "Here you go, Ms. McDonald."

"Kate, please." Kate took the bag from her.

Lynn smiled. "Katie."

Kate took it philosophically. She'd just about given up getting people here to call her Kate. All her colleagues at the think tank called her Kate. All her friends in Alexandria called her Kate.

When she'd first returned to Granville, she'd insisted her name was Kate. She'd been Kate since her first year in college. But the good people of Granville had long memories, and it was beginning to look like she would always be Katie to them.

So far, Harry and the chief were the only ones who didn't call her Katie, but they hadn't known her since she was knee high to whatever. At first, just hearing the name Katie conjured up unhappy memories of being a childhood geek. *The misfit. The weirdo. K-K-Katie. Katie-did.* Or the worse one, *Katie is a ge-ek. Katie is a ge-ek,* sung to that taunting cadence that any unpopular, isolated child shudders to hear, regardless of the words.

She still heard that taunt in her mind sometimes, especially whenever she'd done or said something socially inept or geeky. Which she did whenever she was not concentrating. But the taunt was getting fainter. Maybe someday the memory would disappear altogether.

She became aware that the entire café had become quiet, and they were all giving her surreptitious looks.

"What's going on?"

Rayette looked embarrassed but just lifted her chin toward the newspaper Kate was holding.

Kate looked down at the front page. There was a photo of the alley—after the arrival of the police, since yellow tape was stretched across the entrance. Next to it was a pen-and-ink drawing of the murder scene—pretty accurate, Kate could see, even at first glance. Either Finn or Fast Eddie knew how to make detailed drawings.

And below that—her stomach fell; a slow burn ignited in her gut and spread first to her cheeks, then to the rest of her. A picture of her and Brandon in the museum's kitchen. His hands gripped her shoulders. She remembered it. When he'd stopped her from going outside.

That's why everyone was staring at her.

It had been totally innocent, until the new owner of the *Free Press* put his own imaginative spin on it. The photo's caption read in bold black letters, "Why Is the Chief of Police so Friendly with this Woman?"

The accompanying article did nothing to answer the question. Just raised scurrilous speculation. "Is she a suspect? A witness? Or is there something more personal between them?"

Kate's mouth fell open in astonishment. Blood rushed to her face. "I'd like to strangle Finn Tucker."

She clapped a hand over her mouth as if she could push the words back in. She sounded like Henny Dougan, except for the drunken slur. "That so and so. How dare he?"

"He's a sleazy journalist. Nobody is going to pay much attention.

They know you're not a suspect," Rayette assured her.

Kate shook her head.

"And everyone already suspects you and the chief are . . ."

"Don't say it," Kate said through clenched teeth. "It's nothing like that. We're just . . ." What were they? Friends? Not exactly. Not colleagues. She didn't know how she felt about the chief. And she certainly didn't know how he felt about her. Either way, it was nobody's business.

"Hey Katie, are you helping the chief with this investigation?"

"Sure hope so."

"Ever think about applying for chief of police?"

"We've already got a chief of police."

"Too bad he's more interested in Katie than in catching Henny Dougan's murderer."

"You better watch it or you'll make Sam Swyndon jealous."

Rayette crossed her arms and glared out across the room. Heads lowered to their plates.

"Just ignore them."

Kate stuffed the newspaper into her bag. "That does it." She snatched her latte off the counter.

"Where are you going?"

"To give Finn Tucker a piece of my mind."

She ran out of steam on her way to her car. What could she say that would do anything but antagonize the newspaperman? The damage was already done.

She couldn't prevent him from printing more of the same. She might even goad him into printing worse. She stood by her car, indecisive and frustrated. If Finn Tucker was an equation, she'd know exactly what to do with him. As it was, she didn't have a clue.

Then a worse thought struck her. What if Brandon had seen the paper? He was bound to sooner or later. He'd just ignore it. He always did. But it would be so embarrassing.

Like Aunt Pru always said, no smoke without fire.

Kate wasn't about to add fuel to the flames of speculation. She'd just take her cue from the chief and act like nothing had happened, wait for talk to blow over.

As she unlocked the car door, Carrie Blaine and Beatrice Noakes came out of Rayette's. They were both members of the Granny Activist Brigade and had helped with last winter's Sudoku tournament.

They saw her and waved. Kate smiled and waved back.

"It's nobody's business what you and Chief Mitchell do on your own time," Carrie yelled just as another group came out of the café. Everyone's head turned toward Kate. Carrie must have had her hearing aid turned down, which always made her talk too loudly.

Kate was sure she heard someone snicker before Beatrice herded Carrie away.

Kate jumped into the Matrix, and without a look back, headed for the museum.

She'd never be able to face the town—or Brandon—again.

Unfortunately, she did have to face Alice, who was waiting for her on the steps of the museum.

"You're early," Kate said.

"Thought you might need a little extra help."

Kate unlocked the front door and they both went inside.

Alice immediately sat down at the registration desk and began unloading her bag.

"I guess you saw the *Free Press* this morning."

Alice looked up, all innocence. "No. Bea Noakes called me. She felt bad about Carrie blurting out some nonsense about you and Chief Mitchell in front of everybody."

"Thank her for me."

"I will." Alice folded her hands and rested them on the ink blotter.

"Is there something else?"

"Of course. Are you going to show me a copy of that paper?"

It was hopeless. Kate handed over her copy of the *Free Press*. Alice spread it out on the desk and frowned at it.

"Good heavens." Alice clicked her tongue. "The idea of you being a suspect. Someone should wash that young man's mouth out with soap. If he'd just asked, anybody would have told him you always help the chief solve his cases."

"But I *don't*."

"Of course you do. Not that he couldn't solve them himself—eventually. But it's going to be a long, long time before people are going to trust him enough to actively cooperate with him."

"You trust him," Kate said. "And you didn't even like him."

"Well, I'm more open-minded than most folks around here. And he stepped up to the plate, so to speak, when we were having trouble getting the Valley Assisted Living Home to upgrade their smoke alarm system. A man who cares about old folks is okay by me. I'm going to be one of them some day."

Kate bit back a smile. Alice was eighty if she was a day, but she had more energy and enthusiasm than a lot of people half her age. Kate began to feel better: maybe Alice wasn't the only person who had begun to accept the chief.

"And I think the two of you make a lovely couple."

"Alice!" Kate's smile faltered and she felt the blood rush to her face. "We are not a couple."

"I know that." Alice's blue eyes twinkled. "I'm just saying . . ."

Kate wrestled the paper away from Alice and took it upstairs. She hadn't been able to take a good look at it with everyone watching. Now she planned to study it and stew.

She was tempted to go straight to the picture of her and the chief and fume over the indignity, but discipline made her stop to peruse the graphic representation of the murder scene.

Even though it was rendered in black and white, Finn or Eddie had done an extremely thorough job.

One always heard about a journalist's "nose" for news, but Kate supposed that having a good eye was just as important. In the picture, Henny Dougan lay against a trashcan, looking . . . like Henny Dougan. It was so lifelike that Kate shuddered.

His head lay in the puddle of filthy-looking water, and the artist had even caught the lettering on the newspaper beneath his head. His jacket was open down the front and one side was crumpled beneath his body. One trouser leg was pulled up, revealing a sock-less foot in a holey sneaker.

Fortunately, the other, more sordid, evidence of Henny's demise had been left out. *Except for . . .* Kate looked more closely at the artist's rendering. Across Henny's neck was a faint, thin line: the mark left by whatever killed him.

How on earth did they know about that? Brandon hadn't let them close enough to see that much detail. Kate had barely noticed it herself, and she'd stood next to the body.

Fast Eddie had gotten closest to the body, before the chief stopped him. Was it possible that he picked out that detail so quickly? It would be part of his training to notice detail, just like it was a part of a scientist's or mathematician's training.

She finally let herself look at the photo of her and the chief. The Kate in the picture looked startled, worried maybe. The chief was standing behind her, his hands grasping her shoulders, his head lowered toward hers. It looked like an intensely private moment even to her, and she knew exactly how innocent it had been.

A wave of emotion rolled through her and was gone before she could identify the feeling. But it left her deflated and just a little lonely.

She gave herself a mental shake, concentrated on the caption, and began to rebuild her sense of righteous indignation. She should sue them, except they had stayed just on the legal side of libel. It didn't matter; they'd gotten the effect they wanted. Kate knew exactly what inferences the town would make.

She'd seen it on their faces at Rayette's. They thought she and the chief were having an affair. And that misconception could seriously throw a wrench in his ability to do his job—not to mention what it would do to her family and friends.

CHAPTER

SEVEN

HARRY CALLED TO say he would be late. Kate hoped that he and the chief had finally gone fishing and possibly, just possibly, hadn't seen the latest *Free Press*. Or maybe they had, and she was being ostracized. Either way, she was glad to put off that meeting for as long as possible.

The afternoon went by without any more people asking about her relationship with the chief or accusing her of being a suspect in the death of Henny Dougan, mainly because Kate had to manage P. T.'s place until Harry showed up. Which was okay. She'd rather face a dozen rambunctious children than talk with curious adults.

Sam called around three to ask her to dinner at the Bowsman Inn. From the sound of his voice, he'd seen the photo of her and Brandon and was claiming his territory. She could hardly blame him.

Kate didn't even pretend to have other plans. She never had other plans, much to Aunt Pru's disappointment, but she just couldn't seem to take any interest in dating. Especially when the slightest interest set Pru off on the marriage mantra.

When Kate had turned thirty last month, she'd thought that her aunt would at last give up the notion of marrying her to a nice local man with job security and accept Kate for what she was quickly becoming, at least in Pru's eyes—an old maid.

But Pru had surprised her by merely stepping up her efforts.

So Kate went bowling with Norris Endelman, who owned his own garage, dancing with Louis Albioni, who was the manager at the Market Basket, and to the movies and dinner with Sam Swyndon.

She'd also been skiing with the chief and Harry. It had been the first time on the slopes for both Harry and Kate, and the chief showed more patience than she'd ever seen from him. She'd had fun that day, more fun than she'd had with the others. But it hadn't been a date. It must be that she liked skiing more than she liked dancing, bowling, or the movies.

Harry still hadn't arrived when Kate closed at five, but Kate didn't mind. She was always encouraging him to do other things. He had begun to make friends at school, unlike her as a teenager, and she didn't want him to miss out on such opportunities by tying himself to the museum.

She realized that she would really miss him when he went off to college and for the first time got an inkling of what the professor must have felt when she had left him behind. Whenever she thought about how they'd lost touch, she always felt a rush of remorse. She was thankful that Harry had become his apprentice and companion and wondered if she would take on another apprentice when Harry was gone.

She reapplied makeup in the upstairs bathroom and was standing at the window of the mechanical puzzle room when Sam's SUV pulled up at the curb. She'd asked him to pick her up at the museum, mainly because she didn't want to take the chance of Pru seeing them from her front window.

Kate was getting used to living in a fishbowl, but she had even more qualms than usual tonight. Was going on a dinner date the evening after you had found a dead man just a little bit crass?

"What are you thinking?" Sam asked as he drove down Main Street toward the river.

"Nothing." She wasn't going to even mention Henny Dougan. She wasn't going to mention the *Free Press* photo. So far, Sam hadn't said a word, but she knew that he was unhappy about her being at the scene of another murder. It was all in her best interest, she knew. One, he wanted to keep her safe, and two, he was jealous. It should have made her feel gratified, but it just made her uncomfortable.

Sam was, in the words of her aunt, a great catch. Thirty-three. Owned his own photography shop. Was kind, funny, and good looking, with wheat-straw hair, hazel eyes, a firm chin that was all put together in a delightful picture. She liked him. He liked her. But . . .

Nancy Vance met them in the Bowsman's lobby. Nancy and John had bought the old Revolutionary War inn several years back. They had added a banquet room and enlarged the bar and restaurant since then. They catered to weekenders and weddings and had hosted a good many of the participants in last year's Sudoku Championship.

Nancy widened her eyes when she saw Kate with Sam, but merely said, "Good evening," and led them past the bar and into the restaurant. The restaurant was already crowded. The Bowsman Inn was gaining a reputation, and people came from miles around for the food and the ambience.

Nancy showed them to a table that overlooked the river and took their wine order.

"What was that about?" Sam asked when she was gone.

"What?"

"The look she gave you."

Kate shrugged and looked out the window. Between the recent rains and the spring runoff from the surrounding mountains, the river was swollen over its banks. It looked dark and treacherous as it flowed past the inn. "Did she give me a look?"

"Katie. She was dying to ask you about yesterday morning, wasn't she?"

So here it came. She appreciated his concern, but she chafed under it just the same. It wasn't her fault that Granville was seeing a spate of murders. It was what happened when the outside world encroached, according to Brandon. And it wasn't her fault that she seemed to always be on the scene when the body was discovered.

Except for the first one, there had always been other people with her. No one ever accused Rayette or Calvin or Alice or even Aunt Pru of "always discovering the body."

"Katie?"

Kate sighed. "Probably. People are curious."

Two wine glasses and a bottle of Pinot Noir appeared on the table before them.

"Compliments of the proprietors." The waiter uncorked the bottle and poured a drop for Sam to taste.

When the tasting ritual was over, he said, "My name is Dan, and I'll be your server this evening."

Dan was middle-aged, middle height, with darkish hair combed back from a widow's peak.

"Hi, Dan," Kate said, thankful for the interruption. "I haven't see you before. You must be new."

"Yes, ma'am. We have several specials tonight."

Once they had ordered and were alone again, Sam said, "I don't mean to harass you. It's just that I care about you."

"I know, and I appreciate it, but can we talk about something else?

It's not exactly dinner conversation."

Sam let out his breath. "You're right. Sorry."

During the main course, Nancy came to the table. "Do you have everything you need?"

"Mmm hmm," Kate said. "This lamb curry is delicious."

Dan appeared to refill their water glasses and discreetly disappeared again.

"How do you like our new waiter?" Nancy asked.

"Very attentive," Sam said.

"John hired him from the Brick House after the fire. He's excellent, though I suppose he'll go back once they rebuild. He's living temporarily in the apartment over the garage. He's working out nicely so far."

"Rayette hired a cook and one of their waitresses," Kate said. "Lucky that so many of them got jobs right away."

"We both needed more help, fingers crossed, but I always get nervous when we hire new people. You just never know. There's peach melba for dessert."

Nancy moved off to stop at other tables and Kate and Sam moved on to coffee and dessert.

It was only nine o'clock when Sam dropped Kate off at the museum to pick up her car. He pulled to the curb and turned off the ignition. Kate immediately got butterflies. Dinner had not been the most comfortable they'd ever had, and she wasn't sure whether he was planning to kiss her or reprimand her.

She braced herself.

"Katie, I know you don't like me butting in. But I worry about you."

She squeezed her lips into a kind of smile. No kiss.

"I know."

"Actually it makes me crazy that you keep putting yourself in danger."

"I was just one of several people on the scene. I didn't find Henny. I just happened to be going to breakfast." She thought she probably sounded whiny, though she was never sure about the impression she was making—too many years of dealing with numbers and theories instead of people.

"I know, but still. You're always there."

Kate sank back into the seat and stared out at the darkness.

"Marry me."

Kate jerked toward him. "What?" Her voice was shrill with surprise. She tried to temper it but she could only stare at Sam. He stared back at her.

"Sam, you don't want to marry me. We've only known each other a few months. . ."

He frowned. "Well, I don't *not* want to marry you. And I just don't see any other way that I can keep you safe."

"You've got to be kidding me."

Now he looked hurt. Kate desperately tried to organize her thoughts so she wouldn't say anything stupid. She didn't want to marry . . . anybody.

"It's not that I don't want to marry you, exactly. It's just. Well, hell. Sam. Do you think getting married is going to . . . what? Would you expect me to stay at home, never go to Rayette's or the Bowsman because I might find a body? Turn over the museum to someone else?"

"Well, no, but—"

"Because that's all I do. I have an active life, a presence in the community." And she sounded like a pompous ass. "It's not my fault that I . . ."

"Keep finding bodies?"

"Yeah," she said and lapsed into silence.

They parted a few minutes later. She got her good-night kiss, but it was perfunctory at best. Sam could be as prickly as the chief in his own way. Except that in Sam's case, Kate always ended up feeling awful, whereas the chief just pissed her off.

Pru's porch light was on when Kate pulled into her own driveway two doors away. She parked by the side of the house and hurried up the porch steps to the front door. She hadn't left the porch light on because she had expected to be home before dark, and if a serial killer was out there, she was in big trouble. But at least Pru wouldn't see her and call to see where she'd been.

The door opened; the telephone rang. With a sigh, Kate went to answer it.

"I'm coming over," said Pru and hung up.

Kate shrugged out of her jacket and hung it on a peg in the closet. She unlocked the front door, then went down the hall to the kitchen and put on the kettle for tea.

"Now just look what has happened," Pru began when Kate opened the door.

Surprise. Pru didn't want to pump her about her date with Sam. "What happened?"

Pru beetled her eye at Kate, her Katherine Margaret McDonald look.

"I told you not to give that police chief an inch."

"The chief? What about him?"

"Don't play coy with me. The whole town is talking. It's a disgrace."

"Oh that," said Kate and started down the hall to the kitchen.

"And don't you ignore me . . ." Pru continued as she followed Kate down the hall to the kitchen.

Young lady, Kate finished.

"Young lady."

"I'm not ignoring you. The kettle is whistling."

"And the front page no less."

Kate pulled up short and turned on her aunt. "Aunt Pru. He was at the museum taking my statement, rather than making me wait at Rayette's where the whole town would have seen us."

Kate reached into the cabinet for tea.

"Well, the whole town has seen you anyway. And him holding on to you like that. He should be ashamed." Pru slumped onto a kitchen chair.

"He was stopping me from going outside when I heard a noise. Which turned out to be Fast Eddie, who was spying through the window."

"Well, you should put up curtains."

"I intend to."

"Not that you should be doing anything that shouldn't be seen."

"I don't. Would you like Earl Grey or something herbal?"

"Why couldn't you just marry Sam?"

Kate got out the good cups and saucers.

"Or Norris . . . or Louis Albioni."

"Earl Grey or chamomile?"

Her aunt sighed. "Earl Grey."

Kate opened a tin of English cookies and placed them on the table, then poured water into the cups.

"Tell me about Henny and Tess Dougan."

Pru stopped with her hand in the biscuit tin. "I will not. Not if you're going to run around trying to catch a serial killer."

"There is no serial killer. I just want to know why people think he killed her and buried her body. I've been away a long time and I barely remember them."

"No reason you should remember them. White trash. Well, she wasn't so bad. But Henny was never any good. Married him anyway." Pru tsked. "See what wrong choices can do to a girl's life?" She gave Kate a pointed look.

"Did they . . . uh . . . fight or anything?"

"Poor thing was always 'falling down the steps' or some such nonsense. Didn't fool anybody. Her friends tried to get her into counseling, but she wouldn't have any of it. Said he only got that way when he drank.

"'Course, he drank all the time. We all breathed a sigh of relief when she left. Figured it was only a matter of time till he did something worse. And now it seems like he has."

Kate pushed the sugar and cream toward her aunt.

Pru's hand hovered over the creamer. "Good heavens. What if she isn't buried in the foundation?"

"Aunt Pru—"

"What if she got fed up with him? What if he didn't kill her, but she killed him? She planned it all the time. She's probably hiding out somewhere."

"Aunt Pru, do you have any real reason to believe that's what happened?"

Pru poured cream into her cup. "Well, that would be better than having a serial killer in our midst."

Kate bobbled her cup. "There is no serial killer."

It was the kind of blanket statement Kate knew better than to make. "But I wouldn't spread any theories about Tess," she added quickly. "You wouldn't want people getting ideas."

Pru shook her head. "I wouldn't dream of it."

Kate wasn't fooled; Aunt Pru was the hub of Granville gossip. It would be all over town by tomorrow that they were safe from serial killers because Tess Dougan had killed her husband.

		1			6		5	
	4	5	7			8		
		9		2	3	1	7	
8	7			3	1			9
	2		8				6	
5				4			8	7
	9	8	3	6		2		
		7			4	6	1	
	6		1			7		

CHAPTER

EIGHT

SINCE THE MUSEUM was closed on Mondays, Kate didn't leave her house until nearly two o'clock. The Arcane Masters, the most advanced of the puzzle clubs, was the only one that met on Monday evenings. Kate always went to the museum in the afternoon and stayed to close up after they had adjourned.

She swung by Rayette's, judging that most of the lunch crowd would be gone and she could order a coffee without curious eyes following her every move.

There were no copies of the *Free Press* left, which was fine by her. Only three tables were occupied, one of them by Ted Lumley, who was just getting up to leave.

He saw Kate and waved. Kate smiled back.

Lynn hurried up to her. "Hi, Katie."

"Hi. Where is everyone?"

"Holly called in with the flu. Johnny and Rayette had to drive over to Nanuet to pick up another milk steamer. The old one started smoking halfway through the breakfast rush. It's just me and Calvin. He'll steam the milk by hand if you want to wait. But he's kind of backed up in the kitchen." She sighed. "Never rains but it pours."

"That's okay, regular coffee will be fine."

Ted came up to the cash register and waited for Lynn to return.

Kate tried to think of something to say and finally settled on, "So what are you going to do with all this free time?"

"Not much." He smiled ruefully. "Harry's in school all day, and Bran has his hands full with this murder. I'd kibitz but I don't want to cramp his style. And I didn't come for a busman's holiday."

"It's too bad," Kate commiserated.

"Thought I might come by and take that tour of the museum when you have time."

"Oh. Well, how about now? The museum is closed today, and I don't have a club coming in until eight."

"Sounds great."

Lynn returned with Kate's coffee, then took Ted's lunch bill and rang it up.

As Lynn handed him his change, Ted said to her, "Now, don't you worry about any serial killers. Just don't talk to strangers, don't let anyone you don't know accost you or even come close to your car. If someone does bother you, scream like crazy and run." He gave the girl a reassuring smile. "You'll be fine."

"Thanks. I feel a lot better after talking to you. I mean, you know all about this kind of stuff, right?"

"Unfortunately, I do. Now, you have a nice day."

Lynn tucked a piece of shoulder-length hair behind her ear. "I sure will. Thanks." She gave him a flirtatious smile.

Kate felt a little envious—she'd never flirted in her life.

Calvin burst through the double doors to the kitchen, holding a bowl of soup and a muffin. He looked harassed and overheated. Strands of hair had begun to curl around his face, and his apron was smeared with evidence of the lunch menu.

"Lynn, if you don't mind. Yankee bean soup is not meant to be served chilled. Take this over to table twelve . . . if it isn't too much trouble."

He plunked the soup down on the counter; it sloshed over the sides. "Shit." He took the tail of his apron and wiped up the spill. Which went a long way to explaining the state of his apron.

Lynn made a face at him as he strode back into the kitchen.

"I guess he's a little stressed." She leaned over the register. "Chief Mitchell was back asking him more questions this morning. It sounded pretty tense in there."

Ted walked Kate out. "The whole town's fixated on this murder. Damn journalists. Stirring up needless speculation."

As they reached Kate's car, the sun made a brief appearance.

"Maybe you'll be able to get some fishing in after all," Kate said, "though Brandon says that rain is good for fishing."

"He's the expert."

"Oh," said Kate, surprised. He'd never even mentioned fishing that she could remember. "Does he fish a lot?"

"Isn't that why he's here?"

Kate blinked. "I don't . . ."

"I mean, he left the force to have more leisure time, right?"

Kate shrugged. "He doesn't seem to have much time to do anything but work."

Ted flashed her a smile that she couldn't quite read. Had she sounded like she was complaining? She had no right to. But why that smile?

"Poor guy." Ted's eyes twinkled. "Not exactly what he had in mind when he came here, is it?"

Not knowing what to say, Kate opened her car door. "I have no idea. Do you have a car?"

"I do have a car, but I walked today. Try to get what exercise I can, such as it is." He didn't seem at all uncomfortable about his disability, but Kate felt uncomfortable. Should she offer him a ride, or would he rather walk? And why not just ask him?

"But I'll take a lift to the museum if you're offering."

"Of course." She jumped in and unlocked the doors.

Ted held on to the hood as he lowered himself from the curb, then got in the passenger's seat.

Kate thought it must be so frustrating for someone like him to be held back by a permanent injury. She couldn't imagine not being able to get up and down the stairs without a real effort.

They were quiet during the short ride to the museum. Kate was dying to ask if the chief had discovered anything he'd shared with Ted, but she didn't.

She liked Ted, but she wasn't sure of his relationship with Brandon. He seemed amused all the time, and that couldn't sit well with a man who was under constant scrutiny by his own neighbors and who now had another murder to investigate. And who didn't have much of a sense of humor at the best of times.

"Pretty town," Ted said as they turned in to the historic district. "I can see why Bran might have chosen to move here."

"Hmm," Kate agreed, though she had no idea of the real reason Brandon had chosen Granville over any other place.

Ted sighed. "I can't believe how different he is. Anyone else . . . but Bran?"

Kate didn't want to show any curiosity about Brandon's past, but she couldn't help herself. "You think he's different now?"

"Are you kidding? He was one mean son of a bitch. He could scare the crap out of any perp. I've seen him make guys cry just by looking at them. But here . . ." He gestured out the window with a dismissive flip of his hand. "No offense, but the people are uncooperative, pull pranks on him, and generally make his job a pain in the butt. I've seen some of them in action and heard from Harry about the others. I mean, really. Why does he put up with that kind of nonsense?"

Kate bristled. "Small towns need law and order too."

"Food handlers' licenses? Parking tickets? Confiscating some old man's truck because it didn't have an inspection sticker?"

"Roy Larkins had *never* had an inspection. His truck was a danger to the community."

Ted smiled. "I know these things are important, but any decently trained policeman could handle them. Any one of those boys on his staff could do it. Hell, old man Meany could do it."

"We have worse crimes here than misdemeanors." Though it was nothing to brag about.

"Yeah, I know. You've had a couple of murders. Simple and straightforward."

Kate bit back a retort. She wouldn't point out that they hadn't been so simple at the time. Somehow, that didn't sound like an affirmation of the chief's abilities to keep order.

"Bran was a Boston detective. A *detective*. He dealt with the worst of the worst. He'd be working this serial killer case right now if he was there. He always had his pick of cases."

"Maybe he was tired of all that violence." Hadn't Brandon told her that once? "Maybe he wanted a more well-rounded life." Kate wanted to defend Brandon's decision, but she didn't have any real idea of why he'd left Boston, and she didn't want to ask Ted. It was none of her business, and from Ted's obvious disgust, she wasn't sure she wanted to hear anything he had to say.

Ted bit his lip and said almost to himself, "Not Bran. He thrived on it, and he gave it up for this, just gave it up. What a waste. And all for one little mistake."

Mistake? Kate had never heard anything even hinting at a negative reason for Brandon's being here.

"It was only that one time . . ." He broke off. "Never mind. He seems determined to make a go of it here. Now he's saddled himself with a teenage boy." He shook his head. "I like Harry, don't get me wrong. But if there is one man I never thought would want a kid, it was Brandon Mitchell."

She just hoped Ted wasn't trying to talk him into returning to Boston. What would happen to Harry if he did? Would Brandon take him to Boston or would he be dumped back into the foster care system?

And what would happen to her? *Nope—no—not thinking that way.* She would be fine. She had other friends. She and Brandon weren't even friends exactly. She wasn't sure what they were. It was all the fault of that stupid picture in the *Free Press*. It had gotten the towns-people talking, and it even had her wandering down unfamiliar paths.

They arrived at the museum, putting an end to the conversation. She sipped her coffee while taking Ted through each room on the first floor. Told him the history of jigsaws. Showed him how to view the hidden-picture puzzles by shifting his eyes until the obvious picture blurred and the hidden picture popped into focus. She demonstrated the mechanical puzzles and the box puzzles.

They lingered over the lacquered Chinese puzzle box. "It's never been opened," Kate told him.

"How do you know?" Ted leaned over the lighted glass case and peered intently at the eight-inch-square box.

"If you look halfway around the sides, you can see where it was sealed with the original lacquer."

"So what was the point?"

Kate looked startled. "The mystery."

"So you're telling me that no one knows what's inside?"

She chuckled. "Well . . . of course, it's been x-rayed. But knowing that fact takes some of the fun out of it."

"So what's in it?"

"I'll never tell."

Ted shook his head. "Tease."

As they turned to leave, the toe of his shoe hit something and sent it gliding across the floor. Kate bent down and picked up a pair of reading glasses.

"Incredible what people leave behind." Kate detoured by the registration desk and placed them in the top drawer. "Look. Four pairs of glasses, a pair of sunglasses, an earring, and a makeup bag. We have a huge lost-and-found box in the closet over there: scarves, gloves, umbrellas, large, small and in between, you name it. You'd think someone would claim them, but few people do. Most we just donate to the Vets at the end of the season."

"Not very logical," Ted agreed, giving her his amused smile.

"No, it isn't. What good does one glove do?"

Ted laughed.

"There are more rooms upstairs. If you . . ." She trailed off. There was no handicap access to upstairs. It was in the plans for the addition, but so far only the downstairs was accessible by a ramp off the side entrance.

"I can make it upstairs," Ted said, not appearing in the least offended. "It just takes me a while."

"We don't have to—"

"Kate, it's okay."

She nodded, trying to smile. She was the most socially inept person she could imagine. And it just didn't seem to get any better, no matter how much she practiced or how hard she tried.

She led him upstairs, matching her step to his. She talked as they went, mainly from nerves, but also because she enjoyed sharing her knowledge of puzzles. She explained the origin and methods of each puzzle type. Demonstrated how to drink from a puzzle jug, with their myriad holes, without pouring water down your front.

Ted declared the puzzle jugs his favorite.

The bell over the entrance door tinkled. "Must be Harry," Kate said. "He sometimes comes in on Mondays."

Most Mondays, Kate thought. She and Harry both needed to get a life.

She stopped at the door to P. T.'s Place.

"Who is P. T.?" Ted asked, as Harry slammed the front door.

"Professor P. T. Avondale. He owned the museum. He was my mentor, and Harry's. Harry came up with the idea of an interactive kids' room and named it after him as a tribute. I think I'll let him show you around."

While Harry did that, Kate went into the office to get some work done.

She logged on to her e-mail account. She'd been remiss about dealing with the mail recently, and it had piled up. She attacked the spam folder first and eliminated twenty or so solicitations and advertisements from puzzle magazines, e-zines, and Web sites. She transferred the rest to the museum in-box.

There were letters from other curators asking for advice or inviting her to talk to their board members. Interest in the next Sudoku competition. Questions about joining one of the many puzzle groups that met at the museum. She answered the most pressing and filed the others.

Then she began wading through the puzzles people invariably sent. *Have you seen this one? See if you can solve this.* She knew most of them were from avid puzzlers, many of whom were lonely and just wanted some kind of interaction. She had a special file for these, and she tried to work the puzzles and e-mail them back. But she always did this at night on her own time.

Some were from cranks who just wanted to stump her and show how much smarter they were than the curator of a puzzle museum, but those were rare. Most people just wanted to share their love of puzzles.

She and Harry had talked about putting an interactive section up on the site, but with everything else, they just hadn't had time to do it.

Harry and Ted came in when she was still only halfway through.

Harry turned on the hot plate and began rummaging through the cupboard for cups and tea. "We do this every afternoon," he told Ted.

"I'm honored."

Kate looked up. "There's some of Aunt Pru's maple cream cake in that red tin on the bookshelf. I put it out of reach so I wouldn't eat it all."

"I'll get it. Make myself useful." As Ted reached the bookshelves, Aloysius jumped down from the top bookshelf where he'd been sleeping.

"Jesus!" Ted exclaimed.

"Sorry, I should have warned you," Kate said. "Meet Aloysius."

Al bumped Ted's foot with his head, then flopped onto his back to have his stomach scratched.

Ted knelt awkwardly to pet him. "Lord, he's huge."

"And pushy. We have him on a diet, but since he's an excellent hunter, it doesn't seem to be doing much good."

Ted stood and brushed his hands off on his slacks. He stretched up to reach the cake tin and Kate realized he might have trouble reaching it. Why hadn't she just gotten it herself?

But Ted merely stood on his good leg and curved his opposite side until he could reach the tin. He carried it back to Harry and stood watching while Harry measured out the tea.

Kate realized she'd been holding her breath and quickly went back to her e-mails. More industry newsletters, a couple of notes from friends and colleagues that she could answer later. Some advertisements that had slipped through her spam filter; she deleted them.

Then she came to one with the subject line, "How to Solve a Murder." She didn't recognize the sender. Probably some crackpot who'd read about her in the newspaper. She started to delete it.

"It's pretty amazing," Ted said, suddenly standing right beside her. "Dealing with puzzles day in and day out. Probably what makes you so good at investigating."

Kate opened her mouth to protest, but Ted beat her to it. "Everybody's told me how you've helped Bran solve the murders."

"Wait. I didn't help him. Mainly I just got in the way." She was aware that Harry had stopped fiddling with the tea and was listening. "My—and Harry's—investigations were purely the armchair kind." She meant to stop there, but the truth won out. "At least they were meant to be. But Brand—the chief solved the murders without my help. If anything, I hindered."

Ted's smile said he didn't believe her. What was with him? In one breath he talked about what a badass Brandon had been, and in the next he seemed to think Brandon needed an amateur's help. It was confusing, and she could see that Harry thought so too. Ted was probably just trying to be complimentary, but it felt like he was belittling the chief. If this was how close friends treated each other, Kate was glad she didn't have any.

She turned her attention back to the e-mail. "How to Solve a Murder." *Right. Probably nothing. Still . . .*

She was trained to find answers, so she opened it. A Killer Sudoku grid filled the screen. Not filled out with numbers, but color-coded. Like a paint-by-numbers set, each box was tinted a different color—

except for two areas dead center.

They were blood red and outlined in black.

What the hell? This wasn't a new form of puzzle. It didn't make sense.

She stared at the shapes, trying to make out the meaning, then shifted her focus the way she would viewing a hidden puzzle picture. And suddenly it was crystal clear.

The red boxes transmuted into two bulky letters.

HD

Kate's fingers recoiled from the computer keys; she pushed her chair away from the desk.

"Kate? What's the matter?"

She was aware of Harry hurrying toward her, followed by the slower Ted.

Was this some kind of sick joke? Was it a message? She perused the rest of the puzzle grid looking for more shapes that could be made into letters, but found none.

She scrolled to the bottom of the page. No message. No hint. No name. No tagline. She considered replying to see if she could discover who the sender was, but thought better of it. If this was some sicko, she didn't want to start a dialogue with him.

Ted and Harry hovered over her.

"Christ," Ted said.

"Shit," Harry said.

Kate reached for the phone, then waited for someone to answer.

"Elmira? You'd better send the chief."

		5		4		3		
3					9		2	
	1				2			8
7			9		6	4	8	
9				8				1
	5	6		2				9
6			1				7	
	2		8					6
		3		6		8		

9 1

CHAPTER
NINE

2

HARRY WENT DOWNSTAIRS to wait for the chief while Kate and Ted made a more thorough evaluation of the anonymous e-mail.

"I don't get it," Ted said. "I know Sudoku uses numbers one through nine, and they have to line up vertically and horizontally without repeating, but what are those outlined boxes, the ones that are colored in?"

"This is a Killer Sudoku puzzle."

"The sender has a bizarre sense of humor."

"You think it's a prank?"

"Beats me. Tell me how the thing works."

"Well, normally a Sudoku puzzle is divided into nine regions made up of nine squares. As well as not repeating in the rows and columns, the numbers can't be repeated in the regions. There are a certain number of givens, preprinted numbers, already filled in that serve as clues." She paused. "Are you following me so far?"

"Sort of. Keep going."

"This puzzle is a Killer Sudoku. In Killer Sudoku, there are no givens. Instead there are additional regions that overlap the original nine. You can recognize them by the dotted lines. There's a little number in each of the new regions, and the numbers in that region have to add up to that number."

Ted shook his head. "Lost me."

Kate picked up a pencil and pointed to a two-cell region with the number 16 in the top cell. "The only two numbers that fulfill that number are nine and seven."

Ted looked blank.

"The only other possibility is eight plus eight, but—"

"You can't use eight twice. Got it. But what about the bigger . . . regions, is it?"

Kate nodded. "Some combinations are set, for example this three-cell region that adds up to twenty-three. The numbers have to be nine, eight, six."

"Always?"

"Always. There are others like that. You just have to memorize the combinations. But look at this one." She pointed to a four-cell region that had been tinted green and that added up to twenty-eight. "This could either be four, seven, eight, and nine or five, six, eight, and nine."

"Way over my head. But I can tell that some of the regions overlap the original nine. How do you know which number to put where?"

"You have to use the rule of forty-five."

Ted groaned. "No wonder the sender didn't try to work the puzzle."

"It's simple once you get used to it. Each row, column, and nine-number grid has to add up to forty-five."

"I'll take your word for it. You'd have to be a genius to figure it all out."

"Not really. You just have to understand the internal logic and practice."

Ted laughed. "I'd better stick to detective work. It's a lot easier."

"Which," Kate said, "brings us to Henny Dougan's murder. Who would want him dead, and why send a puzzle with his initials to me?"

The chief and Harry entered the room at that moment.

Brandon was dressed in full uniform with holster and firearm at his side. Daunting, competent, no nonsense. Tough even. But for the life of her, Kate couldn't imagine him the way Ted had described him—one mean bastard.

He saw Ted and hesitated on the threshold. "Ted," he said and stepped into the room.

"Harry and Kate were just showing me around the museum when Kate got this. We thought you should see it."

That wasn't exactly true. Kate had automatically called Brandon, but maybe she was quibbling. Maybe it was some "ceding power" thing men did. *I'm not messing in your yard. Just happened to be here.*

Really, numbers were a lot easier to interpret.

Brandon strode over to the desk and leaned over Kate's shoulder to peruse the e-mail. Kate was hyper aware of his closeness and tried to ignore it, but when Harry and Ted crowded in behind him, she said, "Here, take my chair," and squeezed out of her position so he could sit down.

He slipped into her vacated seat without a word, all his attention on the e-mail. He didn't speak for so long that Kate blurted out, "Do you think it's just a prank?"

"Possibly, but using e-mail for threats or harassment is a federal offense."

"It's not exactly either," Harry pointed out. "He doesn't take credit for the murder, just puts in Dougan's initials. Do you think he's threatening that there will be more murders?"

"I don't think anything at this point."

Ted just shrugged.

Harry leaned closer. "But if it's from the serial killer?"

"There is no serial killer," Kate and Brandon said simultaneously.

"You seem awfully certain of that," said Ted.

Brandon swiveled his chair to face him. "Do you know something we don't?"

Ted threw up both hands. "Not me. I'm just kibitzing."

The chief shot Kate and Harry a look. "I've heard that before."

Ted grinned. "Got yourself a couple a real smart sidekicks."

"Who will *not* involve themselves in *any way* in this case," Brandon said firmly.

"I'm sort of already involved," Kate pointed out. "Why do you think he sent me this e-mail? And what does Henny's death have to do with Sudoku?"

"Probably nothing," Brandon said. "But you do have a reputation for your . . . *investigative skills.*"

"He means you're always poking your nose into his investigations," Harry said.

"Pots and kettles," Kate snapped back.

Harry raised his eyebrows, the epitome of innocence.

"So it would have to be someone we know. But who could possibly think this was funny?"

"I can think of a number of people," the chief said dryly.

Kate hated to think that. And she hated for him to believe it. The town had taken pleasure in hoaxing the chief when he'd first taken over the job, but it had tapered off since he'd settled in and established his authority.

"So what do I do?"

"Nothing." Brandon scrolled down to the bottom of the e-mail.

"I already looked. It's blank."

He scrolled back to the subject line and sender address. "You didn't reply to it, did you?"

Kate shook her head. "I didn't think I should."

"You were right not to."

"I didn't recognize the addy."

"Most likely it's a dummy address."

"Sure," Harry broke in. "He probably used an anonymous server, so the e-mail can't be traced back to him."

"Which shows a certain sophistication with respect to the Internet," added Ted.

The chief merely grunted.

"But you can trace it, can't you?" asked Harry.

"Probably. But it might take some time." Brandon turned to Kate. "In the meantime, you know the drill. Relay any more e-mails to me. Do not answer them, do not download them into your computer, and do not stay here alone at night."

Kate nodded, but she felt suddenly sick. "You don't think—" The rest of the sentence stuck in her throat.

"No, I don't think you are in danger, but until I locate this jerk, I want you to take extra precautions. And that goes for you, too, Harry."

"Me?"

"Kate's not the only one with a reputation. I'll contact the Boston PD tomorrow—just as a precaution—and coordinate what we have here with their detectives on the serial killer case." He saw Kate's face and repeated, "Merely as a precaution. And mostly to reassure you *and* everyone else that the two are not connected.

"Print out several copies of the e-mail for me."

Kate did so.

He clicked the forward button, shifted so that his shoulders hid the computer screen while he typed in an e-mail address, and pressed Send. The e-mail left with a whoosh of sound.

"What's that?" asked Harry.

Brandon pressed a few keys before he said, "A secure server for just such exhibits. And you don't need to know more than that. And don't try to restore the e-mail. It's permanently deleted." The chief pushed the chair away from the desk and stood up. He unclipped his cell phone from his utility belt and flipped it open. Pressed in a number, watched the screen for a few seconds, and closed the phone.

The chief took the printouts and handed one to Kate. "I know this seems simplistic. All the skill it required was the ability to look through puzzles until he found one with an H-shaped region and a two and a three that are positioned to resemble a D. But I'd like you to solve the puzzle, just to make sure we're not missing anything."

Kate sat down at the desk and took a pencil from the pencil caddy. It took her less than ten minutes to solve the puzzle. She looked at the numbers but saw nothing unusual.

"Nothing jumps out at me." She handed it to Brandon, who also looked at it.

"Don't tell me you understand that thing," said Ted.

"I understand the concept." Brandon took the pencil from Kate and wrote a series of numbers next to the puzzle. "Date, approximate time of death, the address of the Bakery and Café. I'll send over any other numbers I can come up with."

"Birthday? Henny's address?"

"Social and phone number," he added.

Ted grinned broadly. "What a team."

Kate had been thinking the same thing. And she was curious as well as surprised. She could see that Harry was having the same reaction, though he was trying hard not to show it. The chief had never viewed her involvement with anything but exasperation.

Now, out of the blue, he was acting like she was a partner in his investigations. Was it for Ted's benefit? Was he claiming his turf the way Sam had done? Not because of any feelings he might have for her, but because he wanted to make it clear to Ted that he wasn't to interfere?

Interesting. She'd have to ask Harry how the chief and Ted were getting along after a week in the same house.

It was one thing to have a close friend for a house guest. It might be another to have a former colleague dogging your steps in a murder investigation.

At seven-thirty, Kate got out the coffee urn and carried it to the boardroom where the Arcane Masters met each Monday night. The other evenings had become so busy with crossword clubs, jigsaw clubs, Sudoku clubs, and peripheral groups like the quilters, scrap bookers, and chess club that the Masters began meeting on the only night that was completely free.

The meetings rarely began before eight-thirty since some of the members came from Nashua and other surrounding areas. They were all Master puzzlers and could only join the group by invitation. Their members had made up the Sudoku team that had competed in the winter Sudoku competition. They'd come in third—not bad considering that teams had come from as far away as Maine, Virginia, and Pennsylvania.

Jason Elks and Erik Ingersoll were the first to arrive. They had taken over leadership after the professor died and the former board president had been ousted. Both were members of the museum's board of directors along with another Arcane member, Obadiah Creek. There were a college professor, a butcher from Portland, a financial planner, and a security consultant. Until recently, there had also been a bank president.

"Evenin', Katie," Erik said, pulling off his gloves and stuffing them into the pocket of his quilted jacket.

"I'm deducing that the temperature dropped this afternoon," said Kate. "I haven't been outside all day."

"Ayuh. Ten degrees in the last hour. Wouldn't be surprised if there's a snowstorm headed our way."

Kate groaned. "No more snow."

"I'm with you there," Jason said. "I'm for spring."

Erik and Jason deposited their hats and coats in the coat closet and went into the boardroom. Erik immediately stuck his head out again.

"We have a new applicant for membership," Erik told her.

"That's great," Kate said, wondering if they would at last admit a woman to their group—

"He's a waiter over at the Bowsman Inn," Jason told her. "We're testing him out tonight."

That answers that question.

"He's new in town," said Erik. "John Vance hired him from the, uh . . ."

"Brick House," Jason said.

"Right, the Brick House."

"I think I met him last night," Kate said. "Sam and I were having dinner at the Inn."

"Is that right?" said Erik.

"Fancy that," Jason added.

Kate hurried on before they could question her about Sam and his reaction to the *Free Press* photo of her and the chief.

"Name's Dan Graves. Crosswords and logic puzzles are his forté. But he says he's proficient in sequentials, Kakuro, Sudoku, and nonograms."

"Nonograms?"

"Yes," Jason rushed to explain first. "You fill in the cells until a picture emerges."

Kate knew what a nonogram was. It just hadn't occurred to her that maybe her Killer Sudoku might have been the result of nonogram techniques, not Sudoku.

"Not that we do much of the latter," Erik said. "Mostly silly if you ask me. More geared to children."

"Oh, they can get extremely difficult," added Jason.

"Hmmph." Erik refolded the paper. "We'll see what kind of expertise Dan Graves has. Ah, here's Maurice."

Maurice Toombs, an English professor at Exeter, came through the door carrying a bakery box. "Stopped by Rayette's on my way by. Hope I'm not late."

"Not at all," Erik said, eyeing the box. "Obadiah was running late on his last job, and I told the new guy to come at nine so we'd have time to discuss his qualifications before he gets here."

It's going to be a long night, thought Kate. Even when they started on time, they tended to lose track of it, and many nights they were still playing at midnight, at which point she sent them home.

A lot of nights, she left and came back before they finished. But not tonight— she'd promised not to leave until Brandon returned to escort her. And besides, she wanted a chance to study the new waiter. She wasn't about to fall into the misguided attitude of not trusting outsiders.

But he *was* new in town. Which meant he was worth checking out.

And she also intended to brush up on her nonograms.

At ten to nine, Kate went downstairs to wait for Dan Graves. Her back was stiff, her neck tight, and her eyes tired from hunching over a computer for an hour trying to master the rudiments of nonograms.

She'd worked Griddlers and Pixel Pictures in her younger days, but had moved on to other less depictive puzzles, and some of the nonograms were way over her head. It would take a while before she could apply the same techniques to deciphering her Henny Dougan Sudoku.

Dan rang the front bell at exactly nine o'clock. Kate went to the door as Erik came out of the boardroom. Dan wiped his feet and stepped into the marble foyer.

"Wow," he said from behind the turned-up collar of his sheepskin jacket. He stripped off gloves, hat, scarf, and coat while looking around at the high ceilings and walnut staircase, newly carpeted in an Oriental runner.

Then he looked at Kate. "Weren't you having dinner at the Bowsman Inn last night?"

"Yes." Kate stuck out her hand. "Kate McDonald. Curator of the Avondale Puzzle Museum. Welcome."

She sounded stilted and pompous, but she'd copied her welcome speech from Marian Teasdale, the museum board president and the professor's long time friend. Marian never sounded stilted, just well-bred, sophisticated, and friendly.

Dan shook her hand. "Nice to meet you, Ms. McDonald."

Kate pulled her hand away—his hand was freezing.

"Just call her Katie," said Erik, stepping up to greet the newcomer. "Everyone does. Now come in and meet the others. Weather caught you unprepared, huh? Does that sometimes. You can hang your coat in there."

Dan hung his jacket on a hanger and tossed a brown knit scarf around the neck of the hanger before cramming it back into the closet.

She watched the two men walk back down the hall to the board room where the club met. Dan was taller than Erik. And younger. Probably mid-forties, Kate estimated. He was in decent shape and had a round bald spot at the crown of his dark hair.

He seemed friendly, and he'd obviously been voted into the club. But as Nancy had told her, one couldn't be too careful. Or words to that effect. It paid to be cautious, but when she began wondering if he was strong enough to garrote a man to death, she knew her imagination had gotten out of hand.

Scolding herself, she climbed the stairs and spent the rest of the night curled up in one of the wing chairs, working Sudoku puzzles and drinking tea while Aloysius dozed in the other.

At eleven-thirty, the chief called. "Are they still there?"

"Yes they are."

"I'm at the station. Go tell them to start wrapping it up. I'll be there in twenty minutes."

She went downstairs and shooed the Masters out.

"We'll wait until you're ready to leave and see you home," Erik said. "I brought my car tonight—too cold for these old bones to walk."

"What he means is he doesn't want to be serial killer bait."

"Jason, don't you go making Katie nervous. You're safe with us."

"Thanks," Kate said. "But Chief Mitchell is coming to make sure I, uh, that the museum gets locked up properly."

"Is he now?" Erik said.

"You don't say," said Jason. "Well, we'll just wait in the car until he gets here."

They shrugged back into coats and hats and left down the front steps as a group.

Several members got into cars. Dan Graves took off toward town on foot. She was surprised no one offered him a ride. A few minutes later, the chief's police cruiser came down the street and Erik and Jason drove away.

The chief pulled into a place behind her car. She took her purse off the registration desk and noticed a glove and a brown scarf on the floor by the door. She picked them up and dropped them on the desk. Men were just big forgetful little boys after all.

She turned off the foyer light and met the chief at the door.

"You didn't have to do this," she said. "I had several cavaliers who offered to watch me home."

She saw his look of amusement and blushed. Had that sounded like she thought of the chief as a cavalier? She was hopeless. "What I mean is . . ."

"I know what you mean. Ready?"

"Yes."

He waited while she set the alarm and double-locked the door, then walked her to her car. Just then, she remembered her idea about the nonogram. She stopped and turned back to the chief.

"I had an idea."

She was glad it was dark, because she bet the chief was rolling his eyes. She couldn't be sure in the eerie light of the street lamp.

"Okay, but hurry up. You're not exactly dressed for the weather."

She stepped away from the car and faced him. "Actually, Erik was talking about them. Nonograms. A kind of pixel picture. Fill in the boxes and a picture emerges."

"That would mean that the e-mailer would have to arrive at the initials HD by filling in the squares. How would he know what the initials would be? Unless he chose his victim because of the nonogram."

Kate shivered. The cold was getting to her. So was the idea of someone randomly killing because of the outcome of a game.

"What do you think?"

"I think you should go home and not worry about it. I'll follow you."

Dismissed. "I just thought I'd mention the possibility."

"Thank you," he said formally, but Kate thought she detected just a trace of amusement.

She turned to get into the car.

He pulled the car door wider and stood back, watching her.

It came from the dark. A hulking shadow, motor gunning. No lights. Aiming right for them. Kate opened her mouth to scream, but nothing came out.

Then she was grabbed, lifted up, and tossed into her front seat all in one motion. The truck sped past. Metal shrieked, tires squealed. Her door crumpled and Kate watched in wordless horror as the chief flew over the hood of her car.

8			5				1	
		7	9			2	8	
3				2		6		
	5			9				7
2			3		4			6
4					7		5	
		4		8				2
	6	5			2	9		
	8				9			4

FOR AN ETERNITY Kate could only stare, uncomprehending, into the darkness as the vehicle sped away. It rounded the corner and her brain recorded *truck*. A truck had hit the chief.

She struggled out of the car, tripped, and cried Brandon's name as she frantically searched the dimly lit street for his mangled body. She found him crumpled against the curb, his legs hidden beneath the bumper of her car, his shoulders wedged between the car and the curb.

She dropped to her knees beside him. *"Chief!* Can you hear me? Brandon?"

He didn't move or make a sound.

Her pulse raced and she couldn't draw a breath to ask again.

Stay calm. You're a mathematician. Stay calm. "Brandon! Can you hear me?"

Still no response. She fumbled in her jacket pocket for her cell phone. It slid from her trembling fingers. She searched blindly until her fingers finally touched the cold metal.

Next door,, Alice Hinckley's porch light came on, and Alice stepped into the doorway.

Kate stood up. "It's the chief, Alice! Call nine-one-one!"

Alice disappeared into the house.

She was afraid to touch him, afraid that . . . *Vital signs. Check his vital signs.*

She had to pull herself together. She knelt down over his unresponsive body, careful not to jar him, and gently felt his neck. Her fingers touched something wet. Blood.

Memories flooded back in one cataclysmic tide, cutting off her oxygen, drowning her in fear. *The professor. His blood on her hands. Beyond help. . .*

"No," she whimpered. "No. No." Her fingers searched his neck for a pulse, but the ringing in her ears overcame her . She shook her head to clear it, moved her fingers. It was there, but very faint, and she was afraid she was feeling the pulse from her own fingertips. She shifted her position. Found it again. This time stronger. He was alive.

She watched for the rise and fall of his chest, but it was impossible to tell between his thick jacket and the dark. Bracing her weight on her hands, she leaned into him until her cheek was close to his face. She thought she felt a slight stirring of air on her skin.

She became aware of Alice running down her front walk, carrying a colorful afghan, and the squeak of the gate as Alice hurried through.

"Oh, dear God." Alice's voice warbled, not in the birdlike way it usually did, but small and afraid. "Is he breathing?"

"I think so. I'm not sure." Kate could barely form the words. Her lungs were pumping way too fast. She couldn't breathe; she was panicking. But she didn't panic. She wouldn't panic. She would stay in control. Brandon's life might depend on it.

"Cover him with this." Alice thrust the afghan toward her.

Of course, Kate thought. *Shock. Keep the person warm.* She arranged the afghan over Brandon's torso, then shrugged out of her jacket and draped it over the afghan.

She strained to hear the sound of a siren. Nothing. "You called nine-one-one, right?"

"Yes, dear. They're coming."

"What's taking them so long?" Then Kate remembered what Brandon had said to do if she were in real trouble. She fumbled with her phone until it flipped open, speed-dialed the station dispatcher. "Officer down," she screamed. "Officer down."

"Who is this?"

"Kate McDonald."

"Katie?"

"Yes. Please! It's the chief. Hit and run. Get an ambulance to the museum. Now!" She gave the address just in case.

"They're already on their way. Stay on the line and I'll patch you through to the EMTs."

Kate did, answering questions until she finally heard a siren, then another, and at last saw flashing lights racing down the street.

She left Alice with the chief and ran into the middle of the street, waving her arms.

The ambulance screeched to a stop. Two men and a woman jumped out and began hauling a gurney and other equipment to where Kate pointed.

A squad car pulled up beside the ambulance. Paul Curtis and Dickie Wilson jumped out. Their faces were pale.

"Is it the chief?" Paul's eyes were wide with fear.

Kate nodded.

"Is he—?"

"I don't know." Her words ended in something close to a wail. She turned to see the EMTs attaching a drip to the chief's arm and connecting him to some machine.

"It looks real serious," Paul said.

Kate could only nod.

The team slid the chief onto a body board, strapped him down, secured his head, and lifted him to the gurney. Moving as one, the two EMTs rolled the gurney toward the waiting ambulance while the third EMT ran beside them holding the serum bag above her head.

The doors closed and the ambulance pulled away, sirens deafening. Kate tried to swallow.

"I'm going too." Kate turned to her car and for the first time saw that her door was accordioned into the side of the car.

She whirled around. "Can you take me to the hospital?"

Curtis and Wilson exchanged looks. They didn't know what to do.

"I'm coming too." Alice took Kate by the elbow and steered her to the squad car. The officers followed them and opened the back door for them to climb in.

A minute later, they were speeding toward County General. No one spoke. Alice sat bolt upright beside Kate, who stared out the front window, keeping the ambulance in sight and willing them to go faster.

Kate sniffed and a Kleenex appeared before her eyes. She stared at it. Alice fluttered it at her, and Kate felt the trickle of tears down her face.

"Thanks." She took the tissue and blotted her face, then blew her nose and concentrated on pulling herself together.

She wondered what they were doing in the ambulance. If they would get to the hospital in time.

She should call Harry, but she was in no state to talk to him. She didn't want to frighten him. . . she was frightened enough for both of them. What would happen to him if the chief—

No. She wouldn't even think the word. *Brandon, hang on. You have to.*

A whole slew of uniformed hospital staff were waiting for them at the entrance to the emergency room. They whisked Brandon through the doors and out of sight before Kate and Alice got out of the squad car.

Paul Curtis escorted them inside. Wilson stayed in the car, speaking to someone over the radio. They stopped at the admittance desk. A familiar-looking nurse met Kate's gaze and frowned.

"Katie. Don't know what this dang world's coming to. People running down the chief of police. Do you know if Chief Mitchell has any next of kin?"

Kate clapped her hand over her mouth.

"Now, now. Just a formality. I'll just put no and make a note to contact you if it's . . . necessary."

"Thanks." Kate couldn't even remember the woman's name.

"I'll call Elmira and tell her what's up. She can give me the insurance information. You go on and sit over there. I'll let you know as soon as I know something."

Kate turned blindly toward the waiting room and heard Alice say, "Thank you, Daisy."

Right, Daisy Cunningham. "Thanks, Daisy," Kate said belatedly.

She promised herself that if Brandon came out of this alive, she'd get the town to hold a huge fundraiser to help build the additional wing the hospital had been trying to build for the last decade. The museum would sponsor it. Marian would lend her support. . .

It was a long wait. The two young police officers leaned against the wall looking lost. Alice went to get everyone coffee.

As she walked away, Kate saw that Alice was wearing an old house dress and furry bedroom slippers. Her hair fell in a long snowy braid down her back.

A sob escaped from Kate. Wilson and Owens jumped, then settled back against the wall, looking anywhere but at Kate.

"I'm calling somebody," Paul said into the silence.

"Who?" asked Dickie.

Yes, who? wondered Kate. The chief had a five-man staff, if you counted Elmira and Benjamin Meany.

"Elmira. Maybe she can get county to send somebody. The sheriff maybe."

"Okay."

Paul walked outside to use his cell phone.

Alice returned with coffee, and Kate knew she had to call Harry. An hour had passed, though it seemed much longer, and they'd received no news. She'd hoped to have heard something positive before she had to call, but she didn't dare wait longer.

Harry has a right to be here if anything . . . but it wouldn't. Still, she had to call.

Thank goodness Ted was staying with them. He could drive Harry over, would be there to support him until he got to the hospital. Hopefully, he would be able to stay with him until Brandon was released to go home.

And if not, Harry could stay with her.

For the hundredth time, Kate looked at the clock and then at the door the gurney had rolled through.

Alice patted her knee.

Kate reluctantly picked up her phone and went outside to call.

She stood under the Emergency Room sign. Paul Curtis paced the edge of the parking lot, gesturing with one hand while he talked.

Kate punched in Brandon's land line. It rang four times and switched over to voice mail. "Harry, Ted. This is Kate, someone answer, please."

She hung up. Called again, left the same message. But this time she added, "The chief has been hurt. He's at County General." She hung up. Called again. They had to be home. It was after midnight and a school night.

This time a groggy voice answered.

"Ted?"

"Who is this?"

"It's Kate. The chief's been hurt. Can you bring Harry to the hospital?"

"Of course. But what happened? How bad is it?"

"Hit and run. He was picking me up at the museum." *The image of a dark monster rising out of the darkness, passing under the street light as it made the turn. A truck. A gray truck. A truck she knew. . .*"I don't know . . . how bad. They're going to let us know. Please. Can you just come?"

"Of course. We're on our way."

She started back inside, but as she reached the door, her cell rang.

"Harry isn't here," Ted said.

"Where is he?"

"I don't know. He said he was going to bed around eleven. Does he often sneak out?"

"I don't think so." Where on earth could he be? With Wynter? She seemed like the kind of girl a boy might sneak out to meet. But Kate didn't even know her last name.

"Don't worry. I'll start out and look for him on my way." He hung up.

Kate called Harry's cell. It went to voice mail. "Damn it, Harry. Wherever you are, whatever you're doing, answer this phone!"

She stood outside, willing her phone to ring. But all she heard was the buzzing of the Emergency Room sign. As she stood there, indecisive, a small red sports coupe pulled into an empty space halfway down the row of cars. Rayette climbed out, reached back in for a large tote bag, and hurried toward Kate.

"Elmira called me. I would have been here sooner, but Calvin went home sick and I had to close by myself. How is he?"

Kate shook her head as tears filled her eyes.

"He's not dead?"

"No. He can't be. I can't find Harry. Ted's out looking for him."

"Did they have a fight?" Rayette asked.

"I don't know. Brandon didn't say anything about it."

"Then ten to one he's out with a girl. And since I just left Lynn, it must be someone else. Well, if Ted doesn't find him soon, I'll go out and look too." Rayette took Kate by the elbow. "Come back inside. I brought coffee. Hospital coffee tastes like sludge."

Daisy Cunningham nodded to Rayette and offered to take them all to a waiting room on the third floor. No, she hadn't heard anything. The doctor would come down to the waiting room as soon as they had news.

They had all just crowded into the elevator when Ted came through the sliding glass doors. Harry was with him, looking scared.

"Wait up." Ted strode toward them, his uneven gait more pronounced than usual. Probably because of the iron grip he had on Harry's shoulder.

"Where were you?" Kate snapped.

"Not now, Kate." Ted pushed Harry into the elevator and followed him in.

Harry yanked his arm away and looked at Kate. His face crumpled. "He's dead. He's dead and I wasn't there."

Kate's anger and frustration evaporated. "No, Harry. He's going to be all right."

"I should've been there."

Ted seemed to have recovered from his own frustration. He gave Harry's shoulder a gentle shake. "Buck up, boy. You don't want Bran to see you crying. He might think he's worse than he is."

Harry blinked at him, his eyes suddenly hopeful. "Can I see him?"

"All in good time."

The nurse showed them to a square room painted institutional green, with a floor of beige linoleum, an orange naugahyede couch and two lumpy chairs upholstered in brown tweed. An old television sat on a frame suspended high in the corner.

Alice and Rayette began unloading two large thermoses of coffee and boxes of baked goods from the tote bag. Alice filled two cups with coffee and plenty of milk and sugar. She handed one to Kate, then went to sit beside Harry, who was crumpled up on the corner of the couch. "Drink this, you'll feel better." She handed him the cup, then sat down beside him.

Ted turned to Paul Curtis. "Are you in charge?"

Paul looked at Dickie, then back to Ted. "Uh. I guess so."

Ted's eyes closed momentarily. "What happened?"

Both men looked at Kate.

"Did you take her statement?"

"Uh, no sir. Not yet."

"Perhaps you should do that now."

"Yes, sir."

Kate was glad to let Ted take charge, and from Paul and Dickie's expressions, so were they. She hadn't even thought about a statement. At first she'd been too busy reliving every moment. Over and over and over. The surprise. Brandon pushing her into the car. The crunch and thud. The blur of movement. Brandon lying curled in on himself, unmoving.

Then she'd been too worried about Harry.

Paul Curtis dispatched Dickie to the patrol car to get the tape recorder.

Ted rolled his eyes and paced until Dickie returned, out of breath. "I brought extra batteries."

Paul took it from him and set it next to the pastries. "Uh, now Katie…"

Ted dropped his forehead to his hand.

The door swung open. Finn Tucker and Fast Eddie Blair squeezed into the room.

There was a moment of pandemonium, Finn firing questions, Eddie getting off shots, Paul and Dickie spluttering and looking toward Ted, who finally took over and forced the two intruders to the door.

Two security guards and an irate nurse were waiting for them.

"I told you you could not come up here. Now please leave the building."

"Was it really an attempt on Chief Mitchell's life?" Finn yelled as he was escorted toward the elevators. "Or on Katie's?"

"Damn press," Ted said and firmly closed the door.

Kate enumerated the events into the small recorder. Her voice caught only once, when she described Brandon's body as it arced across her windshield.

Harry hadn't said a word; he only sat with his head bowed, holding his Styrofoam cup. Alone. Scared and hurting. Now he came to sit by Kate and awkwardly put his arm around her shoulders.

She wanted to have time alone with him, to apologize for her outburst, to reassure him.

"And what were you doing at the museum at that hour?"

Ted had asked the question. Kate glanced at Paul Curtis, who until then had been conducting the interview.

"The Arcane Masters—it's a club made up of the best puzzlers— meets on Monday night. They had just adjourned."

"Can you remember who was in attendance?"

The tone of the questioning had changed. Kate felt Rayette move a little closer.

Alice let out an unladylike snort. "I can give Officer Curtis a list if he comes by tomorrow."

Ted nodded to Paul, who nodded back.

"And they had all left by the time Chief Mitchell arrived?"

"Everyone but Jason and Erik. They waited so I wouldn't be alone, but they left when the chief drove up, so I doubt if they saw anything."

Ted took out a small notebook and wrote their names in it. "Any one else might have seen what happened?"

"No. I don't think so. Dan Graves was walking back toward town. He might have seen a truck headed in the direction of the museum."

At Ted's raised eyebrows, she said, "He works at the Bowsman Inn. He was probably on his way back there."

"So Chief Mitchell saw you to your car . . ." Ted prompted.

"Yes." Kate wondered how he could be so professional when his friend had almost been killed. But she knew the chief would be the same way. Maybe cops had to grow a second, thicker skin.

"You think it was a truck?"

Kate hesitated. She'd seen the truck. She thought she knew who it belonged to. But it didn't make sense, unless he was drunk. And even then, he wouldn't have aimed for them. "It all happened so fast."

"Kate? Did you see what make or model it was?"

She looked at Ted. He was waiting for her answer, almost as if he knew she was vacillating on how much to tell. He wasn't here officially, but he'd taken over the questioning, and neither Paul nor Dickie seemed to mind. In fact, they looked relieved. But Kate wasn't.

She knew he was just as anxious as she was to find the person who had hurt the chief. But still she balked at mentioning her suspicions. And she thought Brandon would understand. Ted might be a good cop, but he was an outsider. He didn't understand the people of Granville and might easily leap to the wrong conclusions.

She'd wait. If Brandon wasn't able to take her statement by tomorrow, she'd tell Ted. And hope she didn't get into legal trouble for withholding evidence.

"Did you recognize anything about it?"

"I couldn't be sure."

Ted's lips tightened. "You're tired. That should be enough for tonight. If you remember anything else . . ." He hesitated. "Notify the Granville PD." He punched off the tape recorder and returned it to Paul Curtis.

"Don't lose it."

"No, sir." Paul shook his head vehemently.

Kate felt a surge of indignation. Brandon's small staff might be young and not very experienced, but they were well-trained. Brandon had seen to it. Kate didn't like the hint of condescension Ted used with them.

Then she reminded herself that he was used to dealing with seasoned detectives and that he was feeling as frustrated and worried as she was. She was acting like a Granvilleite.

And she was being selfish. There was someone else who needed reassurance more than either of them. She turned so that she could face Harry. His chin was hidden in his chest again.

She walked over to him. "I'm sorry I snapped at you."

Harry didn't look up, just shook his head.

"He's going to be fine."

Harry's head lifted slightly; he glared at her. "How do you know?"

Angry, frightened, defiant, needing reassurance. She understood. She was feeling all those things herself.

"I just know he will be."

Because nothing else is acceptable, Kate thought.

8				1		3		6
		7	8			4		
3			5			2		
5			1		4		8	
9				6				5
	8				7			4
		2			9			7
		1			5	8		
6		8		7				2

CHAPTER

ELEVEN

DOCTOR LEONARD WAS a small, wiry African-American man. He looked tired, but not grave. At least that's what Kate was making herself believe. She stood up, but Harry beat her to the doctor.

"How is he?" Harry demanded. His freckles stood out stark against the pallor of his face. His eyes were huge and dark and frightened.

It seemed to Kate that everyone in the room was holding their breath. She knew she was.

"Are you his son?" the doctor asked.

"Sorta," Harry mumbled, casting an anguished glance at Kate. She knew what he was thinking. If the chief's condition were serious, only the next of kin would be able to see him.

Kate weighed her options as she came to stand beside Harry. It would be stupid to lie. Everyone knew the chief wasn't married and didn't have a kid. Or did they? Kate's step stuttered. What did any of them know about the chief?

It doesn't matter, she told herself.

"Hi, I'm Kate McDonald. We don't know of any family at this time. He's Harry's guardian. They live together." She sounded like an idiot.

"We're all his family," Alice piped up. "So don't even think about keeping any information from us or trying to keep us from seeing him when he's up to visitors."

"You'll have to take that up with the powers that be, I just do the surgery." Dr. Leonard said it kindly, almost humorously. Surely, that meant the chief was all right. "But since my friend here is 'sorta' the son, let me say that Chief Mitchell is in stable condition."

"Can I see him?" Harry asked, practically bowling the poor doctor over.

"Not tonight. He's still in ICU. But perhaps tomorrow, just for a minute."

"What's wrong with him?" Alice demanded.

"I really can't—"

Ted reached past Harry and Alice and stuck out his hand. "Ted Lumley, Boston Police Department. We have reason to believe that this incident relates to another case. If you could just tell me the nature of Chief Mitchell's injuries, and give me a heads up on when he'll be able to talk."

"Oh dear." The doctor grasped Ted's hand and shook it. "I'm not sure what the protocol is, but if you're police . . ." He lowered his voice.

Kate strained to hear, but only got bits and pieces. Broken shoulder and collar bone . . . broken ribs . . . superficial . . .

"We'll keep him for a few days to make sure no pulmonary contusions develop."

"Days?" Harry blurted out.

Ted clasped his shoulder. "Take it easy. I'll stick around until he's back home with you. Now I think it's time we all went home and got some sleep."

Harry jutted out his chin. "I'm staying here."

"You can't stay here. Now let's go."

Kate wondered if she should interfere. Ted seemed to be taking over on all fronts. Maybe he felt it was his duty, considering his relationship with Brandon. But Harry wasn't the only one chafing under it. New Hampshireites didn't take kindly to someone else giving the orders, even if they were good friends with the best of intentions.

"Ted's right," Kate said, though she sympathized with Harry. She wanted to stay, too, even if she couldn't possibly do any good.

"We can't see him tonight, and Dr. Leonard said they'd call if there was any change. We'll need to be fresh and alert tomorrow." She gave him a direct, meaningful look. " . . . when we come to see the chief."

Harry looked right back at her, and she saw the dawning understanding. It had been a cheap trick, but he'd bought it. He thought they were really going to find the person who'd run down Brandon instead. She'd make it up to him, but he needed to be in bed, and she didn't want to have to referee any fights between him and Ted.

And besides, she *was* going to find the person who ran Brandon down. And she knew just where to start.

Reluctantly, Harry let Ted lead him away.

"I guess we'll go, too," Rayette said. "I'm dropping Alice off—do you need a ride?"

Kate looked around. She could see the two patrolmen down the hall talking with the doctor. "I think I'll wait for Paul and Dickie."

Rayette nodded. "Well, don't stay too late. Harry's not the only one who needs his wits tomorrow."

Kate hung back trying to listen to what was going on between the two patrolmen and the doctor. But they were merely being reassured that the chief would survive and would be able to resume his duties after a sufficient convalescence.

Good to hear, but we need him now, thought Kate.

The three men walked off together down the hall and turned the corner. Kate lingered for a few seconds before following. But when she turned into the adjacent corridor, it was empty except for a nurses' station and a bank of two elevators.

They had gone, and Kate was about to lose her ride back into town. She pressed the down button and waited impatiently for the elevator to arrive. When the doors finally opened, she jumped in and pressed One.

It let her off in a different part of the hospital, and by the time she followed the signs to the emergency room and stepped out into the parking lot, the police cruiser was gone.

Finn Tucker stepped out of the shadows and gave her his trademark grin.

"No comment." Kate turned to go back into the emergency room.

He slipped between her and the door. "How is Chief Mitchell?"

"Stable. That's all I know." She tried to sidestep him.

He moved with her. "Can you tell me what happened?"

"No."

"Come on, Katie. People have a right to know."

"It's *Kate*. And you'll just make it up anyway." She wouldn't put it past Finn Tucker to make news just to have something to write about.

Finn laughed. The light caught the gleam of a row of even white teeth. "I don't fabricate. I just spin."

Kate wished he'd spin away from her. Right now she had more important things to think about. Like how she was going to get back to town. There was a cab service in Granville. Three cars, and they wouldn't like being wakened in the middle of the night.

"Was the car aimed at you or Chief Mitchell?"

She'd been trying to convince herself that it had been a drunken accident. But what if the driver had purposely aimed at her or the chief? Either way, somebody had a lot to answer for, and they were going to pay.

"I'm really tired. Good night." She slipped past him; the doors opened.

"Need a ride?"

She did, but she didn't want one from Finn Tucker. He'd pump her for information all the way back to town.

"I have to pick up Eddie at the museum. I can drop you off there or anywhere you want."

Kate hesitated. "What's he doing at the museum?"

"Getting photos, what else?"

And mucking up the crime scene. Had they even sent anyone to secure the area? The thought of Fast Eddie climbing around destroying any evidence that might lead to the person who did this made the decision for her. "Okay. Thank you."

Finn bowed slightly. "I'm right over here." He gestured toward a beat-up green Nissan parked in a tow-away zone. There was a cardboard sign with PRESS printed out in block letters.

Finn ran ahead and pried open a dented passenger's door. There were dings and scrapes everywhere—this car had been through the wars. But it hadn't run down the chief.

Kate climbed inside, and Finn threw his weight against the door until it shut. The upholstery was ripped. A long strip of gaffer's tape ran front to back across the seat, separating them. Bits of stuffing spewed out the sides.

Finn hopped in the driver's side. "She's a bit beat up, but she's reliable."

Kate was unimpressed. "Doesn't Eddie have a car?"

"Nah. And I don't have the petty cash for cabs. Normally we trade who gets the car and who has to take the bike. The bike had a flat tonight, so Fast Eddie's hoofing it."

"Bike? Let me guess. A Harley."

"Schwinn."

Kate would have laughed except she was too scared, tired, and angry. Journalism on a wing, a prayer, and a Schwinn. And it wasn't even journalism. She'd never seen a newspaper with so much questionable data. Though to be fair, she'd read a few government edicts that were just as convoluted.

Finn didn't ask any more questions on the ride back into town. He was still quiet as they turned onto Main Street, and Kate began to worry about what she was going to do about her car.

If they had secured the scene, she wouldn't be able to claim it until they were through. If it was even driveable. She didn't relish having to ask Finn to drive her home. Hopefully someone would still be there to give her a lift.

She closed her eyes. They felt gritty behind her lids, and she felt physically beat and emotionally drained. She must have drifted off, because when she opened them again, they were stopping in front of the museum.

The street was lit with generated field lights. Police tape designated a large area that encompassed both sides of the street.

A police cruiser was parked at the edge of the light, and Will Owens leaned against the side. And behind the police car was Sam Swyndon's SUV.

Sam was here. Somebody had been on the ball.

Finn pulled in behind Sam's car and cut the engine and lights.

"Thank you. Good night." Kate wrestled with the door.

"It only opens from the outside," Finn informed her and hopped out of the car to come around and open her door.

Kate ignored him as they walked toward the police car. She wished he'd go away. "Where is Fast Eddie?"

"Around somewhere." Finn didn't stop at the police cruiser, merely nodded at Owens and kept going toward the cordoned-off area.

Kate had to run to catch up. "This is a secured scene," she told him icily.

"It doesn't look all that secure to me." Finn ducked under the tape.

Kate followed him. She could see Sam taking pictures of the Matrix. Benjamin Meany appeared from behind him and ran toward Kate and Finn, shoving in his shirttails. Someone must have called him and gotten him out of bed. Wisps of thin hair stood up from his head, and his shirt was buttoned wrong.

"This is a crime—Oh Katie, it's you. How's the chief?"

"He's in stable condition."

Mr. Meany nodded his head sagely. "I'll have to ask you to step behind the tape."

"Of course." Kate grabbed Finn by the jacket and hauled him toward the tape.

Finn just kept smiling. "Katie love, you're strong for a—"

"If you say geek, you'll be crawling home."

Finn just grinned more broadly.

There was a sudden rustling in the trees, even though there was no breeze to speak of. A pair of legs appeared from a lower branch and dangled in space for a second, and then Fast Eddie Blair dropped to the ground.

He trotted over to where Kate and Finn were standing.

He glanced at Kate, then patted the leather case attached to his belt.

Finn nodded back. "Well, good-night, Katie. We've got a paper to put to bed. If you remember anything—anything at all—give me a call." He reached into his jacket pocket and pulled out a dog-eared business card. "Don't lose it. I don't have many left."

He saluted Kate with two fingers, and he and Fast Eddie retreated to the Nissan.

Kate stood in the semidarkness, clutching her arms to her chest, attempting to ward off the early morning chill, fatigue, and confusion.

Sam seemed to be taking forever. Benjamin Meany had gone back to helping him, which seemed to consist mainly of jumping out of the way when Sam changed positions for another shot.

Will Owens slumped against the side of the police car, asleep on his feet.

At last Sam began gathering up his equipment. He slung his cameras over his shoulder and bent under the tape. He looked up and his eyes met Kate's.

"What are you doing here?"

"Getting my car."

"You won't be driving it anywhere tonight even if they would release it to you. Hey, Will."

Owens jerked away from the car and acknowledged Sam with a jaw-cracking yawn.

Sam shook his head. "A ship without a captain."

Kate agreed, but it was the nicest thing Sam had ever said about the chief. Usually they were at loggerheads. And usually it was about her.

Owens pushed himself away from the car and walked over. "Do you know how the chief is doing, Katie?"

For what seemed like the hundredth time that night, she said, "In stable condition."

He grunted. "I don't know what we're supposed to do without him."

"We'll carry on, just like we do when he's around." Benjamin Meany bent slowly to crawl under the tape. Took even longer to stand up again. "Ayuh. We'll just keep keeping on like the chief expects us to."

Kate was tired, but it hadn't escaped her that people were rallying around the chief for a change. At the hospital. Here. Granted, they were people who had already passed the discomfort zone with the outsider. She was just sorry it had taken this for them to realize how much the town relied on the new chief of police.

Owens yawned again. "Sorry. My second straight shift."

"What about Katie's car?" Sam asked.

Meany sighed. "Might as well call Norris Endelman to come tow it. Can't drive it the way it is. The door's pushed right into the side."

"But have the crime scene people finished with it ?" Kate asked.

"The county wouldn't send the crime van. Not for an auto accident. Told us to take pictures, scrape paint residue, and look for tire marks. Not that we found any. That's because the bast—the *so-and-so* didn't even try to stop or swerve out of the way. Damn drunken driver.

"Is there anything you can tell us, Katie? See anything?"

Kate looked off down the street. It was lit now for most of the block. Her car sat in a pool of light. But she could see the whole scene as it happened. Jason and Erik driving away. Dan Graves walking in the opposite direction. She thought he might have been whistling. The chief opening her door. Her stopping to tell him her suspicions.

If only she'd just gotten in and not delayed him with her suspicions.

No. The truck had been waiting for them.

Waiting for the chief.

If Brandon had been standing farther from the car, he might be dead. Kate shivered. Sam put his arm around her.

"Can't this wait until tomorrow?"

"I'm okay," Kate said. "Just a little cold."

The truck had headed straight for them. A gray truck. Roy Larkins' truck.

Once again, Kate hesitated. If she mentioned Roy, the whole town would know by morning. They'd be taking sides by lunchtime, and there would be no chance of a decent investigation, even if they had someone to lead it. And she still couldn't bring herself to believe that

Roy Larkins would intentionally try to kill the chief. That he'd been nursing that kind of grudge for nearly a year, just because the chief impounded his truck. It didn't make sense.

"It had its lights off until right before it reached us. I remember the lights coming on and blinding me. If Brandon hadn't—" She took a breath. "It turned left down at the end of the block."

"You check that far, son?"

"No, sir." Owens unclipped his flashlight from his utility belt and started off down the street.

"Probably won't find anything but skid marks, if even that. But it'll make him feel like he's doing something." Meany let out a prodigious sigh. "Another murder investigation and the chief out of commission. Things are looking mighty bad."

Kate couldn't agree more. Who would take charge of the force until the chief returned? No one had the expertise to carry out a murder investigation. Benjamin Meany was feisty but really too old to be put under that kind of stress.

They'd have to bring someone in. Another outsider. *And won't the town just love that?*

Another reason not to rat on Roy Larkins. She was born and raised in Granville, but no one would ever speak to her again if she implicated him to the authorities. She'd have to make sure before she said anything.

Sam spoke up for the first time. "What was Chief Mitchell doing here?"

"He was making sure I got home safely."

"You could have called me. I would have taken you home."

Kate gritted her teeth. She was not in the mood to explain her actions to Sam. "Could you take me home now?"

His expression softened. "Sure. You must be exhausted." He turned to Benjamin. "I'll develop these and bring them over to the station tomorrow."

"Ayuh. I'll see about getting your car towed in the morning, Katie."

It was still dark when Sam and Kate reached Kate's bungalow. It was nearly five o'clock, but at this time of year, the sun wouldn't rise for another hour. The street was dark. No lights shone from Aunt Pru's house, not even the porch light. She must not have heard the news.

Sam wouldn't leave until Kate let him come inside to search for intruders. He would have stayed longer, but Kate was dead on her feet. She thanked him and kissed him and sent him on his way. And not once did either of them mention marriage.

Then she locked the door and went down the hall to fall asleep fully clothed on her bed.

The phone rang. Kate could hear it from down the hall, but it sounded distant to her sleep-fogged brain. She rolled over and pulled the blanket over her head. The ringing stopped, then started again.

Kate peered out of the covers. It was still dark outside. It was five fifty-six. She'd only been asleep for a few minutes.

"Damn it, Aunt Pru. If you're calling now...." Or was it the hospital? She pushed back the covers, ran down the hall to the telephone bench in the foyer, and grabbed the receiver. A recorded voice said, "You've got mail." Then a dial tone.

The cold seeped from Kate's bare feet to the top of her head.

She'd left her laptop at the museum, so she reached into the hall closet for a sweatshirt, then went into her dad's old bedroom where his PC still sat on her mother's makeup table.

Kate sat down and booted up the computer. It took forever before the screen lit up. Then it took another forever to connect to the Internet. And all the time, Kate was dreading what might be waiting for her in her mailbox.

She scrolled down the new e-mails, opened a few she didn't recognize, then stopped.

It wasn't a puzzle this time. Just a four-word message. *Try and stop me.*

For a moment she forgot to breathe. Not the same address as before. Having a photographic memory could be a pain in the butt, but it had its uses.

She had to fight the urge to delete the e-mail. But she knew that wouldn't prevent him from killing again. If it really was the serial killer.

No matter who it was, he'd killed before. He might have tried to kill her or Brandon tonight.

And from the sound of his e-mail, he was planning to kill again.

CHAPTER
TWELVE

IT TOOK SOME time for Kate to realize someone was knocking on her front door. The sun was out for the second day in a row—and Brandon had been run down by a gray truck. She was halfway to the door when she remembered the e-mail. *Try and stop me.*

She stood with her hand on the doorknob. "Who is it?"

"Who do you think it is this time of morning?"

Kate expelled a breath. Aunt Pru. She unlocked the door.

Pru breezed past her and whirled around. She'd attempted some sort of half-up, half-down hairstyle today. It was slightly off kilter, which made Kate want to tilt her head to look at her aunt. She was also wearing a green nylon running suit: her nod to spring.

"What did I tell you about job security?"

Kate waited, trying to comprehend the question and figure out the context.

"And now there he is lying at death's door, and if you had your way, you'd be a widow."

Kate shook her head. "Coffee." She padded past Pru toward the kitchen, hearing Pru's sneakers squeaking behind her.

Pru took the coffee canister from Kate's hands and began measuring grounds into the coffeemaker. "You could have been *killed.*"

Elmira had been busy this morning: She and Pru were the grapevine divas. Kate was often astonished that the chief kept Elmira on, except that he probably wouldn't find anybody else who was willing to be both secretary and dispatcher *and* put up with his gruffness.

"He pushed me out of the way. He saved my life."

Pru paused with the scoop in her hand. Grounds floated to the counter. "Well, I'll give him that. But he wouldn't have had to push you out of the way if you hadn't been standing next to him."

Perfect New Hampshire logic.

Kate made a pointed look at the coffee scoop, and Pru dumped the contents into the mesh cone, scooped out more grounds.

"And what would have happened to me if he hadn't been there?"

Coffee grounds flew into the air and the scoop clattered to the linoleum floor. "Oh my Lord, I didn't think of that."

"So maybe you should send him a get-well card." Kate leaned over and picked up the scoop. She nudged Pru out of the way and finished filling the coffeemaker.

"I will *not*. You would never have been someone's target if he hadn't moved here."

Kate turned on her aunt. It was one thing to complain about the police chief. Everyone did—he was new, after all—but not when he had nearly been killed. And Pru never cut him a break.

"What? Granville never had drunk drivers before Br—Chief Mitchell moved here?"

Pru pulled a paper towel off the roll and knelt down to clean up the grounds. "Of course we did. I'm just saying—you think it was a drunk driver?"

Kate looked at her, the soul of innocence. "What else could it have been?"

The coffeemaker belched steam.

The two of them watched the coffee drip into the glass carafe.

"If you'd just marry Norris or Sam or even Louis Albioni, these kind of things wouldn't happen."

"I'm not marrying anybody." Kate carried two mugs to the table.

Pru grumbled her way through the first cup of coffee, but petered out during the next.

Kate stood up from the table and carried both cups to the sink. "Now I have to get to work."

She managed to steer Pru toward the front door—then remembered she didn't have a car.

"Would you mind if I borrowed the Buick today? I'll get a rental once I find out how long it will take to fix the Matrix."

"If you can drop me off at the beauty parlor on your way. I'll call Simon to drive me home."

Kate dropped Pru off at the door of Karen's Kurls, drove another half block, and stopped to call the hospital. As expected, they wouldn't tell her anything because she wasn't next of kin. She asked if a next of kin had been notified, but the nurse on duty didn't know.

She called Elmira.

"The only emergency contact listed on his application is someone named John Clifton. I called, but the number has been disconnected."

"No one else?"

"Nope. But the form doesn't ask for next of kin, only asks whom to notify in case of an emergency. I'm sure there's a more complete dossier, but I don't have it. And I really don't want to hassle Mayor Saxon. He's in a state."

"How are things going at the station?"

"Bedlam would be an understatement. Phone's been ringing off the hook, asking if the chief is dead and if the serial killer did it. I swear. I could knock some folks' heads together. Will Owens' mother called and wants him to come home. She doesn't think he's safe working for the police. Go figure."

"Did he go?"

"No. He's sleeping in one of the cells out back. Paul and Dickie are walking around like zombies. Benjamin Meany is here, and I can't get the old geezer to go home and rest."

"I heard that, Elmira Swyndon—" came from behind her.

"I meant for you to! Honestly, Katie, he's making me nuts. Got some crazy idea that since he's got seniority, it's his responsibility to hold down the fort."

"Good for him," Kate said.

"I know. You gotta respect him for it. But heck. Have you heard how the chief is this morning?"

"I just called. They wouldn't tell me much, just that his condition is stable. The same thing they said last night."

Elmira sighed.

"What?"

"I was just wondering if his mother is out there somewhere worrying about him."

"The chief? A mother?" Kate responded.

"Most people at least start out with one."

"Of course, I just never thought about it before."

"He's a human being just like the rest of us."

"You're preaching to the choir," Kate said. "I'll call if I hear any more."

"You just tell him to hurry up and get better. Everybody's been asking about him."

Like that would be a comforting thought. The chief had a pretty good idea of what most people in Granville thought about him.

Kate hung up. She had to get to the bank for the week's petty cash. It was her least favorite job. Every time she entered the hallowed doors of the Farm and Mercantile, she heard echoes of Darrell Donnelly's childhood taunts. "Katie is a ge-ek. Katie is a ge-ek."

Darrell had been merciless. Kate *had* been a geek, still was, probably always would be. Darrell was now president of the bank. He'd finally gotten his payback for all those years he'd tortured her, but the punishment had been too severe for Kate to feel any satisfaction.

She hadn't been in line for all of thirty seconds when someone said, "Katie. How awful. Are you all right?"

Kate smiled and was relieved to hear "Next" before she could answer.

She had no better success with the teller though. As soon as the girl had counted out the bills, she said, "Is it true the serial killer tried to kill Chief Mitchell?"

"No," Kate said firmly. "It was some drunken driver that took the turn too fast."

The teller looked disappointed.

"Well, it's mighty suspicious." A voice two lines over. Kate fled without looking back. She crossed the street and slipped into Rayette's. She knew Rayette would have saved a copy of the *Free Press* for her.

She had, and she stood close by while Kate read the headlines. "Police Chief Struck Down by Mystery Car. Was he getting too close to the killer?" A photo of Kate's Matrix, the door crunched like an accordion. Another photo of Sam photographing the crime scene. And a third, a long shot. The length of the street that faded into black. The last was pretty impressive, but the story that followed made her forget the artistic merit of the photo.

"I'm going to kill him," Kate said. "He's creating a panic."

"I'd help you, except I've got a truckload of people in here for breakfast, and Calvin's still sick."

"What's he got?"

"Flu, I guess. He said he'd try to come in. But hell, I don't want him making the clientele sick. We'll just have to make do."

Johnny brought Kate her usual latte, gave her a harried smile, and trudged off again.

Kate glanced at her watch. It was almost eleven. She wished she had someone to confer with about the e-mail she'd received the night before. She couldn't take it to the chief, they might not even let her see him. She'd have to wait for Harry to get back from school. Maybe he'd picked up some things about anonymous servers from talking to Brandon.

Until then, she had some questions, and it was time to get some answers.

Roy Larkins lived on the west edge of town. He lived alone—had never married as far as Kate knew. The house was a surprisingly well-kept clapboard cottage, painted a light gray with white shutters. There were several outbuildings, a huge woodpile, an old Chevy up on concrete blocks, and a gray truck in the driveway.

Kate pulled over to the curb and got out of the car. On her way to the front door, she slowed down to take a look at the truck. She walked around to the front fender. The right headlight was smashed, the bumper was hanging nearly to the ground, and there was a long scrape along the side right above the front wheel.

She'd been right. This was the truck that someone had used in the hit and run.

Kate knelt down to get a closer look. She didn't know a lot about forensics; it was a subject that had not come her way until recently.

She ran her finger along one of the scrapes, then repeated the motion with her fingernail. Her hand came away with dark residue under the nail. She fished in her purse for a piece of paper, found the tissue that Alice had given her the night before, and scraped the residue onto it.

She folded it and secured it in a zippered pocket before standing up and proceeding to the house.

She knocked. From inside the house she heard a dog bark. She knew Roy had a beagle named Hound—Roy's sense of humor. The dog was pretty old, but still capable of biting if Roy sicced him on her.

Maybe she had acted prematurely. What if Roy *had* been drunk and failed to stop? What if he was still drunk? He might get belligerent. She stepped back from the door.

This had been a stupid idea. Then again, she couldn't see Dickie or Paul questioning Roy.

The door opened a crack. Roy stuck a disheveled head out and squinted at her. "Yeah?"

"Mr. Larkins?"

"That's me."

"I'm Kate McDonald."

"Pru's niece? Thought you looked familiar." He worked his mouth like he was rinsing toothpaste. Kate had to force herself not to dodge in case he spat.

"What time is it?"

Kate looked at her watch. "Nearly noon."

"Dang. One too many beers last night. You taking up a collection or something?"

"No. I wanted to ask you a couple of questions, if I might." No way could this man have cold-bloodedly run down the chief. But he had been drinking last night—could it actually be a case of drunken driving? She had really hoped she'd been wrong about the truck and that Roy and his truck had an alibi for the night before.

Scientific method, she reminded herself. *Facts first. Logic later. Feelings, never.*

"What kind of questions?"

"About your truck."

"My truck?" He groaned. "Yeah. I remember."

This was too easy. Was he actually going to confess to hitting the chief? And would his admission hold up in court if there wasn't a law officer present?

"Weird. But I didn't file a complaint or nothing."

That stopped her. "What do you mean?"

"What do you mean, what do I mean? I didn't file a complaint."

"Why were you going to file a complaint?"

Roy scrubbed his head. "Why do you want to know?"

"Chief Mitchell was the victim of a hit and run last night. It was a truck. A gray truck. I think it was your truck."

"My truck?" Roy looked out into the yard. "Well, dang. There it is. Right in my own driveway. And it hit Chief Mitchell? Damn kids. Oughta be tanned good and hard."

"What kids? Was someone other than you driving your truck last night?"

"Well, heck. The chief of police and I never seen eye to eye, but I wouldn't run him down, if that's what you're thinking. Musta been those damn kids."

"What kids?" Kate repeated.

"I dunno. It was the dangest thing. I was out at Jumpin' Jack's with some of the guys. We had a few beers. When I come out, my truck is gone. Ned Jensen had to give me a ride home. And now there it is, in my own driveway. Dang."

"Have they stolen your truck before?"

"Nah, but they took Noah Zumwaldt's tractor out of the barn and left it in the middle of town, right underneath Abelard Granville's statue. The town made Noah pay to resod. Made him mad as crabs. Can't blame him. It wasn't his fault."

"Do you know who the kids are?"

"Nah. Could be any of 'em, the way they dress, and talk back, get away with murder. If I had any, I'd give 'em what for."

Kate didn't doubt it.

"The police will probably want to look at the truck. Your headlight's been smashed. And the side's scraped."

Roy suddenly came to life. He trotted down the steps and stopped in front of the truck. "Damn those juvenile delinquents. Someone is gonna have to pay for this." He lifted up the broken bumper.

"Mr. Larkins. I don't think you should touch anything until the police search it for evidence."

"Oh, no. Nobody's impounding my truck. I got my inspection, and it's not my fault that some damn kids go for a joyride and hit somebody. I'm sorry about Chief Mitchell, but they're not getting my truck."

He swung around and strode back to the house, went inside, and slammed the door behind him.

He'd probably be waiting for poor Paul Curtis with a shotgun on his lap.

Kids, Kate thought as she drove back to the center of town. Not some serial killer trying to stop Brandon from capturing him. Not somebody out for revenge. Just a bunch of drunken kids.

Which was even worse in a way.

She tucked away an idea to open the museum to teens on weekend nights. She'd run it past Ginny Sue—when things got safe again.

And someone should tell Finn Tucker to back off. Even Kate, the logical mathematician, the rational, unemotional geek, had succumbed to his lurid articles.

She called the station and told Elmira what she'd learned. "Tell the guys to be careful if they go question him."

"Maybe you should be the new interim chief of police," Elmira said.

"You're getting an interim chief?"

"Well, we'll have to, won't we?"

CHAPTER
THIRTEEN

FEELING SHE HAD done her duty and ruminating on Elmira's words about finding a replacement for the chief, Kate drove straight to the hospital. She didn't like the idea of someone standing in for Brandon. It seemed to her it would be one step away from letting him go at the end of his contract in May.

But surely he'd won the town over by now. They still liked to complain and give him a hard time, but look at all the people who'd asked about him—though if he was seriously injured they might have no choice—

No. She wouldn't think like that. She'd go to the hospital and see for herself. How long could a few broken bones take to heal? Benjamin Meany could drive him until he could use his arm again. He could catch up on paperwork, let his staff be his arms and legs. . .

She sighed. If only there wasn't a murderer on the loose.

It took a few minutes before Kate could find a large enough parking space for Aunt Pru's Buick. While she'd been busy, she hadn't thought about the chief and how she was going to tell him what she'd learned. But as she stood in the elevator, she began to feel anxious.

Which was stupid. An emotional, not rational, reaction.

At the nurses' station, a nurse informed her that he'd been transferred from ICU to a private room on the fourth floor—a good sign.

Still, she had to stand outside the door to collect herself as a vision of the chief lying bleeding on the pavement rose up to haunt her. She pushed it away, opened the door, and stepped inside.

The room was dim, the blinds drawn against the weak April sun. A blipping green monitor was the only source of light in the otherwise gray room. Brandon was a mere shadow. She tiptoed toward the bed, which was raised at the head end.

Brandon was a tall man, large-boned and strong, but now he looked smaller, younger, and helpless. One side of his face was nearly the color of the sheet, the other was swollen, black, and dotted with rectangles of white tape.

There was a large swath of bandage across his forehead, a stark contrast to his dark hair. She could see a patch of scalp where his hair had been shaved. She swallowed the lump that clogged her throat. Until now, she hadn't let herself dwell on the state of his injuries or calculate the odds of hit-and-run survival. Sometimes ignorance really was bliss.

Now that she saw him, she realized how close he had come to dying. If he'd been standing a foot farther into the street . . . If the truck had been going faster, if it hadn't swerved away at the last minute . . . She shuddered. *No ifs.* He was alive and he would recover. And Granville would have its chief of police again.

Kate hesitated. *If the truck hadn't swerved at the last minute.* She closed her eyes, remembering. The sound of the engine, the sudden light. Brandon throwing her into the car. She hadn't seen the truck until it was driving away, but she'd seen the headlights. Coming straight at them, then veering away as the front fender hit the chief.

Because the driver had nodded off and caught himself just before impact? Or because the driver had only wanted to frighten them? Or did he want the chief out of the way while he continued to kill? It was getting harder and harder to hold on to the drunken-driver theory.

She needed to find out who had been driving that truck.

A visitor's chair had been pulled close to the bed. She sat down on the edge of the seat, wondering who had already visited the chief.

Kate knew he was heavily sedated, but the nurse said he had awakened several times for short moments. She was kind of glad that he wasn't awake now; she wouldn't know what to say.

His left arm was bent beneath the hospital gown: the broken shoulder and collarbone. His right arm was stretched alongside his body, taped to a board, palm up. An IV feed ran down from a hanging bag. His fingers curled slightly against his palm, and Kate longed to put her hand in his. Just to let him know someone was there and cared about him.

But it seemed way too intimate a gesture. Just sitting here alone in the dusky light seemed to draw her too close. To wrap a cocoon around them, separating them from serial killers, nosy aunts, museums, and police departments.

She leaned forward. "Hi, it's Kate." She spoke softly, trying to sound reassuring. She really wanted to yell, "Get up, dammit," even if she had to buy the pizza.

The town needed him. Needed him to secure washed-out bridges, confiscate uninspected trucks, give out tickets to people who rolled through stop signs—needed him to protect them from a killer.

She needed him to tell her what to do. To help her find out what the Sudoku puzzle meant. Who had sent her the *Try and stop me* e-mail.

Hell, she just needed him.

The realization sent her reeling.

"Kate?" Barely a whisper.

Kate jumped. "You're awake."

"Is that what it's called." A tilt of his mouth. Probably meant as a smile, but hardly making it.

"You'll feel better soon."

His eyes closed.

"No—" Kate cut off her words. She needed his help, but he needed his rest. And he didn't need to know that his department was in chaos without him or that Kate was being taunted by a serial killer.

His fingers opened slightly as they relaxed in sleep, and Kate found herself slipping her hand in his. Gently, slowly, like a whisper. He probably wasn't aware of what she was doing and wouldn't even remember if he was.

He sighed, his breathing regular, slow, drugged. But alive.

They sat that way until Kate heard the door open behind her. She pulled her hand back. Brandon didn't stir.

Ted and Harry came through the door. Harry stopped just inside. His eyes flew from the chief to Kate. She motioned him forward, stood up, and pushed him into the chair. He shot her a look of panic and grabbed her wrist.

"He's okay. He was awake for a second. Be patient. He's fine. You'll see." She gently pried his fingers away and went to stand with Ted.

Ted nodded in the direction of the door, and they went out into the hallway. "He really woke up?"

"Yes." And he'd tried to make a joke to reassure her. Kate blinked away sudden tears.

"What is it?"

"Nothing. Just tired."

"Damn. I wish he could tell us what he saw." Ted frowned, almost angry. "I don't mean to cast aspersions on your version of the incident. It's just . . ." He trailed off, ended with a slight shrug.

"That you trust the chief to be a better witness and you're mad as hell and want to catch whoever did this?" Kate ventured.

Ted relaxed. "Well, he's trained to notice details. And you're right, I'm angry. And frustrated. You said he woke up for a bit. Did he say anything? Anything at all that might help us find the SOB who hit him?"

Kate shook her head. "He didn't say anything. He saw me, knew me, and closed his eyes again. But that's a good sign, right?"

Of course it was. It wasn't like her to need useless reassurance. She was just tired and jumpy from the lack of sleep. Brandon was going to recover—barring any unusual complications. And the odds of that were. . . really big.

She deliberated about telling Ted about Roy Larkins' truck, but decided to leave it to somebody else. Maybe she was being ridiculous, insular, and prejudiced, but what could he do anyway? He had no jurisdiction in Granville.

Kate watched a nurse tread quietly down the hall toward them. She knew they were about to be kicked out. Ted saw her coming too.

"I'll go get Harry," he said and left Kate in the hallway.

The nurse stopped and nodded her approval, lifted two fingers—two minutes—and returned to the nurses' station.

Ted was gone several minutes, and after the second look from the nurses' station, Kate slipped inside to drag the recalcitrant visitors home.

Harry was sitting in the chair just as she had left him. Ted was standing behind him, his hand resting on the chair back.

Kate stopped as she took in the scene: three men—friends, partners, ward. Frozen in time like a photrograph—a finished work that kept you from ever entering their world.

An overwhelming sense of aloneness swelled inside her. Suddenly it didn't seem as if Brandon was the outsider everyone said he was. It was her. Forever on the outside, not fitting in anywhere except with a bunch of government geeks and eccentric puzzle freaks, most of whom were just as isolated as she was.

She'd come home in part to learn how to be a people person, but so far she'd earned one big goose egg in the human relations department.

Harry turned in his seat and shook his head at Kate. "He didn't wake up."

Kate's momentary self-pity evaporated.

Harry was still in limbo—he was the one who needed reassurance.

"Tomorrow," she whispered.

Harry's lip quivered, and Ted put a hand on his shoulder.

Harry shrugged it away, stood, and left the room.

Kate gave Ted a rueful smile. She didn't envy him. Harry wouldn't accept his overtures easily. He'd just begun to trust the chief. She doubted if he was ready to trust anyone else.

Ted lingered behind, and as Kate opened the door, she heard Ted say, "Don't worry, old buddy. I'll take care of everything. You can count on me. Like always."

Kate quickly shut the door and glanced at Harry. He hadn't

heard, but she knew he would feel as if he were being shut out too. She could feel his tension.

Was he jealous of Ted and Brandon's relationship? That was possible, probable even. He was used to having the chief to himself.

"I'm going with Kate to the museum," Harry announced as soon as Ted joined them.

Ted pressed the elevator button, but instead of getting on with them, he stayed outside. "Okay. I have some things to do around here."

"Visitors' hours are over," Harry said.

"Other things." Ted smiled.

Kate was glad he had a thick skin. Harry was being a brat.

"See you later." Ted walked away from them toward the nurses' station. His limp seemed more pronounced than usual, Kate thought. Maybe hospitals did that to a person.

"I'll bring him home," Kate called after him.

Ted waved and kept on walking.

"That wasn't very nice," Kate said as soon as the elevator doors closed behind them.

"He treats me like a kid."

"Funny, I've heard you say the same thing about the chief."

"That's different."

"I thought you liked Ted."

"He's okay, I guess."

"I thought he was wicked cool."

"He is. But he's kind of weird. Always around, helping out. Minding our business. Treating the chief like . . . I dunno. He's nice and everything and he jokes around, but it's like he thinks he knows more than the chief does."

"Maybe he's just compensating for not being as physically capable as the chief."

"You mean like he's angry because the chief's okay and he's crippled?"

Astute, thought Kate. "There's bound to be some awkward times between them, considering their past history."

The elevator opened on the ground floor.

"I guess. Now, can we figure out who hit the chief and why?"

"Why don't we wait until we get to the car."

Kate stopped at the Buick. Harry kept walking.

"Whoa. It's here."

Harry turned. "Oh, man. You're driving your Aunt Pru's Buick?"

Kate winced, seeing the old Buick through Harry's eyes—not the sleek little Matrix, but a big blue clunker. "Yeah. You can just scrunch down in the seat so you won't be seen."

"No, man, it's the bomb. Can I drive it?"

"Harry, you're fourteen."

"Fifteen in May, and I'll be able to get my permit in October."

"Still."

"The chief let me drive his SUV once. When we were out in the country. He said I should start getting the feel of driving, so I wouldn't be a dumb f— stupid when I got my permit."

Kate stifled a laugh.

"So bring me up to speed."

Kate deliberated about the danger to Harry if she told him about Roy Larkins' truck, then decided that it couldn't hurt. She'd already told the police, right after she'd left Larkins' house.

"Here's what's happened. The police department is kind of a mess right now."

Harry nodded. He looked a little frightened. Was he, too, wondering what the future held?

"Anyway . . . I kind of stepped in to help out"—without their knowledge, but Kate didn't think any of the three young officers would mind.

Harry wasn't fooled. "What did you do?"

She told him about recognizing Roy Larkins' truck and going to his house to check it out.

"You should have waited for me," Harry said.

"You were in school."

"Only because Ted made me. I thought about ditching, but he'd rat me out to the chief, and it would piss off the chief and he might get worse." Harry sniffed. "Shit."

"Harry, pizza."

"I don't care. I want things to go back the way they were."

"So do I." The two of them getting into trouble and the chief blowing up at them. And all of them going for pizza. Now a part of their trio was laid up with injuries and they were both at sea.

"Do you want to hear about the truck?"

"Yeah."

"It had a broken headlight, a busted bumper, and traces of paint from my car." She shrugged. "It's definitely the truck that hit the chief."

She had his full attention now. "Roy Larkins?" Henry frowned. "I don't know. I mean, he doesn't like the chief, but to run him down— was he drunk?"

"Probably, but he says he wasn't driving it."

"Who was?"

"He says his truck was stolen outside Jumpin' Jack's, this bar on the outskirts of town."

"Yeah, biker bar," Harry said. "Buck used to hang there a lot."

Buck Perkins, Harry's abusive uncle, who'd more than once threatened to take Harry away from the chief on the excuse that blood was thicker than water. No one doubted the real reason: Buck Perkins was after Harry's inheritance from the professor.

Kate hurried on before they started dwelling on the past or angsting over the future. "Anyway, Roy said he drove there, and when he came out his truck was gone."

"Joyriders."

"That's what Roy thinks. They returned it to his house, so they must be someone he knows or who at least knows where he lives."

"Anybody with a phonebook," Harry pointed out.

Kate sighed. "Yeah. Do you know any guys who are in the habit of drinking and stealing cars?"

Harry's eyes widened in mock innocence.

"And none of them will ever be you," she added.

"No worries. The chief already made that perfectly clear." His expression clouded over. "I could ask around."

"Be discreet."

"*Duh.*"

"And," Kate added more slowly, "I guess those guys could also include some girls."

Harry bristled. "If you're thinking it's Wynter, forget it. Just because she's borrowed her dad's Beamer a few times."

"Crawl off, I wasn't accusing Wynter."

"Well, *Ted* did. He already asked me about her. Said he didn't know if the chief would approve. Like the chief was gonna answer to him. I didn't tell him, but the chief said she was cute." He made a disgusted sound. "Cute. That's so lame."

"I see your point," Kate said dryly. "But he probably meant—"

"I know what he meant. He was busting my chops and letting me know that he'd already checked her out and that he decided she won't get me in trouble."

"Does it bother you that he checked her out?"

Harry thought for a moment. "Nah, it's the chief."

"There's something else. I got another e-mail."

Harry's head snapped toward her. "Another murder?"

"No. A taunt. A challenge, maybe. It said 'try and stop me.' But whether it's from the killer or a crackpot is anybody's guess."

She slowed down in front of the museum and pulled to the curb. "I'll meet you back here in an hour or so."

Harry stopped with his hand on the door handle. "Where are you going?"

"I think I need to talk to the owner of Jumpin' Jack's."

"I'll go too." Harry settled back in his seat.

"I can't take you to a place like that."

"I'll stay in the car. I'll scrunch down so nobody will see me." He grinned. "Backup."

"I don't know."

"I'm not scared, if that's what you're thinking."

"That's not what I was thinking." She was thinking that it would be irresponsible to take him with her. They might even run into Buck Perkins while they were there. But he was right. She could use the company. "Okay, but stay in the car with the doors locked. Don't get out no matter what. Moral support—not backup."

Jumpin' Jack's was a dive. It sat on a point of land at the south edge of town at the junction of Maple Street and Suggahaw Road. It was a one-storied wood and tin building that had probably been a garage at one time. Three large bay openings had been covered with plywood and painted red. The door was painted black. A plate glass window was covered over by a set of tin shutters.

There were three monster cycles parked side by side in the lot. Two trucks and a rattletrap Jeep were parked next to them.

Kate turned to Harry. "You okay?"

"Natch. Go."

"Lock the doors."

"No sh—"

Kate closed the door, cutting off his last word.

She picked her way across a graveled lot, past discarded beer cans, broken bottles, and crumpled cigarette packages. When she got to the door, she looked back.

Harry was leaning forward, arms resting on the dashboard. He gave her a thumbs up.

She opened the door. It was heavy and scraped against the floor as it opened. The bar was dark, lit only by several wall sconces advertising a brand of beer and an imitation hurricane lantern at each end of the bar—also advertising beer.

A bare bulb hung from the ceiling of a back room, casting the bar into even deeper gloom.

"Hey baby, come on over."

She couldn't see anyone in the dingy light, but she made out bundles along the edge of the room that she decided were people. And she got the distinct impression that they were all looking at her.

Kate hurried toward the bar and the back room. "Mister . . . Fletcher?"

A figure appeared in the doorway, a mere silhouette in the glare of the light.

Kate blinked hard several times to accustom her eyes to the light. She hadn't known what to expect—places like Jumpin' Jack's weren't in her milieu. But she'd imagined a big, muscular, hairy man, possibly with sideburns and a mustache. What she got was Humpty Dumpty.

He gave her the once-over.

"Call me Jack. What can I do you for?" His voice was deep and rough, a strange counterpoint to his round body that gave credence to his reputation as a dangerous bully.

Kate tried to swallow but her mouth was suddenly dry.

There was movement at the edges of the room. A chair fell over, a prolonged belch, scuffing of feet, moving closer. They suddenly appeared on the fringe of the light cast by the back room.

"Oo-ee, Jack! Didn't know what a fine establishment you were running here."

"Now, darlin' what are you doing in a place like JJ's?"

"Come looking fer me?" Another long belch.

His unseen companions laughed.

Jack lifted a pudgy hand and the men dropped into silence. They didn't move away, but stood in place like dogs behind an invisible containment fence.

Kate licked dry lips. "I'm—"

"I know who you are. And I know you're probably looking into Henny Dougan's untimely demise, 'cause I hear tell you're always poking your nose into places where it might get snipped off."

His voice was so menacing that Kate had to will herself not to run for her life. No wonder Izzy was obviously afraid of this man, and judging by the bikers' responses, he wasn't the only one.

Time to put her money and all those speech consultants to the test. She concentrated on the row of liquor bottles lined up just behind Jack's head. "Someone nearly killed the police chief. He barely missed me. The chief is in the hospital—"

"Get out the violins, boys."

Sound of yowling cats behind her.

Kate planted her feet, fisted her hands on her hips, and huffed out a fed-up sigh.

"She's cute when she does that," said one of the bikers.

"You gotta badge, honey?"

"Hell, she ain't no cop."

"I dunno. She might be carrying. Maybe we should check her for weapons."

Kate forced herself not to flinch. What the heck had she been thinking to come here?

She hadn't been. Not rationally, anyway. She'd only been thinking of the chief lying immobile in that hospital bed. Of the police department in disarray while the culprit and possibly the murderer got away. "Could you please just help me?"

Jack raised a sardonic eyebrow. "Okay, everybody—shut it." He looked over his shoulder and spat on the floor. "Now listen up. I don't care that much about the police chief, but you now? It would be a shame to have your pretty little self smeared across the pavement.

"I just need to know if anyone saw what happened to Roy Larkin's truck?"

"Roy left after midnight. His truck was gone. That's all I know."

"Nobody saw anything?"

"You boys see anything?"

"Nope."

"Not a thing."

"Can't even remember. Was I here last night?"

Jack shrugged.

"Who else was here?" Kate squeaked out the question.

"Privileged information. But you'd be surprised the people who stop for a beer and a little pool now and again. I strongly suggest you don't come here at night. It gets real busy and I wouldn't want to lose you in the traffic. Now I gotta get ready for my evening clientele."

Kate swallowed; the sound seemed to echo around the room.

"Go on home now, before some church lady drives by and sees that big blue car in the parking lot."

Kate's head automatically snapped toward the door. *How does he know what kind of car I'm driving?*

Jack tapped his head. "Get to getting. And tell Dickie Owens and the other kiddy cops not to come asking."

Surprised, Kate asked, "Did they already question you?"

Jack snorted and spat again. "Honey, you're way ahead of them. But your welcome is wearing thin."

"Thank you." Kate began edging toward the door. Her instinct was to turn and run, but that might be like tempting a snarling dog. *Just slow, even steps. Don't let them sense your fear.*

She reached the door. "If you hear or—"

"Get. Before I lose my temper."

The shadows moved.

Kate snatched open the door and bolted through it as laughter rang behind her. She was past caring. She didn't look back, but ran headlong toward the Buick.

7				3			6	
	5		6			3		
		9	1		4	8		
		8	5			6	3	
	2			4			9	
	7	4				2		
		7	3		5	1		
		5			8		7	
	6			9				2

CHAPTER

FOURTEEN

IT WAS GETTING dark by the time Kate and Harry got back to the museum. In the ten-minute drive from Jumpin' Jack's they'd gone from sheer terror to relief to laughter.

Kate was rattled, though she tried not to let Harry see it. She was used to people confiding in her. For some strange reason, the townspeople had decided to use her as a conduit to the chief. Which made her neither fish nor fowl, but stuck somewhere between belonging and not.

But the men at Jumpin' Jack's had made her question her ability to even be a conduit. They didn't know her, couldn't have cared less who she was or who she was related to. They weren't going to cooperate—if they even knew anything.

She'd wandered into a no man's land, where evidently men who shouldn't frequent places like Jumpin' Jack's—did. She couldn't even begin to imagine who that might be, but she was certain she would be shocked if she found out.

It had been a total bust and a stupid, dangerous thing to do; something she'd been doing a lot of lately. And she hadn't learned a thing. She called Elmira and told her about her visit to the bar.

"You're crazy, Katie. That place is dangerous."

"I know that now. And the guy who runs the place—"

"Jackson Fletcher," Elmira said. "Doesn't look like much, but he's been in jail. And not the local jail, either. Prison."

Damn, thought Kate. She could have gotten into serious trouble. Not scientific, not even smart. She'd be more careful in the future. And she wouldn't jeopardize Harry's well-being again.

"He said none of the police had been out to question him and I should tell them not to come."

"Don't worry, none of them would. I don't know what the hell we're supposed to do. They're all just sitting around waiting for somebody to goose them into action. If only someone knew which action to take."

"Maybe the chief will have a speedy recovery."

"We can only hope." Sounds of shouting in the background. "Oh damn—You folks all just calm down! I'll get to you in a minute. Damn fools," she said to Kate, lowering her voice again. "Everybody in town's got questions and they've come here to ask them. Now we just need to come up with some answers."

Kate hung up and glanced at Harry, who looked worried.

"Want to swing by Rayette's for dinner?"

He shook his head. "I want to stay here."

Where things were safe. Solid. Known. A place of refuge when he'd been an unloved child, and now when he was a frightened teen.

"Good idea. Museum and tea. I think there's some maple cream cake left."

Museum hours were over. Alice had left a note on the desk saying she'd gone home and not to worry—Izzy had dropped by to see her home safely.

But who will take care of Izzy? wondered Kate. Henny Dougan had been a drunk, but he'd been strong, and he wasn't able to fight off the killer. Izzy was small and older. He wouldn't have a chance.

Kate shook herself. "Alice closed up everything. Let's go upstairs."

While Kate heated the water, Harry sat in his wingback chair and opened his cipher book. Kate waited by the hot plate for the water to boil, steeped the tea, and carried the cups to the table between the two chairs.

She sat down and reached for a Sudoku book just as a ping sounded from her laptop.

Harry's pen stopped two inches from his page. Kate's fingers froze on the book. A new e-mail. She'd turned up the volume on her laptop so she wouldn't miss any incoming mail; so far, they'd all been false alarms.

Kate and Harry exchanged startled looks, then stood as one person and hurried to the desk.

Kate sat down in the swivel chair and pulled up her e-mail account. One new e-mail. No one she recognized. But the subject line was clear. *Who will be next?*

Harry leaned over her, so close that his breath sent a chill up her neck.

"Open it."

She did almost automatically, as if her fingers belonged to someone else.

A Sudoku grid filled the page. She clicked to make the image smaller. At the bottom of the frame was the question. *Can you guess?*

"Guess?" said Harry. "We don't guess. Which must mean it's from someone who doesn't know us." He sounded relieved.

"Unless they're just using guess as a figure of speech."

Harry let her know how he felt about figures of speech. "It's a Killer Sudoku, right? That's what those interior shapes are."

Kate nodded.

"But they're not colored in this time."

"Right. So the question is, has he upped the difficulty level or changed the rules?"

Harry grunted. He was bent over so closely that Kate had to lean forward. "Harry, get another chair."

"Right," he said distractedly. He moved away, slid a straight-back chair across the floor, and sat down beside her.

"So how do we start? If he's changed the rules . . ."

There was enough of an edge in his voice to make Kate want to pat his hand. She knew better.

"We'll start with what's worked before."

Harry sighed.

Kate's cell phone rang, and they both jumped. Kate answered it.

"Hi, Kate."

"Hi, Ted." She shot a look at Harry, who shook his head vehemently.

"I'm picking up Harry. I'll be there in five minutes." He hung up.

"That was Ted," Kate said and flipped her phone shut. "He's on his way to pick you up. He sounded upset."

"I'm not going with him. He'll try to make me a better person all night and send me to bed at eleven. It sucks."

Kate didn't doubt it. "He's just trying to help until the chief is back up and running."

"He's not the chief. I'll stay here. In the professor's apartment."

"Harry, we've had this discussion before—"

"Then I'll stay with you. Or even at your aunt Pru's."

Alarms went off in Kate's head. Was Harry protesting for other reasons? Was something going on that she should know about? How was she supposed to deal with this? She didn't know anything about teenagers—not that Harry was an ordinary teenager.

"Does Ted treat you okay?"

Harry groaned. "Too okay. It's like he's the perfect parent. Always telling the chief that he should do this with me or that. We were fine until he got here."

"But he doesn't hurt you or make you . . . uh . . . feel uncomfortable in any way."

Harry frowned at her, then slowly his expression changed. "Kate, that is so lame. Nuh-uh. He doesn't make me feel uncomfortable in the way you mean. And I'm not going to act shit out with dolls or any of that crap. He just isn't one of us."

Kate knew she was blushing as furiously as Harry. "Give me a break. I never had to give that talk before. And as for being one of us, that's such a typical Granville—"

Harry stopped her. "I mean one of us, you and me and the chief."

"Oh."

Brandon's answering sardonic *oh,* the one he always echoed when making fun of her, ran silently in her mind. She missed it. She even missed the sarcasm. Maybe he would be more lucid in the morning and could tell her what she should do.

The doorbell rang.

Harry flopped down in the chair and crossed his arms. His chin stuck out so far that Kate was tempted to cuff him one.

"I'll try to get you a reprieve." Kate went downstairs to answer the door.

Ted was not a happy camper. As soon as Kate opened the door, he pushed past her and turned on her. "Where is Harry?"

"Upstairs. He told you we were coming here. What's wrong?" Suddenly the image of Brandon dying while they were out at Jumpin' Jack's flooded her mind. "It's not Br—the chief?"

"No, it isn't Bran. But I just happened to be at HQ when your call came in."

Kate was having a hard time understanding. Was he talking about the Granville police station? HQ? Call came in. The call to Elmira. And what was he doing at the station?

"Did you stop to think before you went haring off to interview witnesses in a dive like Jumpin' Jack's that you might have been putting yourself, not to mention the investigation, in jeopardy?"

"Is there an investigation?" *You could've fooled me.* No one had done a thing since the chief had been run down. "What were you doing at the police station?"

"Seeing if they had learned anything about the hit and run."

"Had they?" Kate had a temper, but she very rarely lost it. She was in danger of losing it now. Harry was right. Ted was poking his nose into places it wasn't wanted: At least she and Harry didn't want it.

Ted expelled a frustrated sigh. "No. You're right. Nothing's getting done. It's just so damn infuriating."

"I know," said Kate. "And I'm sure you're right about going to Jumpin' Jack's. But it wasn't dangerous really." *Liar liar, pants on fire.* She caught a glimpse of movement at the top of the stairs. Harry was eavesdropping.

Ted started to pace. "Well, don't do anything like that again."

Kate bristled. She didn't intend to do anything except help find a murderer who was using her favorite puzzle as a taunt. And what right did Ted Lumley have to tell her what to do?

"How do you think Brandon will feel when he hears what you've been up to?"

Kate shrugged uncomfortably. She could hear it in her mind, and she knew Brandon would be buying a lot of pizza after he finished with her.

"You've made him look like a fool."

Her thoughts were jerked back by Ted's words. She automatically shook her heard. "I'd never do anything to belittle him."

Ted stopped briefly in front of her. "No? What about your professor's death? You thwarted him at every turn and then made him a laughingstock at the end."

"I did not!" Fury rippled through Kate. Ted wasn't the first person to have thought that, but those attitudes had changed long ago. Brandon didn't need her to investigate. She just kept ending up in a position to help.

"Yes, you did."

"How do you know? Did Brandon say so?"

Ted snorted, shook his head in disgust. "I read the *Free Press* articles. The old *Free Press*, before this new jackass took over. He'll have a field day with this. I can see the headlines now: 'Chief of police in hospital. Girlfriend taking over investigation.' Are you trying to get him fired?"

"No." Her words barely came out. "And I'm not his girlfriend." Was that what everyone thought?

"Leave her alone." Harry ran down the steps. "Kate's just trying to help. The chief doesn't need *you*."

"Harry," Kate warned.

"*We* don't need you."

Ted's lips tightened. "Son, I know you're upset. I don't want to take over. I just want to help Bran until he can help himself. We go back a long way, and I owe him at least that."

Ted owed Brandon for saving *Brandon's* life? Kate wondered.

Wasn't it supposed to be the other way around? If anything, shouldn't Brandon owe him?

Ted lowered his head, looked at the carpet. "I've always felt responsible for him."

Kate shot Harry a fierce look. *Don't get into it with him*—though she was having a hard time keeping her own temper. Brandon didn't need Ted watching out for him. He already had people to look out for him.

"Your rampant curiosity, or ego gratification, or whatever it is, could make things sticky for him. And worse than making him look like a fool, you could actually get him killed. Look where he ended up last night, just from trying to protect you because you were interfering."

"You're wrong," she said, fighting to control the tremor in her voice. "I wasn't interfering. I know you don't understand. Sometimes I don't even understand. It's not ego gratification or idle curiosity. I have to know. Harry has to know. It's like a good friend of mine once said: Puzzlers must solve. It's natural, it's necessary, it's an obligation, and you can't stop them."

Ted's scowl deepened. "Are you threatening me?"

Kate stared at him, taken aback. "No! I'm just trying to explain the way it is."

"Well, maybe it's something you should work on changing. Think about it. Harry, are you ready to leave?"

"No."

Kate was horrified to feel the prickle of tears. "Harry, go on. We've caused Ted enough worry already."

"No."

"*Harry.*"

"That is so bogus."

"Come on, son. It's been a long day."

"And don't—"

"*Harry.*"

Harry shot Kate a defiant, hurt look and slouched back upstairs to get his backpack and jacket.

Kate couldn't look at Ted. She felt angry, mortified, and guilty all at once. Could she really have been the cause of Brandon's accident? She leaned against the desk, saw a scrap of brown on the floor, and stooped down to pick it up: the same brown scarf from the Arcane Masters meeting. It must have fallen off the desk before Alice had a chance to put it away.

It was a perfect excuse to avoid more confrontation. She carried it across the foyer to the closet. She could feel Ted watching her, but he didn't speak. She tossed the scarf in the lost-and-found box and closed the closet door.

"More kids leave their stuff behind?" Ted's voice was calm, no longer angry. He was obviously trying to clear the air, which was still thrumming with their heated exchange.

"No, this belongs to a grown man. One of the members of the Arcane Masters. Forgetfulness knows no age discrimination."

Ted chuckled. Friends again.

Harry came slumping back down the stairs, looking miserable. As he followed Ted out the front door, he whispered to Kate, "Don't listen to him. I hate him."

And for that moment, Kate did too.

She closed the door and stood there, leaning her forehead against the smooth, cool wood.

Ted was wrong. It wasn't idle curiosity or ego gratification that made her "butt in." It was a burning need to know. Ever since she could remember, there was always "the big why."

From the moment she learned to count, she had added numbers, first with *Sesame Street*, then page numbers in Dr. Seuss. When she barely could see out the car window she added numbers, street signs: Route 25 became 2 plus 5 equals 7. Everywhere she went, she counted—dates, house numbers, prices—adding, then subtracting, dividing, multiplying until she was pulled further and further into a world where she was alone.

And it had only grown more intense as she grew older. *Why* became *how* and *when*. She discovered science and higher mathematics, reveled in mysteries and puzzles of all kinds. The kids called her a geek. And that just drove her further into her safe, calculable world.

When her mother died, Kate met the professor, whose quest for knowledge complemented and guided her own, and she discovered a whole world filled with puzzles. A world where she felt at home, a world where she could be safe with someone who loved puzzles as much as she did.

And now she was guiding Harry—though, she added honestly, sometimes it was Harry who took the lead.

If there was a question that interested them, they followed it to the answer.

And the question of who killed Henny Dougan and tried to kill the chief was the most important question she had ever faced.

"You're wrong, Ted," Kate said. "You're wrong." And she slowly climbed the stairs.

Aloysius was sitting on the desk, grooming his furry neck. He let out a "Yeow" when Kate walked into the office.

Kate plopped into the desk chair. "Does that mean you heard?"

Al stretched, yawned, and flipped over onto his back to have his stomach rubbed. Evidently, Kate didn't move fast enough to please him; he wriggled on the ink blotter to get her attention. His tail twitched, then smacked the computer keyboard.

Kate's cosmos screen saver blipped off and the Killer Sudoku puzzle appeared on the screen.

Good Lord. In all her angst, she'd forgotten the puzzle. She blinked at it.

And just like those blasted hidden-picture puzzles, a new image came into focus: two initials.

r L. The lower-case r was one horizontal two-cell row set at right angles at the top of a three-cell vertical. The L was a vertical column made from four cells and a horizontal line of three cells.

r L.

Roy Larkins? It had to be. She'd just been at his house that day. She'd been asking questions about him. His truck was stolen. Or was it? He could have been lying.

Kate took a breath and stopped her thoughts. It didn't make sense. Why would the killer want to harm Roy?

Had the killer seen him talking to Kate? Had Roy seen the person who stole his truck? Roy blamed it on kids. But if it had really been someone he—and the men at Jumpin' Jack's—knew, a local, they might be protecting him. Or blackmailing him.

If the hit-and-run and Henny Dougan's murder were even related. Though she was pretty sure by now that they were.

She looked back at the puzzle. Or was she just seeing things? If Ted hadn't shown up and taken Harry away, she would have Harry as a second pair of eyes and a second opinion.

The r and L blurred, then snapped back into focus. Adrenalin raced through her veins. The killer must be planning another murder. For tonight? Why else send her these new initials? She had to do something.

She picked up the phone and speed-dialed the Granville police station.

"Hi Elmira, it's Kate. I've got a problem."

"Are you okay?"

"Yes. But I received . . ." She hesitated. Had Brandon told anyone about the original e-mailed puzzle? She might be starting a wholesale panic.

"Honey, are you sure you feel okay?"

"I . . . I have reason to believe that Roy Larkins' life may be in danger."

"Why on earth?"

"I just do. Do you think Paul and Dickie or Will could just keep an eye on him for tonight?" Until she could have another chance to rouse Brandon.

"I guess so. But they're like walking zombies at this point."

"Tell them to be careful and to just watch. I don't want them to get hurt."

There was a long pause, then a sigh. "Katie, they're police officers. Paid to uphold the law. They're trained, thanks to the chief. It's their job."

"Yeah, but their mothers would kill me if anything happened to them." And Kate would never forgive herself.

"Then they should never have let them apply for the job and go through the training."

Kate smiled just a bit. Elmira was Brandon's staunchest ally, even though she gave him a rough time. She busted his chops for every little thing, then excused herself on the pretense that she was just toughening him up to withstand the Granville "weather."

"Anything else I should know?"

"No. I'm working at a disadvantage here."

"You *are* working on the case."

"No," Kate protested. "I just keep getting sucked into these things."

She hung up and leaned back in the swivel chair, staring at the screen. Had she gone off half-cocked? Made a snap judgment, instead of a completely researched decision?

She knew how alluring it was to get one's teeth into a theory and follow it to its conclusion. If it was the wrong conclusion, one just started again at the point of misdirection.

She didn't have the leisure for that now, though. Someone out there was going to kill again. He wanted Kate to stop him, and she couldn't afford to screw up.

She leaned forward and braced her elbows on the desktop. *rL.* It might be a false clue, but the two areas were side by side and almost dead center, the strongest focal point of a page.

Kate shifted her eyes until the two initials were out of focus, let the other shapes float across her vision. Slowly, as if in a trance, she moved her eyes barely a centimeter.

The telephone rang. Her body levitated from the chair, her heart pounding. Al reacted with a disgruntled growl.

"Hello?"

"Katie. It's Paul Curtis. We're sitting outside Roy Larkins' house."

Hopefully out of sight, she thought. Al jumped down from the desk and curled up on her lap.

"There're a bunch of cars outside. Looks like a poker game to me. Do you want us to keep watching?"

Me? They think they're taking orders from me? "Do what you think best," Kate said. How on earth had she gotten stuck in the middle again? Things were so out of control.

"I thought that since there're so many of them, Roy would be safe while we go make a few rounds. Make sure everybody else is safe too."

"Good idea," said Kate. Al bumped her hand. Absently, she scratched his ruff of fur.

"We'll swing by on our usual rounds until the party breaks up."

"Good, good." Kate hung up. She felt like such a fool. She'd just assumed that the e-mail had come because the killer had planned something for that night. And, as she well knew, assumptions invariably got you out on a metaphorical limb.

But what was she supposed to do? How could she stop someone she didn't know from killing someone she didn't know at some time she didn't know?

This character was not following the rules of fair play.

Kate's stomach growled. She hadn't eaten since lunch, and it was nearly nine o'clock. Rayette's might still be open. She usually kept the kitchen open until nine if she had the business.

Kate reached over to click out of her e-mail, and her eyes snagged on the rL.

Only this time she wasn't seeing Roy Larkins, but Rayette. Her last name was Lansing.

Rayette Lansing.

He wasn't going after Roy Larkins: He was going to kill Rayette.

HE WAS GOING to kill Rayette and she'd nearly missed it.

Kate reached for the phone and started to dial the police station. Hesitated. She'd sent the police running to Roy Larkins only to find him playing poker. How would they feel about running off on another of her wild tips? She was becoming the boy who cried wolf.

She was reacting instead of acting. She needed to stop and think. The killer might not be after Rayette or Roy. There might be others with the initials rL.

And pigs might fly—to hell with rational thought. She picked up the phone and dialed the bakery. It rang five times before the voice mail picked up and started giving her the hours of operation.

She wouldn't panic. Rayette might be too busy to pick up the phone. If Calvin still had the flu, she might be doing double duty, cooking and waiting tables.

Kate took a breath, then called Rayette's cell phone. No answer there either.

Okay. *Now* it was time to panic. Kate grabbed her jacket and purse and ran for the door.

Not bothering to turn off lights or readjust the heat, Kate locked the front door of the museum and raced toward the Buick. She was dying to call Rayette's cell again, but she needed both hands to maneuver the unwieldy car out of the parking place. She made a cumbersome three-point turn and screeched off toward Main Street and the Café and Bakery.

Downtown Granville looked like a ghost town. Not that this was unusual. It wasn't exactly the hot-spot happening center of New Hampshire. At nine o'clock, most of the inhabitants were either in bed or relaxing in front of the television. Until recently, the Granville Bar and Grill and the Bowsman Inn were the only places open past six o'clock.

The month before, Rayette had decided to serve dinner four nights a week. People came in dribs and drabs, but she was slowly building a solid business.

Except that tonight, the street was deserted. One lone car was parked in front of the bakery: Rayette's sporty red Corvette. As Kate barreled toward it, the lights in the cafe winked out. She screeched into a parking place just as Rayette, arms loaded with bags and boxes, struggled out the front door.

She turned back to lock the door. A dark figure loomed in the shadows. Kate threw herself against the heavy car door and nearly tumbled to the pavement as she yelled, "Rayette! Watch out!"

The boxes fell from Rayette's hands. Her big leather tote bag fell off her shoulder. She grabbed the straps and swung it just as the figure approached her.

It hit the assailant with a whack, and he went down. Kate and Rayette fell on him, pinning him to the ground.

He writhed beneath them, arms battering at them, guttural cries piercing the air. He was a wild man, fighting with everything he had. Arms, legs, nails, teeth.

Nails, teeth. Kate knew immediately that something was wrong. The figure was small, fine-boned. And female.

She reared back. "Rayette, wait."

Rayette stopped, looked down at her assailant. "Holy cow. Aren't you—"

"Nobody you know."

But Kate knew. "She's a friend of Harry's. Wynter with a Y." But what the hell was she doing wandering around town by herself?

Rayette slowly stood up. She and Wynter eyed one another, each sizing the other up, until at last Rayette held out her hand to help Wynter up.

Ignoring it, Wynter scrambled back onto her hands and feet, crablike, then pushed to her feet and scowled at Kate. Her body was alert, ready to make a break for it.

What is with her? Kate wondered. *Is she in trouble? Did we catch her doing something illegal? Or* about *to do something illegal?*

Kate reined in her imagination. She had probably just sneaked out of the house to hang out with some friends. Something Kate had never done.

"I wasn't doing nothing."

"Anything," Kate corrected automatically.

Wynter made a face and slapped at the knees of her black jeans where two wet patches made perfect circles.

Kate and Rayette moved in on her.

Wynter hopped nimbly to the side. "Get out of my fuckin' way."

Kate grimaced. "Hasn't Harry told you about the pizza rule?"

"Yeah, he told me, but I'm not playing any bogus baby games."

"Well, playing or not," interjected Rayette, "you'll watch your mouth around here."

Wynter sank into one hip and cracked her gum. "Then get out of my *freaking* way. Puh-lease."

"You know," said Rayette. "People come from miles around for my sticky buns."

"So."

"So it's important for me to keep my pots and pans nice and clean."

Wynter worked on looking bored.

"It's sort of like mouths. If one starts getting dirty, I just put it in the sink and give it a good scrub and it's all spic and span."

"You're a fu—freaking nutcase."

"Maybe, but if I hear one more obscenity out of that mouth, you're gonna get a taste of my best soap."

"Nobody really does that."

"They do in New Hampshire."

"I hate New Hampshire. So up yours."

"Winter, huh?" said Rayette. "Brr."

"With a Y," Wynter bit back defiantly.

She was all bluff and bravado. Kate didn't condone the attitude or the language, but it was fascinating. The girl was unhappy and acting out, and in a strange way, Kate respected her courage to do it.

The only thing Kate had ever done was to withdraw further into her world of numbers and puzzles.

"I'm outta here."

Kate and Rayette stepped in front of her. Wynter feinted to the right, Rayette grabbed her by her low-slung chain belt, and Wynter rebounded back.

"My parents will sue."

"Bet your parents don't know you're roaming around at night when there's a killer loose."

A flash of the dark eyes. *Fear?*

"So?"

"So, maybe we should call them."

Wynter smirked. "You don't know my number or my last name."

Rayette yanked at the chain. Wynter tried to wrench away, but Rayette held on with a terrier's grip. "Would you like me to call the police instead?"

Now a real flash of fear. Wynter shook her head sharply, once.

"Then why don't we all go inside. I'll fix some sandwiches and hot chocolate."

Kate thought that sounded pretty good. Now that she knew Rayette was safe, her hunger had returned with a vengeance.

"Only dorks do hot chocolate."

"Well, sorry, but I don't have a liquor license, so you'll have to cope." Still holding her captive by the chain-link belt, Rayette fumbled in her tote and pulled out a substantial key ring.

"Dude." Wynter said appreciatively. "Serious key ring."

Kate began picking up the packages Rayette had dropped.

Rayette raised an eyebrow. "Why don't you give Kate a hand?"

Wynter crossed her arms and snapped her gum.

"Or not." She pushed Wynter none too gently through the door. The three of them crossed through the bakery and into the kitchen, where Rayette pulled a stool up to the butcher block work center and shoved Wynter onto it. "Stay."

It was so much like a command to a disobedient puppy that Kate puffed out a laugh.

Wynter rolled her eyes and then glared at Kate, but sat.

Rayette rummaged in the industrial-size fridge and came out with a plate of hacked chicken, lettuce, tomatoes, homemade mayonnaise, and a loaf of bread. Kate pulled up two more stools. She sat down and took a good look at Wynter.

Tonight was a replay of her black ensemble. Tight low-slung jeans with chain belt. A black slashed T-shirt and the leather jacket. Slumped on the stool, she reminded Kate of a rather gawky black widow spider. All arms and legs.

She ran her tongue over her black-lined lips, and Kate caught a flash of brilliance off her teeth. The girl had a diamond stud on her front tooth.

"What are you looking at?"

Taken off guard, Kate blurted, "You."

"Thinking you don't want me hanging around and getting your precious Harry in trouble?"

"Actually, I was wondering how you got that diamond to stick to your tooth."

"Crazy glue." She watched for Kate's expression, then added, "You have to be very careful."

"Not me," said Kate, taking her literally.

For the first time, Wynter smiled. Her tooth flashed, and she didn't seem nearly as odd as she had a few minutes before.

Rayette slipped a plate with a chicken sandwich in front of Wynter and another in front of Kate. The teenager's eyes drifted toward the sandwich; she caught herself and pushed the plate away.

Rayette sighed and turned back to the stove.

Wynter's eyes strayed back to the sandwich.

"So, Wynter, what were you doing skulking around outside my bakery?" Rayette asked over her shoulder.

"Are you gonna harp all night?"

"No. I can make that call."

Wynter snorted. "The only real cop in town is in the hospital. Those other guys wouldn't know what to do with me."

Rayette cut her a look.

"And I wasn't skulking."

"How old are you?"

"Old enough."

"Fourteen," Kate said. "She's in Harry's chem class."

"Fifteen. I'm a dumbass and had to take it over again."

"Well, you better call somebody and tell them you're okay. They're probably worried to death." Rayette placed a steaming mug of hot chocolate in front of her. "You want whipped cream or marshmallows?"

Wynter tightened her mouth like a kid refusing to take medicine. Rayette sprayed a mound of whipped cream on the top of Wynter's chocolate and topped it off with a handful of marshmallows.

Kate had already tucked into her sandwich and nodded for Rayette to fill her cup with whipped cream. Wynter moved her hand toward the mug of hot chocolate.

She had to be cold and probably hungry. Her bad girl façade was beginning to slip.

Rayette brought her own cup over to the work table and sat down. She took a sip of hot chocolate and sighed. "Damn, I'm good."

Wynter's hand edged closer to her cup until finally she picked it up. Kate and Rayette consciously ignored her.

She took an experimental sip and came up with a dot of whipped cream on her nose. It went a long way to erasing the angry Goth girl image. Behind the makeup and the chains and the unrelieved black was a normal adolescent.

Not normal, thought Kate. Another misfit, trying to find a place in the world.

She was acting out. But whether trying to get attention or looking for help, it didn't explain why she happened to be around Rayette's at closing time. Obviously, she wasn't the killer; had her presence scared him away?

Kate sneaked a look at the girl through half-closed lashes.

Wynter had finally picked up her sandwich and was devouring it as if she hadn't eaten in days.

"You still haven't told us why you were standing out in front of Rayette's at closing time."

"I was just hanging," Wynter mumbled around a mouthful of sandwich.

"At nine o'clock?"

Wynter shrugged and concentrated on eating. "No place else to hang. The chief throws everybody off the Green at seven."

Only the chief wasn't there tonight. . . Suddenly Kate was very tired.

"Do you know that a man was murdered in the alley right behind you?" Rayette lifted her chin toward the door.

Wynter cast an anxious glance at the back door. "Out there?"

Rayette and Kate nodded.

Wynter had a harder time keeping her sangfroid this time. "I can take care of myself."

"That's probably what Henny Dougan said."

"The dead man? Harry said he was a drunk."

"He was," Rayette said. "But he was still mean as a snake and strong as an ox, even when he was staggering drunk. And *he* couldn't take care of himself."

A visible shiver ran through the girl. "I just wanted to see her."

"Who?" Kate and Rayette asked at the same time.

"That waitress. Lynn."

"Ah," said Rayette with of nod of understanding.

Kate blinked, knowing she was missing something. "Why?"

Wynter gave her a you're-such-a-geek look. "If you must know, Harry was supposed to meet me in the park in front of the Bowsman Inn. He didn't show. I figured he stood me up for that waitress and I was going to come kick her butt."

Rayette quickly hid a grin behind her napkin.

"Did you see her?" asked Kate.

"Yeah, but some guy was with her."

"Harry?" She couldn't believe that Harry would actually sneak out of the house to see a girl. Or for any other reason—the chief would never countenance it. Of course, the chief wasn't at home. And Harry might disobey just to aggravate Ted.

"Nah. I don't see what's so great about her—the guy was kind of hot, though."

Kate glanced at Rayette for clarification. "It must have been Calvin. I told him to walk her to her car, make sure she got in safely."

"Calvin's back?" asked Kate.

"Yeah, looking like death warmed over, but he swore he wasn't contagious."

"Gross," said Wynter. She'd finished her sandwich and hot chocolate.

"And while we're on it, why are you here, Kate?"

"I," Kate glanced at Wynter, "I was hoping to get dinner before you closed."

"Well, you got it."

"Thanks for the sandwich. Come on, Wynter. I'll drive you home."

Wynter hopped off the stool. "No way. I've got wheels."

"You're not old enough to drive."

Wynter rolled her kohl-rimmed eyes to the ceiling. "Tell it to the chief."

She sauntered toward the door that led to the café, but slowed as she reached it.

Courage failing, thought Kate. And no wonder.

"Well, I for one think we should all leave together," said Rayette, rinsing off the last plate. "All this hype about serial killers. I don't want to be out there alone."

"Me neither," Kate said.

Wynter just did her one-shouldered shrug, a habit Kate was quickly growing to despise.

Rayette locked up while Kate and Wynter waited. "So where are these wheels?"

Another shrug. "Don't have any."

"You said—"

"I lied."

"Then how the hell did you get here?"

"Walked."

A cold chill seeped straight to Kate's bones. "Where do you live?"

Wynter fidgeted. "Out by the high school."

"That's over three miles away," said Kate. The girl was just asking for trouble. "You walked into town?"

"I hitched part of the way. No big deal."

"It's dangerous for a young girl to be out like that at night. And to hitchhike at any time."

"The parents moved us here because it was *safe*. They're all health freaks and back to nature." Wynter made a sound halfway between a groan and a gag. "'Walking is healthy,'" she quoted.

"Do your parents know about these little hikes?"

Wynter had thawed slightly, but now she pokered up. "Well, they grounded me for borrowing the Beamer, didn't they?"

Kate assumed this was a rhetorical question, so she didn't bother to answer.

"Are you gonna rat me out?"

"I'm going to take you home. We'll decide what to do on the way." While Kate could decide how much to tell her about the killer. She didn't want to alarm the girl or start a panic, but the killer intended to kill again, and Wynter was tempting fate.

"Go stand over by that blue Buick. I have to talk to Rayette for a minute."

"Man, that's a dinosaur."

"My car was trashed. I had to borrow this one from my aunt. Go over there and stay where I can see you."

Wynter turned sullen, crammed her fists into her jacket, and dragged her feet across the sidewalk.

"The real reason I came," Kate whispered as soon as she thought Wynter was out of hearing distance, "is that I got an e-mail this afternoon. I don't have time to explain now, but I think it might have been from Henny's killer, and it led me to believe the next victim would be someone with the initials R L."

Rayette's hand went to her throat. "Me?"

"I don't know."

"But why me?"

"I might be wrong. At first I thought it might be Roy Larkins."

"Roy? Why on earth? What the hell is going on? Does someone have a vendetta against the inhabitants of Granville?"

This is why you should never confide pieces of information, thought Kate. One bit led to another until the story was garbled and blown all out of proportion.

Wynter was slowly creeping closer, multipierced ears alert.

"I'll explain this all later. How about if I come to the café early tomorrow?"

"Okay. But I don't know how I'll sleep tonight."

"Maybe you could get someone to stay with you until we know what this maniac is up to?"

Rayette chewed on her lip. "I think I'll call my brother Jake and his wife and see if I can bunk down with them tonight. You've spooked me out."

"That's a good idea. Wynter and I will follow you over there."

"But what about you? If this monster is in communication with you . . ." Rayette fisted her hand to her mouth. "And with the chief out of commission."

"I'll be all right. I don't think he's after me." *Yet*, Kate added.

Rayette rummaged in her tote and pulled out a small canister. "Here, take my extra can of pepper spray. I bought two cans just this afternoon. Everyone is nervous, and I figured I better get a jump on the rush, which there will be once this gets out."

"Don't tell anyone yet. I've told the police—part of the story anyway. I need to talk to the chief before I can figure out what to do. So don't breathe a word." Kate took the canister Rayette forced into her hand. "Thanks."

"Maybe the chief will be better tomorrow."

"I certainly hope so."

They followed Rayette home to pick up her overnight case, then followed her to her brother and sister-in-law's house a few blocks away. With assurances that the car door was locked and that Kate would call Rayette as soon as she got home, Kate turned the old Buick toward the county road.

They drove into the foothills, which looked particularly dark with only a small sliver of moon barely slicing the black sky. The thought of Wynter walking down the side of the road at any time, much less now with a killer loose, made Kate sick.

She should probably tell the girl's parents; that would be the appropriate thing to do. But she hated to get her in more trouble than she was probably already in on a regular basis. Then again, if she didn't rat her out, how could she make sure that Wynter didn't continue to sneak out at night?

For the hundredth time that day, she wished Brandon was here. He'd managed to turn Harry around; maybe he would have the same success with Wynter.

Finally, she said, "I don't want to rat you out, but I have to know that you will not sneak out of the house at night. Period. This is serious. I'm not just being a Nervous Nellie or anything."

A giggle erupted from the passenger seat. "Nervous Nellie? What planet do you come from?"

Good question, thought Kate. "From the planet Geek. You got a problem with that?"

"Nah, I guess not. You gotta be from somewhere. Turn right up here."

Kate slowed the Buick, looking for a turnoff.

"You better let me off here. I'll walk the rest of the way."

Kate could see nothing but trees, not a light anywhere. "I don't think so."

She turned into the drive. No wonder the girl hated New Hampshire. She was living in the wilderness, isolated from her friends, the action in town—what little there was of it, couldn't drive, and probably had to take the county school bus.

"I know," said Wynter, as if reading Kate's mind. "It sucks."

"It's just kind of. . . remote."

"It sucks."

At least the driveway was freshly paved—that was something. Other than that, Kate didn't know what to expect. Then she rounded a bend and was blinded by a flare of security lights.

The central house was made of logs, but there were two large wings that seemed to be recent construction. Two huge Dumpsters were parked at one side of an oval turnaround. *McMansion in the woods*, thought Kate.

"The padre's idea of rusticating. Dickhead."

"Wynter."

"I told you. I'm not playing some stupid pizza game."

Kate pulled up in front of the house. "Is there anybody home?"

"Anybody who couldn't escape."

"Wynter."

"Yeah, my older brother Dave. He's out of here in the spring, lucky dog. And the two runts of the litter. They don't count."

The front door opened and a man stepped out.

"Oh shit," said Wynter and slid down in her seat, out of sight.

CHAPTER

SIXTEEN

9 1

2

INTERESTING, THOUGHT KATE as she watched Oliver Adams escort his daughter into the house. He was tall, thinnish, with salt-and-pepper hair, and expensively dressed.

He'd run the gamut of shock, concern, sympathy, and consternation. All the right parental emotions, at least as portrayed by the Hallmark Channel. Even Kate could sense the anger rumbling just below his p.c. façade.

He didn't ask Wynter where she'd been or who Kate was, just thanked her for bringing his daughter home. For a minute Kate was afraid he was going to offer to pay her, but he merely put his arm around Wynter and led her back to the house in a hold halfway between parental affection and a full nelson.

Wynter looked more disgusted than frightened, so Kate let her go. She wasn't a masked crusader; it wasn't her job to spy on families to make sure everything was as it should be.

But she did think she should consider opening the museum for teen activities a couple of nights a week. Or was it a dorky, geeky thing to do? Would they actually come? She'd have to ask Harry.

Right now she had other things to worry about. First and foremost, she'd left the museum lit up like a Christmas tree and Al unfed. She didn't relish going back there this late—like Rayette, she was spooked. But she had responsibilities, and even a possible serial killer was not going to deter her.

Alice's lights were still on next door. She was probably keeping an eye on the museum and wondering why Kate had left in such a hurry. Watching out the window was a popular Granville pastime, and since the professor's murder, Alice had been as vigilant as Aunt Pru in observing Kate's comings and goings.

Kate pulled to the curb and called Alice to say that she was locking up and would be leaving in ten minutes. Then she sprinted up the walk, keys at the ready.

Al was waiting just inside the door. He let out a disgruntled "Yeow" and turned, tail twitching, to lead the way down the hall to the kitchen. When he was fed, Kate gathered her laptop and briefcase, checked doors and windows, set the alarm, and went home.

She studied the latest e-mail into the wee hours. She consulted the phone book looking for any other names that fit rL, but came up with zip. She began wondering if the latest Sudoku puzzle was really a clue or a distraction.

If so, he wasn't playing by the rules. Which was ridiculous when she thought about it: Serial killers didn't play by the rules.

If this was a serial killer, and not just a copycat of the Boston killer. Someone who'd come up with the idea after the scurrilous reporting of the *Free Press*. And if that were the case, Finn Tucker had a lot to answer for.

But the big question was, why Kate and why Sudoku?

Kate couldn't come up with any correlation between Sudoku and Henny Dougan and Rayette or Roy. None of them did Sudoku. At least she knew Rayette and Roy didn't, and she couldn't imagine Henny working the precise puzzles. And it couldn't be Kate herself. She didn't know Henny, barely knew Roy. Rayette was the only one of the three she was at all close to.

She studied the puzzle, tried working the numbers, tried to dissect them into an address, a date, a time, just as she had the first puzzle—with the same lack of success. She studied. She paced. Studied it some more until her eyes bleared over.

She should compare the second e-mail with the first she'd received, but Brandon had made her delete it. Which didn't mean she couldn't reproduce it.

Having a photographic memory could be annoying, but sometimes a blessing. She pulled up a blank Sudoku grid on her computer screen and entered an HD in the center of the puzzle as if she were generating a new puzzle. She filled in shapes around it, added the number of givens as she remembered them, and then displayed it beside the second e-mail.

HD, rL. The r was lower case, but Kate thought that was because a capital R would be impossible given the nature of a square grid.

She had two puzzles with initials and one e-mail taunt. And she was no closer to understanding what it all meant than she was when she'd begun.

Frustrated, she closed her laptop and went to bed—

But not to sleep.

Initials, numbers, garrotes, and gray trucks rolled around in her presleep mind, keeping her awake. She would begin to drift off, just to be snatched back to wakefulness by an idea or image that led nowhere. At five-thirty, she gave up, showered, and left the house.

The sun was a promise of pink on the dark horizon. The air was chill and damp. Kate buttoned up her car coat, flipped up the hood, and hoped it wouldn't rain—or snow.

She drove downtown. All the stores were closed, the street lamps fading in the morning light. Granville was still sleeping.

One solitary car drove slowly along Main Street, Finn Tucker's Nissan. It pulled to a stop in front of Rayette's. A stack of newspapers sailed out of the driver's window and landed with a thud at the door of the bakery. The car pulled away.

As soon as he'd gone half a block, Kate eased the Buick to a stop in front of the bakery. She hopped out to retrieve a paper, making a mental note to pay Rayette later.

She hurried back to the warmth of the Buick before taking a look at the front page.

It took several tries before her brain connected with the picture that took up a half page. Kate running like a banshee, and behind her the blurred sign, *Jumpin' Jack's*.

Damn. Fast Eddie seemed to be everywhere. And he was becoming a nuisance. Not to mention that his omnipresence was going to get her in hot water. She didn't think Jack Fletcher would appreciate the question the headlines raised. "What's a nice girl like you doing in a place like this?" And she *knew* that the chief would have her hide.

She could throttle Finn Tucker and his pesky photographer. And now would be an appropriate time.

She backed out of the parking space and followed Finn down Main Street. When he turned the corner at the Methodist church, Kate made the turn after him.

She followed him past the VFW hall, past the First Presbyterian church. A block later, he turned into a narrow parking lot on the side of a one-story brick building that housed the offices of the *Granville Free Press*.

Kate waited until Finn went inside before she pulled up beside the Nissan. She let herself in the front door without knocking.

Finn was sitting at his desk still wearing his coat and knit hat. It was even colder inside than it was outside, though the furnace rattled and hissed.

"Katie McDonald. Top o' the morning."

"Cut out the fake Irish," Kate said, attempting to sound stern. She tossed her copy of the *Free Press* on his desk.

He grinned at her. "You look lovely even in midflight."

"I don't know what you think you're going to accomplish—"

"Selling papers, Katie darlin'."

"I'm not your darling, and I'm pissed. This is harassment, and I want it stopped."

"Now, now, when did Fast Eddie get close enough to harass you? Bet you didn't even see him. By the by, what *were* you doing in Jumpin' Jack's? Not having a friendly one with the boys, I wager."

"Ugh. Talking to you is like talking to a free radical."

"Sounds sexy."

"It isn't," Kate said huffily, but she had to fight not to smile. He was incorrigible and funny, but his ill judgment may have pushed an unbalanced person into murder.

"So have a seat—the room ought to start warming up about noon—and tell me how your investigation is going."

"I'm not investigating."

"Darlin', my sources say that you had Roy Larkins' place staked out. Now why would you be doing that?"

"Why don't you ask your source?"

He grinned wider. "I'd much rather talk to you."

"Are you this obnoxious on purpose?" asked Kate, then blushed. This was not the way to win friends and get their cooperation.

But Finn surprised her. He laughed.

The door opened and his laughter cut off. Kate turned to see what had changed his mood so quickly and saw Fast Eddie. Strands of long hair had come loose from his ponytail and fell over his face. His down jacket had a big rip in the sleeve, He was covered everywhere in leaf mold and gunk.

Finn leapt to his feet. "Good God. What happened to you?"

"Fell off the bike." Fast Eddie stopped to lock the front door. He opened the slats of the blinds and peered out, then rushed through the office to a back room.

Finn raised an eyebrow at Kate, then hurried after him. Kate automatically fell into step behind him.

Fast Eddie was already sitting in front of a state-of-the-art computer, plugging in his camera's SD card. Within seconds, a sheet of photos appeared on the screen. They were small, but they seemed to be pictures of tramps or homeless people. A man sitting behind a sign, another scavenging through a Dumpster. He quickly viewed another sheet, then another. Scrolling down the last one, he stopped, clicked on an image, and another photo filled the screen.

The body of a woman, half hidden by leaves.

Kate gagged. Shook her head. *No…*.

"Good God," Finn breathed. "Good *God*."

Eddie clicked on the next shot. A close-up. The slice across the throat, the rictus face. Not Rayette, but the waitress, Lynn.

Kate looked away, fighting nausea.

Finn recoiled.

Not rL but L—something. Kate didn't even know the girl's last name.

Good Lord. The police might not know she was dead. There wasn't a piece of yellow tape or a uniformed policeman in any of the photos.

Kate reached for her phone.

"What are you doing?" Finn asked.

"Calling the police."

Finn snatched her phone from her hand.

Kate grabbed for it but he held it out of reach.

"I don't know what you think you're going to accomplish here," she said. "But you can't just print and disseminate these pictures. They're photos of a crime scene. You have to turn them in to the police."

"No way," said Finn.

Fast Eddie ignored both of them as he clicked through the series, leaning closer and closer to the screen and mumbling under his breath.

"Jesus," said Finn. "You got there before the police."

Eddie shook his head as he fiddled with the resolution. "They were already there. I just shot around the tape and the uniforms. But damn, if I hadn't spent all night looking for homeless people . . ." He paused long enough to give Finn a disgusted look. "I could've scooped the police."

He lifted his chin at Kate. "But I didn't. Your boyfriend was already there taking the official pictures when I arrived."

Kate let the boyfriend remark slide. It didn't really matter what Finn and Fast Eddie surmised about Sam's and her relationship.

She turned on Finn. "Give me my phone back."

"Not if you're calling the police." He slipped Kate's phone into his pocket and sat down at one of the computers.

"You can't put those photos in the paper. What about her next of kin?"

Fast Eddie hesitated and shot a look toward Finn.

Finn winked. "I'm thinking I'll charge two dollars for this edition. We might be able to pay the rent after all."

Eddie's frown disappeared. "And finally get advanced Photoshop so I can download a decent resolution."

"Don't get your hopes up on that one."

"I thought you wanted to do cutting-edge journalism? We can't do that without better equipment."

"We'll have to. Get on it before it grows cold."

"If I had a better program, we'd be printing already."

It was useless. They were two men with only one thing in mind. Scooping the story. Selling papers. Making the *Granville Free Press* profitable. And they were already arguing like a couple of natives.

Finn opened a blank document on his computer. Hands poised over the keyboard, he asked Kate, "Now what do you know about this girl? What's-her-name. Lynn."

"Nothing, and I wouldn't tell you if I did. You're going to cause a panic. It's irresponsible and probably illegal."

"It's a dog eat dog world, darlin'. And we're gonna beat the major media to the bone." He picked up the telephone. God only knew who he was going to call.

"You're disgusting."

"And I'm ahead of the game." Finn winked at her and swung around so that his back was to her.

Kate gritted her teeth. She'd have to rat Fast Eddie out to the police in person. She headed for the door.

"Hey," Finn called.

Kate turned around.

"You forgot your phone." He tossed it to her. "If you get tired of your job at the museum, come see me. You'd make a great investigative reporter."

Kate lifted her chin and slammed the door on his burst of gleeful laughter.

As soon as she was in the car, she speed-dialed the police station.

"I don't have anybody to send to the *Free Press*. Everybody's out at the crime scene. It's just awful. That sweet young girl who worked for Rayette. Garroted just like Henny Dougan."

Kate felt tears burn her throat. The killer had sent her a clue, and she'd missed it. While she and Rayette were wrestling a teenage girl to the ground, the real killer had murdered his next victim.

Her fingers itched to pull out her laptop right there in the parking lot and study the Sudoku again. *Lynn. Lynn . . . Damn.* She redialed Elmira.

"Zimmerman."

Zimmerman. Kate had been so focused on the two initials rL that the rest was a blur. She'd blown it big time. She'd gone for the obvious, because someone she cared about was involved—or so she thought. And another girl had died because Kate hadn't been objective.

The prickle of tears came without warning. She forced them away. If she'd done her job, maybe Lynn Zimmerman would be alive and she wouldn't need tears.

But it *wasn't* her job. Her job was to run a puzzle museum, and it seemed she'd been neglecting it way too much. As soon as this madman was caught, she was never going to get involved in crime again.

She ignored the scientist's voice that scoffed at her decision. Puzzlers puzzled. It was the nature of the beast.

But she couldn't do it alone—she needed help. She drove straight to the hospital.

She strode through the lobby, her briefcase slung over her shoulder. She was passing the hospital gift shop when she realized that she should bring something to cheer him up. He was going to need it.

She stepped inside and wasted several minutes trying to decide on flowers, balloons, or magazines before admitting that she didn't have a clue what he would like. She arrived at the fourth floor empty-handed.

Someone had raised the shade, and Kate's heart sank. He didn't look any better today than he had the last time she'd seen him. The oxygen tube was gone—that was a good sign. But all the other wires, tubes, and monitors were still in place.

Which meant he wasn't going to bounce out of bed and get on the case. But maybe when he woke up, he could at least give her some advice—after he yelled at her. Then again, he probably couldn't even yell, not with fractured ribs.

Kate pulled up a chair, sat down, and unpacked her laptop.

Somehow she'd missed the clue, if the killer had really left one. The whole thing seemed so off base, out of kilter, initials instead of numbers in a Sudoku puzzle. Areas in the shape of initials, colored in, not colored in. The clues followed no logical order.

Not like science and mathematics.

Get over it, she remonstrated herself. Killers had their own kind of logic, one that had nothing to do with reality. She just had to figure out what this killer's *modus logicus* was.

Kate opened the latest Killer Sudoku. rL took front and center attention. She'd gone with her initial reaction because she knew and cared about the victims. Today, in hindsight, she was more methodical, scanning and rescanning, combining shapes, resisting the urge to focus on the rL.

And finally it jumped out at her. Not the L on the right of the r. But an L to the left of it. And one line down and below the original L, an elongated zigzag. Z for Zimmerman.

Anger surged inside her. She hadn't even known Lynn's last name. The only reason she knew her first name was because of the "Hi, I'm Lynn and I'll be your server" spiel she'd brought from the Brick House.

The killer was leaving clues but not playing fair. How was she supposed to *guess* who the victim was? Even if she hadn't been so obsessed by that first recognition of rL, she couldn't have pinpointed the victim. She didn't have adequate information . . . until now.

"Kate?"

His voice sounded horrible, dry and croaky, but it filled Kate with relief. "Do you want some water? Can you have water?"

"Yes."

Of course he could. There was a cup with a straw in it on the rolling cart next to the bed. She poured water into it, then stalled. How could he drink lying down?

"Maybe I should call the nurse."

She turned away as her cheeks heated. There was no hope for her. She couldn't even administer a little TLC to the man she—to a friend in need.

The nurse came almost immediately, pressed a button that raised the bed, then held the straw to the chief's lips. Kate watched, mesmerized, feeling incompetent and out of place.

Before the nurse left, she took Kate aside. "You don't have to be afraid. He's a pretty tough guy. Just don't tire him out. Ring if you need anything."

"I don't feel very tough," a voice behind her said as the nurse left. "I feel like I got hit by a truck."

Kate smiled, her throat suddenly burning.

"Are you okay?" Brandon rasped.

"Not a scratch." *But I've got a serious problem, and I don't know whether I should tell you or not.*

"They find the truck?"

"It belongs to Roy Larkins."

"Roy?"

"Yeah, but he swears he didn't do it. Someone stole it while he was at Jumpin' Jack's, then returned it to his house."

"And you know . . . be . . . cause. . ." The chief's eyes closed.

Shit. She was losing her window of opportunity. "But something else has happened."

His eyelashes fluttered; Kate held her breath. After a struggle, his eyes opened.

"What?"

Kate licked dry lips.

"Tell me, Kate. I need to know."

The door opened and Harry and Wynter slipped into the room like two fugitives. Wynter saw Kate and stopped dead.

Before Kate could ask, "Why aren't you in school?" Wynter blurted out, "I didn't kill her. I swear!"

CHAPTER

SEVENTEEN

KATE HEARD A grunt and turned in time to see the chief struggling to sit up. She jabbed her finger at him. "Don't move." She turned the finger on Wynter. "Not another word."

She immediately felt contrite. Wynter's bangs were spiked up from her face, accentuating her paper-white skin. Her kohl-rimmed eyes were as wide as one of those girls painted on velvet. She shrank back, and Harry put a protective arm around her shoulders.

He was looking even worse. His eyes were puffy, his skin pallid, as if he'd just wakened from a long sleep. Having the chief in the hospital with a killer loose was taking its toll.

"Of course you didn't. Don't worry." Kate nodded surreptitiously toward the chief. *Don't upset him.*

"Kill who? What's she talking about?" The chief's breath sounded too fast and shallow.

"Nothing."

"Kate, goddammit, tell me!"

Harry dragged Wynter toward the bed. "That waitress. The one we like. Lynn. He killed her. And Wynter might have been the last one to see her alive. Except for Calvin."

Kate collapsed into the nearest chair. So much for not upsetting the chief.

"When?"

Harry and Wynter both looked at Kate.

"You knew about this?" Brandon croaked. Kate stood up and held the cup of water for him. He drank, then let his head fall back on the pillow while still managing to focus intent eyes on her. Actually, they looked like they might close any second. And if he nodded out, she wouldn't have to tell him what she'd been up to.

No, that wouldn't help anyone. Hadn't she come here for his advice? No way was she was chickening out now.

"Just listen and don't get upset."

She waited until he nodded, then she told him everything. She could see him fighting off the effects of the painkillers they were giving him. Halfway through her account of getting the e-mail, rushing to Rayette, and discovering that she'd been wrong about the victim, and now Lynn Zimmerman was dead, he began to shake his head.

It was a slight movement and Kate could tell it hurt him to move, but she didn't try to stop him. His free fingers opened and closed as if he were grabbing at something and Kate became frightened.

"Wrong." His voice was failing. "Kate. . ."

She moved closer.

"Not right. Something not right. . ." He made a gigantic effort to open his eyes. "Can't. . ." And he slid back into a drugged sleep.

The three of them waited, and Kate had no doubts that the other two, like her, were willing him to wake up and tell them more. But he didn't.

When Kate was sure that his breathing was steady and deep, she motioned Harry and Wynter into the hall.

"What the hell are you talking about?" she asked as soon as the door clicked shut behind her.

"Pizza," Harry warned.

"I'm declaring a moratorium on the pizza rule until further notice."

"Cool."

"Not for you—just me." She turned on Wynter. "What do you know and how do you know it?"

Wynter flinched, sank into one hip, and crossed her arms in a defiant—or maybe a protective—gesture. Harry stepped closer to her.

Kate gave them both a look. "I am not the enemy."

"The bus driver." Wynter made a face. "Yeah, I have to take the dweeb mobile to school every day. The padre says it will make us thankful for whatever. So this dude always keeps his radio tuned to the police band. Like he's afraid of getting stopped for endangering children by bad driving. I mean, he can't drive worth shit—"

"You are still under the pizza rule."

"Not fair!"

"Tell it to the equality police. So everyone on the bus heard about Lynn Zimmerman being murdered."

"Pretty much. And by the time we got to the school, half the parents were already there to pick up their kids off the bus and take them home." Wynter shifted her weight. "Mine weren't," she said in a smaller voice. "Probably thinks it builds character to take your life in your hands to get an education."

"So you get to school, then you and Harry—"

"It wasn't her fault. I was waiting for her outside our classroom, and she was, like, upset, so we decided to come see the chief. He always knows what to do."

Yeah, thought Kate. But there wasn't one thing he could do to help them now.

"Me and Wynter might be implicated."

Kate's heart stopped before pounding again at twice its regular rate. "Why?" she asked, though she was afraid of what the answer might be.

"I wasn't meeting Lynn, like *some* people think."

"Then where were you?" Wynter demanded.

"I told you, I fell asleep."

"Like I'm gonna believe—"

"Stop it, you two. You're being too loud for the hospital, and flinging insults isn't going to help us figure out what's what." Kate didn't for a minute think that either of them were viable suspects. The idea was ludicrous. But if they had seen something they shouldn't have, they could be in serious danger.

"Come on," she said.

"I'm not going back to school and have my ass hauled off to jail in front of all those—"

"Pizza," Harry and Kate said automatically, though neither of them was really concerned about language at that moment. It was just something normal in a world that suddenly made no sense.

"I'm not going either," Harry said and jutted his chin.

"We're going to my car where we can talk without being overheard. Then we're going to get coffee because I haven't had mine this morning, and I need it. And Harry looks like he needs it too. Are you sleeping okay?"

Harry ran a hand over his eyes. "Like the dead."

Stress, Kate thought. But better than not being able to sleep.

"Come on. And while I'm driving, you're going to tell me exactly what you were doing last night, when and where you were doing it, and with whom. The truth, no matter how icky."

Kate strode toward the elevator, not bothering to look to see if they were following.

They were. So close that they kept stepping on her heels.

They were scared and so was she. Their go-to guy was flat on his back in a drugged state and they had nowhere to turn but to each other.

When they reached the Buick, Harry and Wynter both climbed into the front seat with Kate. Kate turned on the ignition and ramped up the heat. She shifted in the driver's seat so she could see both of them.

"Who wants to start?"

"Me," Harry said quickly. "Wynter thinks I stood her up to hook up with Lynn. Bogus. I didn't even get out of the house."

Wynter gave Kate a look that seemed way too knowledgeable for a girl her age.

"I was going to go to bed early like I was really tired, then sneak out and meet her. I don't usually do that. The chief would be really pissed. And he'd have a right to be, 'cause we have an understanding."

Interesting, thought Kate. She hadn't been let in on any of the male-bonding stuff.

"But Ted? He's such a stiff. And he doesn't have any right to tell me what to do."

"He's just trying to help out in a pinch."

"I don't care. He acts like he's the boss of everything. And then last night he decides he's going to make us a nice dinner. Gag. Like I really want to sit at a table with him, but what could I do?"

Harry wasn't usually so vocal about his likes and dislikes. He was a smart kid, near genius, and his natural state was rational. It must be Wynter's influence, which Kate hated to think, because for some strange reason she was beginning to like the girl.

But Wynter had to learn some respect if she was going to continue to be friends with Harry. Kate and Brandon hadn't snatched him from the jaws of foster care only to have him turn into a juvenile delinquent.

"So he makes dinner, and I'm trying to rush, and yawning so he'll get the point. But he wants to talk." Harry rolled his eyes. "You know in this pals-y, just-us-men kind of way."

Wynter made a gagging sound. "Suck-up."

"I am not."

"Not you, stupid. The Tedster."

"Oh. So anyway, I sat down and let him lecture. And he kept droning on and on how we had to be strong for the chief, but he calls him Bran like he was some kind of cereal, and I couldn't get away to call Wynter to tell her I was going to be late, and then I kind of fell asleep on the couch."

Wynter punched his shoulder.

"Ow." Harry rubbed his arm. "I couldn't help it. Ted just kept yammering about how he and the chief are bros in the blood, and he feels responsible to keep up the side and I should too, and how its important to stick to a routine and study and shit, until I guess I just nodded out.

"When I woke up, it was morning. Weird. I was still on the couch with a blanket over me." He finished with a shrug.

Wynter made violin noises.

Kate gave her a look, which she ignored. She might not want sympathy, but it was clear that the stress and worry had finally caught up with Harry. And he'd succumbed to exhaustion.

"It happens like that sometimes," Kate said. "Your body just takes over when your brain refuses to listen."

Harry looked relieved, but Wynter cut in with, "Give me a break."

Harry snapped toward her. "And. I. Did. Not. Go. Meet. Lynn Zimmerman."

"Whatever." Wynter turned her back to them and stared out the passenger window, which had completely fogged over from the heat.

"I don't even know her. She just was nice to me and the chief when we'd go into Rayette's. So don't be a butthead."

Wynter turned back. Her eyes were red rimmed beneath the kohl. "Maybe if you *had* met her, she wouldn't be dead." Her voice broke. "Shit." A tear ran down her cheek.

Harry stared at it in horror. Kate would have given her a hug, except that Harry was in the way, and she wasn't sure sympathy was going to get Wynter through this ordeal. She seemed to respond better to tough.

"All right, Wynter, your turn."

"You already know what I did. You were there."

"Before," said Kate. "Tell me what happened after you left your house."

Wynter slipped down in the seat until only her eyes and the top of her spiked head showed from above her leather jacket collar.

"I was supposed to meet Harry at eleven." She cut him a look. "I started out early in case I couldn't get a ride, but this truck came along—"

"You shouldn't get into strange cars," Harry told her.

"Yeah, yeah, whatever. It was just some redneck townie boy. He dropped me off outside the quickie mart.

"I was supposed to meet Harry in that park down by the river. You know, the one in front of the Bowsman Inn?"

"Memorial Park," Harry interjected.

"Well, I waited . . . and waited. Harry was a no-show."

"I told you—"

Kate put a hand on his arm. Harry huffed out an exasperated sigh and fell back against the seat.

"So then I guess I got—you know. Well, hell, I was pissed."

"Pizza," Harry said through clenched teeth.

"Okay, okay, I was pizza," said Wynter and nudged him in the ribs. He shrugged her off and moved closer to Kate. Wynter nudged him again.

Ritual teenage courtship, thought Kate. *If you can't kiss them, slug them.*

"So you waited. Then what?"

"I went to look for him."

"But not at my *house*," Harry grumbled. "where I was *the whole time.*"

Wynter ignored him. "I wanted to see if he was hooking up with that Lynn girl when she got off work. I guess I shouldn't call her that now, huh?"

"No," Kate said. "And then what?"

"So I went to the bakery and she and that Calvin guy were coming out the front door. They walked across the street—she was like hanging on him and stuff. Then they stopped at a car and she got in."

"What did Calvin do?"

"I dunno. I stopped looking. I figured I'd go back to the park to see if Harry ever showed, but then I saw Rayette closing up so I figured I'd just go ask her if she'd seen Harry and maybe cop some rolls or something. I was hungry."

"Then you two jumped me."

"I can't believe you and Rayette actually did that," Harry said.

"We weren't expecting Wynter."

"You were expecting the serial killer. Why?"

"We just jumped the gun, okay?"

Harry wasn't buying it, but Kate didn't think she should make him privy to her latest e-mail in front of Wynter.

"And you know the rest." Wynter said.

If only she knew the rest. Unfortunately, she didn't know jack.

"And you didn't see anyone else?"

"No."

Kate turned on the car.

"Where are we going?" Wynter asked, her voice edged with apprehension, her body tense.

"We're going to breakfast. Then I'm calling the school and telling them you're with me. And you are calling your family and telling them that I'll bring you home later."

"We don't have to go back?"

Kate shook her head. "For the record . . . you're both too upset over recent events. Besides, you said half the kids had already been taken home. And Harry is going to call Ted, as a matter of courtesy," she added quickly to forestall his outburst, "not because he's the boss."

"No way," groused Harry.

"Or we can all go to school."

There was unanimous protest.

"Am I going to have to tell the police?" Wynter asked.

"I don't know. I'll tell them what I saw, and maybe they won't need to talk to you. I don't want either of you discussing this with anyone. Understand me? Anyone at all."

"Not even the chief?" asked Harry.

"Not even the chief."

As Kate expected, Rayette's was closed for business. Word had traveled fast. Knots of people stood on the sidewalk, huddled against the spring chill, reading what must be the latest special edition of the *Free Press*.

Kate could only hope that the police had been able to notify Lynn's next of kin before those pictures became public. She wondered if the girl was local. She didn't know anyone named Zimmerman, but she'd been gone for almost ten years, and contrary to popular belief, people did move *to* Granville.

Kate called Rayette to offer her condolences. Her call went straight to voice mail. She left a message.

"Well, I guess it's the Bowsman Inn for breakfast. And on the way there, you can show me where you waited for Harry."

Nancy Vance met them in the lobby, dressed in a hunter-green skirt and twin set and looking very New England bed and breakfast. Except for the expression on her face.

"This is just so awful. Have you heard?" She cast a quick glance at Harry and Wynter, her eyes widening with curiosity when she took in the black clothes and makeup.

"Nancy, this is Harry's friend, Wynter."

"How do you do," Nancy said, and shot Kate a look that said she expected to get the lowdown later.

"This way, please." She gestured them into the dining room. It was a large open room, and most sections were closed except the tables nearest the window and the view of the river.

Nancy snagged three menus as they passed the maitre d's station and held Kate back while Harry and Wynter chose a table by the window.

"She's a Goth. I didn't know we had any."

"Her family just moved here."

"Chief Mitchell must be beside himself. Speaking of which, how is he doing?"

"Okay, I guess. But it's slow going."

"Who's going to stop this madman, with the chief banged up and in the hospital?"

"I don't know. Maybe he'll be able to work in a day or two." Kate knew that wasn't true. It would be a while before he was in fighting form, but that wouldn't keep him from working from home or even from a hospital bed.

"We've already lost three guests because of this. People are afraid to stay. Everyone is scared, Katie. We hardly had anybody for dinner last night. And even with Rayette closed today, and it being Dan's day off, I still had to send one of the waiters home for lack of work. Who could be doing this?"

"I don't know," Kate said. "You said it was Dan's day off?"

"Yes. I wonder if he's heard about that poor girl? They worked together at the Brick House."

Three people from the Brick House: Lynn dead. Calvin, who was probably the last person to see her alive. And Dan taking his day off. Kate couldn't make the pieces fit.

Yet.

		8	5				6	
		9	7		2			8
3					4		7	
	8		4				5	
	4		3				1	
	7		1					9
1			2		6	5		
	2				8	6		

THERE WAS A note with Kate's name on it taped to the museum door. Her heart stopped for a couple of seconds before she recognized the handwriting. She pulled it off and unfolded it while Wynter and Harry crowded to see over her shoulder.

GAB Meeting my house. Eleven o'clock. Light lunch. Please come, we need your expertise.

"Oh, Lord, what are they up to now?" Kate wondered out loud.

"Who are the Gabs?" Wynter asked.

"A bunch of old ladies—"

"Harry."

"Senior citizens. Last year someone was trying to tear down all the old . . . I mean 'senior' houses to build a shopping mall." Harry shot Kate a sententious look.

"Alice—you met her at the museum the other day. She organized the Grannies Activist Brigade—the GABs. They stormed the courthouse and caused a riot. But they stopped the mall from being built. Now they do all sorts of stuff. Right, Kate?"

"Right." She dreaded to think what they were planning now. She'd have to attend that meeting. She looked at her watch: almost eleven.

"Are we going?" Harry asked.

"I am. I think you and Wynter should—"

"Get lost?"

Kate didn't think they would get lost. Knowing Harry, he would start trying to solve the murders while she was gone. He and Wynter might go off half cocked and get into real trouble.

"—come too." Kate finished. "But first Al needs to be fed. And we have museum business to attend to."

Kate watched Harry, Wynter, and Al go off down the hall. Al circled in and out of Wynter's legs as she walked. She didn't falter or trip or even slow down.

Like a witch and her familiar, thought Kate, then chided herself for her ungenerous thought. Wynter was just a teenage girl trying to find her way. She was just different.

Kate could relate to that.

And Al thought she was all right. That should be enough, thought Kate as she climbed the stairs.

Before she even took off her coat or sat down at the desk, she unpacked and booted up her laptop. She scrolled through the e-mails that had come in since she'd checked earlier that morning. Nothing that couldn't wait, thank God.

She opened the latest e-mail from the killer. rL stared right back at her as it had last night. But today she saw the L and Z as well.

He'd told her, and she'd missed it because she'd gone for the obvious, though even if she'd looked more thoroughly, she still wouldn't have been able to save Lynn. She hadn't known the girl's last name.

If only she could communicate with the killer, he might give something away. She was so tempted, but she remembered Brandon's words. *Don't engage him.*

He was right, she knew, but she felt so useless. Two people were dead. There would be more if she didn't get a handle on the clues.

She pushed her chair away from the desk, paced over to the fireplace, and looked out the window.

"What are you—"

Kate yelped and whirled around. Harry and Wynter stood just inside the door. Wynter was smirking, but Harry looked concerned.

"Sorry," he said. "Are you all right?"

Kate nodded. "You just startled me." Too late, she realized she should have closed the saved e-mail. Harry had zeroed in on it.

"Harry."

"Is this another one?" he asked, sitting down at her desk, leaning over the computer screen, and resting his weight on his elbows.

"It's the one from last night. I blew it. I saw the rL and didn't look further."

"Not your fault," he said as he peered at the puzzle. "We didn't know her last name, did we?"

Wynter slid onto the arm of his chair. "What is this shit? Some kind of puzzle, right?"

Kate didn't even warn her about her language. If she was going to stick around, they'd have to deal with her later. There were more important priorities at the moment. Like finding the damn killer.

"It's a Sudoku puzzle," Harry explained. "A special kind of Sudoku puzzle. The killer sent it to Kate as a clue to his next murder."

"You're shittin' me. The murderer sent you an e-mail? That is so random. Let me see." Wynter burrowed in front of Harry to get a closer look at the computer screen.

Harry pursed his lips. "You're sworn to secrecy."

"Sure, cool, whatever."

"I'm not sure this is a good idea," Kate said. "It could be—"

Harry preempted her. "Come on, Kate. You can't just cut her off now."

"Yeah, cause if you do, I'll blab it all over town." Wynter grinned complacently, and her tooth diamond winked.

Kate knew she'd do it. And that could be irreparable. But she didn't want to tempt Harry to include Wynter in any investigation without her supervision. "Okay, but nothing leaves this room. And you don't try to do any sleuthing," Kate added, as much for Harry's benefit as for Wynter's. "We look for connections only. The police will solve the crime."

"They're a bunch of kids with acne." Wynter cracked her gum.

Kate turned her ear away from the noise and nudged the two away from the desk. "Get your own chairs."

Moments later, the three of them were huddled together studying the e-mail.

"That was really sent by the serial killer?" Wynter asked.

"Or some sicko trying to horn in on the excitement," said Harry.

"Someone with a grudge against me?" asked Kate.

"Or someone who knows you and wants you to solve the murder."

"That could be anybody."

"Pretty much. Except the second e-mail came before the second murder. Whoever sent it knew who the victim would be."

"So how does this get to be a clue?" Wynter asked, frowning at the puzzle.

"This is a Killer Sudoku puzzle. It's made up of squares and other shaped regions that you have to complete with numbers. More difficult than the regular nine-region puzzles. That's why they call it Killer Sudoku."

"Kinda ironic, isn't it? Killer Sudoku."

"Yeah."

"So where's the clue?"

Kate gave up. She'd probably be sued for involving Wynter in this, but it was too late to backpedal. Once Harry had his teeth into something, he wouldn't let go. Just like her, she thought. And it was getting more and more obvious that where Harry went, so did Wynter.

Kate nudged them aside so that she could reach the trackpad. She opened her reconstruction of the original puzzle. "The first clue came after the fact and had Henny Dougan's initials colored in." She pointed the cursor to the tinted HD constructed from the Killer regions.

"An H and a D. The technique is simplistic," said Kate. "You don't even need to know Sudoku to leave this clue."

"HD. Like paint by numbers," said Wynter. "That's pretty lame. All they had to do was look for a puzzle that had the right shapes in it, then color them in. Even I could do that, and I'm dumb as shit."

"No, you're not," Harry said automatically.

"That's what we thought," Kate went on. "Simplistic. But he got me on the next one." She had to stop to control her voice. She opened the second puzzle.

"This one isn't tinted. But dead center are the initials—"

"Little r, big L. I get it."

"I thought he was planning to kill Rayette, and I panicked. Her last name is Lansing." The memory of that piercing fear swept over her, and she shivered. "I went racing off to save Rayette, but instead of stopping a murderer, I found you."

"And while you were trying to save Rayette, he was killing Lynn. Wow."

"It was a diversionary tactic," Kate pointed out defensively, "one that I should have thought through. But I didn't."

"'Cause you were obsessing over Rayette."

Kate blinked. "I wasn't exactly obsessing."

"Just an expression," Harry explained. "Kind of a forest and trees thing."

"Oh," Kate said.

"It wasn't your fault. You didn't even know her name."

"I know that," Kate said. "Intellectually. But . . ."

"It still sucks," added Wynter.

Kate looked at her. "Yeah. It sucks."

"I don't want to seem insensitive or anything," Harry said. "But all this emotional angsting isn't exactly the most efficient way to go about solving a murder. It needs—"

"The little gray cells," said Wynter with more enthusiasm than Kate had ever heard from her.

"You read Agatha Christie?"

The façade slammed back up. "The madre reads everything, belongs to one of those book clubs. I guess I must've seen it somewhere. Gotta ring to it, ya know. Little gray cells. Too bad I don't have any."

"I keep telling you, you're not dumb."

"Whatever."

They are going to drive me nuts, thought Kate. How could she think with all this constant teenage badinage?

And she realized that she was a little envious—she'd never had a friend like that. She shook it off. *Murder*, she reminded herself.

Harry was right; she was being emotional. Her friends were in danger. Brandon had almost been killed protecting her. She had every right to be emotional—she just didn't have the time.

"You're right, we need the scientific method." Kate opened a blank document.

"Woo-hoo," said Harry and scooted his chair closer.

Kate arranged the three documents on the screen, the two puzzles and the new blank document. She created three columns on the empty page, one for a time line of events, a second one for notes, and a third for what she called people and motives and Harry called the usual suspects.

"This jerk has been controlling the rules of play for too long. It's time to take action." Kate typed in "*Free Press* article/Boston serial killer/Henny buries Tess in garage foundation." Followed the last with a question mark.

"And Henny ends up dead," Harry added.

Kate held up one finger. "First, someone broke into the Free Press office and trashed Finn's printer." Kate typed "Printer destroyed" and tabbed over to the People column and left a series of question marks.

"Then Henny was found dead." Kate typed in "Henny Dougan/garroted."

"You think Henny busted up Finn's printer, and Finn offed him for it?"

"*Harry*. That's really—"

"Inappropriate," Wynter shrieked and jabbed him in the ribs.

Harry made a face. "Well, do you?"

"Too early to make a hypothesis," said Kate and typed in "Finn and Fast Eddie" across from Henny's name on the time line.

She drummed her fingers on the desktop for a second, then moved the cursor to the top of the timeline to insert "Tess Dougan missing."

"She might have killed him," Wynter volunteered, finally showing some interest.

"Possibly," said Kate and typed in "Tess" beneath "Finn and Fast Eddie."

"But why would she kill Lynn?" asked Harry.

"Maybe she caught her having an affair with her husband," said Wynter.

"No way would Lynn have an affair with Henny Dougan," Harry said incredulously. "He was a drunk. He smelled. And she was . . . well, she was normal."

Wynter merely shrugged at this. "You'd be surprised at what women are attracted to."

Kate's eyes widened. Wynter sounded way too old and experienced for a fifteen-year-old. Kate just hoped she wasn't leading Harry into places he shouldn't be going.

"All possibilities are to be considered until ruled to be impossible," Kate said quickly and typed Wynter's suggestion into the people column. She looked up to see Wynter staring at her.

"You are really weird, ya know that?"

"Hey," said Harry, coming to Kate's defense. "She's a mathematician. They all talk that way."

Funny. Harry had never commented on her speech habits before, and Kate felt the same feeling she'd felt thousands of times before.

Katie doesn't belong. Not like us. Katie is a ge-ek. She shook it off.

"Let's get back on track. What happened next?"

"Someone hits the chief?"

"Not yet." Kate frowned, flipping through her mind for *Free Press* headlines. "The *Free Press* becomes a daily and hints that the serial killer has killed in Manchester and is on his way to Granville." She entered the headlines as she recalled them.

"To draw suspicion from themselves?" asked Harry.

"Or to sell newspapers. They're strapped for cash."

"Wicked," said Wynter. "They're offing the town in order to up their circulation."

"Which would eventually dry up their reader base," Harry pointed out. "So who was the last person to see Henny alive?"

Kate added more questions marks. "That, we don't know. And I don't see how we can find out. We just know that he left Jumpin' Jack's around midnight and his body was discovered on Saturday morning—"

"By you."

"By Rayette, Calvin, and Johnny. I came afterward."

"But the killer contacted you."

"Right. On the following Monday, I get the first e-mail."

"Sent from an anonymous server," said Harry.

"I don't suppose the chief had a chance to trace it before he was hurt?"

"I don't know. I think it's a pretty complicated process. We'll have to ask him."

And she would, first thing the next day.

"The same night as the e-mail, someone runs down the chief while he's walking me to my car.

"It happened really fast, but in afterthought, I'm sure it was aiming at us. Or one of us. I recognized Roy's truck." Kate typed as she spoke, not pausing for comment. "He says someone stole it while he was at Jumpin' Jack's and returned it to his house sometime during the night."

"A killer with a sense of humor," said Harry.

"Or he's creating a diversion away from himself," said Wynter. "Maybe once Tess has killed, she goes on a rampage. She can't stop herself, so she sets up the guy with the truck."

Kate and Harry stared at her, nonplussed.

"What the heck?" exclaimed Harry.

Wynter shrugged and cracked her gum. "I read trashy novels. What can I say?"

Kate shook her head. Their rational investigation was taking a spurious spin.

"And here is when I really stopped thinking rationally." Kate clicked on the second e-mail. "The e-mail from last night."

"So do you think he'll send any more?"

"Probably. But there are only so many letters you can visually make out of the available areas in killer Sudoku. H and D are simple; it would be fairly easy to find a puzzle with those two initials. Others, say Kate McDonald for example, wouldn't be possible. There are no diagonals in this kind of puzzle. And to try to make a K or an M out of rectangles would make them not very recognizable. Which would mean that the killer will have to choose victims according to who fits the puzzle's initials."

Harry and Wynter both looked stunned, and Kate knew what they were thinking. Could their initials be constructed from the Sudoku grid?

And would one of them be next?

Her incoming e-mail alert pinged. The three of them jumped. Kate scrolled to the new arrival, and a chill spread through her. An address she didn't recognize.

Hardly daring to breathe, she opened it.

Tsk. Tsk. You surprise me. That was sloppy thinking. You'll have to do better next time. Much better.

CHAPTER

NINETEEN

NO ONE SPOKE as they put on their coats and left the museum. The last e-mail left no doubt of the killer's intentions. Kate knew she had scared the two teenagers, but maybe it was for the best. At least they might be more cautious than they normally were.

Regardless, she needed to solve this. If they could trace the origin of the e-mails, they might be able to get a line on the killer. She needed help, but help was drugged and in the hospital.

She stopped on the sidewalk in front of Alice's house. "Harry, do you think the chief could trace the e-mail from the hospital?"

Harry looked taken aback. "I don't know. His big computer has all the heavy software. I don't know what he has on his laptop." He thought for a second. "I might be able to download the programs he would need. He lets me use the big one for some stuff, but he has about a million passwords on it."

Kate raised an eyebrow.

"I can get into basic programs for schoolwork and stuff. But after that . . ." He shrugged. "I've seen him use at least seven, depending on how sensitive the information is. I don't think he'll give them to me, and I can't hack into it." Another pause and a grin. "I've tried."

He sighed heavily. "The chief will be back soon, won't he, Kate?"

Kate knew Harry was asking about more than just a timeframe.

"Absolutely."

"'Cause Ted is driving me crazy."

"Just be nice. It will be over soon."

"And we didn't even go fishing. Which was the whole point of his coming for a visit."

"He's definitely a creeper," Wynter interjected.

Kate decided to ignore the remark and walked ahead to ring Alice Hinckley's doorbell.

Alice's house was next door to the museum, separated by a large privet hedge and a monstrous old oak whose leaves were just now beginning to bud. It was three stories high, a typical New England clapboard, and like all the other houses in the historic district, over a hundred and fifty years old.

"Maybe I'll wait for you out here," said Wynter, hanging back.

Harry pulled her up the steps.

Alice answered the door wearing her usual print dress and cardigan sweater. They might be coming to tea except for the raised voices echoing from the parlor.

"Come on in, dear. We've already begun, as you can hear. And you've brought Harry and his little friend. How nice."

Kate felt Wynter tense beside her, and she pressed her foot over the girl's heavy work boot.

When no snide remark ensued, Kate ushered her through the door.

The GABs—ten grannies and one honorary, Pru, who had never married—were crowded around the coffee table where a sterling tea set was surrounded by plates of cookies and cakes. Only Maria Albioni and Elmira Swyndon were missing. Elmira was probably working double shifts at the police station.

They all fell silent when the three newcomers came through the archway. Most eyes, Kate knew, were focused on Wynter.

Beatrice Noakes reached for her magnifying glass and held it up.

Carrie Blaine yelled, "Is that Katie? Who's she got with her? It looks like one of those gothic people."

Wynter snorted.

"Hi, Ms. Blaine," Harry yelled back at her. "This is my friend Wynter."

"Might be, but spring's on its way," she yelled back.

"Turn up your hearing aid." Tanya Watson made a twisting motion at her ear.

Carrie adjusted her hearing aid. "If you girls didn't yell so loud, I wouldn't have to turn the darn thing off. Now Harry, who's this?"

"Wynter," Harry repeated.

"I heard you the first time."

Pru motioned to Katie. "Come over here and sit down. Maybe Harry and Wynter should wait in the kitchen . . . because of the, uh, situation." She gave Kate a pointed look and nodded toward the door.

"Oh, we know all about the murders, Miss McDonald," Harry said as he pushed Wynter farther into the room. "Wynter even has some theories."

"Oh, Lord," Alice said. "Then you might as well come in and sit down. Don't know what this world is coming to, children talking about murder like it was recess."

"They're all weird," Wynter said under her breath as Harry steered her to a couple of straight chairs at the back of the group.

Kate went to sit by Aunt Pru, who was wearing a black running suit, black sneakers, and a black turtleneck. A comment on the atmosphere surrounding Granville lately? In mourning for two people she didn't really know?

Or maybe Wynter had just found a kindred spirit. They did have similar theories regarding Tess Dougan.

"I don't know what you have to smile about," Pru said as Kate sat down.

Kate wiped the smile from her face. "Was I smiling?"

"Hmmph." Pru turned her attention to Alice, who was trying to quiet the room.

"I call this strategy meeting of the Granville Grannies' Activist Brigade to order," commanded Alice in her lyrical, birdlike warble. No one paid the least bit of attention.

Pru put two fingers to her lips and whistled. Kate's hands flew to her ears, and she turned to stare at her aunt in wonder.

Two words rose from the stunned silence. "Freaking wicked."

Kate groaned.

"Thank you, Prudence," said Alice with a slight dip of her head. *Are the two longtime spatters enjoying a momentary truce?* Kate wondered.

"As you all know, we've been beset by two recent murders."

Everyone in the room, including her aunt, turned to look at Kate.

"No use expecting Katie to solve all our problems," Alice said.

"No, it isn't," Pru said. "That's what we hired that snot-potty police chief to do. And look where that got us."

"Prudence McDonald, if you don't have something nice to say—"

"I'm just saying."

"He pushed Katie out of the path of that speeding car. She owes him her life. For shame."

"Hmmph," Pru answered. "Never had a murder before he came."

Kate's cheeks burned, but there was nothing she could say or do to stay the tide. She hung her head and let the squabble run its course.

"Some people have a very selective memory," Alice countered.

"That's right." Beatrice lifted her cane, barely missing Tanya, who had just reached for a cookie. She jabbed the cane at Pru. "What about the Gibson family? Awful."

"That was thirty years ago."

"Like I said." Beatrice smacked the tip of her cane on the carpet and settled back, satisfied.

Kate knew that Alice had finally moved over to the chief's side. She wasn't sure about Beatrice. Granvilleites liked to argue. It didn't always matter which side you took as long as you took a side. It was the Granville way.

"Regardless," Alice continued. "We've got murders now. Just like every other town in America."

"Just what happens when you let in outsiders," groused Pru.

Several "ayuhs" were heard around the table.

"Prudence McDonald, if you don't contain yourself, I'll call you in contempt."

"You can't—"

Kate nudged her aunt. "Aunt Pru, I've got to get back to work soon."

Pru tightened her lips and folded her hands primly in her lap.

Kate sighed. Now Pru was miffed at her. One thing about her family, they never had to yell. They could make their feelings known with a look.

Alice gave Pru a slight nod and consulted her notes. "In view of these uncertain times, we will activate our usual telephone chain in case of an emergency. So everyone remember to turn on your message machines if you leave the house. And Carrie Blaine, keep your hearing aid turned on at all times."

Carrie reached for a piece of banana bread. Tanya tapped her on the shoulder, pointed to her ear.

Carrie dutifully turned it back on. "Too much noise going on," she said and bit into her piece of cake.

"Tanya has graciously volunteered to organize excursions."

"Now she's planning vacations," Pru groused under her breath.

"No one will travel solo until further notice. I've had these sticky cards printed up with the Granville Taxi service number on them. If you can't find a buddy, call a cab."

"They charge five dollars just to get in the backseat."

"And you can just hold your horses if you're in a hurry."

"They only have three cars and there's twelve of us."

Alice held up both of her dainty hands and batted the air. "Ladies, ladies. That is why we're organizing car pools. And you must let your ride know when you get safely inside."

"What about the last person out?"

"She will call the last person she dropped off. And Simon Mack has offered to drive anyone who gets stranded. He'll make sure you get home safely. His number is on the bottom of the card."

"Who's going to make sure Simon gets home safely?" asked Pru in a sugary-sweet voice.

"You can," Alice returned.

A titter bounced around the coffee table. People had their ideas about Pru and the retired lawyer. Pru began her silent smolder.

"Everyone clear?" Alice asked.

They all nodded.

"In that case, let's move to the next item of business. How are we going to help Katie solve this murder before the madman strikes again?"

Kate's stomach flipped over and she began to shake her head. Unfortunately, no words found their way out.

The telephone rang.

"Excuse me." Alice scurried into the hallway to answer the phone.

She came back two minutes later. "That was Elmira. She and Maria are on their way…" she paused for effect, then added, "And they're bringing Tess Dougan with them."

Elmira and Maria Albioni arrived five minutes later, a tanned Tess Dougan standing between them.

The GABs for once were gabless. Everyone stared.

"Well, would you look at her?" Pru whispered and clicked her tongue.

Kate remembered Tess as a thin, stoop-shouldered, middle-aged woman with mousy brown hair that straggled down her back. She usually sported a black eye or swollen jaw.

The Tess Dougan who stood in the archway was not just tanned. Her hair was styled in a shoulder-length bob, dyed blonde with platinum highlights. She was wearing tight jeans, leopardskin high heels, and a magenta puff jacket. A knock-off designer bag hung from her shoulder—she held onto the strap with fingers whose nails were manicured and polished a persimmon orange.

There wasn't a bruise in sight.

Tess Dougan had had a makeover.

Elmira gave her a little shove into the room. "Look who we found coming out of the Market Basket."

"Where have you been?" Kate blurted. She darted a look at Elmira.
"She knows."

"You mean that Henny is dead?" Tess cast her eyes toward the ceiling.

"She isn't going to find him there," Pru said behind her hand. "There's no way that no-good snake made it anywhere close to the pearly gates."

"Pru." Kate gave her aunt a stern look, which she merely shrugged off, turning to say something to Beatrice, who was sitting on her other side.

Elmira gave Tess another push.

Alice finally remembered her manners. "Won't you come in?" She motioned for Tess to sit down in the empty chair next to hers.

Tess balked, and finally Elmira grabbed her by the elbow and steered her across the room.

She pushed Tess into the chair, then stood behind it.

"Elmira Swyndon has definitely been watching too much *48 Hours*," Pru whispered.

"I heard that, Pru. And I'll thank you to keep your opinion to yourself." Turning her attention to the others, Elmira said, "Tess is not exactly thrilled to be here. I told her it was just us girls. And I told her about Henny so you don't have to tiptoe around trying not to say the wrong thing."

"Is that Tess Dougan?" Carrie Blaine yelled and slapped at her hearing aid. "We thought you were dead."

Tess snorted. "Ain't that a kicker? I go off for some R and R and the whole town thinks that no-good son of a bitch did me in." She chuckled. "I'd like to see him show that much gumption."

A collective gasp of disapproval rocketed around the circle of chairs.

Maria leaned around the back of Tess's chair where she'd stationed herself next to Elmira. "You have to admit, it was just a tad unusual for you to leave town. Then when he started pouring the foundation for your new garage . . ."

"We just naturally assumed," Elmira continued. "Though now that you mention it, it wasn't like Henny to show that kind of initiative."

"Yeah, well he didn't," Tess said. "I've been at him to do something about the garage for two years now. So before I left I called L and J Construction. Les is a good friend of mine."

"And we all know what that means," Pru whispered.

"I told him to get started on the foundation and I'd pay him when

I got back." Tess reached for a cookie. "Damn fool."

Kate wasn't sure if she was talking about Les or Henny—maybe both of them.

Alice handed Tess a napkin for her cookie and asked if she'd like some coffee.

Tess declined. "I just had my teeth whitened." She flashed them a grin.

Twelve GABS leaned forward to get a better look.

"Now, could you tell us where you've been all this time?" asked Kate. They'd long ago passed out of proper police procedure, and since there weren't any police around, they might as well find out what they could. And not about Tess Dougan's teeth.

Tess studied her newly manicure nails. "I went over to Bedford to help my sister. She's having twins. I don't much get along with my sister, but I don't much get along with Henny either. I decided to try out somebody else's domestic bliss for a change."

"The police called her looking for you. She said you weren't there and she didn't know where you were."

"That's 'cause when I got there, her mother-in-law was already there. I like her mother-in-law even less. I'm telling you, that woman can talk a splinter off a fence post. I held on for a day and a half and then threw in the towel."

"Where did you go after that?"

"Well, hell. This is the good part. I was out picking up some ice cream and I ran into my friend Stella. We went to beautician's school together. She finished, I married Henny, the more fool me. Anyway. She was just about to leave for this cruise down to the islands. Only her friend who she was going with got the flu, so she asked me if I wanted to go.

"So I thought, what the hell, it was already paid for. I didn't see any need to tell my sister I was ditching her for a cruise to Barbados.

God almighty. You shoulda seen her. A beached whale, I swear—"

"The cruise?" Kate prompted.

"I had a blast. Five days and four nights of fun, fun, fun. I wasn't looking forward to coming back, I can tell you. 'Bout half decided I had to get a divorce. Only now I guess I won't have to."

Throwing caution to the wind, Kate asked, "Can your friend Stella verify your whereabouts?"

"Say what?"

Elmira gave Kate an approving nod before she prodded Tess with a finger. "She wants to know if Stella will give you an alibi."

"Sure, why not?" Belated understanding flickered across Tess's face. "Hey. You girls don't think I killed Henny, do you?" She looked from Kate to the others.

No one spoke.

"That's just plain crazy."

Still getting no reaction, she added, "I don't even know how to use one of those whatchamacallits. Elmira, what's that thing called that you said killed Henny?"

"Garrote," Elmira supplied, just a hint of exasperation seeping into her tone.

"Garrote," Tess repeated. "Am I gonna have to tell all this to Chief Mitchell?"

"Yes," Elmira said. "But it will have to wait. Someone tried to kill the chief a few nights ago."

It is officially an accident, Kate thought. But she decided not to equivocate. It was clear from the nods and murmurs that everyone already believed that someone had tried to kill the chief.

And she was pretty sure they were right.

Tess adjusted her shoulder bag. "Well, that's a crying shame. I hope he's all right. He's not bad for someone from down south. Came out and kept Henny from beating the crap outta me more than once, and I appreciate it."

She started to stand; Elmira pushed her back into her chair. "Did Henny have any enemies?"

Tess barked out a laugh. "Are you kidding me? Name anybody."

"I mean," Elmira said, looking stern. "Someone who'd want to kill him?"

Tess shrugged. "Just about anybody who knew him. But nobody would. What you got is one of them serial killers."

Kate stifled a groan. If Tess had killed her husband, she'd get off on a technicality—thanks to them. This needed to be done legally. Kate stood up. "I'm sure Elmira wants to get you down to the station so they can take your statement."

"Oh no she doesn't. I'm not going."

"It's just for the record—"

"Thank you kindly, I'll just wait for Chief Mitchell to get back. But she can give me a ride home."

Elmira huffed out a sigh and pulled Tess from the chair.

Kate signaled to Harry and Wynter that it was time to go.

"Now what?" asked Harry as they watched Elmira and Tess drive away.

"I'd check her alibi if I were you," Wynter said.

"That's for the police to do."

Wynter sank into one hip. "I thought we did this already. The police are in the hospital. And I gotta say, for a bunch of whackjobs, those old ladies know how to kick butt." Wynter came to a dead stop. "Shit."

A silver Mercedes pulled up to the curb.

"It's the padre, and I am so effed." Wynter assumed her vaguest expression and sauntered over to the car just as the passenger window lowered.

"Yo," she said. Arrogant, bored, in your face. Every reaction but the one that might mollify an obviously irate father.

"I thought she called home," Kate said to Harry.

Harry shrugged. "She called someone. Go help her."

Kate gave him a look but walked over to the car.

Oliver Adams was visibly shaking as he confronted his daughter.

When he finally had to stop his tirade to take a breath, Kate said, "I'm sorry—this is all my fault."

Oliver turned steel-gray eyes on her. One eyebrow lifted. He was a handsome man but intimidating as all get out. Kate stared at his forehead, a technique she'd learned from a speaking coach. "I called the school to let them know Harry and Wynter were with me. They were upset about the—"

"Wynter? *Wynter*? This nonsense has to stop." Dismissing Kate, he snapped his head toward his daughter. "I didn't move to this back of beyond for you to continue this inappropriate behavior." Back to Kate. "Her name is Cindy. Cindy Adams."

"Wynter," Wynter leaned into the window. "With a Y."

"Get in. We're going home."

"No."

"Don't make me get out of this car."

Harry took a protective step toward Wynter.

"And you, whoever you are, stay away from my daughter."

"Mr. Adams," Kate began.

"Get in the car *now*."

"She really—"

"And you stop encouraging her."

"Really, Mr. Adams—"

"Forget it, Kate. You can't talk to him when he gets like this." Wynter reached for the door handle and shot her father a look so filled with unhappiness that Kate was tempted to grab her back.

She slid into the front seat and slumped down, crossed her arms, and stared at the floorboards.

The window rose, and the Mercedes shot off down the street.

It stopped almost immediately. The car backed up, the window lowered again, and Oliver Adams leaned across his daughter. "I must apologize. It's just that we've had, well, it's been a difficult time. I'm sure you understand."

Kate had an inkling. In the few days she'd been acquainted with Wynter, she'd had reason to be exasperated more than once. She couldn't imagine what living with her would be like. But she didn't like his sudden condescension.

He gave Kate a charming smile. "Thank you for taking care of her."

"I'd be happy to have Wyn—Cindy at the museum anytime."

"That's very kind, but Cindy is grounded until further notice."

Wynter slumped lower, tilting her head long enough to give Harry a meaningful look that Kate didn't miss.

Mr. Adams's hardnosed reaction was bound to send Wynter into total rebellion.

"Now we must be going." Another smile. "Thanks again."

For the second time, the window rose and the car took off. Kate and Harry watched until it rounded the curve at the end of the block.

"What an ass—"

"I totally agree," said Kate.

"Like Dr. Jekyll."

"And Mr. Hyde."

	4				9			
6					3		1	
8			7					2
9					8	3	4	
	1						6	
	3	7		5				9
5					7			8
	9		6					3
			3				7	

CHAPTER

TWENTY

THERE WAS ONLY a handful of visitors to the museum that day. Most people were staying home. Kate sent Tanya, who manned the registration desk on Wednesdays, home early. At 4:15, Ginny Sue arrived for her five o'clock Math and Sudoku kids program. By 5:30 it was clear that no one was coming.

Kate called the members of the Crossword Club and told them the evening's meeting was canceled. Most of them had already planned to stay home.

At 6:15, Ted picked up Harry and took him to the hospital for evening visiting hours. Kate and Ginny Sue left the museum together, both a little depressed and both looking over their shoulders as they hurried to their cars.

Kate went home and poured herself a glass of wine while she reheated a plate of Pru's lima bean and sausage casserole. She worked two Sudoku puzzles from her new books while she ate, but after dinner she tossed them aside. She couldn't spend the evening working syndicated puzzles when there was a real puzzle to contemplate.

She had pretty much decided that the two local murders had not been perpetrated by the Boston killer. That relationship had been pure fabrication by Finn Tucker, and he had a lot to answer for, especially if he'd given the local killer the idea.

But she couldn't figure out who had it in for Henny or Lynn—she couldn't imagine what they might have in common. She didn't know anything about either of them, and it was stupid to speculate without having facts.

There was one place she could find out more about Henny, and maybe even pick up a tidbit or two about the waitress. She called Aunt Pru.

"Are you at home?" Pru asked as soon as Kate identified herself.

"Yes. Safe and sound and needing some information."

"About what?" Pru asked warily.

"Henny Dougan."

"Good Lord. I *knew* it. Katie, please don't get involved any more than you already are. It's not your job."

"The police seem to be in disarray, and I'm not doing anything but gathering information." *And not even doing that very well*, she thought.

"It's that damn Chief Mitchell's fault."

"Pru, he's in the hospital. I haven't even talked to him." Hardly.

"That's just what I mean. He ought to be up and doing his job, not depending on you to do it for him."

"He isn't," Kate retorted, then tamped down her temper, which was naturally quick to boil over, especially when she was trying to keep it. "And I'm not doing his job. I just have to know."

Pru let out a heartfelt sigh. "You always did. I don't know why you couldn't just be happy letting things be and not have to try to find out everything about everything."

"I don't know either," Kate said. "It's just the way I was made."

"It was bad enough when you were off working for that Washington think tank. I had nightmares about what you were up to."

"It was theoretical mathematics, Aunt Pru. Nothing clandestine or dangerous."

"You can't always tell when the government's involved. And now, you finally come back and look what's happened."

Kate knew dangerous waters when she heard them. Pru's logic was headed right where it always headed—commiseration on why Kate wasn't married.

"If you would just marry Sam."

Sam. She'd hardly given him a thought. And if Aunt Pru ever found out that he'd actually proposed. . .

"Henny Dougan?" Kate prodded.

"Oh, him. Never worth a hill of beans. Not even Boston ones. Lazy and nasty. Drank when he was a teenager and never stopped. And look where it got *him.*"

"It seems like everyone tolerated him and ignored him," Kate said. "Did anyone really hate him?"

"Nobody that I heard tell. He wasn't worth getting upset about. And nobody's gonna miss him. Not even his wife."

Especially not his wife, thought Kate and jotted down a note to check Tess's alibi as Wynter had suggested.

"Did you hear anything about Lynn Zimmerman?"

"The little waitress at Rayette's? No. Agnes Mortimer said she was a sassy piece, but you can't always believe what Agnes says. She was friendly whenever she waited on me. I did see her flirting with

Erik Ingersoll one lunch time. But she didn't mean anything by it—you can always tell the ones that do. And it made Erik's day. He left the café whistling, the old fool."

"Anything else?"

"Didn't she used to work with the fella that's cooking for Rayette?" Pru asked.

"Yes. They both worked at the Brick House."

"Well, you stay away from him."

"Thanks," Kate said, glossing over her answer. "Lock your doors."

"I think you should stay with me until this madman is caught," Pru said.

"Thanks, but I . . . would you like to stay here?"

"I would not. I'm perfectly capable of taking care of myself. But I'm worried about you alone in that house."

"I'll be fine. The doors are locked, the alarm is on, and I'm staying in tonight."

Pru hung up with a final "Hmmph."

Kate carried her laptop over to the couch, set it on the coffee table, and pulled up the timeline she had created with Harry and Wynter. All the events—the known events—were listed in order. She still had no connections. *If there are connections, and not just random killings.* But there must be. She just had to ferret them out.

She started at the beginning—at least the beginning as she knew it.

Finn writes about the Boston killer.

Next, he practically accuses Henny of killing his wife.

Finn's printer is vandalized.

Henny is killed.

Over a printer? It seemed absurd, but thus far in the list, the only two players were Finn and Henny.

Kate tabbed over to the People and Motives column and typed "Check out Finn's background." She added Fast Eddie's name just to be thorough.

Kate received the first e-mail puzzle. She had nothing to enter in Motives except "Why me?"

She moved to the next event. Someone in Roy Larkins' truck runs down the chief. Was he aiming for the chief or both of them?

According to Roy, someone stole his truck from the parking lot at Jumpin' Jack's and returned it to his yard with the front light bashed in. Everyone knew Roy and the chief had had a major confrontation over Roy's truck the year before. Anyone could have used this knowledge to set Roy up or to merely cover their own tracks. The police still had no leads on the thief.

Kate entered "Who??? Kids? Killer? Motive???"

The second e-mail arrives.

Lynn Zimmerman is killed on her way home from work.

Kate was sure the killer had intentionally misled her with the second e-mail. He wanted her to see rL and rush to save Rayette while he was killing Lynn.

Someone who knew Kate and Rayette were friends. Someone who knew Kate's reputation for aiding the police in their investigations. Someone who knew she was a Sudoku puzzler.

And that could be just about anyone in Granville.

Rayette was taking Lynn's murder hard. Kate had called her several times, but the call always went to voice mail. When she drove down Main Street the next morning, the bakery and café were dark.

There was a sign on the door: *Closed due to death*. A bundle of *Free Press* papers was languishing unopened on the sidewalk. Kate didn't even slow down to snag a copy. She didn't want to see what

Finn and Fast Eddie had made of the latest murder.

And she didn't want to think about her part in not preventing it. *If only, if only.*

Kate knew the uselessness of going down that road. If only she hadn't gone off half cocked. If only she'd known the girl's last name, maybe her initials as well as Rayette's would have popped out at her.

The streets were as empty as the bakery and café. The hardware store was the only business that seemed to have any customers—there were cars and trucks parked at the front door.

As Kate passed by, two more cars slid into spaces. It didn't take a rocket scientist to know why. Everyone was adding extra locks to doors and windows, outfitting their cars with alarms, buying pepper spray, and probably carrying handguns. It *was* the Live Free Or Die state, after all.

Kate just hoped that they didn't start shooting each other by mistake.

She considered going straight to the hospital to see if Brandon was better, but her daily visits were already becoming a source of gossip. She'd call instead or wait until Harry got to the museum after school. Taking Harry to visit the chief would be innocent enough.

Gloom settled over her as she turned toward the museum. It stayed with her while she waded through paperwork. Al eventually jumped down from the bookshelf and came over to keep her company. He soon lost interest in the account books and entertained himself by batting the pencils out of her pencil caddy and nosing her papers onto the floor.

Around noon, she took a break for lunch, then realized she should have gone shopping or brought some of the casserole from home, only she'd finished it the night before.

She drove to the Bowsman Inn.

Nancy Vance waved from the registration desk. "Hang on, Kate. The Town Council was just having a breakfast meeting. Sit down and I'll be with you as soon as I give them their change."

"Doesn't the council meet on Tuesday nights?"

Nancy pursed her lips and nodded. "An emergency meeting." She sighed and gathered up a stack of leather credit card receipt folders.

And that's when Kate got her first look at the morning's *Free Press*. It was sitting on the counter. "Killer Strikes Again. No one safe."

No wonder people were staying home in droves.

Kate stepped inside the dining room. It was virtually empty except for a large round table in the corner where the town council was meeting.

She chose a table by the window and sat down just as Charlie Saxon, the mayor of Granville, stood up.

"Welcome aboard." He shook hands with the man next to him.

Kate did a double take. What was Ted Lumley doing at the town council meeting? But Kate thought she knew. The mayor must be asking Ted to help with the investigation. How was that possible? You couldn't just borrow a cop from another state, could you? What about the county and state police?

And what about Brandon? Had he been consulted?

He wasn't in any shape to physically lead the team, but he could certainly coordinate it from a hospital bed or a chair.

Her appetite gone, Kate shoved her menu aside. How could they do this?

Wait, she told herself, *you're jumping to conclusions again*. A bad habit she had picked up since returning home to Granville.

The other council members started pushing back chairs and gathering bags and briefcases. Most of them gathered around the mayor and Ted.

Marian Teasdale spotted Kate, excused herself from the group, and made a beeline to Kate's table.

"May I join you for a minute?"

"Certainly," Kate said.

Marian sat and placed her handbag on the table. "Charlie just appointed Ted Lumley to head the investigation of the recent murders."

"I thought it might be something like that."

"He's convinced that the chief isn't in any shape to lead it, though when I visited him yesterday, he seemed a lot better. Charlie's up for reelection in the fall, and I think he's in a panic because the murders might reflect on his service.

"Quite frankly, I think he's acting prematurely. It's taken long enough for everyone to put their faith in the chief. Now they're about to have another Bostonian shoved down their throats."

"When was this decided?"

"It came as a fait accompli at the meeting," Marian answered. "Executive leeway or some such. He's already had flyers posted calling for a special town meeting tonight."

"Can he do that? Just replace the chief?"

"Normally he would appoint someone already on the force, but Charlie thinks no one on the force is experienced enough to handle the situation. And I must say, I do have to agree with him on that point. It was inevitable that he might appoint someone in the interim, but I think he's made an odd choice."

"Ted doesn't know anything about us," Kate said. "He hardly knows any of the townspeople. Certainly not Henny or Lynn. Wouldn't the county send anyone?"

"I have no idea. We were left out of the process. If you ask me— and this isn't just because I like Brandon Mitchell—someone has been lobbying for the position."

"Ted?"

Marian gave a noncommittal "Hmm."

"Why would he want to do this? He came to fish for a couple of weeks."

"I don't know. A busman's holiday? A chance to help out his old partner?"

"Does Brandon know?"

"I have no idea, but knowing Charlie, I doubt it."

"Kate." Ted strode toward them. She watched and wondered bitterly how someone with such a pronounced limp could carry out an investigation better than someone with a few bruises, a couple of fractured ribs, and a broken shoulder.

Stupid comparison. She wasn't being realistic. Or open-minded or fair. She was being a Granvilleite, she realized.

"You've probably just heard." Ted cut a meaningful look at Marian.

"Yes. Congratulations." Kate supposed that was what one was supposed to say under the circumstances.

"I'm just trying to help Bran out while he's down. I have to be at the town meeting tonight. Do you think you could keep Harry with you until I'm free?"

"Sure."

"Kate, I'm not trying to take Bran's job, if that's what you think." She wasn't thinking that. But she knew there were still people who didn't like the chief and who might use this as an excuse to get rid of him.

"Of course not. I'm sure Chief Mitchell will appreciate it." *Right up there with getting hit by a truck.*

"I sure hope so. Well, see you later. And thanks for watching out for Harry." He followed the others out.

Kate turned to Marian.

Marian raised her already arched eyebrows.

"At least Harry might get a breather," Kate said.

"Meaning?"

"Ted's been trying to play surrogate while the chief is in the hospital. Harry's not having any of it."

"Then he certainly won't like this latest development."

"No," Kate said, "I don't think he will at all."

Kate dragged a sulking Harry to the town meeting that night. He'd come in that afternoon already upset because Wynter's parents were holding firm on the grounding thing. She wasn't even allowed to take the bus, instead being driven to and from school by their housekeeper.

When he heard about Ted's appointment, he blew up. "It's not fair. He's taking over everything. He bosses me around like he's my . . . my . . . parole officer."

Kate fought a smile. "You don't have a parole officer."

"Or anything else," Harry mumbled and shuffled out of the room.

She didn't see him again until they left for the Town Hall.

The meeting room was filled when they arrived at the courthouse shortly before eight o'clock. The council was sitting at a long table on the stage at the front of the room. Marian caught Kate's eye and nodded. Ginny Sue stood and waved at Kate and Harry and pointed to two empty chairs next to her. She was sitting near the back, which was just as well. She hadn't told Ted that she and Harry were planning to lend a hand.

Kate squeezed past the knees of people already seated and fell into a place next to Ginny Sue.

"Thanks for saving us seats."

"I'm surprised how many people are here."

"Yeah," said Kate. "The Granville grapevine is an amazing thing."

"You sound unhappy."

"Two murders, the chief in the hospital, and a stranger taking over the police force?"

Ginny Sue patted her knee. She always—almost always—managed to see the silver lining. Kate took a good look at her friend. Maybe it was all those years of working with fourth-graders. Maybe she just saw it as her duty to make people feel better.

"Sorry. I'm just feeling a little stressed."

More than a little. Harry was not the only one upset by the announcement. Kate's New Hampshire stubbornness had flared to life with a vengeance. At least she called it that. If she let herself look more closely, she would know that it wasn't just Yankee stubbornness—it was also her fierce loyalty to the chief.

And Harry, she reminded herself. *Don't forget Harry*. Any change would be bad for him.

The mayor stood, and the screech of a microphone cut off further conversation.

"Glad so many of you could come at such short notice, and I hate to take you away from your busy lives—"

"Get on with it, Charlie. My missus's got dinner waiting."

"Thank you for sharing, Thaddeus Pike. We've all got things to do tonight. So if you'll just let me get on with it, we'll get out of here all the sooner."

"That'll be the day," Ginny Sue whispered.

"As you know, Granville has been beset by a spate of violent deaths recently—"

"Use plain English and we'll get outta here sooner."

"Let Charlie speak."

A smattering of applause.

Another typical town meeting in Granville, New Hampshire,

thought Kate. They could be here all night just to listen to one announcement.

"Unfortunately, our Police Chief, Brandon Mitchell—"

"We know who he is."

"A Beantowner."

"No, he ain't. He helped my Althea when her car swerved off the road. Didn't even charge her."

"That's right. He's helped lots of folks, so you stop your bad-mouthing, Pete Gulasky." Alice Hinckley had come out to speak her piece. Kate should have thought to ask if she needed a ride— *time to stop being so self involved,* Kate admonished herself. She gave Harry an encouraging smile and returned her attention to the mayor.

The mayor banged a gavel. Alice sat down.

"I've decided, in view of the situation and Chief Mitchell's accident, to appoint an interim chief of police to carry out the investigation. Fortunately, we have a visitor to the area who is well qualified to lead our small police force."

The room exploded. Kate stopped breathing. Not just aiding the investigation, but interim chief.

"Not another outsider."

"Give it to Ben Meany!"

"Get Roger Blanchard out of retirement."

"Roger couldn't find his fishing rod in a canoe!"

"Why can't county take over?"

"After carefully considering all angles," the mayor shouted, "I decided that an expert will be able to bring this to a conclusion quickly and return our fair town to safety. And Ted Lumley has graciously accepted. Ted is a high-ranking detective with the Boston Police Department."

A collective groan rose from the seats. "Not another one."

"What's the matter with you, Charlie?"

The mayor banged on the table. "I give you Ted Lumley," he shouted at the top of his lungs, then sat down.

Ted, who was sitting next to the mayor, stood up.

Arguing broke out in the seats. Ted waited calmly until there was a lull and said, "A serial killer is preying on your town. He won't stop at two murders."

The room instantly fell into silence.

Harry looked at Kate. If the panic had been marginal before, it would escalate exponentially by tomorrow.

Ted looked over the crowd. "I know you don't like this, and it's not exactly the way I intended on spending my vacation. But facts are facts. He's here and I can stop him before he kills again."

"What do you know—" The heckler was yanked back into his chair.

"What do I know about catching murderers? It's a good question. I've been a detective on the—" he smiled slightly "—*Beantown* police department for twenty-five years. I've seen my share of murders. Have sent a few killers to jail. But more than that, I worked several investigations that were instrumental in bringing three separate serial killers to justice. None as famous as The Boston Strangler, but just as deadly."

Kate couldn't control the shudder that rippled through her. Harry inched closer to her.

Ted held up his hand. Everyone watched, mesmerized, as he left his place at the lectern and walked slowly, obviously limping, around the table until he was standing at the edge of the stage.

Murmurs tumbled around the room. "The man's a cripple." "What's Charlie Saxon thinking?" "Oh, that poor man!" "In the line of duty, I heard. . ."

"I know you don't know me. But you know your police chief,

Brandon Mitchell. We were partners once. On one particularly nasty assignment, Bran got separated from the rest of the team. He needed my help then, and I was glad to give it, even though it got me this gimpy leg." He smiled deprecatingly. "Now his town needs help, and I'm here to do what I can."

A choked sob erupted from Harry, who sat rigidly beside Kate.

Kate's stomach turned sour. What was Ted doing? Win over the town by making Brandon seem incompetent? And he dared to lecture her!

"You need help. I'm willing to give it." He opened his hands. It was a theatrical gesture, but it worked. A smattering of applause started at the front of the room. It spread. Some people stood, and others began putting on coats and gathering in knots to opine about this latest change.

Harry cried, "No!" He pushed to his feet, scrambled past the other people in the row, and ran out of the room.

Kate lost sight of him immediately. "I've got to go."

"Run," Ginny Sue told her. "He shouldn't be out there in the dark."

CHAPTER

TWENTY-ONE

BY THE TIME Kate fought her way out of the courthouse, the green had begun to fill with people. She saw Simon Mack talking to her aunt and ran up to them. "Simon, did you see Harry? He just ran out of the meeting."

"Taking the change of command hard, is he?"

"Yes, did you see him?"

Simon shook his head. "Maybe Erik and Jason. They're standing over there."

She ran to where they were talking with Dan Graves. "Did you see Harry?"

"Ayuh," said Erik. "I called out to him, but he just kept running."

"Tough to see your hero taken down a peg," Jason added.

Kate had been about to run, but she stopped. "What do you mean?"

"Kinda talked like he saved Chief Mitchell's butt. Kinda sounds like maybe it was the chief's fault."

"Ayuh," agreed Erik. "Happened ten years ago. The chief was probably only in his twenties. Easy to make a mistake when you're that young."

"What are you talking about?"

"Just sayin'."

Kate gritted her teeth. "Which way did Harry go?"

"Cut across Main and took off up Morrow," said Jason.

Erik nodded. "Hell of a long walk if he's headed home."

"Thanks." Kate sprinted across the green and the street to the Farm and Mercantile Bank where she'd parked the Buick. She screeched out of the parking lot, hoping Pru hadn't seen her, made the immediate right and another right at the corner.

She cruised First Avenue looking for Harry, then stopped in the intersection at Morrow and peered down the darkened street back toward Main Street. The street was deserted.

Panic seized her. Her fingers were locked to the steering wheel, but she couldn't seem to move. Had he made it this far? Should she wait for him here, or go ahead? She looked to the left and saw a shadow of movement crossing Morrow at an angle.

It was too dark to really see, but she knew it was Harry. Everything about him was so familiar to her. She turned left, slowing down as she reached him.

She lost valuable seconds stopping and leaning over the seat to roll down the passenger window and cursed the Buick for not having power windows.

Harry saw her and took off at a run. Kate sped up and brought the Buick alongside of him.

"I know you're upset, but please get in the car."

"Go away."

"I can't go away. There's a killer out there—"

"So what? He's ruined everything."

"Harry, please. I'm not any happier than you are about the situation."

His step faltered. He stopped, leaned over, and braced his hands on his knees while he gulped in air.

Kate braked to a stop.

Finally he looked up. "I hate him."

She knew that Harry was feeling his world slip out of his grasp. It had taken months for him to start trusting Kate and the chief, but he'd made the effort and it had worked. Now everything was blowing up in his face.

Kate felt the same way. It wasn't Ted's fault, but she wasn't about to say so. She just wanted to get Harry in the car.

"Come on. We'll go get some dinner."

"I'm not hungry." But he trudged toward the car, yanked the door open, and slumped on the seat. "It sucks."

"It does."

"I want the chief back."

"So do I."

Rayette's was closed, Harry was too young for the Granville Bar and Grill, and Kate didn't want to meet anybody they knew at the Bowsman. They drove to the next town, where there were several fast-food restaurants to chose from.

"Fried chicken or burgers?"

"Burgers."

Kate pulled into the parking lot and they walked into the restaurant, not speaking, both feeling forlorn.

"It's not fair," Harry said as soon as they sat down to their burgers and fries. "I wish Ted had never come. Now we'll never get rid of him."

"Of course we will. You heard him. He's on vacation. He has his own job back in Boston." She frowned.

"What?" Harry asked.

"What what?"

Harry heaved a sigh. "You looked like you'd thought of something."

"No. But . . . has the chief ever said anything about what happened when he was shot?"

"Not before Ted came." Harry frowned at his burger. "He doesn't say anything about it now. Ted's said some things. Not outright, but like he thinks the chief made a mistake and it was his fault that Ted got shot."

Kate grunted. "I got that impression too." She saw Harry's face fire up and hurriedly went on. "The impression that *Ted* thinks so. Doesn't the chief stick up for himself?"

Harry shook his head. "I even asked him why he didn't say something. He just said, 'Water under the bridge' and asked me about my homework or something."

Changing the subject, thought Kate. Why? The Brandon she knew wouldn't make that kind of mistake. But he *had* been young, though it was hard to imagine him as anything but an adult, tough and taciturn, now lying in a hospital bed because he'd shoved her out of the way of a speeding truck. Not the kind of man who would let another man take a bullet for him.

Not now anyway. And it was fruitless to speculate about the past.

"If you're finished, I'll drive you home."

"I don't want to go home. I'll sleep at the museum."

"Harry, I'm tired. Let's not do the sleep at the museum discussion again, okay? When you're eighteen, if you want to move out of the chief's, we'll talk."

"You mean like if he's still here even."

"He'll be here." If Kate had to chain him to his squad car. No way was he leaving. Harry needed a home. Harry needed the chief.

It took them twenty minutes to drive back to Granville, and another ten to get to the chief's house. He lived in the north of town, where residential blocks turned to woods. The front of his house was set back from the winding road and the back opened onto a view of Otter Creek. A light blazed on the front porch and several security lights shone down from the eaves of the garage.

The house itself was what the locals called a New Englander, part Cape, part bungalow, with a big stone and clapboard central part and a one-story addition off to one side.

Kate pulled into the driveway. Ted's old black sedan was parked in front of the garage.

Harry let out a groan. "You want to come inside?"

Kate had dropped Harry off numerous times, but she'd never been invited inside. And she certainly wasn't going in without the chief's knowledge.

"Thanks, but I'll just wait here until you're inside. And be nice."

Harry gave her a look and got out of the car.

She waited until he was safely inside before driving away. While Harry had been with her, she'd listened and commiserated but tried to convince him that Ted was in an awkward position and was only trying to help. But once she was driving back across town to her own bungalow and had time to look at her own feelings, she had to admit that she, too, wished Ted had never come.

She understood what it was. Jealousy. She was jealous that Ted had stepped into Harry and Brandon's lives, and she felt left out. Jealous that he would get the glory if he caught the killer, which would belittle Brandon in the eyes of the town. They might not even want him to stay on as chief of police.

Jealous that she would have to turn over her evidence to Ted instead of working with Brandon.

She'd been saving her information about the e-mails to give to Brandon when he was up to speed, but now it looked as if she would have to cooperate with Ted. And that burned her. She liked Ted, but she didn't trust him.

He was an outsider, and though she'd been away for almost a decade, it seemed that you could take the girl out of New England, but you couldn't take the Yankee stubbornness out of the girl.

Erik, Jason, and Dan Graves were having breakfast at Rayette's when Kate went in for her latte the next morning. They were all reading the *Free Press*.

Erik saw her and waved her over. Kate grabbed her own copy off the counter and went to join them.

"Mornin', Katie," Erik said.

"Katie," echoed Jason.

Dan nodded.

Erik gestured to a seat. The gesture was as much order as invitation. Kate sat down.

Erik stabbed his copy of the *Free Press* with his fork. "Have you seen this?"

"Not yet." Kate laid her copy on the table.

"'Ted Lumley Appointed Head of Serial Killer Investigation,'" Erik read out loud. "Makes it sound like he's the new police chief."

"Ayuh," Jason echoed.

Erik continued to read out loud. "'Mayor of Granville, New Hampshire, Charlie Saxon'—does he think we don't know where we live and who our mayor is?—'appointed Ted Lumley, Boston Police Department detective, to head the investigation into the recent murders of the local citizens.'

"'Detective Lumley comes with excellent credentials. He has served in the BPD for thirty years, and actually mentored

Granville's permanent Police Chief Brandon Mitchell, who is out with injuries . . .' blah, blah, blah."

"Get to the good part," Jason said.

If there is a good part, Kate thought.

"I'm getting there." Erik ran a pudgy index finger down the column.

Jason nodded. "Ayuh. Read her the part about how that investigation him and the chief were on, got him crippled."

Erik pushed the paper toward Kate. "You'd best read what he says for yourself." He pointed to the place.

Kate started to read. "It was a major drug bust. We knew that this particular group had a contract out on a warring drug lord. We were spreading out to surround the apartment building. Brandon, Police Chief Mitchell, was the first into the alley. Impetuous, young, he wasn't thinking clearly. He went down. And all h— broke loose. It was all I could do to grab him and drag him out of the line of fire. That's when I got hit. Of course, it was my responsibility. He was just a rookie."

"Now what do you think of that?" Erik asked.

Kate was speechless.

"He makes Chief Mitchell sound incompetent. Ayuh," Jason said.

"It gets worse. They asked him if he had worked with Mitchell since then and he tells them no, but not because of what happened, and he's sure the chief is very competent."

"What?" Kate almost choked on the word. "What a condescending—ugh. If he thinks he'll get people to cooperate with him by putting down the chief, he should think again. The people around here might not love the chief, but he's closer to being one of us than Ted Lumley."

Rayette came up with Kate's latte. She looked pale and harried.

"How are you?" Kate asked, though the answer was obvious.

"I tell ya, it's bad enough that that filthy, scumbag, evil whoever killed my waitress, but now." Rayette slapped her hands on her skirt. "An hour ago, Ted Lumley walks in here cool as you please and takes Calvin in for questioning."

"Ayuh," said Erik. "Took him away like a common criminal."

"He sure did," Jason seconded. "Said he was going to take him down to the station. Hmmph. Just shows ya. You don't go down to the station in Granville. You go across the street."

Rayette glared at him. "Now we're working without a cook and a waitress. There's no way Calvin could have killed Lynn—it's absurd. And while Ted Lumley's wasting time, the killer is free to kill somebody else. I sure hope Chief Mitchell makes a quick recovery."

"Hey, Rayette. Can we get some coffee over here?"

"Grrr," Rayette said and hurried away.

"It's going to be a witch hunt," said Dan.

It was the first thing he'd said, and Kate stared at him. His eyes didn't meet hers. He and Calvin both had worked with Lynn. Was he afraid he would be questioned next?

Kate knew how hard the locals could be on newcomers. "I'm sure they are just questioning him because he was one of the last people to see Lynn alive."

"A witch hunt," Dan mumbled and poked moodily at his half-eaten eggs.

Jason and Erik eyed Dan with curiosity and—Kate was afraid—with suspicion.

Was it starting?

Dan was new in town. Calvin had worked at the Brick House, but he'd lived in Granville for the last three years. Would they turn on Jason next? He'd been here for over fifteen years, and they still sometimes razzed him about being new.

Kate sucked in her breath. This could get nasty. It was difficult for any town to believe that one of its own might be a killer. And it was even harder for an insular town like Granville that kept to itself and didn't suffer strangers, even tourists, lightly.

Kate had been guilty too. When she'd made her list of suspects, she'd listed the newbies first. But the more she thought and theorized, the more she came to believe that a serial killer hadn't suddenly taken up residence among them.

It was someone who knew them. Knew her. Someone who wanted her involved.

Kate picked up the *Free Press* and continued to read the rest of the article.

There was an account of the decade-old police sting in a sidebar to the article. It was bare-bones: number of police injured, number of arrests. But as Finn had told her, he spun stories to sell papers, and his expanded account blossomed into something right out of *Law and Order*. Two policemen cornering a drug gang, waiting for backup. Brandon attempting to rush the gang and getting caught in the crossfire. Going down. Ted dragging him to safety and taking the bullet that crippled him.

By the end of the story, Ted was the hero and Brandon just another screwup rookie.

Kate didn't believe it. Even at his greenest, Brandon would never do something so stupid, and certainly not for the glory—unless he'd really changed. And Kate didn't believe that either.

But was this Ted's version of what happened, or Finn's spin on it?

It didn't matter, she realized, not to her anyway. What did matter was how Brandon would react if he saw the article. He'd probably feel humiliated, since there was no way he could justify himself. He might have a relapse. He might even resign.

She'd just have to make sure he didn't see it.

"I've got to run." She shrugged into her jacket and stood up. "Oh, I found a brown scarf at the museum Monday night after the meeting. With everything else, I forgot about it. Does it belong to one of you? It's in the lost-and-found box."

Erik and Jason shook their heads. Dan touched his collar as if he expected to find the scarf there. "I have a brown scarf. I might have left it there. I haven't worn it since the rain let up."

"You can pick it up or I'll keep it until the next meeting." Kate took her latte and headed for the door.

Rayette caught up to her in the bakery.

"Kate, wait a minute." She hooked her hand in Kate's elbow and practically dragged her through the door to the kitchen.

Calvin stood at the center island, chopping celery like there was no tomorrow. He stopped, knife poised in the air, when he saw Kate.

"Listen, I didn't kill Lynn. I mean, why would I?"

Kate eyed the knife.

Calvin glanced at it. "Oh." He quickly laid it on the cutting board.

"This guy, Lumley, thinks just because I knew Lynn . . . I mean, jeez, we worked together. You have an in with Chief Mitchell. Tell him I didn't do it."

Kate didn't have to tell Calvin that the chief was in the hospital; the whole town knew. At the moment there was nothing he could do to help Calvin or anybody else.

And besides, something wasn't ringing true in Calvin's story. The way his eyes flitted from her face to the table and back again made her think he was holding something back. That he knew more than he'd told the police.

Kate felt totally out of her league. She didn't know how to break a suspect into confessing—she could barely carry on a normal conversation. She gave him a look. "I'm sure it was just information gathering. Not to worry."

But Calvin was worried. "I wasn't exactly forthright with them. I mean, it's none of their business."

"Oh, Lord. I guess you'd better spill it all, and I'll relay it to the chief."

"Okay." Calvin hesitated, using the knife to form the celery pieces into a square mound. Finally he looked up. "Lynn and I had a thing for a while when we were at the Brick House." He let out a depressed sigh and scattered the pile of celery bits.

Gone was the brash, in-your-face, seen-it-all chef of a few days ago. Calvin Jones was scared.

"Did you tell this to the police?"

"Hell, no," he said with a little of his old bravura. "It was months before we came to work for Rayette.

"Lynn was just working until she saved enough money to go back to school. She was living with her aunt near the restaurant. She didn't have a chance for much fun. We started kidding around, went out a few times. One thing led to another, you know, like it does. Then it was over." He shrugged. "Poor kid. How could they think I would hurt her?"

He raised his head. "You'll help, right? Rayette said I should talk to you."

Kate had never intentionally investigated in opposition to an official investigation. Well, maybe when she'd been the chief suspect, but then she'd had no choice. Her other involvements were mere happenstance. But if she helped Calvin, she would knowingly be interfering, maybe even obstructing.

"Please?"

Oh, rats. He sounded so pathetic. But if she were honest—and she always was—she'd known all along that she would help him, because no way was she going to help Ted make the chief look bad, even if he didn't mean to. And besides, there was the sticky issue of those undisclosed e-mails.

"All right, but just between you and me. Don't tell anyone you've spoken to me."

Calvin nodded and leaned forward on his elbows.

"You and Dan and Lynn all worked at the Brick House before you came to Rayette's?"

"Until the fire. Then, we were all out of work, and Dan got the idea we should apply for jobs over here. He'd already applied for a job at the Bowsman, even before the fire. He's kind of a brain and is always working crosswords and stuff, so when he heard about the Puzzle Museum and all the clubs, he decided to move closer so he could join."

Interesting. "When was that?"

"About a month ago. Shouldn't you be writing this down?"

Kate shook her head and pointed to her temple.

Calvin looked skeptical.

"And?"

"And so we did. Lynn and I got hired by Rayette just about the same time Dan was hired at the Inn. Worked out great—not everybody was that lucky." His features twisted. "God. Not so lucky for Lynn."

"Did you all get along?"

"Sure. It's like I told the cops, I hardly ever saw Dan or Lynn except when I was passing plates through the service window. Except for that really short time with Lynn."

Kate couldn't help it. She was suckered in. Lynn was dead, and this man had been her lover.

"Do you mind if I ask why you, uh, broke up?"

Calvin laughed softly. "She's really sweet, but too damn perky for me."

Kate got a flash of the cute, bouncy waitress and was hit by a pang of sadness. It wasn't fair that someone took away her life, her hopes, her future. She remembered Harry's infatuation, how he told her that Lynn was nice and he and the chief liked her.

"Okay, tell me exactly what happened the night she was killed."

Calvin scraped fingers through his hair. "We closed up kind of early because there were no customers. Everyone's too spooked to stay out late after that Dougan guy got killed in the alley out back.

"Lynn was parked down in the public lot, and Rayette asked me to walk her to her car and see that she got in safely." Calvin sucked back a sob. "She got in and I left. I would've gone back for Rayette, but she'd already moved her Vette around front, so she told me not to bother.

"So I got on my bike and rode out to Jumpin' Jack's for a couple of beers."

"Motorcycle?"

"Kawasaki."

"And there were people there who could vouch for you?"

"Witnesses? Sure. I don't really know who the hell they were, but somebody ought to remember me."

"Do you go to Jumpin' Jack's often?"

"It's either that or the Bar and Grill. I sort of alternate between them."

"When did you leave?"

"Around eleven. I went home." He shook his head. "I should have followed her home. Why didn't I follow her home?"

A rhetorical question that would probably haunt him for years to come. If he was telling the truth.

The chief needed to know about this. Maybe she should question Dan, too, then take what she learned to the chief.

Kate would have to be his eyes and ears until he was on his feet again.

He'd yell at her—if he could stay awake long enough. But he would have enough facts to start investigating.

The chief would solve this case, not Ted Lumley.

CHAPTER

TWENTY-TWO

KATE WASN'T SURE if visiting hours had begun, but she was too impatient to wait. She walked purposefully down the corridor and stopped at Brandon's room. She tapped lightly on the door, then slipped inside.

A nurse was leaning over the bed. "Now stay put or I'll have to ask everyone to leave." She flicked the end of a syringe, and though Brandon protested, she flipped his arm over and slid the needle deftly underneath the skin.

Kate looked away and into a sea of flowers. They were on the dresser, on the floor, even on one of the chairs. Balloons filled with helium stretched to the ceiling.

Harry stood at the far side of the bed holding a laptop computer. Elmira Swyndon stood at the foot of the bed clutching a large manila envelope behind her back.

"Don't upset him," the nurse said and left the room.

The chief had stilled, and he lay motionless on the bed, his eyes closed.

Kate swallowed, anxiety making her mouth dry. She went to stand next to Elmira. "What happened?"

"Some fool candy striper showed him a copy of today's *Free Press*. He tried to get up. Someone oughta teach Finn Tucker a thing or two about legitimate reporting."

"Damn," said Kate.

"Katie," Elmira said in surprise.

"Pizza," said Harry, but his eyes were on Brandon.

The chief's eyes fluttered open and a brief instant of amusement filled them. Kate smiled back just before they closed again. The surge of relief she felt fled as exasperation replaced it.

"Brandon? Chief?"

He forced his eyes open. "Don't . . ." He tried to push himself up on his good arm.

"Cuss, I know. I'll buy the darn pizza. Now lie down before you break the other shoulder. And just listen."

"Don't . . ." His voice trailed off on a faint, "damn."

The three of them waited, but the chief didn't rouse again. After several frustrating minutes, Kate motioned toward the door. Elmira followed her out, but Harry hung back.

"Harry," Kate whispered.

Ignoring her, Harry pulled a chair close to the bed, but instead of sitting in it, he placed the laptop on the seat where Brandon could reach it when he woke up. He slid a bulging backpack off his shoulder and placed it on top of the computer, then scribbled a note on the pad on the bedside table and placed the pad on top of the backpack.

He followed Kate and Elmira into the hallway.

"I tried to get here before he saw the article," Kate told them. "I knew someone was bound to have a copy, and I didn't want him to get upset."

"Which he was," Elmira said.

"It's a lie," whispered Harry, barely managing to get the words out. Kate saw how pale he was, and she wished she could put her arm around him, but she knew it would only embarrass him and make things worse.

"It didn't happen that way. It couldn't."

"It doesn't matter, Harry. It's in the past."

"Everybody will believe Ted because they don't like the chief."

"That's not true," Kate said. "Plenty of people like the chief. Look at all those flowers and balloons."

"It's just the GABs and a few others."

"And what's wrong with our flowers?" asked Elmira with mock indignation.

It won her a slight smile, which just as quickly dissipated.

"Whether it's true or not, that's not what upset the chief," Elmira said.

"What upset him then?"

"Beats me. He was reading the paper when I came in. He tried to get out of bed, I called the nurse, and that's when you came." Elmira straightened the envelope she held and frowned pensively at it. "I brought this for him."

Kate craned her neck to look at the face of the ten-by-fourteen manila envelope. It looked liked it contained a lot of paperwork. "What is it?"

"A copy of the police report from Lynn Zimmerman's murder. I thought maybe it would help him pass the time. You know, like that mystery novel where the detective is in the hospital."

"*Daughter of Time*," Harry said automatically, then looked at Kate. "Are you thinking what I'm thinking?"

Kate was, but she didn't want to admit it. Her fingers itched to snatch the envelope from Elmira's hands. But she was pretty sure that the report was confidential and that showing it to Kate would be highly illegal. She didn't want Elmira to be some kind of accessory to whatever crime they might be about to commit. And she knew for sure that she shouldn't involve a fourteen-year-old boy.

Then again, this was no longer an armchair investigation. It was for real, and though it went against the grain, it seemed a perfect time to resort to situational ethics.

She had to see that report.

"Well, I don't know about Kate, but *I'm* thinking what you're thinking." Elmira waved the folder. "There's a nice empty waiting room just down the hall. I checked it out on my way in." She lifted her eyebrows in a question.

Without a word, Harry and Kate followed her down the hall.

The waiting room was empty. Elmira led them to a far corner before she opened the overlarge envelope and handed it to Kate.

Kate glanced through its contents with Harry and Elmira peering over her shoulders. There was a series of color photographs beneath the written report. They were more detailed and a lot gorier than the ones Fast Eddie had taken.

"Poor Sam," Elmira said. "He really hates being police photographer."

Of course. Sam must have taken these. He was probably feeling pretty down, and Kate hadn't even thought about him or his proposal since dinner at the Bowsman. As soon as this was over . . .

She passed over several wide shots of the scene, each so clear that it could have been daytime.

"Infrared photography," Harry said as if reading her mind.

Trampled weeds, a pile of tire irons, a half-standing barbed wire fence, and farther back, the abandoned railroad tracks. Why on earth had Lynn gone there?

Unless someone had forced her.

She slid the photo to the back and her breath caught. Lynn, her body propped against a tree, her uniform twisted at her waist. Her legs were stretched out in front of her, covered in matted, wet leaves. Strands of hair were pulled from her ponytail and hung limply over one side of her face. A long purple bruise bisected her throat.

Kate's stomach lurched.

Elmira sobbed. "Oh."

"Bastard," Harry whispered. "Bastard."

What had she been thinking to let Harry see these? Although how she could have prevented him once he knew what was in the envelope was beyond her.

She passed quickly over the rest of the photos until she came to a close-up of the driver's door, partially opened.

Where the killer had pulled her from the car?

An even closer shot of the driver's door: a thread of some kind was caught in the handle.

Kate lifted the picture and looked more closely. Excitement vibrated through her. A clue?

She flipped back to the printed report and quickly read the stats. Place, time, victim's description, and a list of forensic evidence that had been sent to the lab.

Plaster casts had been made of the surrounding ground, which was wet from the recent rain. Chunks of sod had been churned up. They were only able to get partial footprints.

It seemed that Lynn had struggled.

But not enough, thought Kate and instinctively touched her throat.

Fingerprints of the victim. Several other sets as yet unidentified.

Interiors of car and trunk had been vacuumed.

A two-inch section of brown yarn was found caught in the handle of the car door.

Brown yarn, Kate thought. It must have broken off from a larger piece. Had it been the murder weapon? It seemed so cruel.

DNA samples per the coroner.

The report was signed by the county crime scene detective, and the first officer on the scene, Dickie Owens.

He'd done a good job: kept his head, secured the area, and called the county police. Brandon had trained him well.

Kate sighed and closed the report.

Elmira reached for the papers. "I can't let you keep them. I shouldn't have even brought them to the chief, seeing how his partner has taken over the investigation."

"Ex," snapped Harry. "Ex-partner."

"Yes, well. I thought he should see these. And now thanks to that busybody candy striper, they sedated him again, and I have to get these back before they're missed. Now what do I do?"

"Make a copy before you turn them in," Harry said.

Kate and Elmira looked at him.

"The chief should see these. He's still the chief."

"You're absolutely right. I'll drop by the library on my way back to town. The copy machine is in an alcove by the water fountain. I don't dare take them to Kinko's."

They rode back to the museum in tense silence. Harry had skipped school and informed Kate that he wasn't going back until further notice. "Ted will be busy with the investigation. He probably won't even notice. He was gone before sunrise this morning. I'm going to help you solve the murders."

"We should let the police handle it," Kate told him halfheartedly.

"You keep saying that, but Ted is not the police. He's an outsider. He has no business poking his nose into our business and screwing up everything."

"Maybe not, but he's in charge, and there's nothing we can do."

"Bull—"

"Harry."

That's when the silent treatment began. Harry stared out the passenger window until they came to the turnoff to school. Kate slowed down.

"Keep going or I'll jump out of the car," he threatened.

Kate drove past the turn but pulled to the shoulder and brought the old Buick to a stop.

Harry, expecting a lecture, hunkered down in the seat and crossed his arms defensively over his chest.

"Harry," Kate began, hoping she would find the right words to get through to him. "The chief means a lot to me, too. But we can help him best by not getting involved with the investigation. That's what he would want."

No response.

"I want to stop these killings just as much as you do. And yes, I'd rather it happen without Ted's interference."

A flicker of interest.

"But—"

"You don't like him either."

That caught her off guard. "It's not a question of like. It's a question of . . ."

Jealousy. Pure and simple. She didn't want Ted horning in on their way of life any more than Harry did. She wanted Brandon to solve the case, she wanted to help him, and she wanted Harry to be happy again. She wanted things the way they had been.

Stunned, she tried to rationalize her response. It was a question of inertia. Everyone liked things to stay the same. It was comfortable. As a citizen of Granville, it was logical for her to question a stranger's ability to gain the cooperation of the townspeople during the investigation.

It only made sense that she felt this way. She started up the Buick and pulled back onto the pavement.

"Kate?"

"Uh-huh."

"The chief likes you."

Kate's hands slipped on the wheel. She pulled the car back on track.

"I know he doesn't always act like it. But he does."

"Well, that's good to know."

"I mean really likes, you know?"

When Kate didn't answer, he went on. "It's okay if you and him, you know. I mean. It would be cool. Then you could be—" He stopped abruptly.

Kate panicked. She knew what he meant. She'd figured out a while ago that Harry was beginning to look on the chief as a role model. That had been her intention all along, when she'd forced Brandon to let Harry live with him.

Now she realized that it had become more. Harry was beginning to think of the chief as a father figure. And if the chief liked her . . . He'd caught himself before he'd said what she was afraid he might have said. *You could be my mother.*

She had no idea how to respond—she was way out of her comfort zone. She dealt with facts, with numbers, with information. Not only was she not old enough to be Harry's mother, but it was a subject that had never come up between Brandon and her.

He'd never made any kind of move that made her think he was anything more than a harassed police chief, certainly none that would indicate she meant any more to him than the next person. And she hadn't given the matter any thought . . . until Sam's proposal.

"It doesn't matter." Harry slumped back in his seat and went back to staring out the window. Covering his bases, not getting his hopes up. Protecting himself.

It broke Kate's heart.

She let out a slow breath. "I like the chief, too. And that's why I think we shouldn't do anything to upset him." And what he didn't know . . .

"Yeah, whatever."

They fell back into silence, caught up in their own thoughts, for the rest of the ride to the museum.

As soon as they were inside, Harry bounded past her and up the stairs to P. T.'s Place. He spent a lot of time there experimenting with his favorite interest: codes and ciphers. Kate guessed he also went there to think, maybe even to feel close to the professor. And to wonder about life.

Alice was sitting at the reception desk.

"You're here early."

Alice smiled. "The early bird catches the worm."

"Good advice," Kate said. And a wake-up call for her to stop mulling over her love life and start finding a killer. She climbed the stairs, put water on the office hot plate, and sat down at the desk.

She had to admit she resented Ted as much as Harry did, and if she were honest, for much the same reasons. She'd told Harry they shouldn't get involved, but she *was* involved. The killer was sending her clues, using the things she loved—Sudoku puzzles—to bait her. She knew she should turn over everything she knew to Ted, but she couldn't.

She was so lost in thought that she yelped when Aloysius butted open the old dumbwaiter chute and glided into the room. He performed a figure eight around her ankles, but instead of jumping to the desk, he leapt to the windowsill where he stretched out and began to wash his paws.

The kettle whistled, making her jump. She got up to steep the tea, then wandered to the window and looked out. It was overcast again and getting colder. Pretty normal for early spring, but if she looked closely, she could just see a touch of green on the branches of the tree that grew just outside the window.

Spring. A time of birth and growth. It shouldn't be a time of murder.

She turned away, paced the length of the room, scanned the bookshelves without any purpose in mind. Stopped at the pedestal with its crystal ball. She placed her hand on it, felt the glass cool beneath her palm.

"If you were a real crystal ball, you'd help me catch this killer," she said.

Al let out a derisive "Yeow" from across the room.

"I know. Logic, not crystal balls, will help me figure this out."

She checked the tea and pressed the intercom to P. T.'s Place.

"Tea's ready."

The telephone rang.

"Avondale Puzzle Museum."

"Kate, it's Elmira." Her voice was low and muffled as if she had a hand pressed over the phone.

"They found a brown scarf belonging to Dan Graves in the Dumpster behind the Bowsman Inn. Ted Lumley has taken Curtis and Wilson to the Inn to bring him in. All hell will break lose when the town finds out."

A witch hunt, Dan had said at Rayette's after Ted had taken Calvin in for questioning. So far two new residents had come under suspicion. As far as Kate knew, Ted hadn't even bothered to question Tess Dougan, which would have been the most natural thing to do and what the chief would have done.

This really could turn into a witch hunt.

A piece of brown yarn found at the crime scene. A brown scarf found in the Dumpster at the Inn. Dan had a brown scarf. He worked at the Inn. It was incriminating but not conclusive. And besides, Dan had left his scarf at the museum.

Kate had found it on the floor the night Ted chastised her for interfering. She'd put in the lost-and-found box. It must still be there.

She jumped up just as Harry came in. She ran past him.

"Where are you going?"

"Downstairs."

She took the stairs two at a time. Alice hung up the phone as Kate ran past her.

"Anything the matter?"

"Hmm," Kate said. She threw open the closet door and dragged the lost-and-found box out into the foyer. Pulled out piece after piece but found no brown scarf. She went back, knelt down and searched the closet floor, then rifled through the coat hangers.

She dumped the contents of the lost-and-found box onto the marble floor and went through each item one by one before returning them to the box. There was no brown scarf.

She nearly jumped out of her skin when Harry said, "What are you doing?" not a foot behind her.

"Looking for Dan's scarf. Have you seen it?"

Alice had started on another phone call, but she placed her hand over the receiver and asked, "Who's Dan?"

"The new waiter at the Bowsman. He left his scarf here after the Arcane Masters meeting Sunday night. Have you seen it?"

Alice shook her head and went back to her phone call.

"A brown scarf?" Harry asked, already up to speed.

Kate pushed the box into the closet and closed the door. "A brown scarf." She paused. "A brown scarf left at the museum—a brown scarf found in the Dumpster behind the Bowsman Inn—the Granville homeless. Harry, get your jacket."

"Where are we going?"

"The *Free Press*. Alice, you'll have to—" Kate stopped.

Alice was standing by the front door, her purse in her hand and her coat draped over her arm.

"You'll have to close up, Katie. I can't stay."

Both men were in the office when Kate and Harry arrived at the Free Press. Finn Tucker was sitting behind a cumbersome computer console opened to a half-filled layout page.

"Katie darlin'," Finn said, standing up. "And the noble Harry. What brings you to our humble establishment?"

"I'm looking for Fast Eddie."

"Right with ya," came a voice from the back room.

Kate didn't wait, but marched through the door, Harry on her heels. And Finn right behind him.

Eddie looked up from where he was cropping a picture of an old man sitting outside the Market Basket, looking forlorn and holding a sign printed in quavering letters, I'm Hungry.

"Make-work," he said, disgusted. "Tell me you've discovered the identity of the serial killer and I can get a reprieve from articles on the Granville hungry."

"That's old man Brewster," Harry said, stepping closer to the picture. "How did you con him into holding that sign? He owns the dry cleaners. He's not homeless."

"Forgot his glasses that day. Told him he was collecting for charity. He made five bucks and change while I took a few fast ones of him." Eddie shrugged. "So entertain me."

Kate didn't see any way she could get what she wanted without letting him and Finn in on what was happening. And she was certain that making them swear to secrecy would be futile, not to mention naive. But she had no choice.

"Remember when I was in here the other day?"

"The fiery Valkyrie," said Finn and grinned.

"You had pictures of the uh, crime scene."

"Yeah, I remember," Eddie said.

"*But,*" Finn interrupted, "if you want to see them again, you'll have to let us in on the whys and wherefores."

"I don't want to see them. I want to see the other ones you took that night. For the article on the homeless in Granville. Do you still have them?"

"Yeah, you never know when you'll need some filler." Eddie clicked into his photo gallery.

"Now wait just a minute, darlin'." Finn moved to cut off her view of the screen. "What's so important about those photos?"

"It's a hunch," Kate said. "If I find something useful, you'll be the first to know."

Finn eyed her speculatively. "You really ought to come to work for me. We could go national if we had a reporter with your tenacity. Go ahead, Eddie, and let the lady see."

A strip of pictures appeared at the bottom of the screen. They were pictures of the crime scene.

"Scroll back to the ones of your homeless people."

The photos moved across the screen, one series replacing another until they finally came to the ones she wanted.

"Can you make these larger?"

Fast Eddie's fingers moved across the keyboard. The series disappeared, and a larger photo filled the screen: an old woman sitting with a battered shopping cart in the vacant lot of the gas station outside of town.

Kate frowned, momentarily distracted. Did they really have homeless people in Granville?

"The next one."

A click. The "I'm Hungry" photo at the Market Basket.

Fast Eddie raised his eyebrow at Kate.

Kate shook her head.

Again the screen changed.

"This one?"

Two skinny children playing down by the river.

Kate shook her head.

"This?"

"No."

Fast Eddie blew out air. Brought up another photo, then another.

And there it was. Dark and shadowy, but she could definitely make out Eddie's homeless man rummaging in a Dumpster.

"That one."

CHAPTER

TWENTY-THREE

IT WAS THERE—right in front of her, most likely the convicting evidence that would bring the Granville killer to justice.

If only it were readable, the figure recognizable. What she saw was the dark rectangle of the Dumpster, the shadowy wall of the inn in the background, and a white starburst from a security light just out of frame.

The photo was obviously taken in color even though it appeared in various shades of black and brown. The figure was an indistinct silhouette, a man or a woman in a formless coat.

His body curved as his left arm stretched up to hold the lid of the Dumpster open. His other hand held something that might be a crumpled bag, a half-filled garbage bag, or a brown scarf. Was he taking something out or putting something in? Impossible to tell.

Kate could feel Harry beside her. Close. His attention focused on the same details she was focusing on.

"Can you get better resolution?" Harry asked.

Eddie threw up one hand. "Sure. If I had equipment that didn't come over on the Mayflower. I've got the pixels in the camera, just not enough dpi on the screen."

"If you had better equipment and software?" Harry asked.

Seeing where this might be going, Kate warned, *"Harry."*

"How much better?" Eddie was hooked.

"State of the art."

"Where?"

"What's this about?" Finn, who had been hovering close by, muscled his way into the group.

When neither Kate nor Harry answered him, he reached over and pulled the plug on the computer.

"Hey," cried Eddie. "You could lose important data that way." He reached for the cord, but Finn stopped him.

"First I want to know what these two are up to."

"And how you can cash in on it," Kate said, letting her disgust show.

"I'm a journalist."

"Is that what you call it?"

Finn's nostrils flared. "Do you want to play or do you want to leave?"

Kate deliberated. If there was a chance those photos could be enhanced enough to be used as evidence . . .

She should call the police and tell them to confiscate Eddie's equipment; it might help wrap up the case. Help Ted wrap up the case.

On the other hand—

"I'm growing gray here," Finn complained.

"I'm thinking." It was her duty to report this to the police, and yet . . . hadn't Tess said that the police were in the hospital? Wynter had pretty much said the same thing. And Kate agreed with them.

She'd get the information and pass it along to the chief. Not to an outsider, no matter how well-meaning, who would go back to Boston when it was over and leave them to live with the consequences.

"We'll make a deal."

Finn broke into that grin she was learning to know and detest. "I'm all ears."

She looked at Harry. He dipped his chin. Yes.

"We think those photos might be evidence in the recent murders."

"No shit?" Fast Eddie leaned over and flipped the surge protector. "You better hope that nothing got bollixed when you pulled the juice on me."

The screen appeared. Fast Eddie rapidly clicked through his row of photos. All appeared unharmed and everyone, including Finn, breathed a sigh of relief.

"And why do you think this?"

Kate studied Finn's face. She didn't trust him, and he could really mess up the case if he leaked information too soon. Not to mention what it might do to her—jail maybe?

"I have my reasons. Here's the deal. If Fast Eddie can get a definable photo, one with enough detail, I'll tell you the rest."

"Like I'll go for that."

"Take it or leave it."

Finn glanced at Fast Eddie. "You'll have to do better than that."

Kate bit her lip.

Harry stepped forward. "Let's go, Kate. I knew it would be a bust. They don't have the equipment to do it, but they don't want to cooperate with us." He started walking toward the door.

Hoping he had a plan, Kate followed him.

"I can find the equipment," Fast Eddie boasted. "Somewhere. Manchester or Nashua probably."

"Go ahead. You pedaling your Schwinn to get there?"

"You have a high-res monitor?"

"Yep. We've got the business and we're willing to let you use it." Harry turned. "On our terms of course."

Kate smiled in admiration.

"How high is it?"

"Synchmaster three oh five. That should do it. Or if not, we've also got Apple Cinema, plus we have Photoshop Extended."

"Jeez. Your dad?"

"My, uh, roommate."

Eddie closed out the photos and disconnected the SD card. "Let's go."

Harry held up a hand. "Only if you swear not to use the information we get, if any, until Kate says it's okay."

"Sure. Whatever." Fast Eddie was already shrugging into his jacket.

"Wait," said Kate. "Is it a deal or not? I need to hear more than 'sure.'"

"Deal," said Fast Eddie.

She looked at Finn.

Finn's smile had turned sour. "I guess, but I want an exclusive."

"Okay."

"Before it leaks out."

"I'll try."

Kate stopped the Buick a block and a half from the chief's house.

"What are you doing?" asked Harry, who was leaning forward, elbows resting on the seatback between Kate and Fast Eddie.

Kate felt sick. She knew they must be breaking all sorts of laws, and they were definitely obstructing justice. On the other hand, what they had was a useless picture of someone putting something in a Dumpster.

"It might be John Vance throwing out the trash."

"What?" said Fast Eddie.

Kate started. "Sorry. Must have been thinking out loud."

"She's having a moral dilemma," Harry told him. "It always happens."

Eddie yawned. "You'll get used to it. Always one foot *ahead* of the authorities and just *short* of federal and state statutes. I love it."

"Well, I don't." Kate got out her cell phone.

"Now what are you doing?"

"Calling Elmira to make sure Ted isn't going to walk in on us and pack us all off to jail."

"Detective Lumley is not available at the moment," Elmira said in her most deterring voice.

"I have a favor to ask."

"Certainly."

Kate frowned. Was Elmira mad at her for some reason? "Can you just call my cell if Ted decides to go home—go back to the chief's house, I mean—for any reason."

"Certainly." Then in a whisper. "He's questioning Dan Graves about the murder. You don't think he did it, do you? You're investigating on your own."

"No. Of course not. I just need to use the chief's computer and I don't want to, uh, bother Ted if he was going to be around."

"You go, girl. Hold on." The sound of Elmira giving directions to someone. Then she was back, whispering to Kate. "I hope they've got the wrong man. It'll look bad for the chief if this upstart solves the murders in one day."

"Just call me, okay?"

"Copy that," whispered Elmira and hung up.

Shaking her head, Kate closed her phone and started the Buick. Three minutes later, they were climbing the steps to Brandon's house, Harry in the lead. He used two different keys to open the door.

Kate had never been inside Brandon's house. He'd never invited her, even though she often dropped Harry off when evening clubs were meeting or Brandon had to work late. And she had to admit she was curious to see how the two of them lived.

Harry turned on the lights, then hurried to turn off the alarm system that blinked from an adjacent wall.

Kate looked around the room. The décor was nice but about what you'd expect for the style of architecture—bungalow basics. Rich wood floors and woodwork. An arch that led into a square living room with a big window that overlooked a landscape of rocks, trees, and dried grasses. Below the lawn, Otter Creek twisted and churned its way past the house and disappeared into a clump of trees.

There was a huge HDTV along one wall, a brown leather couch and two club chairs oriented around it. And oddly enough, an oval rag rug in hues of blue, green, and yellow.

Beyond another arch, the dining room had been turned into office space. One glimpse inside the room and Kate understood the reason for the alarm system. A bank of electronic equipment filled one wall: monitors, computers, printers, fax machines.

A long, light wood desk wrapped around one corner of the room, and a smaller yet substantial desk ran along the opposite wall.

Brandon was connected twenty-four-seven.

Fast Eddie let out an appreciative, "Dyn-o-mite." He shrugged out of his jacket, dropped it on the couch, and went inside.

Harry grinned at Kate. They dropped their coats next to Fast Eddie's and followed him into the office.

Eddie stood in the middle of the room taking in the equipment. He whistled through his teeth. "Get *out.*"

Kate hesitated, confused.

"He doesn't mean get out." Harry rolled his eyes and pushed her into the room.

Fast Eddie was practically doing a jig. "This is incredible. He buy all this on a cop's salary?"

Harry frowned. "He didn't steal it, if that's what you mean."

"Chill. I didn't say he did. I was just asking." Fast Eddie sat down at a thirty-inch LCD monitor and cracked his knuckles. "This is amazing."

"You can't get in without the password," Harry told him.

"And you have the password, right?"

Kate looked a question at Harry. She now remembered him telling her that he was locked out of the chief's computer. "Harry?"

"I have first-level clearance. It lets me do Internet, Photoshop, and Word, also some basic math programs. All his work stuff is seriously secure."

Harry leaned over Eddie and typed in the password. The screen changed, displayed a series of official-looking info boxes, then turned blue. "Voilà."

Fast Eddie plugged in his SD card, opened Photoshop, and went to work.

The blurry sepia-toned photos of the Dumpster appeared lined up across the screen. He chose the one they had gleaned the most information from at the *Free Press* office.

It didn't look any better than it had before, just larger. Shape of Dumpster, halo of security lights, dark silhouette of a man—or woman.

Kate let out a disappointed sigh.

Eddie's fingers began to fly over the keyboard, moved to the mouse, then back again to the keyboard. Numbers and broken lines appeared and disappeared on the screen until he stopped on a close-up of the figure.

"This is the best I can do."

The three of them peered at the figure. He was clearer but still not identifiable.

"He's wearing some kind of long coat. A rain or all-weather coat. But even so, he's too stocky to be—" Harry clamped down on the word.

"Too stocky to be who?" asked Fast Eddie.

"Nobody."

Eddie sat back and crossed his arms, trapping his hands under his armpits. Stalemate.

"Actually," Kate said. "The police took, um, Calvin in for questioning. He's the chef at Rayette's. We're just eliminating suspects as we go." *And trying to keep you at this computer instead of rushing off to scoop the arrest of Dan Graves.*

"Old news," Eddie said. "Finn interviewed Calvin. He was pretty closed-mouth and pretty pissed. You know anything else we might want to know?"

"Nope. They took him in for questioning and let him go. How tall would you say this guy is?"

Eddie shrugged. "Regular, not too tall and not too short. Quite frankly, I wasn't paying that much attention. I knew I had to fill the page with something, and this looked like a shot I could segue into the homeless article, so . . ."

"How far away were you when you took this?"

"About fifty feet."

Kate pulled out her own laptop and placed it on the desk. It looked pretty puny next to the wall of state-of-the-art electronics, but it would do what she needed.

"Okay, fifty feet." She entered the numbers. "The Dumpster is— we've walked past that Dumpster lots of times, Harry. About six feet."

"A little over."

Kate entered the Dumpster height. "How tall are you?"

"Six-two."

"And were you standing up or kneeling when you took this?"

"Standing, though I had to lean around a tree." Getting into the spirit of the investigation, Eddie jumped up and stood behind his chair. He leaned around it, then mimed taking a picture.

"Subtract five inches." She entered the data and let the program calculate the figure's height. "So the figure is probably five feet ten-ish."

"Five-ten—ish?" Harry gave Kate a look.

"It's just an estimate," Kate said. "It's the best I can do under the circumstances."

"Do you know the average height of men in the United States?"

"Let me guess. Five-ten?"

Harry nodded.

"Which means," said Eddie, "this guy could be just about anybody."

Once again, they all stared at the photo.

"Can you get any resolution on the face?"

Eddie moved them aside and sat down again. His hand moved to the mouse; a box appeared around the man's head. Several more clicks and the head came into focus with higher contrast. But he was facing away from the camera.

"His head is covered. A hat?"

Eddie enlarged the area.

"No," said Harry. "A hood, probably wearing a hoodie beneath the coat."

Fast Eddie zoomed in on the collar. "Black hooded sweatshirt, dark brown coat."

"Oh great," Kate said. "The back of a head is the back of a head. And black hooded sweatshirts are not exactly rare. Is there any way we can see the face?"

The black hood grew larger. Eddie fiddled with the settings; no identifying features appeared. He brought up the other photos and played with the controls, trying to get a glimpse of the man's face, but at the end of twenty minutes he admitted defeat.

"Sorry. Why is this so important? What does it have to do with the murders? That's what you're after, right? The murderer?"

Harry looked at his watch. "Shit, I just remembered. I have something I have to do. I'll be right back." He raced out of the room. A minute later they heard a door slam.

Kate and Eddie turned back to the photo.

"Move to the object in his hand."

Eddie repositioned the edit box and zoomed in.

A gloved hand—and grasped in the hand was a piece of fabric. Eddie continued to type, and the part of the photo inside the quadrant grew larger. The gloved hand became more distinct.

"Beautiful," Eddie breathed.

They were looking at a typical driver's glove as far as Kate could tell. But the fabric he was holding was knitted—and brown.

A brown scarf. Kate got a rush of pure adrenalin. They had evidence that showed Dan—or someone—getting rid of the scarf the night of the murder. It had to be the same scarf the killer was wearing when he killed Lynn.

"That what you wanted?" asked Eddie.

Kate tamped down her excitement. "Maybe."

"You're not going to go back on our agreement, are you? Finn will have a coronary. It was all I could do to keep him from coming. I convinced him it might take hours and still might not be usable. He can be really annoying when he's impatient."

"We're solid," said Kate. But she wasn't ready to divulge her information yet, and she was beginning to worry about Harry. "Can you save those close-ups? I just want to check on Harry."

She went out to the living room. "Harry?" His jacket was missing from the pile on the couch. The door she had heard slamming must have been the one to the outside. She glanced automatically toward the picture window. It was already growing dark; the woods were shadowed and, she had to admit, spooky.

Kate fumbled in her coat pocket, grabbed her cell phone, and called Harry, looking out the window as it rang. A movement at the edge of the trees caught her eye. She peered into the growing dusk and saw a thin figure in black standing at the back of the lawn.

Wynter. She must have sneaked out of the house to meet Harry. That's where he'd gone. But he should have met her by now. And the two of them shouldn't be out there when it was getting dark.

Kate skirted the couch and club chairs and unlocked the door to the deck. A blast of cold April air sent a chill through her, but not as much as the second figure that stood partially hidden behind a thick maple.

Someone wearing brown. Not Harry—Harry's jacket was brown, but short. This was a long brown coat. Just like the one in the photos they'd been studying.

Fear clogged her throat as she screamed. "Wynter, watch out!"

Kate was afraid it wasn't loud enough for the girl to hear. But Wynter turned, seemed to look Kate straight in the eye, and then ran into the trees.

"Wynter. No!"

A blur of brown. And both figures disappeared into the woods.

		8			6	5		
	3			1				6
	5			4				
4			6	2				9
		6		7		3		
7					3			8
				6			5	
3				5			1	
		7	9			4		

CHAPTER

TWENTY-FOUR

KATE TOSSED HER cell phone onto the chair just as it rang. Harry, calling back. But she didn't have time for Harry now. "Eddie, answer the phone," she yelled. "Tell Harry to get inside. I've gone after Wynter."

She yanked open the back door and sprinted across the deck, took the steps to the lawn two at a time, trying to keep her eyes on the woods where she'd last seen Wynter. But the grass was rimy from the cold front and she had to concentrate to keep from sliding down in her panic.

"Wynter!" she called as soon as she reached the trees.

She looked, listened, trying to make out which way to follow. Heard leaves and branches cracking to her right and plunged after the sound.

Hoping she wasn't too late and not thinking about how she would stop the killer, just knowing she had to, she pushed into the woods.

Evergreens closed in above her. What little light was left in the dusk was snuffed out. Shadows rose up around her, confusing and taunting.

She felt utterly alone, but she knew she wasn't. They had come this way. She stopped again, heard nothing but the sounds of the woods. Was she too late? Had he already killed Wynter?

No. She could still save her. She had to save her.

Kate shot forward, slid on a patch of wet, mildewed leaves, and flailed her arms, trying to keep her balance. She fell to one knee; the earth gave way beneath her. She caromed down an incline, leaves, branches, dirt flying. She tucked and rolled and finally came to a stop. She was in a clearing. Otter Creek roiled past just below.

She pushed to her knees, then to her feet, and staggered. "Wynter!" she called, looking desperately around her. She turned left, right. Saw nothing.

Then it hit her that Wynter might be running because she thought she was in trouble. "Wynter. It's okay. Come out. You're not in trouble."

Kate began following the creek downstream, looking into the woods and calling Wynter's name.

She didn't feel the presence of another person until she was grabbed from behind and crushed in powerful arms. She couldn't breathe, and for a moment everything stopped. The world grew dim. She began to struggle, but the dusk turned to black. She was going to die. . .

Then the tenacious voice of reason prodded her. She couldn't let this cretin win, couldn't leave him to kill again. She couldn't leave Harry and Brandon.

She clutched at the arms, but only managed to get a fistful of coat sleeve. The fabric was loose and thick, and she lost her grip.

She twisted, squirmed, and finally kicked back. Her boot heel connected with a shin.

The grasp loosened in reaction to the blow.

Kate sucked in air, but before she could run, she was lifted up. For a second she saw only sky, then she was tossed away. The world turned to a blur as she hurtled downward toward the swirling water of the swollen creek.

She'd escaped the madman.

Then she hit water with a giant splash that knocked the air out of her. Her lungs seized up and water rushed into her mouth and nose. Bone-chilling cold crept up her arms and legs, paralyzing them.

And she was being dragged downstream by the current. Frigid water buffeted her, eddied around her, grabbed her, and pulled her under. Her bulky sweater grew heavy and wet. She fought to free herself, but it clung to her like a giant limpet. She went under and was spat out long enough to gasp a breath before she was wrenched down again.

The current pummeled her, propelling her forward. She tumbled and sank, fought back again, but the spring current was relentless.

Once, she was pulled teasingly toward the shore. Her knees scraped the jagged stones of creek bed. She grabbed at a rotten log, but it came apart in her numb hand. Then the current swept her up again, dragging her to the middle of the creek where the water ran the swiftest and the deadliest.

She felt weak, helpless—she couldn't fight much longer. She was going to drown. *Aunt Pru will be sad. Harry and Brandon . . .*

She heard her name. Someone was calling her.

No. Not yet. I'm not ready.

"Kate!"

Harry's voice. A splash.

Kate sputtered, kicked, forced her unfeeling arms to keep her afloat.

Harry grabbed her, and they both went under. But Kate was alert now. No way was she going to let Harry drown with her.

Together they kicked and struggled and pulled themselves toward shore. They dragged each other up the narrow rock-strewn bank and collapsed in the leaves.

Kate began to shake. Her teeth threatened to crack from chattering.

"H-H-Harry?"

"Y-yeah."

"Y-you okay?"

"Uh. . ."

Running footsteps.

Fast Eddie slid down the embankment. "What the hell?"

"W-Wynter. She's out there. He's after her."

"Who?"

"The killer."

Harry struggled to get up. "She was supposed to meet me at the corner. I was waiting for her."

"She's in the woods—with the murderer. We have to find her."

Fast Eddie hauled Harry to his feet, then reached back for Kate. "We have to get you both to the house and into dry clothes."

Kate stumbled on cold numb feet. Fast Eddie grabbed her.

"You have to find Wynter."

"After you get inside."

Harry ran ahead, with Fast Eddie half carrying and half dragging Kate behind him.

They reached the living room just as the front door opened.

Ted hurried forward, his eyes on Kate. He tripped on the rag rug but regained his balance without breaking stride.

"Kate, what happened? Good God, you're soaked through."

You're supposed to be at the station, Kate thought, before she felt Fast Eddie ease away from her. She remembered the photos on the monitor.

"Thank God, Ted," Kate said, grabbing both his arms and maneuvering her body away from the entrance of the computer room. "Wynter is out in the woods. There's someone out there. He's after her. He pushed me into the stream. You've got to get some men. It may be too late." She had to stop as a violent spasm took hold of her. "H-hurry!"

Ted was already radioing for backup.

"I'll help." Fast Eddie appeared behind her. He winked and pulled his jacket off the pile on the couch. Kate glanced toward the computer monitor—a nice even blue screen saver. They didn't call him Fast Eddie for nothing.

Harry came running down the stairs, already changed. He barely looked at Ted as he ran out the back door.

"Come back here, you young hellion!" Ted started after him. "Going to get himself in trouble one of these days." Then he, too, was gone.

Fast Eddie pointed a pistol finger at Kate. "Find some dry clothes. We need to talk." He triggered his finger then followed Ted into the yard.

Kate stood at the window and watched as they separated and ran into the woods. She seemed to be rooted to the floor, barely aware of the tremors of cold that coursed through her. It was superstitious, but she was afraid that if she didn't watch, they wouldn't find Wynter in time.

That was stupid. She needed to get dry and join the search.

Harry had changed upstairs. Kate climbed the stairs. There were three doors on the second floor—a closed one on her left, an open one on the right. She could see Harry's wet clothes lying in a pile on the floor.

She went into his room, and apologizing for invading his privacy, she rummaged until she found a pair of sweats, some heavy socks and a sweatshirt with a big stain down the front.

She gathered up her clothes and Harry's and carried them to the end of the hall where she found the bathroom. The whole room was newly tiled with new fixtures. And she wondered for a moment if Brandon owned the house or just rented.

Then she pulled herself together, dumped the clothes into a large new bathtub and, ignoring the other closed door, hurried downstairs. Only to realize she couldn't join the search since she had no dry shoes.

She could make coffee, though. The searchers would need it when they brought Wynter back. She passed through the computer room into the kitchen. It was 1950s vintage with white wooden cabinets and light green walls stenciled with red maple leaves along the ceiling.

The chief obviously didn't spend much time in the kitchen.

She found coffee and the coffeemaker. She measured the grounds, poured water into the carafe, and turned the coffeemaker on, keeping one eye on the window that looked out over the creek. Which is why she saw them when the searchers returned, Wynter limping between Harry and Ted. Fast Eddie brought up the rear.

Kate pushed away from the counter and ran to the deck to meet them.

"I saw him!" Wynter told Kate as soon as she saw her. "I saw him come after you, but I couldn't stop him, and by the time I got there he was gone and you were—"

Harry pushed her into the club chair.

"Did you recognize him?" Ted asked. "Can you give me a description?"

Wynter frowned at him.

"Withholding information is. . ."

Kate knew immediately that even if Wynter had seen who it was, she wouldn't tell Ted. He had switched into police mode. Not only was he wearing a black police jacket and full belt, but he stood with his feet parted, confrontational even with the slight weakness of his crippled leg, he exuded cop—not the way to encourage a rebellious teenager to talk.

Wynter shut down, her jaw slightly jutted, her eyes wary. "No. He was wearing brown. That's all I saw."

Ted raised both eyebrows. "Anything that would help you recognize him if you saw him again?"

Wynter looked dumb. Shrugged. "Nope."

"This is very serious business. There is a killer out there. If he thinks you recognized him, he might consider making you his next victim."

Wynter flinched.

"Stop it," Harry said.

Wynter looked at Kate. "I didn't see anything."

Ted scored the group with a long penetrating look. Kate wondered what he was seeing.

She saw two belligerent teenagers. One not-too-honest newspaperman. And one mathematician who knew better than to obstruct justice, but who was just as determined to give information only to the chief.

The sound of sirens made them jump, all but Ted. "I'll be outside if anybody thinks of anything." He gave them one last piercing look before leaving.

No one moved until the door closed behind him.

Kate was the first to speak. "What did you do with the photos?"

Eddie patted his jacket pocket. "Safe and sound. The Photoshop stills are in a file called Christmas Vacation on the desktop."

"Sorry," Wynter said, glancing up at Kate. "It was these freaking boots." She tugged one off and dropped it on the floor. "I could have had him, but. . . "

"Did you hurt your ankle?" Kate asked.

Wynter shook her head, but held up her boot. "Damned heel broke while I was running."

Kate sank onto the couch and started to laugh. The laughter turned into shudders, and Harry found a blanket to throw around her. She pulled it close. "Thank God you're all right."

"Yeah. But I really didn't see who it was, not that I'd tell the Tedster if I did. He really burns me with that attitude. The I'm-such-a-good-cop shit."

"We need the chief," said Harry and sat down on the edge of Wynter's chair.

"We sure do," said Kate, just as the front door opened again.

"Speak of the devil," Fast Eddie said.

Kate turned around. The chief was standing in the doorway, flanked by Alice and Tanya Watson. Several more GABs were crowded in behind them.

Brandon stepped inside. "Are we having a party?"

"Shit," said Kate under her breath.

"Double shit," Wynter said.

Harry jumped up from the chair arm and ran toward him. "Chief! You're just who we need."

Alice gave Harry a little push away. "Don't you go bothering Chief Mitchell. He needs his rest."

"Not as much as I need an explanation."

His voice sounded tight. Kate knew he must be in pain. And she marveled that Alice had been able to talk the doctors into releasing him. If she'd bothered to ask.

"How did you, uh. . ."

"I just told Dr. Leonard to stand aside. We were springing the chief."

Kate glanced at Brandon, who seemed to be listing to the left. "Maybe you should lie down for a while," she said, coming toward him, feeling just a tad of trepidation.

He was frowning. One of his most ferocious ones.

"Are you wearing Harry's clothes?"

Kate pulled up short. She'd forgotten about everything else as soon as he walked through the door. Now, the first thing she thought about was that her hair must look awful. She touched fingertips to it. Pretty bad.

"I fell in the creek."

"This I've got to hear."

"You can hear it once you're lying down," Alice said firmly. "The doctor said to look after you, and that's what we're here to do." She took his arm and nodded to Tanya, who took his other. "Come along, girls."

Brandon only got one panicked look off before the GABs surrounded him. Maria Albioni and Carrie Blaine headed for the kitchen, their arms filled with grocery bags. Beatrice Noakes, nearly invisible behind flowers and balloons, pushed her way inside.

Zeroing in on Fast Eddie, she said, "You, young man—there are more of these in the car." She shoved her bundle at him and followed Alice and Tanya as they trundled the chief up the stairs.

"Now what?" Harry asked.

"I think you'd better run upstairs and see if you can help."

"Right. Don't talk about anything until I get back."

Harry ran up the stairs and Kate turned to Wynter and Fast Eddie.

"Anyone for coffee?"

Since Maria and Carrie were busy heating soup for the chief, Kate took the coffee pot and mugs out to the living room. She met Harry coming down the stairs.

"They're going to drive him crazy, fussing all over him. He'll blow and we'll all be in trouble."

"He'll be patient," Kate said. "It's that or go back to the hospital. Now, we need to discuss a few things before we fill him in."

She dispensed coffee, then sat back on the leather couch. It was firm and manly and she felt safe just being there.

"First, Wynter. What were you doing in the woods?"

Wynter lifted her chin.

"Look," Kate said, losing patience. "If you're going to be part of this, you're going to have to stop being so prickly. Deal?"

Wynter gave one of her half shrugs.

"I'll take that as a yes."

The sound of car doors slamming stopped her next sentence. The front door opened and Ted came back in. He looked at the group, but didn't come any closer.

"Has either of you remembered anything that might help catch this pervert?"

Kate and Wynter shook their heads.

"Chief's back," said Harry, without even trying to keep the elation out of his voice.

Ted nodded. "I thought I saw him. I'll have a word." He slowly climbed the stairs. Kate found it hard not to stare. She suddenly felt guilty for the way she was acting, especially when she thought of him out combing the woods searching for Wynter.

It couldn't be easy and was probably embarrassing for him to be seen like that in front of his men.

But they aren't his men, Kate reminded herself. *They're the chief's.*

They fell silent, everyone sipping hot coffee and waiting. It was several minutes before Ted returned. He gave them a long look, then went out the door. A minute later a car door slammed and the car drove away.

"I wonder what he said to the chief," said Harry.

Kate wondered too. It couldn't have been pleasant, telling your friend that you'd taken his job while he lay unconscious.

Fast Eddie put down his mug. "All right, he's gone. What's all the subterfuge about? And don't shine me on. I want everything."

"I'm not sure I—"

Eddie overrode her. "First of all, why didn't you tell Lumley about the photos? Yeah, and while I'm thinking about it, what about those photos? What do they have to do with the two murders? That's what this is all about, isn't it?

"You're trying to solve this case before Lumley does. Why is that? Besides the fact that's he's an officious prick."

Wynter snorted out a laugh.

Kate gave her a quelling look.

"Because it isn't his job," said Harry. "He's screwing up everything."

"Yeah, I'm getting that you and Katie don't like the guy much. I'm not so hot on him myself. Tried to badger Finn into confessing he'd killed Dougan. What crap."

"How come you don't yell pizza at *him*?" Wynter asked sullenly.

Eddie looked confused. "What pizza?"

"Nothing," said Kate.

"So what gives?"

Kate let out a long breath. "I think it's time we let Eddie in on what we suspect."

Eddie's eyes rounded comically. "You know who the killer is?"

Kate shook her head. "I was hoping that your shots of the homeless man would tell us."

"What does some bum have to do with the serial killer?"

"You have to swear not to leak this to Finn until we say so." But Kate had no illusions about Finn's ability to ferret out news; he might already know the police had a suspect in custody.

"What?"

"They arrested Dan Graves for murder this morning."

Fast Eddie reached for his cell phone.

Harry snatched it away.

"Hey—"

"Tit for tat," Kate said primly. "Just listen. The police found Dan's scarf in the Dumpster this morning. There was a piece of brown yarn found at the crime scene."

"How do you know all this?"

Kate half smiled. "I have my sources, too."

"Damn, Finn was right about you. Go on."

"Pizza, wise ass."

Kate pointed a finger at Wynter. "If you don't cut it out—"

"No way am I leaving. I'll cut the attitude."

In for a penny, in for a pound, thought Kate. She returned her attention to Fast Eddie. "Dan left his scarf at the museum Monday night. I found it and put it on the chair for Alice to put in the lost-and-found box. Alice never saw it. Later, I found it on the floor and put it in lost-and-found in the closet. Either Dan came and picked it up before Lynn was murdered or—"

"Somebody lifted it and is framing Dan. Damn, this is good

stuff."

"Which you will not print a word of until I say you can."

"Finn will have a fit."

"I'll make it up to him."

"An exclusive on how you solved the murders."

"I'm not negotiating. And I haven't solved the murders. I'm merely gathering evidence for the chief."

"Except he'll have an even bigger fit when he finds out," Harry interjected.

Kate threw up her hands. "Well, what else am I supposed to do?" she asked, exasperation, guilt, and the fear that she was making a huge mistake making her shrill.

"Chill," Harry, Wynter, and Eddie said in chorus.

Kate closed her eyes, regrouped. "If Dan is the murderer, it doesn't matter what we do, and if he isn't . . . I doubt that Ted will believe us."

"But if Dan whosit is in jail, who was in the woods?" asked Wynter.

"Good question." Kate reached for her cell phone. One missed call. Elmira, not Harry. She'd probably called to tell Kate that Ted had left the station. Kate pressed redial and listened to Elmira without speaking. She hung up and faced the group.

"They released Dan Graves an hour ago. He had an alibi for the night of Lynn's murder."

Her statement was met by total silence.

"My guess is they'll be picking him up again, alibi or not," Kate said.

Wynter snorted. "Kinda blows the Tedster's 'I'm the big authority on serial killers' attitude."

"But he'll still figure out a way to take all the credit," Harry said.

"So, Katie," Fast Eddie said. "What do you think? Is he guilty?"

"Me? I think it's strange that Dan would have time to get out of jail, collect his killer outfit, happen to see Wynter walking toward the woods, and decide to come after her. All in less than an hour."

Eddie blew out air. "So where does that leave us?"

"With the real killer still out there," Wynter said. She shot a quick, fearful look at Kate. "And he'll kill again. Won't he?"

9   1

CHAPTER

TWENTY-FIVE

2

THE DOOR to the chief's bedroom was ajar when Kate went upstairs to gather her wet clothes before going home. She looked in. The shades were lowered and Brandon lay beneath a black comforter on one side of a black king-sized bed.

She tiptoed to the bed to leave a note, but she couldn't resist the temptation to look around. A long double dresser of black lacquered wood, and nothing else, no television, no piles of dirty clothes, not even a pair of shoes by the bed. The room was spotless and Kate wondered if . . . no, she didn't.

Leaning over the bed. she touched his shoulder. "I'll be back tomorrow." Kate propped the note she'd written against the bedside table lamp and went downstairs.

She offered to give Alice a ride, but the GABs were taking their nursing duties seriously. Their hovering was bound to irritate him.

Kate only hoped he would keep his temper and not send them

packing. It had taken long enough to win them over. Their support could easily be lost, and then where would he be?

She left Harry and Wynter eating Maria Albioni's homemade soup in the kitchen while Maria cut thick slices of Italian bread that disappeared as soon as they touched the plate. It smelled wonderful, but Kate was too anxious to sit down and eat.

Wynter refused to let Kate take her home. Alice promised to take care of the two teenagers until Wynter's father came to pick up her up. Coward that she was, Kate was happy to leave the situation in Alice's hands. She was not eager to face that angry father again.

Fast Eddie was champing at the bit to get back to the *Free Press*. Kate gave him a ride, but only after he promised not to use the Dumpster photos and to attribute any information he and Finn printed to an undisclosed source. She didn't trust him, but she had no choice.

So far, their hours of work had done nothing to further the investigation. They were still no closer to identifying the "homeless" man. And she'd already known that he was holding a brown woolen scarf, because the police had found one in the Dumpster.

"I guess this means Lumley will rearrest Dan Graves," Fast Eddie speculated as they drove to the *Free Press*.

"Probably."

"You don't sound too enthused."

Kate glanced at him. She couldn't trust him not to print anything she said, so she said nothing.

"Come on, Katie. Spill. You got a theory?"

"Kate," she corrected.

"Man, the whole town calls you Katie. So you don't think Graves is the serial killer?"

"I don't know."

"Then who is it?"

"I don't know."

"Well, if you get any ideas . . ."

"You'll be the first to know." *In your dreams.*

Eddie jumped out of the car and Kate watched him sprint inside. She backed the Buick out of the narrow parking lot and headed for home, praying that Eddie would show some responsibility and not print those photos.

Kate was stymied. Maybe she was wrong and Dan really was the killer. He and Calvin and Lynn knew each other from the Brick House. Calvin had said that he kept pretty much to himself. *He was a bit of a loner* was what the neighbors of serial killers always said.

He knew Sudoku, even moved to Granville so he could join the Arcane Masters puzzle group, and lived alone. Every newspaper article she'd ever read about serial killers said pretty much the same thing. "He was a quiet man, intelligent, didn't bother anybody."

But Jason and Erik had taken to him, and they were good judges of character. They not only admired Dan's puzzle-solving skills, they saw him socially.

But if it were Dan, why the simplistic Sudoku puzzle clues? Anybody with a colored pencil could have left those clues in the e-mails. *Why use Sudoku at all?*

She caught herself rolling past the stop sign on Maple and slammed on the brakes. She looked both ways, then proceeded across the intersection.

What was she missing? What were the police missing?

She had more questions than answers, just like every math problem at the inception. So many paths to follow, so many mistakes to make—and so little time.

Kate pulled the Buick into her driveway and got out, making a mental note to call Norris Endelman to see when her car would be ready.

Her bungalow was much smaller than the chief's, and as she walked up the front steps, she realized it was looking a little shabby. Inside, her furnishings seemed old and outmoded. Of course it was the same furniture she'd grown up with. She couldn't redecorate. Her dad might decide to come home from Florida someday.

She opened a can of soup, grabbed an apple off the counter, and set up her laptop on the kitchen table.

She took a breath and opened her e-mail. Just a file from Fast Eddie, who had e-mailed her his Photoshop enhancements with a message that he and Finn were being discreet.

"In *my* dreams," Kate muttered and opened the file.

While her soup heated, she scanned each photo, trying to find some detail that would point her to the identity of the killer. But no matter how hard she looked, it was still just a homeless man with his back to the camera, standing on one foot while his left hand shifted the lid and his right hand held the scarf.

It just doesn't feel like Dan Graves. . . She gave herself a mental slap. No feelings, just facts. She hadn't paid inordinate attention to the waiter the few times they'd met. But . . . she couldn't put her finger on it. The shape was wrong.

She studied the photo for so long that it began to take on a life of its own, became familiar, like an old acquaintance.

Or is he really familiar? Someone she knew, or had seen before. Someone who had killed twice and would kill again.

She memorized the cut of the coat, the collar, the head covering. Black hood, nothing unusual. Brown coat. Long enough and square cut enough to camouflage the person underneath. Pants mostly hidden in shadow. Shapeless. It was like the killer had put on the most innocuous clothes in which to kill.

Well, of course he had, duh.

He was no dummy, even if he didn't know squat about Sudoku. He was toying with her. And yet he'd tried to kill her. Or had he? He'd come at her from behind, had trapped her before she could even react. He could have slipped a wire around her neck, and that would have been the end of Kate McDonald.

Instead, he'd pushed her into the creek. Which could also have killed her. Did he want her dead, or had the attack on her just been a part of the game?

She heard the soup boil over and sizzle on the stovetop. She turned it off and sat back down.

Stood up again, mimed opening a heavy Dumpster and throwing something in. Went back to her photos, no closer to an answer than she was before.

The whole exercise was futile. There was no way to tell if he was thick or thin, dark or fair. The coat and hood concealed everything.

She scrolled down to the shoes. Heeled? Sneakers? The feet were shadowed and it was impossible to tell. She leaned back in her chair, defeated. She couldn't even tell if the figure was male or female.

Had Ted questioned Tess Dougan? They only had her word for it that she'd been out of town. She did have a tan, but there was a tanning salon as close as Manchester.

Tess might have gotten fed up with Henny and finally struck back. Nobody would blame her. But somehow Kate couldn't imagine Tess knowing how to use a garrote, much less being able to choke the life out of someone.

And what reason would she have to kill Lynn? Regardless of Wynter's far-out theory, Kate couldn't see Lynn even being civil to someone like Henny Dougan, much less having an affair with him. *Ick*. Kate's skin crawled at the mere possibility.

The police found a brown scarf in the Dumpster. It had to be a match for the fragment found at the scene. Which meant either Dan had tried to dispose of it or someone else had put it there to incriminate its owner.

She'd seen Dan at Rayette's after Lynn was killed. She'd asked him about his scarf—he hadn't missed it. Obviously it was no longer at the museum. So if Dan hadn't taken it, that left the killer.

Even with the museum traffic off because of the murders, plenty of people had the opportunity to come in and rifle through the lost-and-found box, somewhere between Monday night and Wednesday night. Two whole days.

But who would want to incriminate Dan? And why?

Calvin? He had been out with the flu those two days, though Kate supposed he could have slipped into the museum and found the scarf. Maybe he and Dan had a history. A common interest in Lynn?

Wait. She was thinking in circles. Kate slapped her hands on the table, pulled herself up, and paced over to the stove, where she ate the now-cold soup out of the pan. She needed to slow down, organize the possibilities as she thought them, not let them take over and batter her around like the creek had that day.

Ted had joked about sticking to means, motive, and opportunity when Kate had tried to explain Sudoku to him. And that's what she needed to do.

So who had a motive to kill Henny? Unless Henny had just been a diversion, to take attention away from the real intended victim, Lynn.

Or vice versa, she told herself. Which meant it could be someone who wanted Henny dead.

"Aargh," she said into the empty room. "Why can't somebody just confess?"

She didn't understand how detectives had the patience to follow leads day after day. Of course, she had done the same thing herself when she worked at the think tank, but that was different. People's lives weren't put in jeopardy while they waited for the eureka moment—at least not at the think tank level.

Maybe she should just give the evidence to Ted and let his forensic people analyze it.

Not his *people*, she corrected. The state's forensic people.

She was obstructing justice, and she was afraid her recalcitrance to cooperate with Ted might allow the killer to kill again.

She'd sleep on it and consult the chief first thing in the morning.

And do what he told her to do. Whatever it was.

Maybe.

There was a note attached to the chief's front door when Kate arrived at his house the next morning. "Door's open. Come on in."

So much for his state-of-the-art security system.

Kate stepped inside and heard activity coming from the kitchen. She decided to bypass the GABs and head straight to the chief. She just hoped he was awake and ready to help.

She tapped lightly on the door and, getting no answer, poked her head in just in time to see a flurry of covers from the bed. Slowly, the chief's eyes appeared over the top of the blanket.

"Thank God," he said. "Where are they?"

"The kitchen, as far as I could tell."

"Good." He pushed the covers away.

Kate quickly looked away, looked back again. "You're dressed."

"*Shh.* Help me downstairs."

"No way. You're a couple of bruises away from a serious condition."

"Well at least hand me my shoes. If I bend over, I might keep going."

"What are you planning to do? Where's Ted?"

"He moved out."

"What?"

"He was afraid his long hours would disturb me. He moved into the Bowsman."

There wasn't a hint of irony in his voice. How could he be so complacent? *You invite a friend to come fishing and he tries to take your job? Okay, maybe he hadn't planned it that way, but . . .*

"Did he really save your life?"

The chief, who had managed to ease his feet to the floor, stopped. "Is that what he said?"

"Yeah. He was quoted in the *Free Press*. You were reading it at the hospital. Don't you remember?"

He shook his head. Thought better of it. "I remember getting hit by a truck."

He gave her a lopsided smile that made her tear up. She blinked furiously and pulled herself together.

Brandon eased forward until he was sitting on the edge of the mattress. When he rocked forward, Kate grabbed his good arm. He teetered for a hideous second, then balanced upright.

"Shit," he hissed. "Oops."

"That's a freebie," Kate said. "Now what?"

"Downstairs."

He was heavy and not too steady on his feet, and by the time they made it halfway down the stairs, Kate was sweating. She bet the chief was too.

"This is really stupid," she said.

The chief just grunted and lowered one foot slowly to the next step.

"Of course," a strident voice said from the bottom of the stairs. "Just what you'd expect from a stubborn, hardheaded—"

Kate's head snapped up. "Aunt Pru? Why aren't you in church?"

"It wasn't my idea. Alice can be a real pain in the patoot."

"I heard that, Prudence McDonald!" called a voice from the kitchen.

Kate glanced at the chief, who had stopped midstep, his face frozen in an expression somewhere between pain and hilarity.

"Don't laugh," she whispered. "It will hurt their feelings."

"Not to mention my ribs," he mumbled, and attempted another step. He swayed forward.

Kate hung on. "Aunt Pru, could you help me out here?"

"The man oughta be in bed, where he belongs," Pru groused and crossed her arms.

Kate's arms were beginning to shake with the effort of keeping Brandon upright.

"He needs to catch this killer or we're going to be stuck with Ted Lumley forever," Kate said desperately. "That's *two* Bostonians telling us what to do."

"Oh, for heaven's sake." Pru mounted the stairs. She was wearing a bright orange jogging suit and looked like a demented crossing guard.

"I'll push from behind," she said.

The chief sputtered. "Please say that was a joke."

"Stop complaining, and start putting one foot in front of the other."

Together, Kate and Pru maneuvered the chief downstairs and deposited him in the chair in front of his bank of computers. Pru gave him a final scowl and a "Hmmph" and marched back into the kitchen.

Brandon booted up his computer. The first thing Kate saw was Fast Eddie's Christmas photos file.

The chief saw it, too. "Christmas?"

"Don't get mad."

"I just get even." He clicked on the file. Twelve photo icons appeared on the screen. He opened each one, not saying anything, just studying them in turn. He spent more time over the close-up of the scarf, but even then he didn't comment or ask questions.

Then he went back to the photo she and Fast Eddie had been working from, the full-length figure of the man. He scrutinized it for a long time.

It was maddening. Kate thought she would rather have him verbal and accusatory than this studied silence. *What is he thinking?* Had he picked up something she and Eddie had missed?

Finally, he turned to look at her. He was pale, the skin beneath his cheek bones sunken and ashen. She began to worry.

"Who took these?"

"Fast Eddie." She told him about the homeless study and how Eddie had also been at the murder scene after the fact.

"They found a fragment of yarn at the crime scene."

He cut her a sharp look. "Elmira."

Kate nodded. "She brought the police report to the hospital to show you, but you were in no state to look at it."

"So she showed them to you."

"She was trying to help."

"By leaking information to the public." He seemed to deflate. "I can't even trust my own force."

The public? He considered her the public? Kate bristled. "She was trying to save your job, you big galoot! Because, strangely enough, she's totally loyal to you. And even stranger is the fact that the people of Granville would rather have you as chief of police than Ted Lumley. Don't ask me why."

A ghost of a smile. "Is Ted after my job?"

"I don't know. He's awfully chummy with Mayor Saxon, and

after that stupid *Free Press* article about what happened when the two of you were partners . . . it sure feels like he's making himself at home."

"Harry was complaining about him too."

"I know he's just trying to help, but—"

"I could do with less help."

She stared at him. "Some people can be so . . . ungrateful." Maybe she really would be better off back with her numbers. "So sorry. Our mistake." She turned to leave, feeling the most appalling need to cry.

He grabbed her wrist, hard enough to stop her cold.

"No, I'm sorry. It's just so da—so frustrating not to be able to do anything."

"It must be. So you should let us help."

He released her wrist. Ran his fingers through his hair and winced at the action.

"Okay, what else have you learned?"

It took a second for her to come up to speed. He was asking her to help?

"I know you've been busy, so just cough up what you have."

"Well . . ." She told him about Roy Larkins' truck, which earned her a nod. About going to Jumpin' Jack's. This warranted a stifled expletive.

Kate held up her hand. "You don't have to say it. I won't be going there again."

She told him about the two additional e-mails.

"Can you retrieve them from here?"

She reached past him and logged into her e-mail account through the Internet. As soon as she connected, he eased her out of the way. He studied the e-mails in silence while she pointed out the initials and confessed to her misinterpretation—and how it had cost Lynn her life.

He didn't tell her it wasn't her fault or try to make her feel less guilty. And she appreciated it.

She gave him a full account of Tess Dougan's return and her story of where she'd been.

"Did Ted question her?"

Kate shook her head. "I don't think so. He, uh, may not know that she's in town. She said she would only talk to you." She smiled. "Like I said, everyone wants you back."

He lifted a skeptical eyebrow. Probably the only reaction he could make that didn't hurt.

"Besides, Ted hadn't been appointed to head the investigation yet, and we didn't think Tess talking to Paul or Dickie or even Mr. Meany would do much good. The station was sort of in chaos at that point."

"Benjamin Meany is back at work?"

Kate nodded.

The chief closed his eyes. When he didn't open them again, Kate said, "Maybe you should lie down for a while."

"Can you just hand me that computer case over by the door?"

Kate picked up the laptop and placed it next to the desktop computer.

Brandon slid the laptop out of the case and opened it. "I tried tracing the e-mails while I was in the hospital, but between being in Never Never Land and the lack of available search programs, I didn't get very far. Things should go faster now."

"What do you want me to do?"

"Be very careful and stay safe." He looked at her long and hard. "I'm serious. There's more to these killings than the obvious. I need time to figure it out. And I need you to make sure Harry stays safe too."

Kate realized he was not dismissing her but asking her to enable him to concentrate on his work and not have to worry about her and Harry. And that made up for having her hands tied.

"All right. I'll leave you to it." She rested her hand on his uninjured shoulder for a second, then walked toward the door. "You never did answer my question."

"Which question would that be?"

"Did Ted really save your life?"

"He pulled me out of the line of fire."

She didn't want to ask the next question. She knew it wasn't her business, and she'd made the excuses for him already. But she needed to know. "Does he blame you for his leg injury?"

Brandon shrugged. Winced. "He might, though it's hardly logical."

"Why?"

"He pulled me out, but he was also the one who sent me in."

	1				6	9		
	4		9			8		
				4				3
4			3					1
	5		1	8			7	
2				7				5
9				6				
		2			8		5	
		5	7				6	

CHAPTER

TWENTY-SIX

"SO IT ACTUALLY was *his* fault you were in the alley in the first place?"

Brandon sighed. "There was no fault. He was the senior detective. It was his call. A miscalculation. A misjudgment. Shit happens."

"Why do you let him get away with making it out to be your fault?"

"What does it matter? We both survived. There was an internal investigation. Ted was transferred to a desk job in media relations. I went back to homicide."

"That had to be tough on Ted."

"At first. He liked being in the field, but his femur was shattered. Turns out he was good with the public. Could talk with the press. Made a place for himself."

No kidding, thought Kate. *Looks like he's trying to do it again.*

"He's very well respected. And he enjoys the limelight."

"And you stayed friends all these years?"

"Sure. It was police work, and in police work there are no guarantees. Now if we've finished with this little trip down memory lane, I want to get on these e-mails."

Kate stopped by the kitchen to say good-bye and found Tanya, Alice, Pru, and Maria sitting around Brandon's big oak table. Conversation ceased as she walked in, which made Kate think the talk had been about her or the chief, or both.

She was wrong.

Pru lifted a copy of the *Free Press*. "Did you know about this?"

Kate tried to read the headlines, but Pru was shaking it too violently. She finally grabbed her aunt's hand and read. "Local Waiter Arrested in Two Deaths. Evidence found at the crime scene."

An unidentified source close to the police department . . . So far so good, thought Kate and read on. She was off the hook. Finn and Fast Eddie had actually kept their word.

Pru took the paper back and gave it one last shake before dropping it to the table. "Just what happens when you start letting outsiders in."

"Honestly, Pru," Alice said. "That poor man came from less than twenty miles away. You can hardly call him an outsider."

"Hmmph. That's not who I'm talking about."

"Well, just who are you talking about?"

"Gotta run," Kate jumped in. "Hopefully we'll have more visitors at the museum tomorrow now that the killer is caught, and I want to get caught up on paperwork."

"Have a nice day, dear," Alice said offhandedly. "And, Pru, don't you dare say anything about the man sitting in the other room. Someone tried to kill him. He should be in bed, and he's in there trying to solve the murders—"

"Well, if he'd stayed in Boston—"

Kate fled.

The museum was wonderfully quiet, like a haven from the terrible things that were going on outside. Kate loved being there when it was closed. It was as if she could feel the professor's presence.

Instead of going directly upstairs, she wandered through the exhibit rooms. Today there were no spectres hiding in the corners, no accusing faces glaring back at her. Just a feeling of safety and peace.

She would have lingered longer, oblivious to the outside world, but she couldn't. Outside, things weren't safe, and even though Brandon was investigating, she felt restless.

In the office, she put water on the hot plate to heat and set up her laptop. But instead of sitting down at the desk, she wandered to the window, letting her hand linger on the back of the professor's chair— her chair—as she passed.

It was going to rain again. Black clouds were scudding in and congregating, it seemed, right over the museum. The wind had kicked up and the tree branches scraped against the window panes.

She didn't mind. The office, with its dark wainscoting, was the perfect place to be on a rainy day.

She made tea and sat in front of the cold fireplace while she worked a Sudoku puzzle. But instead of settling into the familiar pattern, her mind kept racing.

In the distance, thunder rumbled, followed by a loud "Yeow." Aloysius jumped from his place on the bookshelf and padded over to jump into her lap, then he tried to bury his head in her armpit.

"You are just a big scaredy cat," she told him as she scratched behind his ears. Soon his distinctive rumble rose from the depths. He poked his head out and lifted his chin so she could scratch there.

They sat together, her puzzle and tea forgotten, until a click told her that someone had come in. "Harry?"

"Ted."

Kate stood up, dumping Al onto the floor. With an affronted spit, he padded away.

"How did you get in?"

"Someone left the front door ajar. Not very safe, Kate."

She never left the door unlocked when she was alone in the museum. "Is Alice downstairs?"

"I didn't see her. She might be in the back somewhere. But even so, you should really keep things locked when there's no one at the front desk."

"I usually do," Kate said, wondering what he wanted.

"I just left the *Free Press* office."

Ah, Kate thought. Now she knew why he was here.

"Did you see the paper this morning?"

"Yes, I did."

"I read those two the riot act. Irresponsible journalism. An information leak like that could spoil the prosecutor's case." He paused, thinking. "You wouldn't happen to know who that source close to the police is by any chance?"

Kate shook her head and tried to look innocent. She wasn't the best liar in the world. "Would you like some tea?"

"I'd rather have coffee."

"We'll have to go downstairs unless you don't mind instant."

"Instant's fine."

Kate went to the cabinet to get a cup. "The coffee's in that wardrobe, top shelf. If you can reach it, I won't have to get the stool to stand on."

"I'll get it."

"I think about those poor Victorians, shorter than us by several inches as a rule, and surrounded by gigantic furniture. It must have been so maddening to have things out of reach all the time."

Ted chuckled and opened the doors of the wardrobe.

"Top shelf on the right, I think."

"Ah, I see it." Ted shifted his weight to his good leg and stretched up to get the coffee. His right foot came off the ground as he curved to reach the coffee tin.

And Kate finally got her eureka moment.

It was the same way he'd reached for Pru's maple cake. It was the same stance she had been studying for the past two days. The "homeless" man.

She was such an idiot. It was Ted in the picture. Ted putting the scarf in the Dumpster.

"Here you go." Ted handed her the jar of coffee. Frowned at her. "What is it? If you're worried that I'm going to chastise you for carrying on your own investigation, don't be. Dan is back in jail. He won't be getting out on bail. The case is cracked. Everyone is safe again and life can get back to normal."

He sounded so logical, so pleased, that Kate wondered if she had imagined that superimposed image. No. She had a photographic memory and Ted was the man in the photo.

She busied herself making the coffee, opening the jar, searching for a spoon while she thought. She needed to approach this logically.

Ted had knowingly arrested the wrong man. Because he had been putting the scarf in the Dumpster, not taking it out, the night of Lynn's murder. He seeded the evidence. But why? To make himself look good?

After all those years at a desk job, he comes on vacation and seizes the opportunity to be actively involved again. Understandable, if not ethical. But if he framed Dan, that meant the killer was still at large and people would get a false sense of security. And Dan might be convicted of a crime he didn't commit.

And he called Finn and Fast Eddie irresponsible.

She wanted to tell him that he was putting people at risk, convince him to come clean, but she couldn't bring herself to do it. Better to let Brandon handle it. And how could Ted face his old friend after pulling a stunt like that?

Stay out of it. Not your business.

Ted took his cup and walked over to the desk. "Nice set-up you have here."

"Mmmm," Kate said.

Ted leaned against the desk and rested his hip against it. Cocked his head at Kate, who had stopped in the middle of the carpet.

"You're a smart girl, Kate."

Kate shrugged. "I'm a mathematician."

Ted smiled, a wistful sweet smile.

"So what do you think of this whole serial killer thing? Do you have any theories for why Dan Graves went on a killing spree?"

"No." She drew the word out. "Not really."

His smile broadened. He walked around the desk. Looked down at her computer. Clicked something on the keyboard.

Kate took a step forward. People didn't just open up other people's files. And she was afraid she knew which file he'd just opened.

Ted pursed his lips and nodded.

"Bran said you were brilliant." He puffed out a laugh. "I thought he was exaggerating because of the way he feels about you. But I should have known better. Bran doesn't exaggerate."

Kate was feeling decidedly uncomfortable. Something wrong here. Why was he talking about her intelligence and Brandon's feelings? Where was this going? And what were Brandon's feelings for her? She didn't know that he had any beyond exasperation—*Pay attention!* She knew she was missing something but she didn't know what.

"I know it's been hard for you—and Harry —to accept me. Too bad. I just wanted to help Bran out. I didn't want to see him mess up again."

Kate gritted her teeth, vacillating between telling him she knew the truth and staying quiet. She was beginning to get really scared. Why was he rambling on about feelings and stuff? She didn't believe that Brandon had been in the wrong all those years ago. Ted had warped the past as a way of coping with his disability and his inability to work as a detective.

The ping from an incoming e-mail made her jump. She glanced involuntarily at her computer.

"Go ahead and open your mail, Kate. I can entertain myself." Ted put down his coffee cup and wandered over to look at the crystal ball. She wanted to tell him not to touch it. It was too special.

He didn't touch it, just turned around, watching her.

Kate's stomach dropped. This was not normal behavior. Ted had finagled his way into the investigation, knowingly arrested the wrong man, because—No, it couldn't be true. . .

"Go ahead, Kate."

Slowly, she sat down. Pulled up her e-mail. She glanced at Ted.

His smile didn't waver. "Open it."

It was from Brandon. *E-mails originated at Harry's computer. It has to be Ted.*

Ted was setting Dan Graves up to protect himself. Ted was the killer.

Kate longed to fire off an SOS, but she didn't dare. She jabbed at the delete key just as Ted moved closer to the desk.

"Just spam." Her voice sounded dull in her ears. "Amazing how much solicitation a museum can get. Then add all the personal ads. So annoying." Her mouth was dry.

Her laptop pinged again.

"Open it." Ted was standing almost beside her now.

She did, knowing with total clarity that Ted already knew what was in the e-mail. He'd been waiting for it, had come to be here when it arrived. Her breath hitched as she read, "You're not taking me seriously. Do I need to get closer to home?"

Slowly Kate raised her eyes to Ted. Sheer fright pulled her to her feet. "I don't understand." Though she did.

She inched from behind the desk, but Ted stepped toward the door and turned the lock.

Kate took a step backward, trying to put the desk between her and Ted.

Thunder rattled the windows.

Ted calmly reached into his jacket pocket and pulled out two metal handles with a line of nylon.

He held it up. "At least I got some use for this."

Fishing line, she thought and fought to keep on her feet. "The museum will be opening any minute."

"The museum is closed today." He took a step toward her.

Kate stepped back. At least he hadn't caught her from behind—she would be dead by now. She would be dead soon anyway if she didn't start thinking clearly.

"Don't you want to know why, Kate? Isn't that what mathematicians do? Find answers. Solve puzzles. Can you solve this one, Kate?"

How about you're totally nuts?

"I do want to know why, Ted."

"Serial killers are fascinating, Kate. Take this guy in Boston. Nobody got what he was up to. Killed six people before they caught him. They. Not me, or we, but they.

"They got all the excitement, the buzz, the glory, while I talked to the media. Gave them information that was laundered and spun until it was meaningless. All because of this stupid leg.

"And for what? For saving Bran's life. It was worth it at first. He was brilliant in his own way. Moved right up the ladder. He was close to making bureau chief. But he threw it all away. He walked away from everything that was important to come to this Podunk and sit on his ass.

"What a waste. I should have let him die in that alley. I've been waiting years for him to take a fatal bullet in the line of duty. I could have felt vindicated." He snorted. "But here? He'll die of old age." He pulled the line tight between his two hands and stepped closer.

Kate shook her head and kept stepping back. It was an automatic response. She didn't think it would stop Ted.

"I could kill him myself. I really could, you know. But I have a much better plan. Let him suffer. Let him have something that he cherishes taken away like I did."

Kate stepped back and bumped up against the pedestal that held the gypsy's crystal ball. The ball rattled in its frame. "W-what?"

Ted smiled. "Bran was always a loner. Never let people get close. Except me sometimes. We were partners. But seeing you two together . . . it's perfect."

"He doesn't care about me. We're hardly even friends."

Ted shook his head, still smiling. "You and Harry. Bran's got himself a perfect little family in a perfect little town."

"It's not like that."

"Oh, Kate. Too bad you're not as smart emotionally as you are intellectually—it would have afforded me so much more entertainment. And I really wanted Bran around to witness, but I hit him a tad too hard. Difficult to judge in a stolen truck, especially with this useless leg."

The trees outside were banging against the window. A storm was brewing. Kate just hoped she would still be around to see it.

Ted took another step.

Kate eased around the pedestal, but there was no place left to go. "But why Henny and Lynn?" she asked desperately.

What good did it do to keep the murderer talking if you couldn't come up with a plan while he was doing it?

"Icing on the cake. It upped the ante. And I thought it would be a nice touch. Bran's little 'family' becomes the latest victims of the serial killer. This town will never forgive him." He chuckled again, and this time it sounded sinister. "And now . . . I'm sorry, Kate. I kind of liked you."

Lightning flashed, lighting the room. Thunder cracked. The window rattled. The branches slapped violently against the panes.

Not branches, Kate realized. Fast Eddie. He was straddling a tree branch and wildly waving his arms.

Ted stepped toward Kate.

Eddie drove his fist through the pane. The glass shattered onto the floor.

Ted whirled toward the sound.

Kate snatched the crystal ball from the pedestal and hurled it at Ted's head. It hit him square on the temple. He went down just as Fast Eddie dropped like a human acorn from the tree.

CHAPTER

TWENTY-SEVEN

WHEN DICKIE OWENS, Benjamin Meany, and the EMTs arrived fifteen minutes later, they found Ted Lumley, their interim chief, trussed up like a bagged deer. Fast Eddie was taking photos with one hand while nursing a broken arm; Aloysius was standing guard.

"I hope I didn't kill him," Kate told them as she met them at the office door.

"Nah," Fast Eddie said. "Finn will be so pleased. You'll have to let us interview the prisoner. After all, I was instrumental in his capture." He lifted his broken arm, then let out a groan. One of the EMTs sat him down in a chair.

Minutes later, Kate was seeing the whole cortege out the front door—the prisoner and the police to the station and Fast Eddie and the EMTs to County General.

Reluctantly, she closed the door. She didn't really want to be alone. And she really, really didn't want to go back upstairs to the scene of her near demise.

She sat down on the steps. Al sat down beside her.

"I suppose you're hungry after all that guard duty," she said as she stroked his fur.

"Yeow."

She stood up as a key rattled in the lock; the front door opened.

Alice hurried in. "My word. I can't believe it. Are you hurt?"

Kate shook her head as tears of relief filled her eyes.

"There, there," said Alice and put her arms around her. "I'll make you a nice cup of tea and some lunch as soon as the others get inside."

"The others?"

The door opened. The chief, flanked by Harry and Wynter, moved stiffly inside, followed by a bevy of GABs carrying grocery bags and totes.

"Take everything back to the kitchen," Alice told them. "We'll have lunch in the boardroom just as soon as we get the chief settled."

Brandon's eyes met Kate's.

"You saved my life," she said.

He frowned.

"Your e-mail gave me just enough warning to fend him off."

"I can't believe we missed it," Harry complained.

He and Wynter maneuvered the chief down the hall and into the boardroom. Kate followed close behind. They lowered the chief into one of the new padded chairs, then turned toward Kate.

"It was Ted all along?"

"I'm afraid so."

Harry laid a hand on Brandon's shoulder. "Sorry, chief. But he wasn't really your friend."

"I figured that one out."

"God, Harry, you're gonna give the chief a serious case of self-doubt and fear and loathing," Wynter said knowingly.

"I am not."

"No doubt," the chief said. "Not much fear, but a hell of a lot of self-loathing. I'm sorry I brought this on the town."

"Oh puh-*lease*." Wynter rolled her eyes. "Next you'll be saying it's all your fault."

Faint color appeared on the chief's cheekbones. It made him look a lot healthier. "Aren't you grounded or something?"

Wynter gave him one of her half-shrugs and a smartass look.

"I told the familias I had to do community service. Overseen by you." She snapped her gum and grinned.

Brandon rubbed his forehead, then looked up at Kate. "I'm not sure what I should do."

"First," said Alice, carrying a tray of sandwiches through the door, "you're having lunch. Then if you're feeling up to it, we're taking you by the police station to make an appearance, so everyone will know you've taken control of things and we'll all be safe again.

"Now what's keeping Pru with that iced tea?" She bustled back through the door.

Harry and Wynter reached for sandwiches.

Kate crossed to stand next to Brandon's chair. "They're both right, you know."

"What?"

"It's not your fault, and we'll all feel safe now that you're back on the job."

"Safe? You were nearly killed. And I brought him here—"

"No, you didn't, chief," Harry said around a mouth full of ham salad. "He invited himself and you were too polite to say no."

"Still."

Pru came through the door. She set a glass in front of the chief. "Which just goes to show you. You should pick your friends from good local folks. Hmmph."

Three stunned faces watched her leave the room.

"What do you think it means?" the chief finally asked.

"I think," said Kate, "the New Hampshire thaw has finally begun."

ACKNOWLEDGEMENTS

Thanks to Gary Brown for his untiring tutorials in computers, cameras, pixels, matrixes, and more. Many thanks to Nancy, Debbie, and Irene, the math and computer mavens; and to the whole GNO group, for being cheerleaders, sales force, and publicists, and always good for a swift kick.

Thanks especially to www.Sudoku.name for the use of their puzzles in this book.

ABOUT THE AUTHOR

Shelley Freydont is a past president of the New York/ Tri-State chapter of Sisters in Crime, and a member of Mystery Writers of America, Romance Writers of America, New Jersey Romance Writers, and Kiss of Death RWA chapter. She is the author of five books in the *Linda Haggerty* mystery series, and writes romance novels under the name Gemma Bruce. An avid lover of puzzles—Sudoku, crossword, jigsaw, and others—she lives in Midland Park, New Jersey.

Please visit her at www.shelleyfreydont.com.

PUZZLE SOLUTIONS

Page 8

3	5	2	4	6	1	9	7	8
8	6	1	7	5	9	2	4	3
4	7	9	3	2	8	1	6	5
6	2	3	8	4	5	7	9	1
1	9	8	6	3	7	4	5	2
5	4	7	9	1	2	8	3	6
9	3	6	1	8	4	5	2	7
2	8	4	5	7	6	3	1	9
7	1	5	2	9	3	6	8	4

Page 28

2	3	9	5	6	4	7	8	1
5	7	4	9	8	1	2	6	3
1	6	8	7	2	3	5	4	9
4	5	2	1	7	9	8	3	6
9	8	3	4	5	6	1	2	7
7	1	6	8	3	2	9	5	4
3	4	1	2	9	5	6	7	8
6	2	7	3	1	8	4	9	5
8	9	5	6	4	7	3	1	2

Page 52

5	3	1	6	4	8	2	9	7
9	8	7	2	3	5	1	4	6
2	6	4	7	9	1	8	5	3
1	9	3	4	2	7	5	6	8
4	5	2	8	6	3	7	1	9
6	7	8	5	1	9	3	2	4
8	4	6	1	7	2	9	3	5
7	1	9	3	5	6	4	8	2
3	2	5	9	8	4	6	7	1

Page 98

7	3	1	4	8	6	9	5	2
2	4	5	7	1	9	8	3	6
6	8	9	5	2	3	1	7	4
8	7	4	6	3	1	5	2	9
9	2	3	8	7	5	4	6	1
5	1	6	9	4	2	3	8	7
1	9	8	3	6	7	2	4	5
3	5	7	2	9	4	6	1	8
4	6	2	1	5	8	7	9	3

Page 110

2	9	5	6	4	8	3	1	7
3	6	8	7	1	9	5	2	4
4	1	7	5	3	2	9	6	8
7	3	1	9	5	6	4	8	2
9	4	2	3	8	7	6	5	1
8	5	6	4	2	1	7	3	9
6	8	4	1	9	5	2	7	3
5	2	9	8	7	3	1	4	6
1	7	3	2	6	4	8	9	5

Page 124

8	2	6	5	4	3	7	1	9
5	4	7	9	1	6	2	8	3
3	1	9	7	2	8	6	4	5
6	5	3	8	9	1	4	2	7
2	7	1	3	5	4	8	9	6
4	9	8	2	6	7	3	5	1
9	3	4	6	8	5	1	7	2
1	6	5	4	7	2	9	3	8
7	8	2	1	3	9	5	6	4

PAGE 138

8	4	5	7	1	2	3	9	6
2	6	7	8	9	3	4	5	1
3	1	9	5	4	6	2	7	8
5	2	6	1	3	4	7	8	9
9	7	4	2	6	8	1	3	5
1	8	3	9	5	7	6	2	4
4	3	2	6	8	9	5	1	7
7	9	1	4	2	5	8	6	3
6	5	8	3	7	1	9	4	2

PAGE 176

7	8	1	2	3	9	4	6	5
4	5	2	6	8	7	3	1	9
6	3	9	1	5	4	8	2	7
1	9	8	5	7	2	6	3	4
5	2	6	8	4	3	7	9	1
3	7	4	9	1	6	2	5	8
9	4	7	3	2	5	1	8	6
2	1	5	4	6	8	9	7	3
8	6	3	7	9	1	5	4	2

PAGE 228

7	1	8	5	9	3	4	6	2
4	5	9	7	6	2	1	3	8
3	6	2	8	1	4	9	7	5
6	8	1	4	2	9	7	5	3
2	3	7	6	5	1	8	9	4
9	4	5	3	8	7	2	1	6
8	7	6	1	4	5	3	2	9
1	9	4	2	3	6	5	8	7
5	2	3	9	7	8	6	4	1

PAGE 252

3	4	1	5	2	9	7	8	6
6	7	2	8	4	3	9	1	5
8	5	9	7	6	1	4	3	2
9	6	5	2	7	8	3	4	1
2	1	8	9	3	4	5	6	7
4	3	7	1	5	6	8	2	9
5	2	3	4	1	7	6	9	8
7	9	4	6	8	2	1	5	3
1	8	6	3	9	5	2	7	4

PAGE 306

1	7	8	2	3	6	5	9	4
9	3	4	5	1	7	2	8	6
6	5	2	8	4	9	7	3	1
4	8	3	6	2	5	1	7	9
2	9	6	1	7	8	3	4	5
7	1	5	4	9	3	6	2	8
8	4	1	3	6	2	9	5	7
3	6	9						
5	2	7						

PAGE 334

8	1	3	2	5	6	9	4	7
5	4	7	9	1	3	8	2	6
6	2	9	8	4	7	5	1	3
4	7	8	3	2	5	6	9	1
3	5	6	1	8	9	2	7	4
2	9	1	6	7	4	3	8	5
9	8	4	5	6	1	7	3	2
			4	3	8	1	5	9
			7	9	2	4	6	8